AMICHEL

A NOVEL OF EARLY AMERICA AND THE ILL FATED NARVAEZ EXPEDITION OF 1528.

PART II

BY

ROBERT CHAMPION WILSON JR.

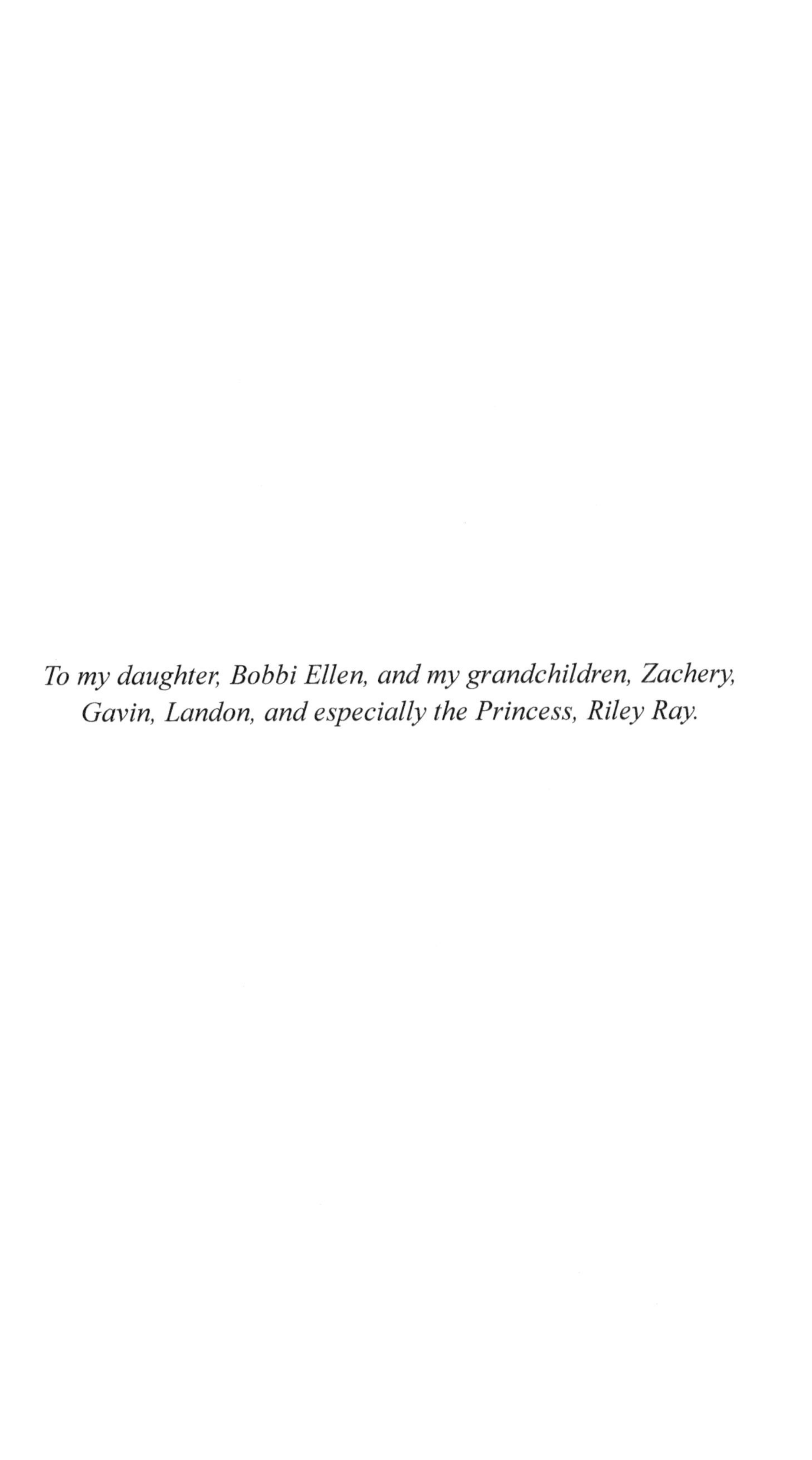

To my daughter, Bobbi Ellen, and my grandchildren, Zachery, Gavin, Landon, and especially the Princess, Riley Ray.

TABLE OF CONTENTS

CHAPTER 01

The Snake Tongue

Lengua de Serpiente

On the sixth day after leaving Apalachan, they came upon a river that flowed to the south. Strangely, the native guides called it Hona-wo-te. Estevan and Carmona struggled with the interpretation but finally settled upon "Snake Tongue" as its meaning.

21 July 1528

On the Trail to Aute

At first, it appeared as if the attacks were over. The first day the expedition followed a well-worn trail to the southwest, crossing small streams and a few shallow lakes, not seeing a single *Indio*. On the second day, Alvar was riding in the lead with Narvaez and Captains Pantoja and Valenzuela when they came to a tangled scrub land and a long meandering swamp that blocked their path. Reining up, the riders surveyed the obstacle in front of them. The expedition stretched far back along the trampled landscape. Those on foot lead the procession. The *rodeleros, musketeers, ballesteros,* and unmounted *cabelleros* walked as a group. Behind them followed the cavalry, twenty mounted at all times. The remaining eighteen animals were either led by one of the mounted *cabelleros* or by the slaves and pages of the expedition. Most of these animals were unfit to ride, being underweight, lame, or injured in the arrow attacks

It made sense to put the horses to the back, for the thick clouds of dust raised by their hoofs made it difficult to breath for anyone walking behind. Besides, stumbling through the piles of horse shit...*mierda de caballo,* was never a pleasant experience.

Captain Pantoja was the first to speak.

"*Adelantado*, I question why these paths we have been following all seem to lead through waterways."

Narvaez thought for a moment. "It seems that way, *Capitan* Pantoja."

By this time some of those on foot had caught up, among them Estevan and La Mancha. Narvaez winked at Pantoja and turned to Estevan. "Estevan, be so kind as to question our guides why all trails lead through these difficult areas."

At first, the guides didn't understand the question. Trails were trails and they had always been there.

"The bearded ones ask strange questions."

Estevan re-framed the question. "Why does water cover the trails and make it difficult to travel?"

At this the guides understood. "Tell the bearded ones that this is the time of much rain and there is water everywhere. As the days grow short the rains disappear, and all of this..." they swept the whole area with his arm, "...all of this will be without water."

As Estevan explained, the *Spaniards* nodded thoughtfully.

"That would explain the charred trunks of all the trees." It was de Vaca. "With no water, this would be a land of fire...*Terra del Fuego*."

"Enough of this!" Narvaez stood up in his stirrups. "*Capitan* Valenzuela bring the *musketeers* and *ballesteros* forward. We have another lake to cross."

These two groups would line up on the near shore to provide covering fire should the column come under attack. More important to many of the *Spanish*, they also kept watch for the dreaded alligator...*el lagardo*, that seemed to frequent every body of water. More than once a *ballestero's* steel shaft had sliced into the water to thwart one of these reptiles on its attack run.

The riderless horses entered the water first led by a contingent of four *cabelleros*. Too large for attacks by *El Lagardo,* the horses served to clear the way of snakes, turtles, and anything else that presented a risk to the soldiers. This lake was particularly wide and strewn with trees, downed limbs, and vegetation. Next in line would be the first group of *rodeleros,* foot soldiers. These would be followed by the *ballesteros* who held their crossbows high to keep the wood and, most importantly, the bowstrings dry. The final group of *rodeleros* then entered the water. Reaching the far side, the *ballesteros* would turn to cover the *musketeers,* officials, and *caballeros* entering the water. The crossing was particularly perilous for the *muskeeters* who had to ensure that their muskets and powder supplies remained dry. In deeper water they became ineffective, having to hold their weapons high overhead.

This lake was deep and filled with obstructions such that the line of crossing meandered to and fro instead of in a straight line. In places, the water was chest-deep. Struggling around the myriad of logs, limbs, and grass, many a *Spaniard* lost his footing and momentarily disappeared under the dark, stinking water only to reemerge sputtering and cursing.

"Hijo de puta."

Most of the *musketeers* had fouled their weapons, saturating powder and extinguishing primer cords. Behind them a crude raft had been constructed to carry the powder reserve, no more than three small wooden casks. Two other rafts had also been constructed, one for carpenter tools, parts, and crossbow bolts. The other was piled with the farrier's supplies...nails, spare horseshoes, anvil, billows, cutters, and rasps. The two small push carts used to land transport all of this material had been disassembled and piled on the rafts as well.

Unseen by anyone, a sinister form arose from behind a submerged log. He was covered in mud and draped with water plants. From his braided scalp lock a single eagle feather hung plastered in mud. Pulling his long bow to its maximum, a hickory shafted arrow was released toward one of the *Spaniards* pushing the powder raft.

Juan de Salvo was struggling to keep his footing and push the raft before him. Shorter than most, the water was almost to his neck. He was forced to half walk, half swim to push the bulky raft forward. With him was Tomas Cisneros who, although much taller than de Salvo, was struggling as well. Coming upon a submerged log, de Salvo raised himself up and paused for a moment to catch his breath.

"Juan, keep moving, I want to get out of here before *el lagardo* bites me on the ass. " It was Cisneros. Reaching for the raft de Salvo felt a sharp pain in his left shoulder.

"Ugh!" Grasping the raft with his flailing right arm he fell forward in the water causing the raft to tilt at a precarious angle. Cisneros struggled to keep the raft upright. He shot a questioning look at de Salvo and saw a spreading smear of blood on his friend's tunic.

"Juan, your shoulder, what is..." Cisnero's question was cut short by a searing pain in his right side. He spun around and fell heavily on the raft which lurched on its side and then flipped over. The precious cargo of gunpowder tumbled into the water. Both men, gravely wounded, struggled to hold on.

All along the column, the call rang out. "A *las armas, estamos bajo ataque*...to arms, we are under attack!"

The *Spaniards,* chest-deep in water, could not see from where the attacks were coming. Unable to fight, they crouched low in the water, holding their bucklers high to shield their head and shoulders as they slogged along. The *ballesteros* on the far shore looked frantically for something to shoot at, but the *Indians* were so well camouflaged and disappeared so quickly that only a few shots were made. Among the few *Spaniards* who had not yet crossed were Narvaez, Campo, Captain Castillo, Alonso Enriquez, Estevan, and La Mancha. Surprised by the attack at first, Narvaez caught sight of two of the attackers and charged into the water after them, closely followed by Castillo and Enriquez. The sight of the three horsemen exploding into the water at full gallop unnerved some of the *Indians* and they retreated further into the lake. One attacker made the mistake of bolting into shallow water. Narvaez seeing this rode him down and cleaved the body from skull to shoulder with his *montante*. Another group of *Indians,* however, had crept up behind Estevan, Campo, and La Mancha. The *Indians* fell on the men, intent on taking prisoners. La Mancha was immediately brained by a war club and fell in a heap. In the melee, Estevan and Campo were able to free themselves and ran toward the water. Three attackers were in hot pursuit. Two other attackers were already dragging the unconscious La Mancha into the grass. Narvaez, returning from his kill, noticed the commotion and spurred hard toward them. The *Indians* hesitated and then ran off. Both Estevan and Campo dove into the water.

Across the lake, Dorantes and five other riders reentered the lake from their side and drove at the remaining attackers while the final few *Spaniards*, including Narvaez, Estevan, Campo, Castillo, and Enriquez, made their way to safety. As the *Spaniards* regrouped on the far side of the lake, the *Indians,* attacked them from the flanks, raining arrows down on the milling columns of men. Narvaez ordered the horses to the rear and for the *caballeros* to dismount and attack the *Indians* on foot. This they did, and drove them back, but the *Indians* hid in another small lake and the *Spaniards* were forced to give up on their pursuit.

Finally, gathering further down the trail and now in a somewhat open country, the expedition took stock of their losses. Seven men had been injured in the arrow attack, de Salvo and Cisneros were the most critical. Many of the injured *Spaniards* had received wounds in spite of their armor, the force of the arrows penetrating the heavy metal *cuirasse* or *corselets* worn by the men. Two horses had suffered deep arrow wounds. Most important, however, was the overturning of the raft. Only one of the gunpowder casks had been recovered and it was saturated. Also lost were carpenter tools that had been carried on the second raft. In their effort to protect themselves, many of the *Spaniards* hid behind this raft as they struggled through the water. Along the way, tools and other materials had slid unnoticed to the muddy bottom below. One of the push carts had also disappeared. Finally, their guide and interpreter, La Mancha, had been captured, for a fate of which they could only guess. For the *Spaniards*, this had been the battle of Gunpowder Lake...*Polvora Lago*.

After Gunpowder Lake the expedition moved quickly to extricate themselves from the attacking hordes of *Indians*, but strangely the arrow attacks began to lessen and then stop altogether. Finally, the attackers seemed to melt away and the expedition was left alone.

Now, with La Mancha gone they had to depend on several of their Indian captives to lead the way to this city of *Aute*. La Mancha himself had been unfamiliar with the route but because of his language and cultural skills was able to act in the expedition's best interests. Now the captives took advantage of their situation and altered course to the southwest. They explained that the land to the south was very harsh and this was the better way to go.

At the back of the column, de Vaca and Captain Dorantes were on horseback directing the rear guard.

"*Senior* de Vaca, it appears that these heathens...*paganos,* have lost their will to fight. They slink among the trees and grasses but no longer fire their arrows at us."

"I think *capitan* that these...*paganos*...as you call them, have exhausted their supply of arrows. During the battle, I saw many searching the ground for spent shafts so they could send them back to us."

Traveling a league the expedition encountered another swamp, much wider and heavily covered with thick blow downs and vegetation. There was a collective groan from the ranks of men. Narvaez sent two squads of *ballesteros* heavily protected by five *rodeleros* to cover their entrance into the lake. This time, however, the crossing went without incident. Not a single *Indio* was even seen. On the far side, the column regrouped and then continued a half league more before going into camp. During the night Tomas Cisneros died of his wounds.

22 July, 1528

On the Trail to Aute

They had buried Cisneros the next morning and then continued southwest. Narvaez sent Alvar in advance with a contingent of five *cabelleros* to scout the path in front of them. Riding forward, they proceeded about a league when another smaller waterway obstructed the trail. Alvar carefully led the men forward to investigate. At the water's edge, there were signs of a recent crossing. Footprints in the mud and a still visible path through the water's vegetation told of at least one hundred warriors on the march. Dismounting, Alvar checked the signs and then gazed across the waterway. It was too open for any kind of ambush. Remounting, he spoke to one of his lieutenants.

"Lieutenant Veresa, it looks as though the *paganos* are just in front of us waiting to turn and fight when the conditions are favorable. We must be on our guard. Take two men and notify the *Adelantado* to strengthen the front of the column."

"*Si Alguacil*, and what of you and the remaining men?"

"I will remain here and continue to keep watch."

With a half salute Cristobal Veresa wheeled his horse and called out, "Alves and Sales, follow me, we ride back to the column to warn the *Adelantado*!"

Astride his horse, Alvar watched the three riders as they shrunk into the distance. They seemed so small in a land so endless. He turned in his saddle, the leather creaking in protest. All around this land of grasses, swamps, lakes, and huge trees stretched as far as he could see. Far to the south, a billowing white thunderhead rose high in the sky, its sun-illuminated top just beginning to flatten. Under it, the darkness blinked imperceptibly with the distant flashes of lightning. To his west, the clear sky radiated with a deep blueness as if painted with an artist's brush. In the east a line of migrating birds extended as far as he could see, their line in the sky distorting to and fro.

Turning back to the north, the riders had disappeared from view with only a dust cloud to mark their passing. For a moment Alvar felt quite alone. He thought of his Maria at home in *Cuellar*...what was she doing at this moment? Did she think of him?

"*Alguacil*, what are your orders?" It was Floriano Bras, one of the remaining three riders.

"Ah Floriano, my apologies. I was thinking of home and my wife." Alvar continued, "Rest yourselves, we will remain here and wait for the column."

22 July, 1528

Crossing a Waterway on the Trail to Aute

They passed over the waterway without a problem. Narvaez had fortified the front of the column in answer to de Vaca's discovery. The *Indians* had made a couple of feints from the front, but seeing the strength of the *Spaniards* they left the trail, swung around the expedition, and regrouped behind the column. Once again, Narvaez shifted the strength and even reverted to the *rana* strategy that had worked so well early in the expedition. A sizable group of *rodeleros* would conceal themselves by the side of the trail and wait for the column to pass. Here they would remain in hopes of ambushing the *Indians* who were following close behind. Once the battle was joined, a *musketeer* would fire a signal shot and a mounted squad of fifteen *caballeros* would hasten to the fight. Twice the *Spaniards* were successful at this tactic, killing two of the attackers.

The day was hot. Alvar was in charge of the relief caballeros riding at the back of the column. He reined in his mount and removed the heavy *morion,* wiping the sweat from his face and hair. Because of the heat, many of the men didn't bother to wear their helmets but, instead lashed them to their waists, only putting them on when under attack.

"*Alguacil,* your brains will explode in this heat if you keep wearing that bucket on your head!"

It was Lieutenant Juan Palacios, a good-natured soldier who had been walking along beside him. Palacios was from *Ribagorza* in northeastern *Aragon.* His speech was lilted with the native *Ribagorçan,* or what Palacios called "the language of the mountains!"

"You may be right friend Palacios, but twice it has protected me from arrows." Alvar pointed to the two deep dents.

"Now I am superstitious and go everywhere with it on."

Both men laughed. A musket discharged on the trail behind them. Alvar quickly called to his fourteen riders, "Quickly *caballeros,* our *rana* team is under attack."

As was the plan, five pikemen...*piqueros* led the charge, the long steel pointed shafts lowered to skewer anything in their path. Behind them, Alvar and the other nine riders followed with bucklers braced on their reining arm and swords drawn.

Moving quickly down the trail at a gallop, they came upon the battle at hand. Two more shots had been discharged by the *rana* musketeer toward the *Indio* threat, but both had done nothing more than slap noisily through the underbrush. Expertly concealed, the warriors released their arrows and then quickly disappeared back into cover. With no visible body of men to attack, the *piqueros* slowed to a trot, jamming up Alvar and the other horsemen who followed behind. Suddenly, another wave of *Indians* descended upon them with a vicious attack from the flank.

It had been a trap. Arrows filled the air and two of the *piqueros* were pulled from their horses. Alvar rode to their rescue, hacking at one warrior who was about to brain the prostrate *Spaniard*. With his arm severed just above the elbow, the *Indio* screamed in pain and fell to the side. Alvar looked to the other downed man, but he had already dispatched his attacker with a dagger thrust. Now with a drawn sword in one hand and dagger in the other, the *piquero* faced off against three warriors who circled him slowly. Alvar spurred his horse forward, scattering the three.

Another barrage of arrows descended upon them. Two careened off his *cuirasse* doing no harm, but a third passed through his left calf muscle embedding itself in the leather stirrup. The pain was excruciating. Alvar severed the shaft with his sword. Looking up he saw the battle forming around him. Some of the *caballeros* had dismounted and were fighting hand-to-hand. More *Indians* were advancing all the time. To his left, the *rana* team was also surrounded, many fighting back to back against the advancing enemy. The situation was becoming desperate. He charged another group of *Indians*, physically bowling over two of them with the momentum of the horse. Hacking to the right and left with his sword, he became aware of another dynamic in the struggle. More *Spaniards* had entered the field. It was Lieutenant...*Teniente* Palacios and the other *rodeleros* from the column's rear guard.

Sensing the battle had turned, the *Indians* suddenly melted away into the trees, leaving two dead on the field and the warrior with the severed arm bleeding to death in the sand. Palacios walked over to the writhing *Indio* and quickly dispatched him with a stroke of the sword. The battle was over. The *Spaniards* had three wounded including de Vaca. One horse had been killed by an arrow that passed completely through it. Five other horses had deep arrow wounds that had to be tended to by the farrier Jorge Nazario. Only the three *Indio* dead could be confirmed, but several of the *Spaniards* had seen wounded or dead attackers being carried off into the surrounding woods.

Narvaez rode up with three other *caballeros* and surveyed the site.

"*Adelantado*, over here!" It was Palacios.

As Narvaez approached, he saw several men staring at an arrow embedded in a small oak tree about as thick as a man's leg. The arrow had almost passed completely through it, with only the fletching visible on the entry side. A bow was brought up from one of the *Indio* dead, and not one of the soldiers could draw it back to its full extent. Looking down from his horse at their futile attempts, Narvaez could only shake his head in disbelief. Dismounting, he walked over to where Alvar and the other wounded men were tending their wounds.

"*Senor* de Vaca, how bad is your injury?"

"*Adelantado*, the arrow passed through my leg and embedded itself in the stirrup leather. I cut myself free. The shaft has been removed and now it bleeds freely. I am certain it will heal without problem."

"Good, good, that is excellent." Narvaez could see the bloody shaft lying on the ground.

Narvaez then spent a moment with the other wounded men. The most serious was Natalo Figueroa who was being tended to by Fray de Palos. An arrow had penetrated his *cuirasse* from the side, skittering across ribs and then reemerging in the front of his chest, finally expending its energy against the inside of the armor. There was a problem with removing the *cuirasse*. Figueroa was sitting upright as Fray Palos and another soldier carefully broke the exposed shaft. Reaching under the armor, he held the protruding shaft steady as the heavy *cuirasse* was gently lifted off. There was a moment of some distress while the shaft, still tightly wedged in the armor, was pulled free.

"Aggh, aahhhh!" Figueroa wreathed in pain, his body sweating profusely.

With the *cuirasse* removed, the extent of the wound was now clearly visible. No organs had been penetrated and the arrowhead lay clearly exposed. While another man held Figueroa tightly, Palos grasped the arrowhead with thumb and forefinger and slowly began pulling on the shaft. Figueroa screamed in anguish and then lost consciousness, his head falling to the side.

"This is good," said Palos, "now he will feel no pain."

Palos pulled harder and the shaft exited the body. Looking at it briefly, he threw the bloody remnant on the ground. Blood streamed from both sides of the wound.

"Good friar." It was Narvaez. "Will he live?"

"I don't believe the wound to be fatal, *Adelantado*, but he will be in great pain when he awakes."

Narvaez nervously looked around for de Vaca. Finding him sitting on a branch, he hurried over.

"Can you ride?"

"*Si Adelantado*, but I will need someone to assist me in mounting." As an afterthought, Alvar pointed out that they would need a stretcher for the still-unconscious Figueroa. Turning to the men still gathered around the arrow tree, Narvaez called out, "Lieutenant Pelacios, detail some men to construct a stretcher...and quickly, we must leave this place."

Stepping over to Alvar, Narvaez helped him to mount and then hurried back to his own horse.

30 July, 1528

Approaching the Indian Village of Aute

The trail remained unbelievably sodden, at times disappearing completely from view beneath ankle-deep water that swarmed with insects, snakes, and *el lagardo*. Even stretches of grassland, viewed as dry, became quagmires of sticking mud. Interspersed among this were myriads of small lakes and thick forests. The *Spaniards* moved slowly through this environment, taxing energy reserves that were rapidly dwindling. Many of the men were belabored with injuries or sickness. Several, like Natalo Figueroa, had to be carried. Narvaez again succumbed to fever. Riding atop the stallion Santiago, bouts of chills and shaking racked his body such that it would almost unseat him. Food was scarce. The corn that had been parched and stored while in *Apalachan* began to run out. The men once again ate the soft pulp of the palmetto stem. Larger animals such as deer and an occasional bear could be seen in the distance but took flight before the *ballesteros* could get a shot off. The *musketeers*, severely low on powder, were instructed not to discharge their weapons.

The health of the horses was becoming critical. Like the men, many had been wounded by arrows. Few of them were now shod, having lost their shoes somewhere along the trail. Nazario, as expedition blacksmith and farrier, did what he could, but now he was short of iron and nails. The hoofs of the horses, subjected to the rivers, creeks, swamps, and lakes of *La Florida* were splitting and rotting. Each day was a struggle. Even completing 2 leagues of travel was difficult.

On the sixth day after leaving *Apalachan,* they came upon a river that flowed to the south. Strangely, the native guides called it *Hona-wo-te*. Estevan and Carmona struggled with the interpretation but finally settled upon "Snake Tongue" as its meaning. The *Spaniards,* unable to pronounce the Indian word, called it *Rio Lengua de Serpiente* The river grew larger the further south they traveled until there was no question that this body of water must empty into the sea. They followed the *Snake Tongue* to the south, for, according to the guides, this was the direction to *Aute*. Surprisingly, the journey to *Aute* was met with a feeling of hope by some of the men. Soon, it was felt, they would reach the ocean and be reunited with the fleet. At night they talked endlessly of what they would eat on the return to *Cuba*. What further bolstered their spirits was the secession of *Indio* attacks. The euphoria would not last.

For two more days, the expedition slogged on without incident.

On the eighth day, Alvar watched as the procession moved slowly past him. All had removed the hot body armor and toted it slung to their backs, their *morions* swinging to and fro by the chin straps. He was mounted on one of the few healthy horses. He crossed his leg in front of him on top of the horse's neck. It throbbed badly and raising it in this manner brought immense relief. The leg was still somewhat swollen. He studied the wounds. The entry wound was all but healed with only a slight discoloration and scab. The exit wound was taking longer. It had finally ceased draining and had begun to scab over but because it was on the inside of his leg was subject to frequent contact with stirrups, saddle, and horse hair.

Now, as he looked, it was bleeding again, small gnats attracted to the moisture of the wound. It itched terribly and he resisted the urge to scratch.

"*Senor* de Vaca, *Senor* de Vaca!" It was Campo running toward him.

Alvar peered down at the young page as he arrived sweating and out of breath. "My young *muchacho,* what on earth could be so important as to make you expend so much energy in this heat?"

"*Senor* de Vaca....ah...the *Adelantado*...ah...requests your presence at the front of the column."

Alvar lifted his leg and swung it back into the stirrup and then offered his hand to Campo.

"It is a long walk back, *Senor* Campo, jump up behind me and we will visit the *Adelantado* together."

"*Gracias.*"

Alvar urged his horse into a slow trot and threaded his way among the column of men.

"Now tell me, what is so important that you were sent to fetch me?"

"*Alguacil*, our advance party has returned with the news that a large *Indio* village is no more than a league ahead."

Ahead, the column had come to a stop. Exhausted men sat down on either side of the trail. Others remained standing trying to determine what was happening up ahead.

One soldier, Alvar recognized him as Gonzalo Ruiz, called up to him. "*Senor* de Vaca, why do we stop?"

"Friend Ruiz, you know as much as me but it appears that we may have reached our destination."

Further forward, Alvar caught sight of Narvaez astride Santiago. The leader was hunched over the saddle and staring at the ground. Enrique Penalosa, who had led the advance party, was in discussion with him. Estevan and two of the *Indio* guides were also present. The other three members of the mission had dismounted and were standing by their mounts.

"*Adelantado*, you called for me."

Narvaez did not look up. "*Alguacil*, less than a league to our south there is a village of some size. It sits on a peninsula bounded by the river we have been following and another that comes in from the west. *Senor* Penalosa encountered no opposition but the size of the village would indicate that they could mount a sizable force. Our guides tell us that these people are also *Apalachees* but of a different band."

From where they stood, the village was not yet visible. It was still too far away, and deep forests shielded their view of the land ahead. It was prime ambush country.

"*Adelantado*, I feel we should proceed slowly and be on our guard until we find out the disposition of these people."

Narvaez was in agreement and ordered both the front and rear guard bolstered. The horses and cavalry would be placed in the middle of the procession, the thick trees and underbrush nullifying their value.

Before riding away, Alvar noticed a spasm descend upon the leader. Holding tightly to the saddle, his whole body shook uncontrollably. Narvaez was sweating profusely. After the spasm had passed, he saw Alvar watching him. For a moment the two traded knowing looks and then Narvaez slowly turned and rode off.

30 July, 1528

Battle Outside of Aute

Yago was nervous. His palms were sweaty and he felt like someone was watching him. He wasn't alone. Most of the fifty men assigned to the rear guard felt the same way. They knew that should an attack come, it would most likely be from the rear. Yago reached down and adjusted his sword. It still felt strange. It was only a month ago that his *patron*, Guillermo Avellaneda, had presented him with it. He had worked for Avellaneda since the age of six after having been sold by his uncle. Yago's peasant parents had died in a fire, and the burden of raising him was too much for the uncle who made a small profit on the sale. Avellaneda's parents lived in *Jaen*, a small city in south-central *Spain*. It was with his parents that he left *Yago* while he was away, for his services as a cavalryman, a *caballero*, kept him busy. At the age of twelve Avellaneda called for Yago. and since that time he had been his constant companion, caring for horses, shining weapons, mending armor, and cooking meals. Theirs had been a *Spartan* existence but Yago had grown to like it, fitting in easily with camp life. Avellaneda had joined the Narvaez expedition to improve his station in life. Then all of *Spain* had been abuzz when the riches of the *Aztecs* had filtered back to the *Spanish* mainland. To accompany Narvaez and share in this bounty of gold from other areas of the New World was an opportunity not to be turned down.

The journey had been exciting and Yago loved it all...that is...until the expedition had gone inland. The constant marching, hunger, and dysentery had been bad enough, but battling the *Indians* and not knowing from one minute to the next whether your head would be cleaved by an arrow was something altogether different. After the drowning of Juan Velazquez, Avellaneda procured the dead man's sword and armor and presented it to Yago.

"You are almost a man now, it is time that you learn to use these. In the days ahead we will need all the able-bodied men we can find."

And so here he was in the middle of a strange and deadly country with a dead man's weapon. He pulled the sword from its scabbard and inspected it by wetting his thumb and running it along the cutting edge. It was plenty sharp. He reached down to return the sword to the scabbard, but just then his foot caught on an exposed root. He fell forward in a heap, the sword skittering across the ground. Laying there, he felt clumsy and stupid. The column had moved on...he was indeed the last one in line. Another soldier, Lope de Oviedo, his friend, broke ranks and hurried back to help him up.

"Yago, what happened?"

Picking up his sword, Yago pointed at the gnarly outcrop of root just behind him. "I was thinking of other things, Lope, and stumbled over..."

Something caught his eye further down the trail--there was movement in the trees.

"Lope, did you see that? *Santa Madre de Dios*, they are everywhere! To arms, to arms...*a las armas*!"

The trail behind them now was filled with savagely painted *Indians* quickly moving toward them. A shower of arrows landed all around and into the rear guard ranks further up the trail. Miraculously, neither man was hit. From the ranks, the *Spaniards* yelled at the two stragglers, "Run, run...quickly!"

The *Indians* were coming fast, too fast. Unable to reach the ranks in time, Yago and Lope turned to meet the charge. At the same time, the *Spanish* line surged forward hoping to help their two comrades. To Yago, everything seemed distant, like he wasn't even there. He could see the sword clenched in his own hand and his buckler held in front of him. From his own lips, he heard a guttural yell that was only slightly audible above the other sounds. One of the *Indians* was almost upon him, his blackened face contorted with hatred, his glistening red body covered in bizarre tattoos. The club he was holding was already beginning its death swing. Yago didn't feel fear, in fact, he didn't feel anything. His mind was clear. As he had been taught, Yago dropped down and swung his sword with all his might at the attacker's legs. He felt resistance and then the crunch of bone and sinew. The *Indio* catapulted over his head, screaming in pain. The death swing of the warrior's club had not found its mark, but it had glanced off Yago's hip, lacerating it deeply.

They were all around him now and he fought like a demon. Only once was he aware of Lope beside him. In a brief pause, he saw his friend lop off the head of the *Indio* that had first attacked him. Now as he fought, the severed head rolled around underfoot and he kicked at it to clear the area. Almost at the same time, the crash of the rest of the *Spanish* rear guard bowled into the battle. For a moment the *Indians* hesitated, but their numbers were great and slowly they pushed the rear guard backward. The rest of the *Spanish* column was just now entering the field and three riders charged into the swarm of red men. One was Guillermo Avellaneda, Yago's *patron.* Through the melee Avellaneda cut a swath, his sword swinging to the right and left. He was unafraid and the soldiers coming up cheered him.

From behind a thick tangle of leaves and branches an *Indio* raised up and pulled his bow to its full extent. Yago saw him then. He was aiming at Avellaneda.

"*Patron, Patron,* to your right!" His voice was lost in the din of battle.

Yago looked back to the *Indio* at just the moment of release. The arrow's flight was true and struck Avellaneda on the edge of his *cuirass* passing almost completely through his neck such that it dangled only by the fletching. Avellaneda rose up in his saddle as a spray of red misted the air. He then fell forward off his horse, dead before hitting the ground. Yago watched in disbelief and then rage. Turning back towards the *Indio* bowman he rushed forward, cutting a path through the mass of bodies now fighting hand to hand. The bowman, still concentrating on his kill, did not see the onrushing *Spaniard* until it was too late, the speed of the charge completely bowling him over. Grabbing the hilt of his sword with both hands Yago drove it hard into the prone man's stomach and then proceeded to stomp on his head. Again and again and again.

Behind him, the main mass of the *Spanish* had now entered the fight. Almost as quickly as they appeared, the *Indians* faded back into the trees, dragging their dead and wounded with them. It was de Oviedo who finally grasped Yago and spun him around. For a moment Lope feared for his own life as the wildness in his friend's eyes did not recognize him.

"Yago, it is over...it is over."

For a moment Yago just stared at his friend and then, sinking down to his knees, he began to cry.

After the battle, the bodies of Avellaneda and three other dead *Spaniards* were placed upon makeshift stretchers and moved to the front. The three were all part of the rear guard and had been struck down in the first few moments of the battle. Miguel de Falla, Manuel Cervantes, and Calderon Gasset had been well-liked by all and their loss brought a deep sadness to the expedition. It was the worst loss of life since the hurricane many months before. With darkness coming on, the expedition sought out a relatively clear area next to the river and assumed a defensive position. Here they would tend to the wounded and face the *Indio* should they return. No one slept that night. At midnight a faint orange glow was seen to paint the southern sky which in no more than fifteen minutes blossomed into a great maelstrom. Tongues of flame leaped high over the distant tree line, sending sparks swirling into the air. The *Spanish* were at first confused by the fire but then came to realize that the *Indians* were burning their own village. There could be no other explanation.

Alvar and Friar Xuarez had watched the burning. It was a spectacle both eerie and fascinating. The *Spanish* campsite was dark and no fire burned. In the calm air only occasionally could they detect the smell of smoke and never once did any noise reach their ears.

"I think, good father, when we enter this village of *Aute* tomorrow we will find the *Indios* have moved on, leaving us little."

"Of this, I believe you are right, Alvar Nunez. Let us hope they are gone and will not meet us in another battle."

31 July, 1528

Spanish Campsite Just Outside the Indian Village of Aute

With dawn, a towering column of smoke still spiraled high into the cool morning air, drifting slowly to the east. The *Spanish* column moved out, cautiously. By mid-morning the leading contingent sighted the village, or what was left of it. Many of the structures were burned to the ground. The *Indians* had even tried to burn the surrounding cornfields, but in the calm air, the fires had not spread too far. As the *Spanish* marched in, not a man, woman, or child was to be seen.

It was all that Narvaez could do to sit upon his horse, so racked with fever had he become. On his arrival to the village, he had weakly called Alvar and Alonso Enriquez over to him.

"*Senors* de Vaca and Enriquez you are my next in command. Before we continue on to the sea, I believe we should rest ourselves here, to bury our dead and recover from the wounds suffered in yesterday's battle."

Both Alvar and Enriquez nodded in agreement. It was Enriquez who next spoke.

"Perhaps *Adelantado*, after resting a bit, we could send a scouting party ahead to find what lies ahead."

Narvaez looked up wearily with his good eye. "Believe me, *Senor* Enriquez, I am more than anxious to get back to the ships, but let us put that decision aside until we are secure in this place."

"*Si Adelantado*, you are right, of course."

Still suspecting another attack, the *Spaniards* quickly secured the village site. Guards were posted and crude shelters were erected to protect the wounded and sick. Some of the fields around the village, not being entirely burned, had maize, squash, and beans. These were rapidly consumed by the men and horses. Cooking fires sprang up everywhere. Defensively, the site was ideal, being on high ground the river formed a partial oxbow around the town so that the location resembled a peninsula. Protected by the river on three sides the open end was covered by maize fields. No *Indio* attack ever came and the *Spanish* rested for two days. On the afternoon of the second day, de Vaca was called to the crude shelter that had been erected for Narvaez. He struggled to sit upright as Alvar approached.

"*Adelantado*, you are looking better today!"

"God has given me a reprieve, *Senor* de Vaca, at least for the moment." He considered what he had to say and then continued.

"I am most anxious to leave this place...as I know we all are."

Alvar nodded in agreement. Narvaez pointed to the water just south of the village. "We have all noticed that the *Rio Lengua de Serpiente* seems to rise and fall with some regularity that could only be influenced by its nearness to the sea and the tides."

"I have observed this myself, *Adelantado*," was Alvar's reply.

"I would entreat you, *Senor* de Vaca, to put together a small force and proceed southward. Determine what is our best route to the sea and scout a location from which we...hopefully...can make contact with the caravels."

"Let us hope, *Adelantado*, that the caravels are still looking for us."

Narvez's one good eye bored into Alvar. He seemed upset and then after a prolonged silence, he sighed and continued.

"Before I joined you in *Trinidad,* after the great *huracan,* I was in *Havana* procuring the caravel *Aqua Azul* which, as you know, was to be our relief ship."

"*Si Adelantado*"

"While there I instructed Alvero de la Cerda, the man who would command the *Aqua Azul, s*hould any unfortunate situation arise, that he would make every attempt to find and resupply us. More importantly, *Senor* de Vaca, and my beloved wife Maria were also at this meeting. She, in the privacy that we later shared, told me if lost she would not rest until I was found."

"*Adelantado*, I have met your wife only briefly, and she seemed the kind of woman not to make idle boasts."

Narvaez seemed to brighten. "She is my one treasure I value more than gold. I know that at this moment she is using every means within her power to find me. That is why we must now regain the sea and await the arrival of the caravels."

For a while, neither man spoke, their thoughts consumed with memories of home. It was Alvar who broke the silence. "*Adelantado*, I will take my leave. The shadows grow long and I have much to prepare for. I will leave tomorrow morning at first light."

Alvar sensed that his visit had worn out the leader. Even as he was leaving, Campo rushed up to help the *Adelantado* lay back upon the crude bed that had been constructed. From behind, Alvar heard Narvaez mutter, "God be with you...*Buena suerte.*"

Alvar had wanted to keep the force as small as possible. He picked the best men who were not encumbered with wounds or sickness. The force, however, had to be powerful enough to ward off any attacks that might occur on the way. He chose Alonzo Castillo and Andres Dorantes as his captains. Seven *cabelleros* would accompany them as their cavalry force and fifty-foot soldiers...*rodeleros* would provide the bulk of the military might. At the last moment, Fray Xuarez petitioned Alvar to accompany the force. Alvar attempted to talk him out of it.

"*Padre* Juan, we will be traveling through a country of which I know nothing. We will be subject to attacks and the hardships may be many. I would ask you to reconsider your request."

Although good friends, Xuarez now took exception to Alvar's request. He addressed him by his official title. "*Alguacil,* I have suffered these last months like all of you. I have walked until my legs grew weak and I have poured my sweat and blood on the ground, but I have kept up. As for fighting..."

Unexpectedly, Xuarez unsheathed the sword hanging at Alonzo Castillo's side and assumed a fighting stance. He swung the sword in large sweeping circles to the left and right, all the time moving in a graceful circle while dancing on sandalled feet. He parried and he thrust with an imaginary foe while de Vaca, Castillo, and Dorantes looked on in wide-eyed amazement. Although somewhat comical in his rolled-up habit, it was obvious that this pious man of God knew how to use a sword. With a flourish, Xuarez finished his routine and passed the sword, hilt first, back to Castillo. He stood there waiting for an answer. Befuddled, Alvar looked to Dorantes who shrugged his shoulders. He turned to Castillo who thought for a moment before answering.

"It looks as if *Padre* Juan will be going with us!"

03 August, 1528

De Vaca Leads Scouting Party to the Coast

Ten horsemen and fifty-foot soldiers left the *Spanish* camp at *Aute* just as the eastern sky began to lighten. They moved slightly north along the *Rio Lengua de Serpiente* to a fording site about half a league from the camp. The river at this point was one hundred feet wide and relatively shallow. The west side of the river seemed to be the better route. Only one raft was constructed to transport men and supplies to this side. There was no opposition and the surrounding countryside remained strangely quiet. Once across, the party turned south and followed the river. As they passed their campsite on the other side, the *Spaniards* waved at each other. Looking across at the accumulation of men, horses, and crude shelters, Alvar was struck by how isolated they appeared. Surrounded by maize fields and thick forest, the little peninsula of land seemed very small indeed.

Past the peninsula, the waterway became much wider. Along its shore, marshes and small tributaries abounded, forcing the party to make many detours. Travel was slow and it wasn't until the hour of Vespers that the exhausted men pulled up onto a spit of land that overlooked a broad mudflat. To the east and southeast the other shore of the river was just visible in the distance, but looking south, there was only open water. At the water's edge, dolphins chased schools of mullet that leaped high into the air to avoid their pursuers. More importantly, the low tide exposed accumulations of oysters. They were everywhere. The *Spaniards* used their swords to pry them loose, greedily forcing the bivalves open and slurping the contents. So starved for protein were they that Alvar had difficulty in setting a defensive guard. The men had to be rotated every half hour so they could join in the oyster orgy.

Late into the night, over a driftwood fire, the men continued their gluttony, roasting the meat on branches cut from trees and denuded of leaves. Gorging until their bellies became distended, many suffered the effects of overeating. Past the light of the fire, the sounds of retching competed with the lapping of waves striking the shore throughout the night. Alvar, Castillo, and Dorantes had eaten their fill, but so busy had they been with ensuring the safety of the campsite that there hadn't been time to overindulge. It was a sorry band of *Christian* warriors that greeted the dawn of the next day. As the sun rose over the bay, the three leaders were already discussing plans for the day when out on the shore a strange lone figure began to materialize in the dim light. Alonzo Castillo reached for his sword, not recognizing the strange apparition. In a few moments, however, the figure materialized as Father Juan squatted down in the mudflat, his white legs and buttocks exposed and in contrast to the dark cassock pulled high over his head. Even from where they stood they could hear moans and foul sounds emanating from his body.

"*Madre de Dios*," muttered Castillo as he disgustingly slammed his sword back into the scabbard. "I thought it was a sea monster crawling from the ocean to attack us."

Both Alvar and Andre Dorantes convulsed into laughter that continued unabated for several minutes. It was a release from the tension and desperation that they all felt. Even Castillo joined in. Not so for the embarrassed Father Juan, who finally cleaned himself and huffed across the mudflat back to the campsite.

It was decided to send out a smaller party to explore a better access to the sea. Here the shallow water, mudflats, and turbulence would not be accessible by the caravels. They needed to find a place more prominent, an obvious site that a rescue mission may choose to investigate, a site where signal fires could be seen far out to sea. For this Alvar picked twenty of the stoutest men, led by Alonzo Castillo, to proceed on foot along the coast to find such a site. The horsemen would remain in camp. In these conditions, inlets, bays and tidal marshes, the horses were more of a hindrance than a help. At mid-morning the scouting party left camp with the good wishes and prayers of Father Juan, who by now had come to see the humor of his sojourn to the mudflat.

06 August, 1528

At the mouth of the Ochlockonee River

It was getting late and the twenty men were just returning. Alvar caught sight of them across the mud flat that extended west from their position. In the lead was Alonzo Castillo making a trail through the scrub grass that marked the higher ground. He stopped for a moment to catch his breath and looked across the expanse to see Alvar and the rest of the men from the party watching him. He halfheartedly waved a greeting and then put his head down and continued the trek. It was another half hour before Castillo and the men had rounded the mudflat and trudged into camp. They were mud-spattered, scratched, and fatigued. Castillo threw off his *morion,* then he unbuckled his sword belt and let it fall to the ground while struggling out of his *curiasse*, the form-fitting torso armor.

"Give me a moment, *Alguacil,* while I catch my wind, for we have been on the move since early morning."

Alvar handed Castillo a canteen. He counted the other men...they were all there.

"Did you see any *Indios, capitan?*"

Castillo wiped his chin with a grimy forearm. "Not one, not even a canoe was seen. What we did see was an endless wilderness, a *despoblado*...inlets, bays, and shallow estuaries all of which had to be crossed or rounded. At midday, the shore turned inland again and

I thought that this may be a bay from which we could wait for the caravels. As we traversed its coast, however, this bay appeared very shallow and fraught with more sandbars and mudflats. We rounded this bay and then followed the shoreline southward for a time until darkness forced us to stop. We ate our fill of oysters and spent the night in much fear that we would be attacked."

Castillo took another long drink, handed the canteen back to Alvar, and lay down on the ground. With his eyes closed he continued his report.

"Today we arose early and continued our march. It was more of the same. Seaward, mudflats extended out for a good distance, and in most places, the water was very shallow. We continued to be hampered in our explorations by the multitudes of shallow inlets that we were forced to navigate around. At mid-morning the shoreline again turned inland to form another shallow bay. Climbing a tree I could look across this expanse of water to the other side. Like the previous bay, it was also shallow and filled with mudflats and sandbars. At this point, we began our return over the same tortuous trails from which we had come."

Squatted down, Alvar had been sketching Castillo's description in the sand. "Is this a fair representation of the shoreline you speak of?"

Castillo rolled over onto an elbow and studied the drawing. He made a few changes, covering the errors with new sand. "This is how it looks, *Alguacil*. I think what we see before us is a broad river delta and clear water is still a great distance away."

Alvar rose to his feet. "You and your men have done well, *capitan* Castillo. Rest tonight and we all will return to this *Indio* town of *Aute* in the morning."

Castillo was asleep before Alvar had finished talking. The next day dawned clear and bright. Just as the sun cleared the horizon, Alvar assembled the reconnaissance party and began their march back to *Aute*. Just as before, the trail was difficult. They had to negotiate the many inlets and waterways that impeded their progress. By mid-morning the temperature had climbed rapidly and the men had divested themselves of helmets and armor. Even Juan Xuarez carried his rolled-up robe with his left hand and a gnarly walking stick in his right. Clad now only with a sword belt and a loose cotton blouse that extended just below his *cajones,* he was, at first, the object of snickers from the other men in the party. Now, as the heat intensified, no one laughed. Each man silently trudged ahead, consumed with the effort to put one foot in front of the other. Even the horses were led to conserve their energy and avoid injury.

It was late afternoon when Alvar called a halt on a dry precipice of land that offered some meager grazing for the horses. Castillo and Xuarez joined him under a tree that offered some relief from the blazing sun.

"If my memory is correct *Alguacil*, we have about another hour of walking until we reach *Aute*, and then it is only a short distance to the crossing." It was fray Xuarez.

Alvar looked up to see Xuarez sitting cross-legged and exposed. He quickly avoided his gaze. "That is as I remember as well, good friar. Let us hope that the time passes quickly."

In the distance, the low rumble of thunder drifted across the exhausted men.

Castillo shook his head. "Just what we need, a little rain to make our journey a little more uncomfortable."

Alvar raised himself and told the men to assemble. The men ambled over to where he stood. "*Senores*, we are only a short distance from the river crossing. Let us continue as quickly as possible and avoid this oncoming tempest."

Turning toward the friar he said, "Come Father Juan, just a little further, and then we can rest."

06 August, 1528

Scouting Party Returns to the Indian Village of Aute

The crossing had gone without incident and the scouting party trudged into the camp at *Aute,* mud-spattered, wet, and exhausted. A strange quietness greeted them. North of the village a column of smoke rose into the humid, windless sky. At first, Alvar thought it was nothing but a campfire, but as flames filled the horizon he realized it was much more than that.

Juan Palacios, one of the soldiers in the camp's advanced guard, rose up from behind a tangle of scrub and tree limbs to address Alvar.

"*Aguacil,* we are truly glad to see you. We were much afraid that you had been killed by the *Indios.*"

Alavar looked around him. The camp was much subdued. There was little movement. The men hid themselves behind anything that was available as if expecting an attack at any moment. Just outside of the corral a dead horse lay on the ground, its already bloated body pierced by several arrows.

"Lieutenant Palacios, what has happened here?"

"*Alguacil,* we came under attack only last night, the savages taking us completely by surprise. The arrows flew so thickly that it is by God's grace alone that any of us are alive. We fought fiercely and drove them back. I killed one of the intruders with my sword, they are fierce fighters and many of our men sustained injuries."

Alvar noticed a deep gash on his left shoulder. Palacios caught his gaze. "I was only able to partially defend myself from a war club wielded by the huge *Indio*. I parried with my sword and cut off his leg. I then stabbed him through the heart as he lay screaming on the ground."s

"Praise God that you are still with us. Were any *Spaniards* killed in this attack?"

"None *Aguacil*, but many are wounded and many more are sick and barely able to defend themselves. It fell to those of us still able to wield a sword to protect the others who were suffering. I hear that *capitans* Pantoja and Tellez each killed ten of the heathens...*paganos!*"

Alvar again scanned the camp. "Tell me, where are the bodies of the dead *Indios*?"

"During the final attack, they drug off all of their dead and wounded, all but the one that I slew." Palacios nodded toward a clump of palmettos just to the side of their position. A leg and part of the torso were just visible.

"God be with you friend, Palacios." Alvar rejoined the column of men.

"And to you, *Aguacil*."

The men of the scouting party rejoined their own units while Alvar and Captain Castello proceeded to the rough enclosure where Narvaez was quartered. The *Adelantado* lay on a pallet of pine boughs sleeping fitfully. Alvar shot a questioning look at Campo who was attending him. Campo walked outside the enclosure and in a low voice said, "*Senor* de Vaca, the *Adelantado* fell sick the night after your departure. The disease of the bowels struck him and many others in camp. He is so weakened that he has trouble standing. During the attack of last night, he could barely manage to hold his sword."

"De Vaca is that you...report to me!" It was Narvaez, now awake and calling from his bed.

"A thousand pardons your excellency, we didn't want to disturb you."

"Never mind that. Were you able to find a suitable harbor?" Now sitting, Narvaez's tone was almost pleading.

"*Adelantado*, we were able to find the river's outlet to the sea, but it is a broad delta that extends out many leagues. From where we stood, the water in this bay is exceedingly shallow, rife with shoals and mudflats...*bajios y marismas*."

Narvaez's countenance seemed to wilt.

"Your excellency, I sent *capitan* Castello with twenty men to further scout the western half of the bay. They traveled outward four leagues and were greatly hampered by the multitude of inlets and swamps that greeted them. On the second day, he climbed a tall tree and saw only more of the same. It is his opinion, and now mine as well, that to reach the true coast we are four or five days distant."

Narvaez sank back down and put his arm over his face. "*Caramba*, this is not what I wanted to hear."

After a long silence, Narvaez spoke again. "You have seen the country we must travel through to reach this true coast...*verdadera costa*, as you call it. To remain here is foolishness, for the *Apalachees* attack us at will and even now set fire to their maize fields to deprive us of sustenance. My mind is aflame with fever and I fear my decisions will not be good ones. I would ask both of you for your recommendations."

Surprisingly, Castillo was the first to speak. Alonso del Castillo Maldonado was known for his straight talk and opinions on matters that most men avoided. He carefully chose his words as he addressed Narvaez.

"*Adelantado*, almost a third of our army is sick or wounded. The horses are in poor shape and our equipment has worn out. The *musketeers* are almost without powder and the *ballesteros* have only a few bolts for their crossbows. I would proceed to the encampment visited by *Senor* de Vaca and myself. After we have slaked our great hunger on the oysters in that bay we can move inland to avoid the terrain that so exhausted my scouting party. After a days march to the west, we should again move to the coast, for by this time we should be clear of this troublesome estuary."

Narvaez looked to Alvar for a comment.

"I agree with *capitan* Castillo. Traveling inland would lessen the burden of our march through this rough terrain. Once we find a suitable location on the true coast, we can concentrate our efforts on making contact with the caravels."

Narvaez remained silent for a long moment. Alvar feared that he had fallen asleep. Then, quite unexpectedly, he sat up once more and looked at both men.

"I will have to put my faith in what you say. Let us make preparations to leave tomorrow for we cannot delay one more day. *Senor* de Vaca, as *Aguacil,* you will notify the expedition officers of my decision, and *Senor* Castillo, you will brief the military captains. Together you will put together a plan so that we may leave this place as quickly as possible.

Narvaez seemed exhausted as he slumped back into his bed. Campo rushed over with a wet rag to cool his fevered forehead. Alvar and Castello hurried out to perform their assigned tasks. Overhead, the storm that had made its presence known only an hour before was almost upon them. There would be rain tonight...heavy rain.

CHAPTER 02
The Bay Of Horses

La Bahia de Caballos

Alvar stood in the bow of boat five. They were underway. Looking back at the campsite he surveyed a wasteland of tree stumps, discarded branches, crude shelters, and piles of discarded rubbish...Further down the beach, the refuse piles attracted scores of buzzards that, even at this early hour, circled lazily in the morning sky. He caught sight of several crude wooden crosses put there by friends and compatriots of the dead. Behind him, one of the men remarked, "It is a most sad-looking place, this Bahia de Caballos...Bay of Horses."

07 August, 1528

Leaving the Apalachee Village of Aute

It had rained all night with no let-up. The morning was wet and still, with a heavy mist enveloping the camp. Rain lightly spattered on the ground as the last of the storm blown up from the Gulf of Mexico moved slowly to the northeast. Shivering sentries, huddled in their hideaways, peered into the gloom as the dull light slowly overtook the mysterious shadows of the surrounding forest. They had been expecting hordes of *Indians* to attack at any moment, but the attack had never come. Now they could relax a little. Behind them, the camp began to come alive.

The sounds of preparation were muffled in the still air. Armor was donned, canteens were filled, horses had their hobbles removed and the meager supplies were stacked onto the remaining two wagons. Each man gathered his possessions. Some strapped them to their backs, others carried them in a pouch attached to their belt. The worst of the sick and wounded were loaded onto the remaining horses. There were not enough. Litters were assembled and the wounded were laid upon them. The litters were carried by four-man teams. In a guarded area, the men relieved themselves, for it was at times like this that they were most susceptible to an attack. Cursing, groans, coughing, spitting, farting and the commands of the captains filled the air.

Narvaez, sick as he was, insisted on riding his beloved *Santiago*, but sitting astride the weakened mount, sweating and coughing, he no longer projected the hulking leader of only a few months previous. He rode head down, holding the saddle with both hands. The fearsome *montante,* hanging at his side, now seemed oversized.

By mid-morning the advance guard of twenty men moved away from the *Indio* village at *Aute*. They were led by captain Alonso Castillo. He would follow the same route as the scouting party the day before. Behind them, another heavily armed contingent of men surrounded the core of the expedition. Encased in this group were the litter bearers, carts, walking wounded, and slaves burdened with the remaining supplies. Immediately behind, ten mounted *caballeros,* heavily armed, were positioned to rapidly respond to any attack. At a distance, forty men divided into two groups of twenty warily protected the rear of the column. They continued to deploy their *rana* defense. The first twenty would conceal themselves until the other group of twenty had passed them by. Remaining concealed for a period of time, they would rise up and pass the second group of twenty who would conceal themselves in turn. Each of the two groups contained several musketeers who would discharge their weapons as a warning should they be attacked.

The river crossing was particularly difficult. Men, horses, and equipment were backed up at the river's edge. Additional rafts had to be constructed to ferry the carts and wounded across the river, now swollen from last night's rain. They were in an extremely precarious defensive position, but still no attacks came. The advance guard and the *rana* teams reported seeing *Indians* at a distance. They were being watched, of that they were sure.

It wasn't until afternoon that the last of the *Spaniards* had crossed the *Rio Lengua de Serpiente*. Once again the expedition started their tedious trek to the south. Almost a third of the expedition was sick or injured. They struggled along the trail, stopping frequently to rest and regroup. The rains had left the trail wet and perilous. Horses stumbled and the stretcher-bearers dropped their loads.

Discontent among the *Spaniards*, before restricted to guarded conversations between friends, now began to surface. Tired and sick as they were, the men talked openly of bad decisions by the expedition leaders and criticized Narvaez in particular. The *caballeros,* all men of some distinction, began to form a plan to desert and ride their mounts to the coast in search of the caravels. In this, they were led by Captain Diego Valenzuela. Unencumbered by the expedition's sick and wounded, they could move quickly in an attempt to save themselves. Three of the cavalrymen melted away and, as planned, set up a rendezvous point a league west of the struggling column where they would wait for the others.

It was Captain Andres Dorantes who discovered the plot. Noticing only seven mounted caballeros at the center of the column, he quickly scanned the formation looking for the other horsemen. They were nowhere to be seen. On foot, Dorantes approached the remaining horsemen.

"Lieutenant Veresa, I count only seven, where are the remainder of your men?"

Cristobal Veresa answered Dorantes in a most evasive manner.

"*Capitan,* I...ah...hadn't noticed." He turned in the saddle as if looking to locate them.

Dorantes grabbed the horse's bridle. "You hadn't noticed? We are surrounded by enemies in an unknown land and you don't know where your men are?"

"*Si capitan*, perhaps they have stopped by the side of the trail to relieve themselves."

"You will dismount, Lieutenant Veresa, and tell me what you are hiding." By this time Dorantes had been joined by Captains Pantoja and Tellez.

Under pressure from the three captains, Veresa related the plot and named Valenzuela as the leader. Narvaez was summoned and a trusted rider was sent to the rendezvous point with instructions to bring the deserters back. Valenzuela was brought before the governor to explain his actions.

Narvaez spoke first. "I am told, *Capitan* Valenzuela, that you would dishonor yourself, your king, and this expedition by abandoning us."

Valenzuela seemed to swell with indignation, but Narvaez, although weak and sickly, was still an imposing figure. Valenzuela chose his words carefully.

"*Adelantado*, we have all suffered greatly on this terrible journey. We were promised great rewards for our efforts but have only experienced dangers, sickness, and death. We have traveled for months in this wretched land and have seen only poor savages. There is no great civilization here such as Cortes found in the valley of *Mexico*. We now wonder aimlessly with only death as our final goal."

There was a reason that Valenzuela was the leader of this movement to desert the expedition. He was an educated *hildago* from a prominent family in *Spain*. With a quick mind, he was a gifted orator. In his answer to Narvaez, he had summed up what everyone on the expedition had come to realize. Narvaez was seized by a bout of coughing. He wiped beads of perspiration from his forehead. Composing himself he looked long and hard at Valenzuela.

"*Senor* Valenzuela, and just where were you planning on going with your band of *caballeros*?"

Valenzuela looked at those around him. Dorantes eyed him suspiciously. Captains Pantoja and Tellez leaned on their swords with no expression. In the background, Campo watched the proceedings with wide-eyed curiosity.

"*Adelantado*, we had made a determination to ride quickly to the coast and seek to meet up with our caravels."

"And then what, *Capitan* Valenzuela? Would you have sailed off leaving all of us, your compatriots, to die here?"

Valenzuela stiffened. His honor was being questioned, and for a moment he lost his composure.

"Not at all! Once contact was made we agreed to return to the expedition and lead it to safety."

Narvaez considered this answer. "*Capitan* Valenzuela, would it not have been better to bring these arguments to me for consideration?"

"With all respect, *Adelantado*, you seem blinded by the promise of gold."

Dorantes, Tellez, and Pantoja looked at one another. They fully expected an explosion by their leader, but Narvaez, obviously tired, seated himself and looked up at Valenzuela.

"What you say is true, *Capitan*. I have been partially blinded by the promise of gold and other riches. But that was the purpose of this expedition. Who would have thought that in this endless land, there is not another *Tenochtitlan* such as Cortes discovered."

All remained silent as Narvaez continued.

"Let us put aside our differences and make every effort to remain united in our venture. When we camp tonight I will call everyone together. All will be heard and we will put together a plan to save ourselves from this dismal country."

Embarrassed, Valenzuela stepped closer to Narvaez. *"Adelantado,* your answer is that of a great leader. I sincerely apologize for my indiscretions and swear fidelity to you from this moment on."

The meeting broke up and Valenzuela hurried off.

Dorantes turned to Pantoja and said, "I thought *Capitan* Valenzuela swore fidelity to the *Adelantado* at the beginning of this expedition!"

Pantoja just shrugged.

07 August, 1528

Arrive at the Bay of Horses

It was late afternoon as the leading contingents arrived at the spot visited earlier by the scouting party. All about were the remains of the campfires and the oyster feast partaken only a few days previous. There was no sign of *Indians*. The receding tide had exposed the vast mudflats. It was determined that the camp would be made at a point some distance from the original campsite. Here the ground was somewhat higher with a broad view of the bay. The location provided a satisfactory defensive position. With their backs to the bay, they would only have to watch for attacks from the front and from each flank. Nearby was grass for the horses and a stream. Firewood could be obtained from the thick stands of sand oak and the abundant driftwood that lay along the shoreline.

Soon, fires were started and the process of securing the campsite was underway. Sentries were posted, horses were unloaded and tethered while the men sought out the best locations. Several were already wading in the mudflats to harvest oysters. It was almost dark as the last *rana* team made its way into camp.

Narvaez had been one of the first to arrive at the camp. Dismounting, the exhausted governor sat down and propped himself against a tree. He fell into a deep sleep while Campo and several of the slaves constructed a crude shelter. It was long after sundown before Narvaez awoke. Somewhat refreshed, he called for de Vaca.

Alvar had been busy setting up the defensive perimeter and ensuring that the horses were protected should an evening attack come. It had taken Campo several minutes to locate him. He rushed over to where Narvaez was sitting.

"*Adelantado*, my apologies, I was assisting *Capitan* Tellez in the placement of the evening guard."

"*Senor* de Vaca, as soon as you feel we are secure I want to talk with all the *capitans* and officials as I had promised. Have them assemble in this clear area in front of me."

Alvar nodded, "*Si Adelantado*," and rushed away.

It was almost midnight by the time all of the leading men of the expedition came together in front of Narvaez's shelter. To the west and southwest bright flashes of lightning illuminated the sinister column of clouds building on the horizon. There would be rain before morning and everyone who was able labored to construct some kind of shelter before it arrived.

Narvaez sat quietly while the men assembled. Some sat cross-legged on the ground, others stood or leaned against trees. There was little talk, the day's march and labor to set up camp had taken its toll. Many of the men were coughing. A few made frequent trips to the dark corners of the camp to relieve themselves. Narvaez arose with some difficulty and began to address the assembly.

"*Compatriotas*, we have searched long and hard for the cities of riches that we know must be here." He stopped and looked at each of his commanders. If they still believed this story, it didn't show on their faces.

Narvaez continued. "Our efforts have been in vain and this dismal country is causing us much pain. We have lost many good men and now we grow weaker each day with hunger and disease. Our horses are spent, our shoes and clothes are rotting and the powder for our musketeers is all but gone. Even the strings for our crossbows are rotting, rendering them useless."

There was bitterness in Narvaez's voice. Bitterness, disappointment, and fatigue. He stopped and coughed. It seemed to drain him of strength and he leaned against a tree for support.

Alvar, standing just to the front of Narvaez, made a run to a dark corner of the camp. Many others had the same problem and it was difficult to step anywhere that hadn't already been used. He didn't care. All that mattered was relieving that terrible pressure in his bowels. He was sweating, and the explosive release made him weak. He had tried hard to clean himself with leaves and grass but he still smelled of feces. The smell made him retch and he sank to his knees trying to gather himself. He heard Narvaez begin again.

"We are now near the sea and it is hoped we will be able to contact the caravels that I am sure are looking for us. If, however, the caravels do not come, we must determine what to do next. As I promised, each one of you can offer an opinion that we all will consider."

Captain Tellez was the first to speak.

"*Adelantado*, we have traveled so far, surely we are much closer to the settlements at *Panuco*?"

Narvaez was slow to answer. "It is true we have traveled far, but there are no pilots with us to read the stars and render a location. So much is unknown between here and the land of New *Spain* that I am loathe to render a guess of how far it is to *Panuco*. Rather, it would be my hope to make contact with the caravels.

The fire in his abdomen somewhat relieved, Alvar approached the group and sat just outside the circle.

Narvaez noticed him. "*Senor* de Vaca, let us hear what you have to say about our situation."

He began slowly. "*Adalentado*, as we already know, this is but a broad river delta, exceedingly shallow and replete with shoals and mudflats. The true coast is much further to the south and fraught with exceedingly difficult terrain. It is my opinion that it will take several days to make this journey, for we will have to round countless inlets, bays, and swamps."

"Do you have a suggestion, *Alguacil*?" It was the comptroller Alonso Enriquez.

Alvar looked around him. One-third of the men were dangerously ill while the remainder displayed an assortment of wounds and maladies. The horses were in poor shape, several being unrideable. His stomach began to burn again.

"*Adelantado*, I have been considering a plan."

"If you have an idea, *Senor* de Vaca, please share it with us."

Alvar cleared his throat and began. "To travel any more in this wilderness is to invite further attacks and misfortunes, yet we must make every attempt to reach a location where the caravels can find us."

There were nods of agreement all around. He continued. "Even now we can hardly transport our wounded, and in but a few more days the horses will be played out."

More nods.

"My thoughts are to remain here and build a vessel by which we can proceed to the true coast...*las cierto costa*. Once there we can follow the shoreline and proceed westward towards *New Spain*. By following the coast we will increase our chances of finding the caravels that I am sure are looking for us."

For a moment the assembly of men was quiet as each considered the idea presented by de Vaca. Then, almost in unison, the meeting erupted in questions and arguments.

"How will we construct this vessel?"

"We have but few men who have any knowledge of carpentry."

"Many of our tools have been lost."

"What will we use for the iron bolts, fittings, ropes, and caulking?"

At first, the idea seemed absurd, but as the individual discussions continued, many entertained the idea that it might be possible.

Alvaro Fernandez, the only carpenter, and his apprentice Bonito Pina were asked to join the discussion.

"*Senor* Fernandez, you have heard the proposal to build a vessel with which we can all proceed to the sea, and if God permits, to the caravels that are surely looking for us."

Fernandez answered. "*Si Adelantado*, the *Aguacil* has discussed this with me on several occasions."

"What then are your thoughts on completing this task with the meager possessions that we now have?"

Fernandez pondered a moment, rubbing his neck as he thought about what he would say. "*Adelantado*, the building of a *barco*...boat requires many special tools of which we have but few. In addition, we will need accessories like bolts, straps, rope, caulking, and sail material."

Alvar spoke next, "*Senor* Fernandez, I myself have taken a count of the tools in our possession. We have several saws, knives, chisels, shovels, an adze, and quite a number of axes. Our blacksmith, *Senor* Nazario, lost his bellows and most of his equipment when we fought the *Indios* at *Polvora Logo,* but still maintains a few hammers, a small anvil, an adze, several pliers, taps, punches, rasps, tongs, and cutters. Perhaps he could fashion some of the necessary items that would be needed."

Narvaez looked around him. "Where is Jorge? Someone find *la Herrero* and have him join us."

Quite unexpectedly Jorge Nazario broke through the crowd into the firelight. "I am here *Adelantado*. I heard someone talking of a blacksmith and decided to join you."

"Ah, Jorge!" Narvaez always seemed to brighten whenever Nazario was around. "We are considering building a vessel by which we could regain the sea and leave this place. To do so, however, will require your knowledge and skills. We must ask if you think this undertaking possible?"

Nazario scanned the faces sitting around the fire to determine if Narvaez was serious. His face hardened.

"*Adelantado*, I can see that you are serious in what you ask. While in *Spain* I assisted in many boat-building projects. I have fashioned nails, pins, chains, clasps, and even whole anchors, many things that you will also need, but these were done with a whole complement of the necessary tools, and, most importantly, a working forge. What I have left is only the most simple tools with no iron stock from which to produce the necessities for building a vessel."

The discussion group fell silent, each consumed in his own thoughts. It was Fray Juan Xaraez who finally broke the silence.

"The Lord will provide. Let us think about what we have talked about tonight and meet again tomorrow morning."

The men moved away. The captains, Castillo and Pantoja, circulated through the camp directing the defensive positions, for it was their turn to perform this function, a responsibility shared by all the captains. The campsite, situated next to the water, was only accessible from one side, the river and mud flats enclosing them in a rough semicircle. Tonight the sky was clear and the brightness of the moon would make it hard for an enemy to surprise them.

His stomach still burning, Alvar found a place to lie down next to the fire and moved the sand and dirt around to suit him. *Las mosquitos* were particularly bad tonight, even the smoke from the fire didn't seem to deter them. He dug deeper into the sandy soil and tried to cover his feet and legs. Tomorrow he would clean himself, but tonight his body ached with fatigue. Carefully, he laid his sword next to him and used his buckler for a pillow. He fell asleep immediately.

08 August, 1528

Expedition Meeting at the Bay of Horses

At morning's light, the camp began to stir. Those who had been on watch were replaced by others still rubbing their eyes to remove the sleep. The main fire pit was now mostly embers, it had been unattended during the night and a light rain had all but put it out. The air was heavy with moisture and a vague haze obstructed the horizon. It was hot and still, not a leaf stirred. The bay was placid as a mill pond. Some of the men were already combing the shallows and mud flats for oysters and clams. One group had waded out into the shallow water to probe the bottom with their bare feet, stooping as they retrieved a mollusk hidden just under the surface.

Alvar sat up and the sand that covered his body cascaded down around him. It seemed as if every part of his body itched. His stomach rumbled and he felt the pressure in his bowels. Rising, he trudged across the mudflat and into the water of the bay. The salt water stung his legs which had been scratched raw in several places. He continued to wade out until the water was just above his knees. Here, the incoming water from a small stream had cut a channel into the bay. Satisfied he was deep enough, he squatted down and let the coolness envelop him. Pulling off what remained of his pantaloons he urinated into the water. He closed his eyes in relief. Now, the pressure in his bowels came again in a spasm that he couldn't ignore. He looked around him. There was no one near. Paddling backward he let it go in a giant gush of relief. When completely out of the area he cleaned himself thoroughly. Rising up, Alvar stepped back into his tattered pantaloons and waded back to the shore feeling much refreshed.

On the beach, a crowd was gathering around the restarted fire. Men were using sticks to roast the clams and oysters they had gathered in the bay. One group included Narvaez and several others. Alvar hurried over.

Capitan Enrique Penalosa was speaking. "*Adelantado*, my man here claims he worked in a tannery as a young boy. Part of his responsibilities were preparing hides for the construction of blacksmith bellows."

Alvar recognized the soldier as Emilano Sandoval, a *balestaro* in Penalosa's company.

Narvaez, who was sitting cross-legged on the ground, looked up at the man who, now in his early thirties, looked as haggard as the rest, his blouse all but rotted away, barefoot, thin as a rail and deeply tanned by the relentless sun.

"Senor Sandoval, is it true what *Capitan* Penalosa says, can you indeed construct *un fuelle*...a bellows, with the meager material we have on hand?"

Sandoval was visibly nervous, "Your excellency, as a boy I prepared the hides for many *fuelle* and even participated in their construction. I think with the hide of *el ciervo*...a stag, that this indeed would be possible."

Narvaez scratched his chin. "If not a stag Senor Sandoval, would the hide of a horse be sufficient?"

Sandoval, somewhat taken aback, considered his answer. "I have never worked with horse hide excellency, but I suppose it would suffice."

By now, a sizable group of captains and expedition officials had gathered around Narvaez. Jorge Nazario, the blacksmith, was next to speak.

"*Adelantado*, with a bellows and a solid hearth I could construct ship-building implements."

"From what? Friend Jorge, as you pointed out last night we have no stock of iron from which to manufacture these things!" Narvaez was clearly frustrated.

Nazario slowly walked over to where Alvar was standing. "Pardon *Alguacil*." He removed the *morion* from Alvar's head and then unsheathed his own knife. Turning, the blacksmith held both items up for all to see.

"*Compatriotas*, we have an abundance of iron. It is all around us. It must only be heated and reshaped."

Narvaez rose up and clasped his hand on Nazario's shoulder.

"It is decided then. We will start immediately to build a vessel by which we can leave this place. Alvaro Fernandez is our carpenter and has extensive knowledge of boat building, but, in addition, we have another compatriot who might be able to help."

Narvaez nodded toward the *Greek*, Doroteo Teodoro, who stepped forward.

"Our *Greek* friend *Senor* Teodoro also has some experience with the design and building of boats. He will advise carpenter Fernandez and his assistant, *Senor* Pina. These three will be in overall charge of this operation. The *capitans* will organize work parties to assist them. All of us will do what we can."

Doroteo Teodora had led a colorful early life. Living outside the *Greek* town of *Paramythia*, he had run away from an abusive father to the seaport at *Igoumenista*. A stout, good-looking boy of 16, he plied the waterfront doing odd jobs and begging for food. Because of his size, he was soon noticed by a local bordello owner, Madam Sophia. He was hired to protect the prostitutes from their waterfront clients. The pay was trivial, but he was promised free room and board, and the services of any of the women that were willing. Doroteo soon became proficient at splitting men's skulls with a lead-filled *cachiporra* and dragging them to the waterfront with pants still around their ankles.

The waterfront, however, was a rough place and one evening Doroteo himself was bludgeoned unconscious by a press gang looking for able-bodied seaman. He awoke on a stinking fishing trawler miles out to sea. Bound hand and foot, he was taken to the stern of the boat and threatened to be thrown overboard if he didn't agree to work. He chose to work.

The work was hard and dangerous but he became acclimated and eventually gained the trust of the captain and the rest of the crew For six months the trawler worked the *Adriatic* coastline netting schools of tuna, amberjack, and mackerel. Gutted and salted, the catches were offloaded at the ports of *Brindisi, Bari, Ancona,* and *Venice.* Doroteo passed his 20th birthday at sea. And so it was until the trawler put in for repairs at the island of *Kerkyra.* Anchored offshore, the captain and mate were drinking heavily. They offered Doroteo a drink and before long he had joined them...only Doroteo feigned drunkenness. A little after midnight he ran to the deck and pretended to vomit over the side. From the cabin, the captain and mate laughed at his misery. Doroteo then lay on the deck as if passed out. Two hours passed until everything was quiet. Crawling on hands and knees to the stern of the trawler, Doroteo dropped over the side taking a small empty cask for flotation. For what seemed an eternity he paddled slowly toward the dim lights on shore, trying to conserve his strength. At last, just before sunrise, he stumbled onto solid ground and freedom.

On *Kerkyra,* he began his new life working as an apprentice for a local boat builder, eventually marrying the owner's daughter and moving the business to *Venice.* It was here he made his fortune and became a gifted designer and a shrewd businessman. From *Venice,* Doroteo expanded his operation to the port of *Cadiz, Spain* where the voyages of discovery supported a lucrative ship-building enterprise. In support of this, he became involved with the timber trade and the acquisition of slaves from Africa. It was at a business meeting in *Jerez* that he encountered Panfilo Narvaez and knew from that moment on that he must travel to the New World.

Everyone began talking at once.

"*Adelantado.*" It was Alonso Enriquez, the expedition comptroller.

Narvaez held up his hands for silence. "The *contralor* wishes to speak."

"We are all in support of leaving this terrible place, but while we are building these *barcos* we will have to protect ourselves from the *Indio* attacks which are sure to come."

There were nods all around.

"More importantly, *Adelantado*, we will have to eat."

More nods.

With this, Alvar stepped forward. "I have thought long and hard about this, and what I am about to say may not be what you want to hear, but it is our only option. We still have eighteen or nineteen serviceable horses. With these our *caballeros* can raid the *Indio* camp for maize and whatever else can be used. This will be dangerous, but necessary."

Alvar paused. "The other mounts will be butchered every three days or as we need them. Eventually, all of the horses will have to be sacrificed. We cannot take them with us and is it not better to use them for our continued nourishment?"

There was silence in the crowd. The horses...the cavalry...*caballeria*, were what defined a *Spanish* fighting unit. There was a bond between these animals and the men that would be hard to break. Still, every man knew the *Alguacil*, Alvar Nunez Cabeza de Vaca, was right. For a while, only the crackling of the fire and camp sounds would break the reverie of the moment. Narvaez had returned to sitting cross-legged on the ground, but now he seemed to sway from side to side. He was covered in sweat. Campo tried to move him back to the crude shelter while several of the captains came over to help the young page.

Narvaez stopped them and looked up at the group. "As you can see I am not well. and for the moment I will delegate *Alguacil* De Vaca to coordinate this effort."

Narvaez stopped and looked at Alvar. "I expect you to report to me on a daily basis."

Bowing slightly at the waist Alvar answered, "As you wish, excellency."

With that, the meeting broke up, but not before Alvar called carpenter Fernandez and Teodoro to his side.

"*Senors*, of boat building I know next to nothing, so I will be depending on you to tell me what is needed.

Fernandez scratched his head and thought for a moment. "*Alguacil*, since this plan was first devised I have been thinking as to what type of vessel...or should I say vessels...we should construct."

"Vessels?"

"*Si Alguacil*, we have not the tools or the capabilities to build a large vessel that could transport..." Fernandez stopped and looked around him. "*Alguacil*, how many men remain in this expedition?"

Alvar hesitated. He knew they had lost people but he was unsure of the actual headcount. "When we arrived in *La Florida* three hundred men and slaves remained to march into the interior with our *Adelantado*. This I know, for we took an accounting by which the comptroller signed his name. Since that time we have lost...uno, dos, tres..." Alvar ticked off each death on his fingers. "Ten men have lost their lives. What remains is two hundred ninety."

Fernandez closed his eyes and thought to himself.

"Six!"

Alvar looked perplexed. "Six what?"

"*Alguacil*, we will need six vessels, each holding about fifty men to leave this place."

Teodoro nodded his head in agreement.

Alvar was worried. "Six vessels...is this even possible?"

Teodoro spoke up, "In the lands along the *African* coast they make vessels out of the most basic of materials. These *dhows*, as they call them, can carry immense loads. I have watched them being built from driftwood and crude planking with only adzes and saws to shape the structures."

Jorge Nazario had joined them. He had been listening intently to what was being said. "I have but one adze, but this is a simple tool and I should be able to construct others if *Senor* Sandoval is successful in his construction of a bellows."

Teodoro nodded, "Good! Let us begin by preparing a construction site for the first vessel. It will need to be close to the bay where the water is deep enough such that we can launch into the bay."

Alvar spoke up. "I know just the place!" He thought of his earlier sojourn to relieve himself.

"Good!" Fernandez answered, "I will begin by laying out the cradle to which the keel of our first vessel will rest upon."

Since the expedition began both Alvaro Fernandez and the *Greek* Doroteo Teodoro had become good friends. Their joint effort now would work well.

10 August, 1528

The Bay of Horses

Two days had passed since the decision to build vessels by which to leave and go in search of the caravels. The camp was a hive of activity. The first concern was for wood, not only to build the vessels but to heat the forge by which the blacksmith Jorge Nazario could shape tools and implements. The sound of axes rang in the woods, interrupted periodically by the crack and 'whoomp" as massive trees crashed to the ground. These were further sectioned and then dragged to the camp by a team of horses. The most difficult was the sawing of these massive trunks into planks. Amazingly, the only two-manned saw on the expedition had not been lost. Depending on the size of the trunk, this was used for half or quarter logs. From here, single-man buck saws (of which there were four) were used to cut the flat planks needed for the sides of the vessels. It was hard, laborious work, especially for men worn down by months of marching and fighting, injuries, and disease.

The best trees were several hundred yards back from the beach, and because of this, the axe men were protected by a strong contingent of soldiers. *Indians* were occasionally seen, but only at a distance. At least for now, they seemed more interested in what the *Spanish* were doing.

Friar Xuarez and his contingent of holy men were tasked with finding a substitute for oakum. This would be needed to pack the seams between the vessels' planking or *"tracas."* As children, several of the soldiers in the expedition had worked in the mountains of *Navarre* collecting pitch from the fir and pine forests. They explained their methods to the friars. Soon, men were scouring the forests for natural collections of pine sap. They further lanced the evergreens with foot-long diagonal cuts that oozed the sticky material. This was all collected and carefully melted down. Teodoro, who had considerable knowledge in the making of oakum, showed the men how to add dried horse dung as a filler. The further addition of animal fat kept the mixture pliable. For the cord, palmetto fibers were pounded until they were supple and then twisted together in a loose weave. Finally, the cord was slowly dipped in a heated vat of the pine sap concoction. The end result produced an oakum product of reasonable quality.

Progress on the blacksmith kiln was delayed for want of mortar to hold the stones together, but this was solved when the slave of Alonso de Solis known only as "El Grande," stepped forward. He was a black *African*, an *Ibo*, who worked for a time with stone masons and brick layers constructing sea walls in the harbor at

Santo Domingo. He recalled that when the lime supplies ran low they would collect sea shells and grind them into powder. Mixed with sand and fresh water they produced a usable mortar.

The boat-building project had a strange and positive effect on the expedition. Men who were sick and debilitated by wounds suddenly had new hope. They seemed to improve. Everyone did what they could to assist. Men unable to withstand the hard labor of wood cutting, hauling logs, carpentry, or soldiering assisted with the more mundane chores of harvesting palmettos, gathering sea shells, boiling pine pitch, and gathering wood for the fires.

Still, the *Indians* did not attack them.

Another problem beset the *Spaniards*. They were running out of food. Alvar called the captains together, the situation was becoming grave.

"We had but a small quantity of maize that we brought from the village on the Snake Tongue. Tonight we will use the last of it. The oysters and clams that we found so plentiful have now become hard to find and we must travel further along the shore to procure them. Some of the men are able to catch or spear fish from the shore, but not enough to feed us all. We dare not deploy hunters into the wilderness for fear of losing them to the roving bands of *Indios* that we know are about."

Captain Castello was the first to speak. "What are your thoughts *Alguacil*?

"So far the *Apalachee* have left us alone. They seem satisfied to watch us from afar. However, if we attack their village seeking food, there is no doubt that they will retaliate in kind."

Captain Tellez spoke up. "We have no choice. We have nothing left to trade. Let us strike *Aute* now while our men and horses are still strong enough."

"I agree," it was Captain Penalosa, "I will volunteer to lead the first raid."

The rest of the captains shook their heads in agreement.

"It is settled then. *Capitan* Penalosa will attack the village at first light tomorrow morning, hoping that your movements are not discovered by the *Indios*." The other *capitans* will concentrate on reinforcing our perimeter for the attack that I am sure will come."

Alvar continued, "Tonight we will kill and butcher our first horse. Emilano Sandoval is in need of a skin for his bellows and we are all in need of nourishment."

The four slaves of Diego de Solis were tasked with the job of dispatching the horse and sectioning the carcass for distribution. One of them, called "Dedos," was the official butcher...*canicero* for the expedition. Trained in Lisbon for the meat trade, Dedos had been bought by Solis to assist with his many cattle *rancheros* throughout *Spain.* As an apprentice, the young *Moor,* born Muhammad al Hassan, had lost the two small fingers on his left hand while learning the trade, a physical characteristic that earned him the sobriquet of *Dedos*...fingers! No one knew him by any other name. While recruiting in Spain, Narvaez had insisted that de Solis bring him on the expedition.

Assisting Dedos was Aldo Salameh, a young man with a smoldering personality. Many times Solis had threatened to sell him, but had always relinquished at the insistence of Dedos who valued him as an assistant. Aldo worked hard for Dedos and gained his trust. He liked Dedo, but more than that, it gave him easy access to the tools of the trade that he hoped to use one day on de Solis whom he hated with a fiery passion.

The other two slaves, also *Moors,* had been recent acquisitions, purchased a month before the expedition left *San Lucar.* Duende was a smallish man of about forty whose *Spanish* name amply described his elfish continence and tireless energy. He was a cook of considerable experience, a luxury that now seemed absurd. The young teen, they called Poco, had been purchased the same day as Duende to look after the horses, weapons, and equipment. Together they now performed whatever menial jobs needed to be done.

The horse was a gelding whose lameness had rendered him unable to carry heavy loads of any kind. Dedos dispatched the animal quickly, cutting its throat. After the death throes had stopped, the four slaves attached a rope to the hindquarters and slowly hoisted the animal into the air, flaying off the skin as it rose. They were particularly careful with the skin on the hind legs, making a circular cut between the gaskin and upper thigh. After sawing off the hoof they rolled the skin off like a stocking, deftly cutting the connective tissue as they went. What remained essentially was a tube of skin open at both ends. Turned inside out the skin was meticulously scraped to remove all traces of fat and other tissue. Dedos had seen this same procedure used with goatskin to make water bags called *botas*. One of the openings would be sewn shut while the narrower end would receive a wooden plug. The *Spaniards* would use these to carry drinking water.

After the much larger main skin was removed it was laid over a log, hair side down, and also scraped clean. Few of the *Spaniards* had any knowledge of the tanner's art. Because of the foul smells and filth, tanneries in Spain were always located outside of town and operated by the poor. Surprisingly, it was one of the padres who was able to impart some knowledge on the process. Fray Pietre de Asturiano had observed the tanning operations outside the monastery, *Convento de Santa Clara* in *Carmona. Spain.* He had been struck by the deplorable working conditions and had done what he could to help the poor people who labored so hard. He had watched in revulsion as the laborers worked the skins in giant vats filled with urine and dung water. The urine process loosened the hair fibers so that they could be removed with a scraping knife. Working the hide in dung water made it supple. This would be the process that the men of the expedition would use in the coming days. All were encouraged to collect their urine in communal piss-pots...*mear ollas*, and animal dung of any kind were collected and put into piles.

Once the horse was skinned, Dedos and Aldo gutted the carcass and quickly sectioned the meat for distribution. In the warm climate, it had to be cooked immediately, there was no salt for preservation. Any uneaten meat was cut into strips and hung above the fire where it further dried and was preserved by the acidic smoke. That night the camp ate well and with it, the men's spirits were somewhat revived. Tomorrow morning Captain Penalosa would ride out to raid the *Apalachee* village.

11 August, 1528

The First Attack on Aute

The camp awoke before dawn to heavy rain and thunder. Those without cover suffered in the cold, unrelenting downpour. Captain Penalosa and his men gathered their equipment and rode into the tempest. Uncomfortable as it was, the bad visibility and noise of the storm masked the Spaniards in their trek. They crossed over the *Rio Lengua de Serpiente* with some difficulty and continued on in the poor visibility. The sky was only marginally lighter as they reached the outskirts of the *Indio* village. Patches of fog drifted through the trees and, the storm had grown in intensity. The camp was unguarded. Penalosa and his 22 *caballeros* split into two columns. One of the columns under the command of Lieutenant Cristobal Verresa would circle the village and begin his attack from the northwest. Penalosa, on hearing the sounds of his attacking comrades would enter from the south. The inhabitants would then be trapped between the cavalry and the river.

It was a good strategy and went exactly as planned. The *Indians* were caught completely unaware and fled from their huts in terror. Penalosa had been instructed to minimize casualties as much as possible, but this directive fell apart when one of the horsemen, a certain Juan Escono, was struck in the mouth by an arrow discharged by a young boy, not yet a warrior, protecting his family. The boy and his family were quickly dispatched, but Escono had fallen from the saddle only to become entangled in the stirrups. The arrow had entered the roof of his mouth and had partially exited just behind his right ear. His wound was mortal and the confused mount, sidestepping to avoid the body, drug him along, leaving a trail of blood and brain matter in the sand. It was Captain Penalosa himself who finally secured the horse while another *caballero* untangled Escono from the stirrups. He was already dead.

Penalosa turned to the other horseman. "Quickly, gather what you can and be on the alert for we are sure to be attacked anew."

But they weren't attacked. At *Aute*, most of the warriors were away at another village on a hunting expedition. What had been left were women, children, and older men unable to participate in the hunt. In all, 26 of the inhabitants had died in the raid and two of the women carried off. Escono had been the only *Spanish* casualty. His body was quickly buried and covered over with grass and branches. His horse would be needed for transport. Even as the *caballeros* gathered up their spoils, however, *Indian* runners from *Aute* spread out in search of the warriors.

It was dusk before the *Spanish* raiding party returned to the camp by the bay. They were delayed by the quantity of maize that they had recovered. Baskets were tied together and thrown over the saddles while the cavalrymen were forced to walk their overburdened mounts. At the river crossing the baskets were carefully floated across on rafts. In all, 95 *fenagas* of maize were received at the camp that day.

That night the guard was doubled for an attack that surely would come. Strangely, however, it did not and the morning of the next day dawned thick, a haze of moisture clinging to the ground. Alvar arose early unable to sleep, the mosquitoes had been especially aggressive during the night, seeming unaffected by the thick smoke of the campfire. The welts covered his arms and legs, their presence marked by blood from prolonged scratching. He ambled down to the water's edge to urinate and noticed three *Spaniards* in the distance. Beyond the safety of the camp, they were probing the mudflats for oysters. A fourth man, further out in the water, carried a pike with which he was attempting to spear fish. Alvar watched with distracted interest as the trio moved slowly along. Finished with his business, Alvar scanned the bay for any sign of sails in the distance. Like everyone else, he hoped that the caravels would appear and take them from this wilderness. There was nothing.

Movement caught his eye. Looking back to the *Spaniards*, the three closest to the shore were down on their knees. One of them collapsed onto the mudflat. At first, Alvar couldn't comprehend, the distance was too great to pick out any particulars. Then he saw them. Ten or more attackers burst from the shore. Alvar watched in stunned disbelief as the *Indio's* weapons rose and fell, hacking the three *Spaniards* to pieces. The pikeman had retreated into deeper water and was attempting to swim back to camp but two warriors bounded into the water after him. Swimming with strong strokes they rapidly gained on the terrified *Spaniard*.

Coming to his senses, Alvar turned and cried out, "To arms, to arms...*a las armas*, we are under attack!"

He turned back to the scene unfolding before him. The *Indians* had caught up to the lone *Spaniard*. A turmoil of splashing water ensued in what appeared to be a terrible struggle, but it was short-lived. The two warriors drug the dead *Spaniard* to the shallows and then proceeded to cut off his head. Holding the trophy by the hair, they made their way to the beach where they were joined by the others. Before disappearing into the trees they placed the head upon a stick at the water's edge.

Alvar stared aghast at the bloody scene. The *Indians* had disappeared as if they had never been there. It was then that Alvar realized he was standing alone, unarmed, and somewhat apart from the main camp. He hurried back and was passed by six armed horsemen racing toward the massacre site.

Shortly after, several of the slaves were called to dig graves for the four men. They would bury them there on the beach, gathering the body parts as best they could. Under guard, Frays Xuarez and Pietre de Asturiano made their way to the site. While they prayed over the graves, the *Spanish* horsemen ranged through the tall grass and trees that bordered the beach ensuring that there were no *Indians* about. Alvar did not attend the burial, he was too sickened by what he had already seen. His thoughts were of the four dead Spaniards, Amodo Ortega, Silvio Tejerina, Rico Redondo, and Guilermo Raez. He thought of their terror in the final moments and then wondered silently if this would be the fate that all in the expedition would face.

This would not be the final attack in this mudflat. Another attack several days later would take the lives of six more *Spaniards*. Gathering shellfish in this shallow bay became extremely dangerous and prompted the name of *Bahia de la Cruz*...Bay of the Cross.

17 August, 1528

Second Attack on the Apalachee Village of Aute

Seven days later the *Spaniards* made another raid on the *Apalachee* camp at *Aute*. This one, however, was hotly contested and two *caballeros* were injured, one gravely. This man, Lieutenant Jordi Avila, had been struck by three arrows while leading a charge. Two of the projectiles glanced harmlessly off his armor, but the third contacted square on, passing completely through his *cuirasse*. He wavered in the saddle and then fell across the horse's neck. The battle continued while the horse and unconscious rider wandered aimlessly about. After the *Indians* had been routed, Avila was gathered up and laid tenderly on the ground. He died only minutes later. The *Spaniards* buried him there and set about the task of gathering maize. This time they had brought additional horses to carry the burden and after a period of an hour hurried back to the river with their spoils. On the opposite side, six additional *caballeros* and ten foot-soldiers had been brought up from the camp to protect the raiding party as they crossed. Here, they would be most exposed. As the rafts were being made ready the *Indians* again attacked, raining arrows down upon the milling men and horses. Immediately the horsemen charged into the bush giving the rest of the party time to hurriedly gather the maize and push across the river. When it appeared that the shoreline was clear, the horseman turned and galloped into the river at full speed, sending huge sprays of water vaulting into the air. The *Indians* moved forward to pick the *Spaniards* off as they swam to the far shore. In this, however, they were somewhat thwarted by the *Spanish Ballesteros* on the opposite bank sending bolts from their crossbows into the raiders. Only one of the horsemen was hit and that was Captain Tellez who had led the raid. He emerged from the water with an arrow dangling from his right arm. It had impacted just below the shoulder and had passed only slightly into the muscle. Until it had been pointed out, he had not even been aware of it. Several horses had been hit by arrows but most of the wounds were superficial. One horse, however, had been mortally injured and died, its body was dragged into camp. It would be butchered for the night's meal.

The raid had procured 104 *fenagas* of maize, much needed by the Spaniards. Most were quickly shelled, dried, and parched, to which each man was given an allotment. Some of the kernels were ground to a fine flour. This flour could be kneaded into flat cakes and roasted on the open fire or mixed with water to produce a thin gruel to which small pieces of horse meat or seafood could be added.

The clams and oysters along the immediate shore had quickly been depleted. To wander further down the bay without armed escort was most dangerous and even hunting parties venturing inland were restricted to a minimum of ten heavily armed men. The *Apalachee* were everywhere. As a result, the surrounding woods and grasslands were quickly depleted of game.

Progress on the boats at first proceeded slowly as the men experimented and learned how to use the tools available to them. Most labor intensive was ripping the downed logs into individual boards. A deep trench was dug to a depth that would allow a man to stand upright. Above, a scaffold was erected to cradle the unfinished log. Working together, two men, one up and one down, would push and pull the long rip saw through the length of the log. Progress was slow, but gradually the number of rough boards of various widths and lengths began to accumulate.

First, to be built were the cradles that would support each vessel while under construction. Once in place, a squared keel log approximately ten *vara* in length was laid down. To this was added the bow post and a single framed internal bulkhead...*mamparos transversale,* located amidship and slotted to receive a mast pole. The transom...*travesano,* defined the aft end of the boat and was also reinforced to receive the rudder post. Another bulkhead, less robust, was added about 1/3 back from the bow post. This was the point at which the planking would begin its bend. Between the bowpost, bulkheads, and transom, spaced at an equal distance, were the ribs...*cuaderna.* These were hand-hewn from specially chosen limbs and driftwood with approximately the same crotch angle as the vessel's deadrise. From the bow post to the transom two internal stringers...*largueros,* one each on the starboard and port sides were added for strength and to support the bulkheads during construction. The center bulkhead represented the widest point of the boat at just over five feet.

The *Spaniards* had considerable disagreement as to the type of planking construction that would best suit their purpose and abilities. It was first decided to use a method of planking called *lapstrake* where each plank, or slat, was overlapped by the one above it. Since each overlapped the next, there was less need for individual fitting and, consequently, savings in labor. However, this method also demanded more material and resulted in a heavier vessel. After much discussion, Alvaro Fernandez successfully argued that *carvel* construction would better suit their needs. Here, the individual slats were fastened edge to edge, and the space between would then be caulked. At the keel, bow post, bulkheads, ribs, and transom the slats were pre-attached with iron nails and then secured with round pegs called "treenails." These pegs were whittled round from soft pine and notched at each end and pounded into pre-drilled holes between the two members to be attached. Into the notches were driven hardwood wedges that expanded the pegs. The protruding residue was then sawed off flush.

The forge and bellows constructed for Jorge Nazario seemed to be working well. The majority of his day was spent manufacturing nails, sharpening, designing, and repairing tools. He worked tirelessly, sometimes late into the night, always protected by at least one swordsman. Nazario's knowledge was indispensable and his loss would be a severe blow to the expedition.

The first vessel began to take shape. It was to be used as a model for the other five, where mistakes were corrected and methods improved. Three others had been started. The fifth and sixth vessels would be built on the cradles vacated by the completed boats. By now, however, a third of the expedition was sick, wounded, or undernourished. Only 10 horses remained serviceable.

Alvar was deep in thought as he inspected the work done on the boats at day's end. It was unusually dark for this time of evening, but he could see a strong line of dark clouds building in the west. The sun had already settled below them and further out he could just make out the ephemeral flashes of light low on the horizon. There would be rain tonight. He absentmindedly stepped off the distance from bow to stern on the first boat which was nearing completion. He was careful to put one foot just in front of the other. He stopped upon reaching the stern...33 steps. Just then a voice came from behind him.

"How many steps *Aguacil*?"

Alvar turned. It was the *Greek* Don Teodoro. "Ah, friend Teodoro, you startled me. Thirty three steps by my count, but my feet are smaller than most."

Teodoro laughed, "We are in agreement then. I counted 30 steps and my feet are larger than most. But, tell me...you are not here to evaluate this vessel. You look troubled."

Alvar sighed, then sat down in the sand. Teodoro did the same.

After a moment Alvar shared his thoughts. "We are losing men every day and all of us are starving. Butchering a horse every three days helps put off the inevitable but the meat is lean and without fat. We will need to raid the *Apalachee* village at *Aute* again to replenish our store of maize."

A deep rumbling sound of distant thunder moved across the bay. Teodoro looked to the west. "We will have to cover a supply of wood for our blacksmith tonight or he will not be able to work tomorrow." Teodoro hesitated. "*Aguacil*, you do what you have to do. Surely we will lose men in the attack but without the maize, we will not have the strength to complete our project, and then...all is lost!"

Wordlessly the two men watched the storm gather strength until tendrils of lightning stabbed regularly at the water and the wind strengthened to a good blow.

"Time to gather wood," were Teodoro's words as he got up and headed off into the dark.

Alvar ambled over to the *Adelantado's* hut to inform him and to begin organizing the raid.

24 August, 1528

Third Raid on Aute

A raiding party of eight horsemen, four pack horses, 28 foot soldiers, and four slaves began the journey to *Aute* just after daybreak. The thunderstorm had hit the camp around midnight and now only a gentle rain was falling while fog still clung to the ground and trees. Everything was wet and the procession made little noise as it headed out of camp. As before, the distance to the crossing site upriver of *Aute* was a little over a league journey. When it was reached, however, the river was swollen by the previous night's rain. Worse, the *Indians* had destroyed all of the rafts used for transport.

A conference was quickly called by *Capitan* Alonso Castillo. There had been rumors of another village further up the *Rio Lengua de Serpiente,* but located on this side of the river. Because of the lack of rafts and the high water, it was decided to parallel the river for a few leagues in search of this village.

Castillo began immediately and posted a strong rear guard to watch for *Indians* coming up from *Aute* that might attack them. Additionally, the captain took four of his best pathfinders...*pioneros*, and placed them far ahead of the main body. Their job would be to give advance notice of an *Indio* settlement or approaching raiding parties. For three hours the *Spaniards* moved along the river, keeping a sharp eye for enemies. Apparently, however, they had remained undetected and continued, unmolested, to the northwest. As the noon hour approached, Castillo considered turning back and had even gone so far as to halt the party and call in the *pioneros*, but no sooner than he instructed two of the *caballeros* to ride forward and retrieve them, the men burst through the tall grass in a run. At first, Castillo was concerned and called the party to arms fearing an attack, but one of the *pioneros*, Juan de Ortega, came up to him breathing heavily.

"*Capitan*, hold the men here, for not more than a short ride ahead is the *Indio* village that we have been seeking."

Castillo dismounted and offered the man a drink from his canteen. He had many questions.

"What of maize...is it ready for picking...how big is this village...is it guarded?"

De Ortega, still gasping, held up his hand. "One question at a time *capitan*. The village is located at the river's edge and appears to be surrounded by three fields of maize that are ready for picking. We could hear women and children talking, but could not get close enough to make a count of the inhabitants."

The other three *pioneros* had now gathered around and given their own impressions of what they had seen. Castillo thought for a moment and then asked all four in turn.

"What would be the best way to approach the village?"

All agreed that the path next to the river's edge would provide the fastest access. Additionally, another path bisected two of the fields of maize and led to the village from another direction. After some discussion it was agreed that the *caballeros* would attack the village from the river path, advancing rapidly on their mounts and taking the *Indians* by surprise. The foot soldiers...*espadachines*, would advance up the maize paths and cut off all retreat. Each of the attacking columns would be led by two *pioneros*. Castillo left a small force of five foot-soldiers to act as a reserve and to guard the rear.

Quietly, the *Spaniards* moved into their attack positions. With a look around to make sure all were in place, Castillo gave the signal to start. First to advance were the *espadachines,* for their movement along the maize path would be slower than the horsemen. When he felt the time was right he ordered the *caballeros* forward. At first, they proceeded at a trot, but nearing the village the *Spaniards* spurred their horses into a headlong charge.

Amid terrified screams and children crying, the horseman burst into the communal area indiscriminately hacking and lancing anything in their path. Fleeing women gathered their children and ran toward the maize path while the few warriors in the camp tried to organize a resistance. The fleeing inhabitants ran into the attacking *espadachines* coming up the maize path. What developed was a bottleneck of humanity. The women trying to save their young ones kicked and clawed at the attacking *Spaniards* only to be cruelly cut down or bludgeoned to death. The soldiers in the rear came to a stop while those in front hacked and pushed their way slowly forward. In the front rank, *pionero* Juan de Ortega tried desperately to clear a path for those coming up behind him. Next to him, a woman tried to wrestle away a lance of one of his compatriots. He grabbed her by the hair and flung her in an arc into the cornfield. There, another *Spaniard* drove his spear through her as she tried to rise. Turning back, *Ortega* was caught full in the throat by a spear wielded by a young boy of no more than 14. Blood gushed out of his mouth and he fought to breathe. His last sight on earth was the ground rushing up as he fell in a heap.

At last, the *espadachines* were able to advance forward and enter the village. Most of the inhabitants had fled, and only a few elderly or infirmed *Indians* remained. These sat in a circle chanting a death song. The *Spaniards* left them alone and began ransacking the huts for anything edible. The *cabelleros* quickly moved into the maize fields and began filling woven baskets with corn. The pack horses were quickly loaded and moved to a staging point by the river trail. Castillo commanded three of the *caballeros* to dismount so that their horse could be used for transport as well. The disgruntled *caballeros* would proceed with the *espadachines*. These foot soldiers and the remaining five horsemen donned crude backpacks to carry maize as well.

Before leaving, Castillo commanded the four slaves to bury Juan de Ortega as quickly as possible. They proceeded back to the maize path and began digging with whatever implements they could find, much of the time scooping the soft earth with their bare hands. Two *espadachines* stood a short distance off, looking warily around to guard the gravediggers. One of them, Miguel de Falla, thought he saw movement in the cornfield. He scanned the area but saw nothing. Suddenly, there it was again. A corn stalk moved ever so slightly. He drew his sword.

The slaves had managed to roll the body of Ortega into a two-foot hole they had hurriedly scooped out. Busily covering the remains, one of them, Rizado, screamed and stood up, frantically reaching behind him. A shaft and projectile point had entered his back and now protruded from his stomach just above the naval. He fell forward into the pit writhing in pain. De Falla saw them then. Ten or more crawling through the corn to conceal themselves. "To arms...*A las armas*, we are under attack!"

The slaves dropped what they were doing and ran headlong towards the main body of *Spaniards* but not before another dropped to the ground, an arrow through his thigh. The other two did not stop. Passing the *espadachines,* the terrified blacks ran as hard as they could. Swords drawn, the two foot-soldiers now faced a horde of angry, charging enemies. De Falla fended off two arrows with his buckler while a third clanged against his *morion,* knocking his head back and spinning him around. His compatriot, Marco Chavez, wasn't as lucky. An arrow struck him full in the mouth, exiting out the back of his neck and severing the spinal cord. De Falla saw him crumple to the ground like a bag of potatoes. Hearing the whoops and yells of the attacking *Indians*, De Falla ran as hard as he could, weaving back and forth to make it harder for them to hit him. Still, he expected a shaft to bring him down at any moment. It didn't, and after what seemed like an eternity of running he reached the *Spaniards* drawn up in a defensive line. They let him and the two retreating slaves pass through. All three collapsed in exhaustion.

The *Indians* didn't follow and only advanced far enough to capture the injured slave who, limping and crawling, was desperately trying to get away. The *Spaniards* had called him Narizota, The *Appalachens* immediately cut the calf tendons on each leg and drug him, screaming, back into the bush. One attacker turned and brandished the sword he had recovered from the body of Marco Chavez. Another hacked off the dead man's head. With that, the *Indians* disappeared as if they had never been there, Narizota's screams gradually fading as they moved further away.

Wary of any more attacks, Castillo immediately ordered the raiding party back down the trail; they wouldn't even make an attempt to recover Chavez's body...it was simply too dangerous. They hurried along, every man on high alert for the attack they were sure would come. A league from the village their trail passed under some exceptionally tall oak trees, while the forest around them was thick with palmettos and undergrowth. Swords drawn, bucklers held high, each man scanned the green hell they were passing through. The party came to an abrupt halt. Up ahead Castillo and his contingent of *cabelleros* stared at the aberration before them. Hanging by his feet from a limb was the naked, mutilated body of Narizota. All ten fingers had been removed and his genitalia had been cut off and stuffed into his mouth. The corpse was punctured by 20 or more arrows. Each man stared hard at the body as they hurried along. Many mumbled a silent prayer and vowed that they would not be taken alive by these heathens.

"Keep the column moving!" Ordered Castillo, but he needn't have worried. The terrified soldiers moved as quickly as possible. The real problem was keeping the column together. Those on horses and those with the lightest load had to be held up for those lagging behind. Two of the horsemen he sent to the rear for added protection and to hurry everyone along.

The raiding party had progressed half a league when another attack came. Passing an area of severe blow-downs, a group of twenty or more *Indio* archers raised up from behind a tangle of limbs and massive trunks, sending a fusillade of arrows at the nearest horseman. Castillo had just proceeded on the other side of the trail to check the rear of the column when the attack came. There were shouts of "*Las Armas...Las Armas*" as soon as the *Indians* had risen up, but by then it was too late. Eighteen arrows struck the horse ridden by Rodriquez Sales. Miraculously none hit the rider, but as the horse spun and collapsed on the ground, Sales was trapped underneath, the force of the fall breaking his neck.

Enraged by the attack and not yet knowing the condition of Sales, Castillo charged the *Indio* archers. Feebly, a few launched arrows in his direction but the others sprinted from their area of concealment to a tall grass swamp. Two were not swift enough. Castillo rode them down, severing one from shoulder to breastbone and splitting the other's skull. The rest crashed through the tall grass and quickly disappeared. Two other *caballeros* quickly joined him.

"*Capitan*, are you all right?"

Breathing hard, his adrenaline still pumping, Castillo muttered "Dirty bastards...*hijos de puta sucia*... I would kill every one of them."

It wasn't until he returned to the column that Castillo learned of the death of Rodriquez Sales.

"We will take our dead comrade back with us and give him a *Christian* burial. The dead horse would have to be left behind, a source of meat that they desperately needed.

31 August, 1528

The Bay of Horses Campsite

Construction of the first boat was complete. It was crude and very much resembled the *Moorish* dhows seen along the coast of North Africa. Internally there were no niceties. No cabin, no raised aft section, strictly an open hull. Attached to the ribs, thin planks were added for strength and for the men to sit on. The mast was internally fitted into the keel and braced at the center bulkhead. It was further braced with a fore and aft stay. A single shroud further braced the mast side to side. A short boom was attached to the mast with an ingenious hook and eyelet device that Jorge Nazario had designed. At the top of the mast, Jorge had attached an eyelet through which the halyard passed to hoist the sail. The ropes were made from palmettos and horse hair woven in a tight braid. Three men stayed busy from dawn to dusk collecting material to manufacture this endless cord that was periodically cut to length for whatever use it was needed.

Now, as the completed boat rested on its cradle, the friars, who had been assigned the task, meticulously caulked the hull. Here, Estevan was able to advise and assist them for he had helped repair and caulk many a hull in his early years as a fisherman.

The health of the expedition continued to deteriorate. By far, the worst malady was dysentery...*las mierdas*, which dehydrated the men and drained them of strength and appetite. The campsite stunk from the foul excretions of the affected. Many were ineffective as workers and lay almost comatose throughout the camp. Others could not be spared to care for them and they pitifully continued to deteriorate. Not even wishing to live, many prayed for death to end their misery. For some, their wish was soon granted. Unnoticed for two days, Emile Fernandez and Andre Villa lay dead in the sand as work continued around them. It wasn't until the bodies began to bloat that they were noticed. Too exhausted to bury the bodies, the men of the expedition drug them downwind on the beach where the crabs, vultures, and wolves quickly devoured the remains.

Since Castillo's disastrous last raid on the *Indio* village, the supply of maize was almost exhausted. Men combed the shoreline for anything to eat, many times venturing far from the safety of the camp. On this day a party of six *Spaniards* picked their way along the shoreline. Here and there they would catch a fiddler crab, eating it whole while spitting out the carapace and claws. At first three would search for food while the other three stood guard, but a large colony of fiddler crabs so excited the famished men that all became involved in digging the crunchy morsels out of their holes.

Still, within sight of the camp, the attack came. A band of *Apalachee* had crawled to within a few yards of the distracted *Spaniards*. The first volley of arrows killed or incapacitated three, the other three, adequately armed, arose to meet the menace but were quickly cut down by a second volley of arrows. As they lay writhing on the beach the *Indians* continued to shoot them through and through until each of the six had no less than ten arrows protruding from their bodies. All of this happened while those in the camp watched helplessly. Long after the *Apalachee* had departed a party of *Spaniards* ventured out to the site to collect any metal that the victims may have had on them. The swords and daggers had all been confiscated by their attackers but three morions, three bucklers, a cuirasse, and a scabbard were retrieved. These would add to Nazario's collection of iron so desperately needed. Prayers were said over the six bodies, but like the others, they also would be left for the scavengers to consume.

That night around the fire many grieved for the men. They had been friends and comrades of everyone in camp. Andres Dorantes wept at their passing. There were the *Portuguese* brothers Heitor and Antonio Coelho, both indomitable warriors. Sonfronio de Huelva, *a musketeer* as good with the sword as he was with his arquebus. Ramon Marias, a smallish man with boundless energy. Miguel Cela and Tirso Jurado, inseparable *ballesteros* whose accuracy with their crossbows was unerring.

In the morning another *Spaniard* lay dead in the sand. Juan Carlos Claver had been injured while watering horses at *Apalachan* many weeks before. It had seemed minor at first, an arrow passing completely through the tricep of his left arm, but the wound had never healed. At first, it was only a nuisance, but as time passed, it began to swell and became increasingly painful. The arm had turned dark over the coming days and he became feverish. It grew worse, exuding pus and smelling of decay. Claver fell into a delirium, talking incoherently to no one in particular. For the last week he had passed in and out of consciousness, waking only to beg for water. It was Friar de Palas who had first discovered the death. The good friar, himself incapacitated by *las mierdas*, had taken it upon himself to care for the injured man. Now, as de Palas knelt over the lifeless body, he gave a blessing that the suffering was over. Like the others, Juan Carlos Claver was dragged from the camp to the location where the bones and decomposed bodies of the others were accumulating.

The first boat completed was taken off the cradle and propped up on the shore. They needed to get started on boat four...*barco cuatro,* as soon as possible. Alvar was concerned that so many men were becoming incapacitated that there may not be enough laborers left to complete the job. He discussed the situation with Fray Xuarez.

"Padre Juan, what are we to do if we have not the ability to complete all of our boats?"

It was a long time before Xuarez answered, his head was bowed and his hands were folded.

"*Alguacil*, if that is the case we must make a decision to send the strongest on the boats in the hope that they may find deliverance in the caravels and lead them back to save the rest."

"But *Padre*, the sick and wounded that remain will not be able to feed themselves and surely will suffer at the hands of the *Apalachee*."

Xuarez looked up and stared into De Vaca's eyes. "Alvar, these are the hard decisions that a commander must make." He thought a moment and then softly added, "I think our lord and Savior has already solved this problem."

"How has he solved our problem, good friar?"

There were tears in Xuarez's eyes as he answered. "We are losing friends and compatriots every day. In another week I think we will not need all of the boats that we had planned for."

This answer took Alvar aback and he sat down to think on it. A good commander must realistically analyze situations. Although he hated to admit it, Padre Juan was right. If their situation continued to deteriorate there would be no need for six boats. Possibly five would do. He again turned to Xuarez.

"*Padre*, your council is always wise. Of course, I will talk with the *Adelantado* about this, after which I will instruct carpenter Teodoro not to begin work on the sixth boat."

Xuarez nodded, "A wise decision *Alguacil*."

05 September, 1528

The Bay of Horses

As the second and third boats neared completion the food stores had dwindled to nothing. All of the men were feeling the effects of starvation. Every day more suffered from scurvy...*escorbuto*, some more than others. The first signs were a general feeling of malaise and fatigue, but this went largely unnoticed because everyone was tired. Soon, muscles began to ache to the point where men became extremely incapacitated. As the disease progressed, the gums became swollen and red, bleeding at the slightest touch. Teeth became loose and the skin began to yellow. Appetite faded, and diarrhea, already rampant in the camp, became worse as the victim slowly wasted away.

It was early September and another five men had died from disease and wounds. These were good men with whom all had lived and fought. They were *musketeers* Emilo Fernandez and Juan Marquez. *Ballestero* Jose Dominquez, *caballero* Niceto Azana whose wounded leg, swollen with infection, burst open spewing pus and fluid across the sand. His suffering, was so immeasurable, that he used his own dagger to end his life. Swordsman...*espadachin*, Aitor Moreno's passing had been much swifter. He was found one morning at the camp's perimeter lying in a pile of his own excrement; his skull crushed from behind as he squatted to relieve himself.

Alvar had just left the crude hut that had been erected for *Narvaez*. Although meeting with him frequently to discuss the progress on the boats and the status of the camp, he was always taken aback by the physical deterioration of the once-powerful *Adelantado*. Today they had discussed the necessity of another foraging expedition to the *Apallachee* village of *Aute*. Although vitally necessary, this raid would be a challenge, for all that remained were four serviceable horses. The number of *Spaniards* able to withstand the rigors of a raid such as this had also been substantially reduced. They needed a plan. Alvar spotted Captain Castello working with an adze to shape some timbers on boat four.

"*Capitan* Castillo, I need to have a word with you."

"*Si aguacil.*" Castillo gladly dropped the adze and hurried over. Alvar related to him the necessity of another raid and his doubts that it would be successful unless they were somehow able to catch the *Apalachee* unaware. Castillo scratched his chin and sat down. He pulled out his dagger and began to draw a crude map in the sand.

"*Alguacil*, I have an idea."

The last few weeks had been dry, and the *Rio Lengua de Serpiente* should be relatively easy to ford. They would stage another attack on the village on the west side of the river, the village that the *Spaniards* had come to call *Pequeno Aute*. A column of broken-down horses and as many men as they could spare would make a show of force as they slowly moved along. Hopefully, this would pull many of the warriors away from the big village of *Aute* where a second column of *Spaniards* would quickly cross the river and attack. Since it was his idea, Captain Castillo asked to lead the raid.

As Alvar relayed the tactics to Narvaez he saw in the *Adelantado's* eyes the fighting spirit that had so long been depressed by sickness. "*Capitan* Castillo has devised a good plan. De Vaca, who will you assign to lead the diversion column?"

"I think *Capitan* Telles, *Adelantado*; he is still strong and will make good decisions."

Narvaez was consumed with a fit of coughing after which he spit a mouth full of phlegm into the dirt beside him.

"Ahhh, if I could only go with *Capitan* Castillo." Narvaez paused for a moment.

"When will this attack occur?"

"Tomorrow morning, *Adelantado*. We are making preparations now."

06 September 1528

Fourth Indian Village Raid on the Rio Lengua De Serpiente

It was well before dawn as Captain Tellez led his column of men and horses up the trail. From a distance, the column looked intimidating, but on closer inspection the condition of the horses and most of the men was startling.

Tellez took note of those around him and muttered to himself, "Invalidos *y jamelgos*...invalids and nags!"

Back at camp, Alvar could still hear the noisy column as they passed out of sight.

"Good, good! That should catch the attention of the *Indios*."

He spoke to Captains Dorantes and Pantoja who would be assisting him in the defense of the camp while the raiding parties were away. They would remain on high alert, for undermanned as they were, an attack by the *Appalaches* could go badly. Exactly two hours after the departure of Tellez the main raiding party left camp and hurried to cross the *Rio Lengua de Serpiente*. Captains Valenzuela and Penalosa assisted Castillo in moving the column along as rapidly as possible. They were able to cross the river without incident at a location where the men easily waded across. On the other side, Castillo regrouped and set off as rapidly as they could for *Aute*.

Captain Tellez continued to lead his noisy column along the west bank of the river toward *Pequeno Aute*...Little *Aute*. So far the ruse was working; on the other side of the river, large groups of *Indians* could be seen following them. By his side, Fray de Asturiano carefully maintained the sand glass...*reloj de arena*, for as soon as the last grains passed to the bottom, the column would turn and hurry back to assist Castillo as they returned from the raid.

Castillo's column burst upon the village of *Aute* in a headlong charge. The diversion had worked, virtually no warriors opposed them. The men were under strict orders not to engage the noncombatants but to concentrate on collecting maize and anything that was edible. Amongst the confusion of the fleeing women and children of *Aute,* the *Spaniards* quickly searched the village and then moved to the fields of ripening maize. Castillo was everywhere, hurrying the men. He even dismounted and helped fill the baskets. Remounting his horse he saw that they had collected all that they could carry.

"*Montar, montar*...regroup!" The column, heavily laden with the spoils, began their trek away from the village. Castillo and the other three horsemen remained in the rear to guard against attack. The rest of the party didn't need to be urged along. Everyone expected an attack at any moment. Exhausted, they made their way to the river crossing and passed quickly to the other side. The last man across was Castillo who looked anxiously around for the column led by Captain Tellez. They were nowhere to be seen. It was past noon, the day had turned hot, very hot, and Castillo's band of raiders struggled mightily under their load of maize. All craved water, but even with the river so close at hand, they dared not tarry for fear of attack. The attack never came, and now Castillo feared that the diversion column, somewhere behind them, was in danger. He was right.

Alejandro Tellez was worried. Across the river, the number of *Indians* was growing in number. Walking along the opposite shore, they no longer tried to hide themselves, taunting the *Spaniards* and losing an occasional arrow. Tellez had turned back an hour ago and was moving as quickly as possible. Reaching the river crossing they saw a rough cross carved into a tree. By agreement, a sign from Castillo that he had preceded them. Now they were on their own. Certain that the *Apalachee* would cross and attack, Tellez doubled the rear guard.

Their pace was maddeningly slow. Of the three horses in the column, only his was of any use. He rode the *Adelantado's* stallion *Santiago*, the one animal on the expedition who had been given preferential treatment. Although thin, the horse was still strong and Narvaez had agreed, reluctantly, to allow Tellez to ride it in the relief column. Ahead, the way looked clear, with a broad grassland spread out before them. Hurrying the men along, he returned to the rear of the column. Behind them, it was obvious their enemy had crossed the river and become more emboldened. Forms could be seen moving through the grass behind and to the side. Halfway across the grassland, the *Apalachee* staged an attack on the rear of the column. Under a shower of arrows, they fell quickly on the rear guard who, after a short encounter drove them back, killing two. Tellez recognized it as a feint, for during the attack the *Indians* on the flanks had increased in number. He quickly moved more of the rear guard forward and shortened the column as much as possible. Their pace slowed even more.

Juan Delgato was sick and scared. Sword in one hand and using the buckler to conceal as much of his upper body as possible, he moved shoulder to shoulder with his comrades. The distress in his bowels momentarily forgotten, his eyes nervously scanned the path ahead. All was quiet except for an occasional comment from one of the soldiers as they spotted a form moving through the grass.

"*Lo veo*"...I see one!

"Por ahi"...over there!

The grassland now began to dissipate as the path moved closer to the river. Clumps of shrubs and palmettos gave way to stands of live oak and hickory, their bases five feet in diameter. Overhead, the thick canopy shaded the sun and blocked the wind. It became eerily silent. Even the sounds of the column moving along the trodden path were sucked up in this twilight world. Suddenly, the man next to Juan screamed in pain, an arrow protruding from his thigh.

Juan watched the man sink to the ground only dimly aware of a burning in his own abdomen. The air was pierced with the screams of the enemy as they attacked the column from three sides. An *Indio,* hideously painted and covered with tattoos, ran straight for him brandishing a war club. He parried the blow and managed to inflict a savage wound that opened the warrior's shoulder blade to the bone. But somehow his strength was ebbing away and his vision began to blur. He was aware once more of the pain in his lower body. He looked down and gasped. Just to the right and below his naval was a neat hole that was oozing blood and fecal material. The arrow that had struck his companion's thigh had first passed through him, entering his abdomen and exiting through his right kidney. Unable to stand, Delgato sunk to his knees as the battle raged around him. Still holding his sword he struggled to remain upright. His vision was gone, he didn't see the warrior who smashed his skull and ended his life.

The *Indio* attack was now in full force. They rushed upon the column screaming most frightfully. They seemed to be everywhere. The starving *Spaniards*, on their backs to the river, fought in desperation. All were injured. Captain Tellez had taken an arrow to his left arm, but the shaft had passed through his tricep without hitting bone or large blood vessels. Another had struck his kneecap and deflected off, leaving a large gash that spewed blood down his leg. Miraculously, *Santiago* remained untouched. Tellez rushed back and forth, using the large stallion as a battering ram to disrupt the *Indio* charge. He slashed right and left with his sword until his arm ached. Just as quickly as the attack had come, it now dissipated. The *Indians* melted back into the cover dragging their dead and wounded back with them. From the right side of the column, Tellez watched helplessly as a wounded *Spaniard* was dragged into the brush. His terrified screams went unheeded.

"Ayudame, Ayudame...help me!"

It became deathly silent. Only the moans of the injured permeated the thick air. It began to rain. Tellez knew that the *Apalachee* would attack again and that this time his group of *Spaniards* would probably be overrun. Dismounting, he did what he could to aid the wounded and prepare for the next attack. The stillness was shattered by the ghastly screams of the *Spaniard* who had been captured. They recognized the man as Thiago Cazorla, a well-liked *ballestero* from *Malaga*. The effect was terrifying, but Tellez and the rest of the men resolved that they would never be taken alive and that the *Indio* would pay dearly for their lives.

The attack came with a suddenness that almost overwhelmed the *Spaniards*. The *Apalachee* rushed at them from all sides. Arrows and stones rained down as the *Indians*, in a full run, rushed upon them. It was a wild melee of brutal hand-to-hand combat. Unable to remount *Santiago* in the swirling fight, Tellez used both sword and dagger to fight off the attackers. Two more *Spaniards*, already grievously wounded, fell. Alvaro Mata and Juan Silva, best of friends from the quaint little town of *Badajoz* on the river *Guadiana,* died together. Just when all seemed hopeless, Tellez was startled by four horsemen rushing into the throng. It was Castillo!

Concerned that the diversion party was in grave danger, Castillo and his three horsemen had left the raiding party and ridden back along the trail. After a twenty-minute ride, they could hear the sounds of battle in the distance. Approaching unnoticed, they had spurred their horses and waded into the attacking *Apalachee* at a full gallop. The effect was devastating. The *Indians* began to retreat in confusion. Buoyed by this turn of events, Tellez and his men surged forward, hacking and clubbing the retreating *Indians*.

As the battle subsided, Castillo rose up in his saddle and called out, "Quickly, *Capitan* Tellez, gather your men and proceed down the trail."

Tellez, once again mounted on *Santiago*, moved the men along. Castillo and his *caballeros* protected the rear of the column should another attack come. It never did. Two hours later the embattled column limped into the camp. That night, two more men died of their wounds sustained in the battle. Victor Morata, his right arm hanging by only a sliver of muscle and tendon, lapsed into unconsciousness and died quietly. Alvaro Valdes, speared in the abdomen, screamed in continuous pain before finally succumbing to his wounds around midnight. The rain that had started falling during the battle continued through the night.

11 September, 1528

The Bay of Horses

The fourth raid on *Aute* had been costly. Six men had died as a result of the battle on the trail...*batella en al camino*, and almost all were injured. Boats two and three had been completed and boat four was well along in construction. The keel and bulkheads for boat five were in place and work was now progressing on the ribs. From their shirts and other clothing they made sails, sewn together with horse hair thread. Each man now walked about with only a loincloth to cover himself. Some still wore their armor, but this was rapidly being consumed by Jose Nazario as he heated and pounded out nails, brackets, and fittings.

The *Apalachee* continued to harass the camp, but no longer did they attack *en masse*. Instead, they satisfied themselves with guerrilla tactics. It was obvious to them that the *Spaniards* wanted to leave this place and they would do what they could to hurry them along. Even weak and starving, the bearded ones fought like demons with their iron weapons, and the *Indians* chose not to confront them again in direct battle. The guerrilla tactics were effective, however, and three more *Spaniards* died at the hands of the *Apalachee* in the five days since the raid.

Felling savins for the construction of oars, Santi de Agudo had strayed a bit too far from the guards. As he stood next to a bush relieving himself, four *Apalachee* rose up with their bows drawn.

Agudo saw them then, but as he turned to run, four arrows impacted with deadly force. He was dead before hitting the ground.

Jordi Pique had died in the middle of camp tending the fires. His body was found the next morning lying amid the bundle of sticks and branches that he had been carrying, a single shaft protruding from his back. The lone shot had pierced his heart and he too had not suffered long.

Gerard Casillas was a *caballero* of undaunted courage, some would say too much so. While collecting palmetto fronds, he had spotted an *Indio* hiding in some tall grass. Casillas grabbed his sword and rushed to dispatch the man, but it was a trap. When no more than ten feet from his quarry three other warriors rose up and bludgeoned him to death with their war clubs. It was over in less than a minute. The *Apalachee* quickly disappeared into the surrounding cover.

Wounds, disease, and sickness had also taken their toll.

The black slave, El Pato, named for his strange duck-like walk, had been injured in the foot during the first raid on *Aute*. A minor laceration, El Pato had not thought much of it. Over time, however, the wound had festered, turning a dark purple and swelling to twice its size. Foul of smell, the skin on his foot split open. Feverish, El Pato had lapsed into semi-consciousness as the infection invaded his body. Lingering in this state for days, he had died in a final fit of agony, screaming incoherently in his native tongue.

Both Sebastian Mores and Felipe Cabanas, caballeros from *Cuenca*, had suffered the debilitating effects of dysentery. With the loss of blood and fluids, they had become incapacitated, dying quietly in their own filth.

19 September, 1528

Boat Building at the Bay of Horses

The fifth boat was complete, save for caulking and final preparations. The frays Juan de Palas, Pietra de Austuriano, and Augusto Alaniz busily forced the cord between the planking, a time-consuming effort that progressed slowly. The sails were also a problem. The first two boats were of fore and aft design, but as it became apparent that lack of material would limit the size of the remaining sails, they were square-rigged. All available clothing had been collected for the material, being sewn together with sinew from the butchered horses. As reinforcement, the head of the sails had been strengthened with a strip of hide attached to both sides. Into this, a series of holes had been cut from which loops of rope attached the sail to the mast or spar. Other reinforcement backings were added to the luff, foot, and clews depending on the sail type. With the completion of the boats, rope production became one of the most pressing necessities. All that were able labored at interweaving the strands of horse hair and palmetto fronds. It was during this time that the expedition suffered another grievous loss, that of their blacksmith Jorge Nazario.

Working late into the night, Nazario had been backlit by the kiln fire when three arrows impacted him. Two had struck the thick rawhide apron that he wore and deflected harmlessly to the side. The third passed under his right arm into the chest cavity. His lungs had been pierced. The three attackers then rushed the injured blacksmith. In pain, but still with presence of mind, he drew his knife and disemboweled the first of the attackers. The second swung his club but missed as Nazario stepped to the side and severed the man's windpipe. The third attacker managed to plunge his knife deep into the blacksmith's left shoulder, but Nazario countered, catching the *Indio* in a headlock with his other arm. Years of pounding steel had developed immense arm strength and the *Indio* flailed about, unsuccessfully, trying to free himself.

Feeling his strength ebbing, Jorge reached up and grabbed the hot poker that was embedded in the coals of the kiln. Bringing it down he held the orange hot tip just in front of the attacker's face. For a moment he enjoyed the look of sheer terror in the man's eyes and laughed aloud.

"Open wide my little friend, I have something to give you!"

He plunged the poker down the *Indio's* throat, the loud pop of steam, frying flesh and the man's stifled screams splitting the air. The body twitched spasmodically for several seconds as he forced the poker deeper and deeper; then it went limp. Nazario relinquished his hold and rolled onto his hands and knees. Blood was flowing out of his mouth staining the sand below him. He rose up to a sitting position and caught sight of Alvar and several men rushing to assist him. He gave them a smile. His head fell forward onto his chest. He was dead.

20 September, 1528

The Bay of Horses

Three horses remained of which one was Narvaez's prize stallion *Santiago*. He had given explicit orders that *Santiago* would not be butchered except by his order. Dedos, slave of Alonso de Solis, now led one of the other horses, both mares, to the butchering place...*la lugar carniceria.* Dedos quickly cut the mare's throat. A spray of arterial blood spouted forth. The mare, eyes wide with fear and breathing heavily, bolted backward and then stood transfixed for a moment on splayed legs. She wavered and then caught herself. Again she wavered. This time her hind quarters gave way and she sunk to the ground. Still alive, but barely, the mare lifted her head ever so slightly as if trying to get up again. With a final gasp, she fell silent.

Dedos attached ropes to the rear legs with the help of Aldo Salameh and Duende. His other young helper, Poco, had died of fever two days before. The horse was skinned, gutted, and sectioned. All viscera, except for the liver and heart, were thrown onto the beach. The sections of meat were immediately set on a spit before the fire and carefully tended by Duende. The smell of the cooking meat was intoxicating to all in the camp and Alvar had set up a guard to protect it. They would eat well tonight and then once more before leaving this place. Five boats had been completed. Three were afloat and teams of men were straining to get the other two in the water.

On this day a strange thing happened. Julio Alves had been an active and energetic cavalryman who had been injured during the first raid at *Aute*. The injury was minor, but he had contracted dysentery and like most, suffered immeasurably from its effects. After days of near immobility, he appeared to be recovering, but grew increasingly reclusive. For hours he would sit in the sand and stare off into the distance. He would talk to no one. Even Alvar had sat before him and tried to communicate but with no success. Quite unexpectedly Alves rose from his stupor, armed himself, and walked to the edge of the camp, disappearing in the treeline. He was never seen again.

The fourth and fifth boats had been floated with great effort. They rode high in the water while the men began loading what remained of the supplies. Of high importance was the assortment of beads, bells, and trinkets that could be used for trade as they traveled along the coast. The bolas sewn together from the flayed leg skins of the horses were filled with fresh water and distributed evenly to each boat. What remained of clothing, weapons, and tools were also added. Finally, their meager supply of parched corn, secured in horsehide bags, was transferred to the boats.

Narvaez, now somewhat recovered from the sickness that had plagued him, began to take an active part in the planning once again. Like the rest, he was a mere shadow of his former self. Watching him move among the men, Alvar thought to himself that the *Adelantado* would be almost unrecognizable to someone who had known him before. But then, looking down at his exposed ribs and sunken stomach, he thought, "Who would recognize me?"

Even as hungry as he was, the eating of horse flesh was repugnant to Alvar. Only once had he tried it, cutting off a wel-cooked piece as it roasted on the fire. As he chewed, a feeling of revulsion overwhelmed him and he spit it into the fire. He subsisted only on corn and the occasional fish, crab, or mollusk that the sea offered up. As evening approached the campfires were tended and the men gathered tightly around them to avoid the scourge of mosquitoes that rose from the grass and woodland at this hour. For a week the *Apalachee* had left them alone and tonight the *Spaniards* were uncharacteristically lax in their vigilance. As darkness enveloped them, a score of canoes moved quietly along the bay toward the boats at anchor. There was no moon, and a heavy overcast left the night extremely dark. Narvaez had posted two men on each boat as guards but on this night most were asleep, their heads resting against the gunnels, their swords laying loose by their sides.

Manuel Alvarez drifted between sleep and consciousness. His thoughts were of home, his family, and the girl he had left behind to find fame and fortune...especially the girl. He envisioned her face, her touch, and the last time they had made love in the garden behind her father's house. He tried to remember everything about her body and the pleasures each gave to the other. He drifted off and was only slightly aware of a noise behind him. Suddenly, a hand clamped over his mouth. Startled to awareness, Manuel brought both his hands up in a reflex action. The knife, intended for his throat, sliced across his forearm. He bit down heavily and the attacker relinquished his hold.

He yelled out then, as loud as he could, *"A las armas, a las armas...*to arms, to arms!"

Rolling to his right Manuel fumbled for his sword, but it clattered to the bottom of the boat just out of reach. He felt rather than saw the *Indio* attacker moving closer to him. Only the dim light of the campfire far up on the beach provided any light. He flailed about only able to see vague forms in the darkness. Manuel Alvarez's last earthly vision was of the attackers advancing up the beach towards the campfire. But his cry of warning had alerted the camp. *Spaniards*, swords in hand, advanced to repel the attack. From behind him, a war club found its mark, crushing his skull and ending his life. His lifeless body fell in a heap at the bottom of boat four.

21 September, 1528

The Bay of Horses

The attack on the camp had been costly. Of the ten guards placed on the boats, eight had been killed. The remaining two had fought their way clear before diving into the water. Only a determined charge by Castillo and 20 men had cleared the beach of the attackers and saved the boats that the *Indians* tried to burn. In the morning they began repairing the damage and loading the remainder of their meager supplies. All in the camp were eager to get underway and much afraid of another attack.

With the help of the comptroller Alonso Enriquez and notary Jero de Alaniz, Narvaez assigned the men to the boats. Choosing the healthiest and strongest, he would command boat one and carry 49 men. In boat two, 49 would be commanded jointly by Enriquez and Fray Xuarez. Boat three was assigned to captains Castillo and Dorantes and would carry 48. Boat four would hold 47 and be commanded by captains Tellez and Penalosa. Finally, boat five would carry 49 and be commanded by Cabeza de Vaca.

Of the original 40 horses only two remained, Narvaez's stallion *Santiago* and a mare. Unable to see his fine animal killed, Narvaez ordered it released. The remaining mare was butchered as the men prepared to leave the next morning. At midnight, however, a storm of the severest intensity blew in and continued throughout the next day. Standing on the shore, the *Spaniards* looked out at a bay fraught with angry white caps and swirling winds. The boats, floating at anchor, were blown parallel with the shore, such that each incoming wave pushed them further onto the beach until all were grounded. This weather continued until Vespers. By midnight the clouds passed and a bright moon illuminated the now quiet bay. They would leave in the morning.

22 September, 1528

Leaving the Bay of Horses

Alvar stood in the bow of boat five. They were underway. Looking back at the campsite he surveyed a wasteland of tree stumps, discarded branches, crude shelters, and piles of discarded rubbish. The boat cradles still remained in place and last night's campfire emitted a spiral of smoke that rose vertically in the calm air. Further down the beach, the refuse piles attracted scores of buzzards that, even at this early hour, circled lazily in the morning sky. He caught sight of several crude wooden crosses put there by friends and compatriots of the dead. Behind him, one of the men remarked, "It is a most sad-looking place, this *Bahia de Caballos*...Bay of Horses."

Alvar answered for all the men. "God willing, I hope to never see it again."

"Somewhere out there," Alvar pointed at the horizon. "Somewhere out there, are the rescue ships of Captain de la Cerda looking for us. Of this I am sure. Let us hope that providence will smile and deliver us from this terrible misfortune."

As an afterthought, he added, "Until we are rescued we must strive to reach *Panuco*. It will be a long journey, but God willing, with favorable winds it is within our reach." Alvar knew the distance to *Panuco* was beyond their capabilities, but many believed it much closer. He would not, at this point, discourage them.

There was not enough wind to raise the sails, so, using the ends of the oars the five boats polled along in the shallow bay which never seemed deeper than a few feet. They proceeded single file, the lead boat watching for sandbars and obstructions. The vessels were so overloaded that the sides of the boat rose no more than half a foot above the water. More than once they had to offload and push the lightened vessel through knee-deep water. It was backbreaking work and the boats filled with mud and water as the occupants clamored over the side. Bailing was a constant ritual while the men at the oars struggled to keep the boats moving. Even the simplest movements were difficult, so stacked together were the men. Those that were able could stand and urinate over the side. The others, sick or injured, without the strength to stand, pissed in the boat. Others with dysentery sat in their own filth. Frequent stops were welcome so that the men could walk about in the shallow water and clean themselves.

29 September, 1528

The Five Boats Make Their Way to the Open Ocean

For seven days the little flotilla proceeded along the bay, using the makeshift sails when they were able. Many times they made wrong turns into blind inlets only to reverse course and seek another route to the open sea. Shoreward, there was no sign of a beach, the dense vegetation growing down to the water's edge and fringed with vast mudflats that stunk of decay. There were occasional oyster beds in the bay, however, and the boats would stop so that the men could feast upon them.

At noon an island was spotted close to the shore. Alvar's boat, being in the lead, headed toward it. As they closed on the island five *Indio* canoes were spotted coming towards them. Men reached for their weapons, but the *Indians*, on seeing the strange fleet, abandoned their canoes and ran. Approaching even closer, several lodges came into view. They appeared to be abandoned.

Alvar called out to the boat captained by Dorantes and Castillo, "Offload your best men so that we can investigate this village."

Sword in hand, Alvar jumped into the water which was only waist deep. Several others from the five boats joined him and together they waded toward the huts.

Indeed, the village was deserted, but only recently. Drying on poles were scores of mullet, split in two and gutted. Many were with roe, their eggs supplying the *Spaniards* with much-needed protein. All of this was collected and divided up among the five boats. On leaving, Alvar collected five of the abandoned canoes and assigned three men to each which alleviated, somewhat, the crowding in the boats.

They called the island *Isla del Pescado*...Fish Island.

A brisk breeze propelled them along for two leagues until they reached a strait. Ahead, the sea opened up, clear and unfettered. To the west, a broad sandy beach glistened in the distance. They had reached the coast. Relieved to finally be out of the river delta, all of the *Spaniards*, led by the *padres*, gave thanks. By their calculations, today was *Saint Michaels Day* and for this, they christened the strait *San Miguel*. By evening, all the boats had landed on the beach. It seemed uninhabited, and for the first time in days, they built a raging bonfire to warm themselves and consume the dried mullet procured at the *Indio* camp. The canoes gathered from the village were disassembled and used to extend the height of the gunnels on each of the five boats.

That night as Alvar stood on the beach and looked out to sea, he watched distant lightning playing across the horizon. Overhead, the skies were wondrously clear and the stars seemed to be close enough to touch. One constellation stood out, Bartalome Valdez's favorite. It was Orion, the hunter, standing strong and formidable, the three belt stars shining brightly. Alvar grasped the medallion around his neck. He looked to the west and in the blackness wondered what awaited them. Would he ever see his Maria again? He whispered a silent prayer and returned to the campfire.

CHAPTER 03

Big Muddy River

Gran Rio Fangoso

Alvar, reaching over the side, scooped up some of the water and tasted it. It was brackish and gritty. He stood up and gazed to the north.

"This big muddy river is nothing like I have ever seen! The land that it flows through must be immense."

29 October, 1528

Somewhere Along the Coast Near Florida's

Panhandle

The sun was setting in the west. Only a small arc of its fading brilliance lingered above the watery horizon and, in a moment, it was gone. Crepuscular rays radiated skyward in a magnificent display of orange and blue hues that seemed to paint the sky. Against this dazzling backdrop, a squadron of pelicans winged shoreward in search of a nocturnal roost.

A quiet sea, disturbed only by gentle swells moving endlessly toward the fading shoreline, spread in all directions. The only noise was the gentle lapping of waves against the hull and the quiet creak of the boom as the tattered sails responded to an intermittent wind that puffed out of the south.

In the bow of *barco de cinco*...boat five, Alvar Nunez Cabeza de Vaca took in the scene before him. It was magnificent and he reveled in its beauty forgetting, for a moment, the plight they all were in.

"A truly wondrous sunset *Alguacil*, is it not?"

Alvar was shaken from his revere as he turned to answer Alonso de Solis who, a moment before, seemed to be sleeping beside him. He tried to answer but only managed a croak from the dryness that permeated his throat. Swallowing twice, he struggled to wet his lips with a tongue that felt more like beach sand.

"*Si* Alonso, it hints of a calm night but I would rather see a rain shower from which we could collect drinking water."

Behind the two, forty seven other men were crammed into the small vessel with barely room enough to turn around. So overloaded were they that the boat rode heavy in the water, only moving forward slightly in the light breeze. Many of the men behind them were asleep, others just stared blankly into the distance, and all were in extreme need of water.

Alvar called out to the rear of the boat. "*Senor* Oviedo, bring us closer to shore, it grows dark and I don't want to be blown out to sea if the wind changes."

Lope de Oviedo roused himself and pushed the tiller to larboard. Slowly, ever so slowly, the bow moved shoreward. In front and to both sides the other four boats, of what remained of the Narvaez expedition, made a similar course adjustment.

They had begun their sea journey 37 days before, launching the five boats into the bay fed by the *Rio de la Magdalena*. They had called this bay, *La Bahia de Caballos*...The Bay of Horses, for it was here they had made the determination to abandon their land journey and proceed by sea. The horses of the expedition had served to feed the men during the boat-building process and, one by one, they had been consumed until only two remained. One was the pampered stallion, *Santiago*, of expedition leader Panfilo de Narvaez, the other, a mare of no distinction. On the eve of the departure, the mare was butchered for a final feast. Narvaez, unable to see his prize stallion killed, had released him into the wilds of *La Florida*.

They had built 5 crude boats resembling the eastern Mediterranean *badan* or *dhow,* handcrafting each component from the materials at hand. Metal tools, fasteners, nails, and brackets were fabricated by the expedition blacksmith using the expedition stirrups, spurs, crossbows, and armor as a source of iron. From the husks of palmettos and the manes and tails of the butchered horses, they braided ropes. From the remaining shirts and clothing sails were sewn together. A mixture of pine sap, horse manure, animal fat, and palmetto husks produced the oakum needed to caulk the hulls. The legs of the horses were carefully flayed and sewn together to make leather pouches for carrying water.

Early on, the expedition raided the surrounding *Apalachee* villages to get food. Four raids had procured four hundred *fanegas* of corn, but at a price. The *Indians* had retaliated, raiding the *Spanish* camp and repeatedly ambushing soldiers that wandered too far from camp. All manner of disease had also taken its toll, the worst of which, *las mierdas*...dysentery, claimed many a life. Typhus, malaria scurvy, drowning, snakebite, lightning, and suicide had also contributed to reducing the three hundred that had originally set out to two hundred and forty two that now manned the five boats. Of these, many were injured or sick. All were suffering from malnutrition and exposure.

In the bow of the fifth boat, Alvar etched another mark into the soft wood to mark the number of days they had been on the water. He counted them.

"Thirty seven days Alonso, thirty seven days we have been hugging the coast since leaving *La Bahia de Caballos.* "

Since reaching open water at *Saint Michael's Straight* most of the days had been involved with investigating the many estuaries and blind bays in the search for food and drinkable water. In their trek westward to *Panuco* they had only made marginal progress.

Alonso de Solis did not answer, for he had again fallen asleep, his head resting on the gunnel. Alvar looked at him and shrugged. To the west, the afterglow of sunset was fading, and behind, to the east, the darkness was rapidly approaching. The shoreline was now close, but not too close for there was always the fear of raids by *Indians*. At a signal from boat one...Narvaez's...all five lowered their single sail and threw out a makeshift anchor...a rock tightly tied to the braided horsehair and palmetto frond rope. Alvar noted that the rope only played out a few feet...they were in shallow water. In the fading light, he scanned the shoreline. There was no sign of anything moving. There was no wind and the water was as calm as a duck pond.

The five boats were positioned in a loose line with Alvar's boat being the most easterly. Nightfall came, and with it a dropping of the temperature. A damp fog began to drift in. The men, already packed tightly in the boats, huddled even more closely together. The last of the water was distributed and Alonso de Solis agreed to take the first watch.

At about midnight, Alvar was gently jostled awake. de Solis whispered to him,

"Someone is approaching us."

Still groggy, Alvar tried to blink himself awake. His mouth was dry and he managed to croak out,

"Where?"

"Astern. I can hear the sound of paddles and movement."

Hoping it was one of the other boats that had drifted close, Alvar peered out into the blackness and listened intently, cupping his hands behind his ears. At first, only the sounds of the sea were distinguishable, the gentle lapping of the water against the hull, a wave breaking on the shore, and an occasional seabird calling out. Then, ever so faintly, another sound...or did he just imagine it?

There it was again, this time louder. The sound of a paddle in the water and then a whisper, almost inaudible and definitely not *Spanish*. Alvar reached for the sword that was at his feet and set it on his lap.

He whispered to de Solis, "I hear them now. Wake the men...quietly...and have them arm themselves."

The boat stirred to life. The few men with weapons, for most had been used for iron in building the boats, gathered them up and made ready. The sounds grew nearer and then seemed to stop. In the blackness, Alvar could see nothing but felt the presence of the *Indio* craft only a short distance away. He turned to de Solis.

"I am going to call out to them, perhaps they are friendly. Besides, it will also alert the other boats."

Alvar recalled the *Apalachee* word for friend...*taysato*...or was it *taysa*? He would try both.

Cupping his hands in the direction of the intruder he called out, "*Taysato*, we are your friends. *Taysa*."

There was silence and then the faint sound of whispering. Alvar could almost imagine the *Indians* as they faced the quandary of what to do next.

From behind them, another voice in the night. "*Cuya embarcacion llama*...Which boat calls out?"

Alvar recognized the voice of Captain Alonso del Castillo in boat 3. "*Capitan* Castillo it is I, de Vaca. We have visitors not more than a few yards from our boat. I know not their numbers but think it is only one canoe."

In the night the sounds of the third boat came to life. Men were awakening. There were calls to the other boats as well.

Again from Castillo, "*Senor* de Vaca, are they threatening?"

"No, they are standing off." Again Alvar called out to the intruder. "*Taysato...Taysa*, we are your friends."

Apparently, the sounds of the other boats awakening had spooked the *Indians* for now Alvar could clearly hear paddles striking the water and the movement of the craft away from them.

He again called out to Castillo. "The *Indios* are moving away, I think to the northwest."

There was more communication between the boats. Finally, from boat one, came the unmistakable voice of Panfilo Narvaez. "Let us proceed away from here should the *Indios* return in greater numbers."

A slight breeze had begun to blow from the southeast. Overhead, stars made their appearance and the fog moved away, its presence a receding shadow in the east. A half moon waxed in the west, its meager light reflected off the water. To the north, the dark profile of the shore materialized against the sky.

A sail from one of the boats punctuated the darkness, and then another. Overhead, Alvar watched as their own sail was hoisted into place. The anchors were hauled and the boats of the expedition, taking advantage of the southeast breeze, moved slowly westward.

30 October, 1528

Somewhere Along the Coast Near Florida's

Panhandle

Waves buffeted the overloaded boats. Since leaving their anchorage earlier the wind had freshened and was now blowing with some force from the south. The sun rising behind them showed an angry sky and the promise of worse weather. On board the boats the thirst of the men was overwhelming, for the last of the water stored in the horse hide bolas had been consumed the day before. Now rotting and useless, the bolas were thrown overboard.

Although they were now in the open ocean the coast was a maze of mangroves, inlets, and coves. They had ventured into many of these in search of water but all were shallow and dangerous. The few *Indians* they met were retched individuals, fishermen mostly, who avoided them and stayed out of reach with their speedier canoes.

From his position in the bow of boat five, Alvar watched as a man dipped his hand into the salt water and rubbed the moisture on his lips. Unable to resist, the man cupped his hands and drank deeply. Alvar tried to call out for him to desist but all that came from his dried lips was a coarse croak. Pointing at the man and waving his arms he managed to attract the attention of those closest and they restrained him, but not before he had consumed a belly full of seawater. The man, Alvar recognized him as one of the youngest ballesteros, began to convulse, the contents of his stomach spewing over the side. He continued to retch. Too weak to hold himself erect, the man seemed to collapse into a state of semi-consciousness.

They had been coasting among a line of barrier reefs and wind-swept islands that lay offshore by no more than half a league. The wind was increasing. Sea-spray blown from the whitecaps that dotted the bay formed a surface haze and the sky grew darker with every minute. They would have to come ashore or risk sinking because the freeboard of these overloaded vessels measured no more than a *xeme*. Ahead, a small island covered with sparse vegetation stood out from the shore. Boat three, now in the lead, seemed to be making for it. At mid-morning they hauled onto the desolate beach dragging the crafts past the wave line.

The wind had now reached gale force and the fine sand from the beach blew sharply against the skin. The men shielded their eyes and moved away from the shore. Those who were sick or wounded were aided by their comrades. Some stayed on board the boats, too weak or not wanting to move. Most of the island was covered in coarse grass that reminded Alvar of the vast fields of oats grown in *Andalusia*. A search of the island for water was in vain, for there was none to be had. The men hunkered down for the coming storm that now threatened in the extreme. Lightning split the sky and the thunder seemed to come in one continuous wave, but the rain fell only fleetingly. As best they could the men struggled to collect moisture. Ringing out their meager clothes they sucked on the cloth. Some dug holes in the sand and scooped the collected water into their mouth. Alvar, who had kept his *morion,* used the helmet to collect the rainfall, but this only provided an occasional mouthful.

The storm continued unabated throughout the day and into the night. Twice the men were forced to haul the boats further on shore, for the strong seas threatened to wash them away. At midnight the storm intensified, dazzling the Spaniards with continuous lightning that illuminated the island in wild bursts of energy. The unending din of thunder made it difficult to speak. Finally, in the darkness of early morning, the rain began to fall, lightly at first and then progressing to torrents that passed over the island in waves. The men lay in the sand with their hands cupped around their mouths relishing each swallow of water. At morning light the tempest had moved further inland. The line of inky black clouds was visible in the half-light of dawn and extended across the entire western horizon. Even in their condition, the *Spaniard*s watched, spellbound, as the sky seemed alive with the electrostatic discharges. Overhead, low clouds swirled by as if being sucked into the maelstrom. The wind continued unabated, actually increasing throughout the day. By evening the blackness in the west had disappeared but the angry turbulent skies continued. They did not see the sun this day nor for the next five.

On the third night, the wind shifted to north northeast, dropping the temperature to just above freezing. With no relief from the relentless wind on the barren island, the men suffered severely, huddling together for protection and warmth. They dug holes in the sand to protect themselves from the wind and there they remained while the wind and turbulent seas continued. They could not risk launching the boats. On this night the young *ballestero* who had drunk seawater died.

On the fourth day, the weather worsened again, such that a man could hardly walk upright without leaning into the strong gusts now blowing directly from the north. Blown sand permeated everything, it was in their ears, their nose, and their mouths and ground against their teeth. Every few minutes Alvar would run his index finger across his gums to remove the accumulated grit. That night two slaves died of exposure. Zuno was a black African from Captain Tellez's boat, owned by Garcia de Oaredes. Dedos was the official expedition butcher...*canicero*...a slave owned by Diego de Solis.

By the evening of the fifth day, a young sword and buckler man...an *espadachine*...from the Friar's boat and two crossbowmen...*ballesteros*...from the Castillo/Dorantes boat had died. As darkness fell on this day, however, the winds and high seas began to abate. There was an indication that the cold northerly that had been blowing continuously was dying away and moving around to the west. In a meeting between the boat commanders and Narvaez, it was decided to launch in the morning and take their chances in making for the mainland. So critical was their need for water, they would entrust themselves to God and risk the dangers of the sea.

06 November, 1528

Somewhere Along the Coast Near Florida's

Panhandle

The morning dawned sullen and overcast. The bay between the island and the mainland was punctuated with whitecaps and windblown spray. The men struggled mightily to push the heavy craft into the water. It wasn't until afternoon that all five were again afloat. Six days previous they had landed on the windward side of the island, today they sailed easterly to round the point before turning toward the mainland. Once in the bay, the flotilla pointed their bows to the northwest, taking the route of the canoe they had encountered the night before reaching the island. Their need for water was so great that even the threat of attack by *Indians* could not deter them.

The wind had moderated only slightly, waves still buffeting the five craft. The tattered and rotting sails were coming apart and the heaviness of the boats made them slow to respond. Taking his turn at the tiller, Alvar, shivering violently, was soaked by the waves that surged over the stern. He tried to anticipate the movements of the boat and bring the bow as close to the wind as possible, but the wind, blowing off their aft quarter, slowed progress to the mainland and they slipped further west. Overloaded as it was, the bow wondered about, requiring constant corrections. Too close to the wind and they stood the danger of broaching. This, almost certainly, would end badly, for turning sideways in these conditions would surely cause the boat to capsize.

 Just before noon, Fray de Palas took his turn at the tiller, and, like Alvar, struggled to maintain direction. A particularly strong gust slammed into the vessel, and despite the fray's best efforts, the stern came around, presenting the side of the vessel to the wind-blown swells. The starboard side rose high and the men struggled to shift their weight. Those that were able hung as far over the windward gunnel as possible. On the port side, green seawater began to spill into the boat. The fear was great and many on board began to lament their sins to the virgin, for surely they were about to die. On this day, however, God was with them, for another gust blew the vessel leeward and, once again, de Palas was able to regain control. This happened twice more during the journey across the bay. So convinced that he would die this day, Alvar had resigned himself to suffering a watery death.

This struggle continued until near sunset when, at last, all five boats neared the mainland. The wind had blown all day, but now there was somewhat of an evening lull. The wind had shifted, and now a soft breeze blew from the east. They coasted along looking for a site to land the boats, but the shore was a tangle of mangrove trees and tidal swamps and no good place to come ashore. Suffering greatly from thirst, the *Spaniards* looked for the telltale signs of a river delta.

The sun was just touching the horizon when the boats of the expedition rounded a point of land that jutted into the bay. In boat two, which was slightly ahead of the other four, it was Fray Xuarez who first saw the *Indians.* There, spread across the water were twelve canoes slowly moving toward them.

"To arms, to arms!" Fray Xuarez's voice carried across the water.

So suffering where the *Spaniards* that only a few prepared themselves for battle. Alvar, standing in boat five, looked across the water and studied the approaching foe. They were tall, well-built men with skin the color of dark copper. Their heads were adorned with feathers and tattoos covered their forearms and chests, but as he looked at each canoe there was no sign of weapons, they carried neither bows nor arrows.

Within hailing distance of all the boats, Alvar called out, "Hide your weapons, for they appear to be unarmed."

As the two groups approached, Estaban, in boat three, called out to them and made a sign of greeting. This was immediately answered by one of the *Indians* in the lead canoe.

Estevan called out, "Stand easy for they appear to offer no threat."

The lead canoe made for Estevan's boat and thestrange-looking black man called out to them. Pulling alongside, they again made the sign of greeting. Their language was different and Estevan could not make it out. They jabbered rapidly, talking as much to themselves as to the strange visitors. Again, Estevan made the sign for peace which the *Indians* seemed to understand. He now pantomimed their need for water, cupping his hands and making slurping sounds. At first, they looked at him strangely and then seemed to comprehend. Reaching down to the floor of the canoe their lead spokesman produced a gourd that was stoppered with a wooden plug. He offered it. Taking the gourd, Estevan removed the plug and saw that it contained water. So great was his thirst that he raised it to his lips and took a long pull of the liquid within. This produced an immediate clamor aboard the boat.

"Water!"

"Pass the gourd, for our need is as great as yours."

"Give it to me!"

Thinking better of it, Estevan replaced the plug and offered the gourd back to the *Indians*.

The clamor aboard the boat, however, caused the *Indians* to pull back slightly and their spokesman indicated that Estevan should keep the gourd and pass it around. Estevan handed it off to Captain Dorantes who took a guarded drink before passing it to the other men on the boat. The gourd was drained in seconds.

The *Indians* had now backed away a boat length. They seemed peaceful and through gestures indicated that the *Spaniards* should follow them, for their village contained much food and water to drink. Boat one had now come up to the gathering and Narvaez, standing in the bow, took in the situation. He addressed one of the captains.

"*Senor* Dorantes, have you been able to communicate with these *Indios*?"

"Si *Adelantado*, they seem to want us to follow them to their village."

So great was their need for water that Narvaez ordered the boats to follow them, but he instructed the men, "Keep your weapons close at hand and be alert for treachery."

Without waiting, the twelve canoes turned back and proceeded shoreward. The five boats struggled to keep up. Close in, the *Indians* continued westward until rounding a weathered point that jutted out towards the sea. On rounding the point, the party then entered a broad bay into which a river flowed. The water in the bay, fed by the river, was sweet and the *Spaniards*, crazy with thirst, dipped their cupped hands into it and drank.

Not far from the inlet the *Indio* lodges appeared on the shoreline, the people of the village lining the waterfront. Some held back and observed the approaching flotilla from further up the beach. In all, Alvar estimated it was a village of a hundred or more with about twenty lodges drawn up in a rough circle. The lodges appeared to be permanent structures with corner poles sunk into the sand and raised floors covered with a matting of grass and woven palm leaves. A much larger lodge dominated the center of the village.

Closing on the beach, Alvar and several of the stronger men jumped overboard to lighten the load. Hanging to the sides they helped guide the craft through the light surf and onto the sand. Off to the right, boat three lay at an angle, its hulk broadside to the waves. Further up the beach, boats one and two had already come ashore and the crews were making an effort to secure them. Boat four ground to a stop not more than twenty feet from where Alvar now stood. The twelve *Indio* canoes had already been dragged further up onto the beach. It was an awkward moment, for the two parties now stood apart, the *Indians* and the *Spaniards* eyeing each other.

At that moment a tall, well-built man adorned with a feathered headdress and a robe of rich skins emerged from the crowd and made his way to the location of the twelve canoes. He talked briefly with these men and then with an entourage of five approached Estevan's boat. It was obvious that this man held a position of importance within the village, a *cacique*. Estevan, standing near the bow used the hand talk to convey a greeting. The *cacique* returned the salutation and stepped close, looking at him in wonder. He grasped Estevan's arm and rubbed the skin, lightly at first and then harder as if to rub the blackness away. When it became clear that this would not happen he conversed rapidly with the men in his entourage. One of them pointed out that there were other black men distributed amongst the boats and they seemed to take great pleasure in identifying them, even coining a descriptive word.

"*Teocoute, teocoute,*" they repeated. Estevan assumed it was their word for "black."

Narvaez's boat had come ashore the furthest away and now as he neared the gathering other officials of the expedition joined him. A group of five including Narvaez, Alvar, Alonso Enriquez, Friar Xuarez, and Captain Castillo now faced the *cacique* and his entourage. From the *Adelantados* boat, Marino Carmona stepped up to assist Estevan with the translation, but this new language was foreign to him as well. Through hand talk, they determined the chief's name was C*e-onto-ada-la,* carefully speaking each syllable until they got it right. Estevan and Carmona struggled with the pronunciation, much to the amusement of the *cacique* and the men around him.

Estevan introduced Narvaez as their leader who, in turn, ordered that several trinkets, carried in the boats for just such an occasion, be distributed to the *cacique* and his men as gifts. This seemed to please Ceontoadala who took great interest in ringing the small hawk bells that had been given him. He turned and ordered the women of the village to bring water to the *Spaniards,* for he could see that they were much distressed. The women brought the water in large earthen jars and placed them on the ground in front of the boats. Ceontoadala then took Narvaez by the hand and led him to his lodge where great quantities of cooked fish were offered to the guests. Narvaez, in turn, instructed Estevan to bring a quantity of the stored corn from the boats. This he presented to Ceontoadala in return.

"Tell him that this is all we have."

As the sun set the men of the expedition began to relax. Their bellies were full and their rasping thirst had finally been quenched. On the beach, the men lounged on the sand, while others stood around in small groups and talked. The sick and wounded remained on the boats, many unable to even raise themselves. Seated near boat 2, Santo Corral leered at the bare-breasted women as they continually replaced the empty jars of water and brought baskets of cooked fish. He even reached out and pinched one on her bare buttocks. Appearing not to notice, the woman continued on, only looking back when she had rejoined her companions. Corral, watching her, grabbed his crotch. She quickly turned away.

The sun had long disappeared and with an overcast sky, the light was almost gone. Strangely, the women did not return to collect the last of the water jars that lay empty and strewn across the sand. Even the sounds coming from the village seemed subdued. Only one small fire glowed in front of a distant lodge. Something wasn't right. Captain Dorantes, sensing the subtle change, felt uneasy and instructed the men around him to arm themselves. Quietly, he passed the word to the other boats to be on guard. His greatest concern, however, was for the *Adelantado* and the men with him. They had been gone for some time. The remaining captains quietly talked amongst themselves.

Dorantes expressed his concerns. "I fear something is amiss and we could be in great danger. The governor and five of our comrades are, even now, far from our protection. I would ask for ten volunteers to accompany me into the village."

Captain Alejandro Tellez was quick to respond. "Andre, these natives have shown no aggressive behavior...yet, if we send armed men into their village they will surely attack us and kill the governor."

There were nods all around.

Captain Penalosa was next to speak. "Let us not forget that the *Adelantado* has *senors* Castillo, De Vaca, and Enriquez with him, all good swordsmen."

"But, what if they are taken unawares." It was Dorantes again.

Penalosa. "Alonzo Castillo trusts no one, I have a hard time believing he will be taken unawares."

Captain Pantoja, who was listening intently, raised his hand. Everyone looked to hear what he had to say.

"I also have a feeling that something is not right, but I agree with *Capitan* Tellez; we cannot march into the village without repercussions...we must wait until there is cause."

Dorantes was frustrated. "What are we to do then?"

Pantoja continued, "Let us put together this ten-man force so that we can be ready should the *Indios* betray us. If they do we will be ready. I would also suggest that we make the boats ready to launch."

07 November, 1528

Indian Village on Florida's Coast

Seated with Alonso Enriquez by his side, Alvar wanted to return to the boats. It was well after midnight. Across from them,

Narvaez was questioning Ceontoadala about what obstacles may lay further west. It was a tiring process of hand talk and a mixture of common words from other *Indio* languages. Sitting between the *cacique* and the governor, Estabanico and Marino Carmona struggled to make sense of the strange language.

Standing by the entrance and just to Alvar's left, Captain Alonso Castillo watched over the proceedings. They made eye contact, and from the look that Castillo gave him, Alvar felt his uncomfortableness. It was very dark outside. They were a good 1000 *yara* from the boats, in a strange village, surrounded by its inhabitants. Still, the *cacique* and his people had shown them nothing but kindness.

Alvar quietly rose and sidled up next to Castillo. He spoke quietly. "You look troubled, *capitan*."

His eyes continuing to scan the room, Castillo answered in a whisper, "We have been here too long. Have you noticed that the women serving us have all disappeared and we are now alone with this *cacique*?"

Alvar looked around. Indeed, all of the women had disappeared, even the ones serving Ceotoadala...and something else...the sounds of the village outside had quieted. There were no sounds of children playing, people talking or moving about...nothing. Slowly he felt for the pommel of his sword. Cross-legged on the floor, Enriquez, still gnawing on a piece of fish, looked up at them with a questioning look. Alvar nodded ever so slightly. He dropped the fish and began to rise. As Enriquez stood Ceontoadala caught notice of him and the two *Spaniards* standing at the entrance. He stopped talking. Narvaez and the interpreters looked around to see what was the matter.

At this moment Ceontoadala bolted upright and yelled a command. The thatched door that covered the entrance flew aside and several armed warriors rushed through the opening. Quick as a cat Castillo drew his sword and cut the first man down, almost severing his shoulder. The second man threw a rock that hit Narvaez in the face, knocking him senseless. Alvar skewered this man through the kidneys. The warriors continued to pour through the opening as de Vaca, Castillo, and Enriquez fought to keep them back. Alvar yelled at the top of his lungs, "To arms, to arms," hoping that the men on the beach would hear him.

Narvaez, falling to the side and bleeding profusely managed to grab hold of Ceotoadala's leg. The *cacique* wrenched himself free but was immediately tackled by Estevan. While Carmona protected Narvaez, the fight swirled about them. The stronger of the two, Ceontoadala, managed to escape Estevan's grasp, but not before losing his sable robe. Head down, the *cacique* lunged for the entrance and disappeared into the night.

The close quarters of the lodge benefited the *Spaniards,* for it restricted the number of attackers. In the melee, Castillo had dispatched four and Alvar three. Carmona and Estevan wrestled on the ground with a particularly large warrior until Narvaez, still blurry-eyed and covered with blood slit the *Indian's* throat. Outside the lodge, the crowd of warriors pounded on the walls and began a frightful howling. They would pass through the opening of the lodge only to be cut down by Castillo and De Vaca. Several times the *Spaniards* were almost overwhelmed and only the assistance of Estevan, Carmona, and Narvaez, now somewhat recovered, kept the *Indians* at bay.

Those on the beach could hear the sounds of battle and Dorantes quickly turned and called to the men he had assembled. "Follow me, *conquistadores*, the governor is under attack!"

They moved rapidly into the village, for all of the warriors were gathered at the *cacique's* lodge and none had yet arrived on the beach to oppose them. So focused were the men of the village on the governor and the *Spaniards* within the lodge that they didn't see

Dorantes and his men until it was too late. Hacking and thrusting the *Spaniards* crashed into the crowd of warriors. So devastating was the attack that the *Indians* fled in terror.

Dorantes called to those in the lodge, "*Adelantado*, we are here. Quickly, we must return to the boats!"

Castillo was the first out. "You are a most welcome sight *capitan* Dorantes."

Stepping over the slain bodies of the *Indians*, the group of *Spaniards,* now numbering sixteen, made their way back to the beach. Narvaez, with blood flowing into his one good eye, had to be led along by Estevan. Halfway there, the *Indians* regrouped and began pressing the *Spaniards*, trying to cut them off. Another fierce battle ensued, and only the intervention of a force led by Captain Penalosa, coming up from the beach, broke the *Indio* attack.

Narvaez was quickly put aboard his boat which was pushed off the beach and into the water. The other boats were floated as well. The bay, however, was a cauldron of high winds and whitecaps, and the boats were forced to remain close to shore. A stormy nor-east wind was blowing seaward and to venture out would have been disastrous. The clouds above were moving fast and only briefly would a patch of clear sky show itself to let the meager light of a quarter moon show through. The temperature also began to drop and the men aboard the boats huddled together to keep warm.

On shore, fifty *Spaniards* remained to guard the boats from attack until the weather would allow them to proceed. Another strong force of *Indians* attacked once again. A barrage of arrows proceeded the onslaught and many of the *Spaniards* were injured. Still, they held together and met the wild charge whose momentum down the beach almost overran them. The fighting was fierce and the *Spaniards* were driven back a stone's throw before it was checked. The *Indio* force melted back into the darkness.

An hour passed and from his position on the beach, Alvar could hear the men of the village preparing for another assault. Fiendish shouts and taunts emanated from the darkness. Occasionally a warrior would make a lone attack to show his bravery, running forward and loosening an arrow.

Alvar, crouched in the sand near the left flank of the *Spanish* line heard the attacker running toward him. He tightened his grip on the sword and prepared to meet the charge. But, the attacker stopped, still out of sight. Alvar cocked his head to the right hoping to pick up some telltale sound in the darkness. Suddenly, a searing pain enveloped him and he fell backward onto the sand. Dazed, he wondered what had happened and for a moment remained still, trying to collect his thoughts. Everything was spinning around and little fireflies of light exploded in his vision. Laying there he could hear the sounds of another attack. In the darkness, men stepped on him as they moved forward. The clatter of steel swords against stone weapons and the cries of men in battle filled his senses but they seemed far off. Alvar gingerly moved his left hand to his forehead. He felt the stickiness of blood and stopped for a moment, afraid of what he would find. He probed further and ran his index finger over a deep gash just above his right eye. An arrow dispatched by the lone attacker had evidently careened off his forehead. Finally managing to sit upright he continued to check himself for additional wounds, groggily becoming more aware of the struggle going on around him. The blood from the wound ran down his face and he could taste its bitterness as it trickled into the corner of his mouth.

Someone fell over him.

"*Caramba*, who is there?" The voice sounded like Captain Telez.

His mouth dry, Alvar managed to croak, "It is de Vaca, I've been wounded."

In the darkness, Alvar felt Telez grasp his tunic and pull him toward the beach. Stumbling, both men fell several times before Alvar was at the water's edge. Here Telez left him and returned to the fight. The sky opened up and momentarily the beach was bathed in lunar light. Alvar could make out the line of *Spaniards*, now advancing and the *Indians* beyond, retreating back to their village. He struggled to stand and stood there for a moment swaying back and forth. Amazingly, he still grasped his sword in his right hand. Slowly he moved forward to assist his comrades.

The *Indians* were in retreat, but they would attack again, of that Captain Dorantes was sure, and they could not sustain such a fight with their backs to the sea. In the fleeting moonlight, he had noticed a line of shrubs and trees to the right of their present position. These, he thought, could shield a flanking force that could do great damage to the next *Indio* attack. He quickly called the other captains together and outlined his plan.

"I would ask for fourteen men to accompany me."

"And what if you are discovered, Captain Dorantes?" It was Alonso Pantoja.

"Then, God willing, we will fight our way back to the beach." As an afterthought Dorantes added, "If we are overwhelmed we will kill as many of the heathens as possible."

It was agreed upon, with Captains Dorantes, Telez, and Penalosa leading the flanking force. Twelve of the fittest men were chosen to accompany them. Staying behind to defend the beach would be Captains Castillo, Pantoja, Valenzuela, and the still shaky *Aguacil*, Cabeza de Vaca.

With faint moonlight still illuminating the beach the fifteen men studied their route and tried to commit it to memory. Once the clouds obscured the moon it would be almost total darkness. So as not to draw attention, the fifteen moved to the back of the *Spanish* line and slowly made their way to the right flank. The wind was blowing harder now and the temperature was continuing to drop. Overhead the moon slipped behind a cloud and Dorantes addressed his men.

"Hold to the man's shoulder in front of you and advance single file. I will lead."

Silently the fifteen moved out into the darkness.

At the beach Captain Castillo addressed Alvar. "*Aguacil*, are you able to defend yourself?"

Although still somewhat disoriented, Alvar's biggest problem now was a pounding headache.

"*Capitan* Castillo, I don't think I will be leading any charges, but I can still fight."

"Good, good, we will need everyone to help turn back the next attack."

The next half hour passed in anticipation. The *Spaniards* could hear the *Indians* working themselves up for another attack. In the leaden sky to the east, the first faint signs of dawn began to show, but only a little. They knew the attack would come soon. Hopefully, the flanking force had escaped detection and was now in position.

It started with the usual onslaught of arrows. In the darkness, injury or death could come quickly and the *Spaniards* had learned to lie low on the ground as the missiles whistled overhead. This time, however, the arrow barrage did not last long. All was quiet once again.

Castillo whispered to Alvar, "I think they have spent their supply of arrows."

Suddenly, there was the sound of men running and the frightful war cries.

Captain Valenzuela stood and shouted, "Rise up *Christians*, we are under attack, kill them, kill them all!"

Mercifully the clouds parted and the beach was bathed in moonlight just as the charging *Indians* crashed into the *Spanish* line. The *Spaniards* gave but did not break, forced back by the momentum of the charge almost to the water's edge. Some warriors broke through the line but were quickly cut down by the friars and wounded men standing in reserve. Fray Xuarez, brandishing a large wooden club, brained one of the heathens making his way toward the boats.

Now, only feet from the surf the two sides locked in a desperate battle. Castillo fought like a man possessed and the sand around him was covered with dead or dying men. Alvar, bowled over in the initial charge and was now holding his own, having dispatched or injured several savages. Others, fighting desperately, many with injuries, continued to fight on.

Captain Pantoja, his left arm injured, called out. "Where is Dorantes," and all along the line the *Spaniards* began chanting "Dorantes, Dorantes."

Another line of *Indio* attackers now appeared, reinforcing those on the line. The *Spanish* began to give way, now fighting in water up to their ankles. To Alvar, it appeared that all was lost and surely Dorantes and his men had been discovered and dispatched. The half-light of predawn now partially illuminated the beach. The line of battle began to deteriorate into knots of individual combat when Alvar clearly heard the *Spanish* battle cry.

"Santiago!"

Dorantes's force slammed into the rear of the attackers. They only numbered fifteen but the result was dramatic. Twenty savages were immediately cut down as the *Spaniards* hacked and cut their way through the *Indian* ranks. Their attention diverted by the threat behind them, the *Indians* on the front line were overpowered by the defenders, now surging forward with renewed hope. Terrified, they retreated in a route, leaving their wounded to fend for themselves. Dorantes and his men, their blood up, chased the stragglers, killing as many as possible and dispatching any wounded they came across.

08 November, 1528

Indian Village on Florida's Coast

Hampered by the thick layer of clouds, the translucent light of sunrise revealed a scene of desperate struggle. Scattered about were the contorted bodies of the *Indians* cut down by the *Spanish*. Blood trails left by the wounded veered off in all directions only to stop where the mortally injured warrior had bled out or been slain by Dorantes and his men as they walked the battlefield.

The village was deserted. Men, women, and children had fled into the countryside. Alvar, walking among the bodies, counted 44 dead. There were signs that many more of the injured had been carried off by their comrades. Amazingly, only three *Spaniards* had died as a result of the fighting. Injured during the second attack Jose Menaldo had been surrounded and clubbed to death as his comrades fell back toward the beach. Looking down at his lifeless body, Alvar shuddered, what had once been the man's face had been pounded to a pulp. He had died bravely though, for about him were the bodies of two of his attackers. Another *Spaniard,* near the boats, had had his throat cut by a lone usurper. One other *Spaniard* would die from his wounds this day as well. Hermanos Larraga, already sickened with fever, had bravely taken his sword and joined the ranks. An arrow had punctured his lung during the first attack and now he lay in much pain while Fray De Palas administered last rights. All of the *Spaniards* had suffered during the attack, not one had escaped unhurt.

Following a blood trail, Alvar came across a cache of about thirty canoes. Hidden from view, a tall, *Indio* raised up from behind one of the canoes, a spear in his hand. The other hand was pressed tightly against his slashed abdomen from which the intestines protruded. Their eyes met, and, in this instant, Alvar felt compassion for this warrior who surely would die. Yet, the man showed no sign of pain and crouched down, ready to defend himself. Others had noticed the confrontation and rushed to Alvar's aid. For a moment the lone warrior parried the thrusts of the *Spaniards* but was soon overcome. He fell there next to the canoe. Still, his eyes burned with hatred as he struggled to breathe.

One of the *Spaniards* stepped up and cut off the *Indian's* head. "*Hijo de puta*!"

Alvar turned from the grisly scene and returned to the boats.

The weather was unrelenting. The temperature dropped and the gray sky was punctuated with periods of cold rain. The wind continued to increase and the bay was flecked with angry white caps. On the beach, windblown sand swirled about such that a man could not walk without shielding his eyes while the inhaled particles, gritted between the teeth.

Narvaez, his face bruised and discolored, called a meeting of the leaders. He addressed the men.

"*Compatriotas*, with this weather we will quickly perish should we venture out to sea." He motioned toward the bay behind him now partially obscured by mist and fast-moving squalls.

"The wind and the cold are almost more than we can bear, but if we remain here we are subject to further attacks."

Captain Pantoja spoke up. *Adelantado*, the enemy has abandoned the village. Even now I have teams entering each lodge to recover anything of value. Perhaps we should inhabit their dwellings until this abominable weather passes."

Captain Castillo rose and motioned in the direction of the village. "Their lodges are close to the beach. If we inhabit their village we will have shelter and be able to easily guard the boats."

All nodded in agreement.

Alvar spoke. "Of course, there is always the possibility the *Indios* will return, but they suffered grievously and I think their fighting spirit is gone. I agree with *Capitans* Pantoja and Castillo, we should camp here until this tempest is past."

For the remainder of the day, that night and the next day they hunkered down in the village while the storm raged. The destroyed canoes were used to build a great fire. By the afternoon of the third day, the final remnants of the storm had passed to the south. Overhead, the sky became brilliantly clear and the wind, though gusty at times, dropped measurably. From the village they had collected everything of value; food, clothing, skins, and, most importantly, a few vessels to hold water. Many, however, had been carried away or destroyed by the *Indians*. What remained were ten clay pots, two per boat, that could be used. Everyone drank their fill before embarking. The next morning the temperature remained cool as the men struggled to push the boats out. Those on board had to be offloaded, many too sick or weak to climb over the gunnels by themselves. Even empty, it was with great effort that each vessel was finally put afloat. Once in the bay the five boats dropped their sails and moved slowly to the west, struggling to make headway in a beam reach, the wind blowing almost directly starboard.

14 November, 1528

Somewhere off the Gulf Coast

For three days the expedition sailed west not daring to go ashore for fear of another encounter. The temperature remained cool during the days and very cold at night so the men crouched down in the boats as far as possible to avoid the chilling sea breezes. The nights remained clear and the outline of the coast was vaguely visible so that they were able to sail on during these evening hours.

His teeth chattering and struggling to stay awake the Greek carpenter, Doroteo Teodoro, watched the coast slide by in the first light of morning. It was his turn at the watch and he scanned the shore for any sign of movement. There was nothing, still, he couldn't shake the feeling that somewhere out there in the tangle of reeds and woodlands someone was watching them. He sensed that the boat was getting closer to the shore and shifted his eyes seaward to check on the other vessels. All were much further out. Looking astern he saw the man steering the boat, Santo Corral, fast asleep and slumped over the tiller.

"*Senor* Corral, wake up and move us away from shore!"

There was no movement from Corral. He continued to sleep, oblivious to the commands from Teodoro. The others on board seemed equally oblivious as well, only a few stirring as he continued to holler out. Finally, exasperated, Teodoro drew his sword and began beating the flat of the blade against the boat. They were now uncomfortably close to the shore.

"Wake up, damn you...someone wake up!"

A few of the men began to move. Alonzo Castillo, rubbing sleep from his eyes struggled to make sense of what was happening. Teodoro, seeing Castillo rouse himself, directed his admonishments toward him.

"*Capitan*, the tiller...someone needs to steer us away from shore...quickly!"

Castillo, now fully awake, and able to reach Corral from his position, roughly grabbed the sleeping man and dragged him off his seat. Corral's head slammed into the side of the boat. The movement awakened the others around him. Someone grabbed the tiller and swung it to port. Slowly, the boat turned away from shore, just in time, for up ahead waves broke over a length of sand bar that would have grounded them.

Santo Corral, still dazed, tried to speak. "What has happened?"

Castillo grabbed the man's tunic with his left hand and slapped him hard against the face with his right. "*Stupido*, your carelessness almost grounded us...I should throw you overboard."

Corral, visibly shaking, thought for a moment that Castillo would carry out his threat. He pleaded, "I am sorry *capitan*, it won't happen again."

Disgusted, Castillo shoved him backward and released his grip. The other boats by now had noticed the commotion. As they drew closer, Narvaez called out from boat one.

"What is the problem?"

Teodoro answered, "We had a man fall asleep at the tiller *Adelantado* but we have corrected the problem."

All five boats were now grouped tightly together and Narvaez addressed the small flotilla. "We are all suffering greatly from thirst. Today, if a suitable location presents itself, we must endeavor to go ashore and relieve our suffering."

All were in agreement as the boats continued on, each scanning the shoreline for the telltale signs of a river that could provide a source of water. At mid-morning the coast opened up into a very large bay that appeared to be fed by a river. So desperate for water were the *Spaniards* that they could smell the fresh water that entered it.

His boat in the lead, Narvaez headed directly for the inlet. The wind was favorable and the men aboard the boats revived with the anticipation of finding water to drink. Rounding a point of land the whole breadth of the bay came into view, its entrance a league wide.

It was enormous. Looking north, the coastline disappeared into the distance.

Pointing to the northwest Narvaez called out. "See there, how the coastline seems to fall away...that surely is where a river enters this bay. Let us move towards it as quickly as possible."

Each boat adjusted its sail and turned in the direction that Narvaez had indicated. The wind still fair and favorable, they continued in this direction for some time when in the distance a single canoe was spotted approaching them.

"To arms...*a las armas*! The call rang out between the boats. Although only one canoe it was a large one, a war canoe, the type the *Indians* used to transport a number of warriors. This one had ten men, six of which were paddling. They made directly for Narvaez's boat which was in the lead and flying the *Adelantado's* personal pendent. Although armed with bows, the *Indians* gave no sign of aggressiveness as they approached and slid up alongside.

Marino Carmona, being in Narvaez's boat, immediately tried to establish communication with the visitors while the other boats dropped sail and drew closer. In boat 3, Estevan was called upon to assist Carmona in the translations. Over the months, both men had become quite good at deciphering the languages of the various groups they encountered. Estevan had even become proficient at mastering the hand talk that seemed to be universal among the *Indians*. It was not long before a lively discourse was under-way.

As the talks continued the warriors aboard the canoe sized up the *Spaniards*. Thin and haggard-looking, many of the men aboard the boats were sick and weak. Still, they eyed the lethal metal swords that the *Spaniards* made clearly visible. Most of these strange bearded men showed the scars and injuries of previous battles.

The *Spaniards,* in turn, evaluated the men in the canoe. On boat three Alonso del Castillo met their stares unflinchingly. All were well-built, tall, and heavily muscled. A variety of tattoos covered their bodies, mostly a collection of jagged lines and circles. Some had the likenesses of animals or even fish. Most had facial ornaments. Rawhide strips passed through piercings in their ears and noses secured a variety of decorations including shells, bones, feathers, and crude wooden carvings. Around their waists, a braided belt secured a deerskin breechcloth. From the waist up the men were naked and seemed unaffected by the cool wind.

Estevan, conducting a lively discourse, was the subject of much interest by the *Indians*. They seemed mesmerized by the blackness of his skin. From boat one an impatient Narvaez called out to him. "Estevan, tell them that we are in much need of water and will give them presents if they will take us to it."

"*Adelantado*, their language is very strange, unlike any we have heard before, but they seem to understand the hand talk. They call themselves *Hacha hatuk*. I think, in their language, this means People of the River."

"Ask them about the water!"

"I have done that *Adelantado*, and although they will not allow us to go ashore they have offered to get some provided we supply them with containers."

On the boats, the *Spaniards* scurried to collect the five containers that had been liberated from the *Indio* village three days previous.

It was Doroteo Teodoro, the *Greek* boat builder who spoke next. "What guarantee do we have that they will return with our containers?"

The *Spaniards* looked at each other. It was a good question. These were the only containers they had, for the horse skin *botas* had long since rotted. No one spoke.

"I will go with them to ensure the containers are returned." It was Teodoro again.

Narvaez tried to dissuade Teodoro. "Friend Doroteo do not put yourself in harm's way such as this."

"*Adelantado*, we must have water. My servant Loannes will accompany me. I would ask these *Indios* to leave two of their men with us as hostages until we return."

Many of the *Spaniards* protested Teodoro leaving, but he was determined and soon the exchange was made. Teodoro and Loannes along with seven clay containers were transferred to the *Indio* canoe while two of their men boarded boat 3 under Castillo's watchful eye.

Loannes was an *Ibo*, his blackness contrasting markedly with the deep amber of the *Indian* warriors. and once aboard the large canoe, the *Indians* reached out in a vain effort to rub the blackness off his skin. There was a moment of tenseness as Loannes, becoming irritated with the attention, roughly pushed one of the *Indians* away. The man fell backward landing in the laps of two other warriors. For a moment all was quiet. Then, quite unexpectedly, they broke out in laughter, slapping the downed man on the back and pointing toward Loannes. The moment passed.

Teodoro took his seat in the front and watched quietly as the large canoe pulled away from the *Spanish* boats.

"*Vaya con Dios amigo* Doroteo Teodoro." It was Narvaez himself who called across the water. "Watch your back and return to us."

"By the will of God!" was Teodoro's reply.

Proceeding toward a point that jutted out from the land Doroteo turned frequently to check on the position of the *Spanish* boats. They were now mere specks in the distance. The *Hacha hatuk*, paddling with precision and great strength, seemed to make the large canoe skim through the water. After rounding the point the boats disappeared from view and Teodoro concentrated on the shoreline.

From his position at the center of the canoe, Loannes watched as one of the paddlers behind Teodoro set his oar down and reached to grab a stone war club. Seeing the danger Loannes rose from his seat but was pulled backward onto the floor of the canoe by those around him.

He called out in vain, "*Senor* Teodoro!" but his warning was cut short by a blow to the head which rendered the *African* unconscious.

Teodoro, hearing the commotion, began to turn, but an explosion of light and pain shattered his consciousness...and then darkness. The blow from the war club had shattered the right side of Teodoro's skull. Blood and brain matter spattered the boat and those around him. The warrior that had delivered the blow quickly lifted his body and threw it over the side. Loannes still alive, but unconscious, was also thrown over the side. The canoe continued on the *Indians* rejoicing that they had procured five containers so easily.

14 November, 1528

Somewhere off the Gulf Coast

Alvar had watched the *Indian* canoe as it rounded the point and disappeared from view. Those aboard the boats were much in anticipation of the water that they had promised. Holding their position in the shallow bay, the men eagerly stared at the point of land the canoe had rounded. An hour passed. Then two. The mood of the *Spaniards* deteriorated.

In the west, the sun had sunk behind a line of clouds that lay low on the horizon. The temperature dropped. The wind, which had been light all day, became decidedly cooler and the men began to shiver once again. Overhead, seabirds, pelicans, cormorants, and gulls made their way towards evening roosting sites.

Narvaez, in boat one, addressed the others. "It looks as if the *Indios* have deceived us and we have lost two of our own."

From boat three Castillo spoke to Narvaez. "*Adelantado*, what should I do with the captives?"

From all five boats, the men seemed to cry in unison, "Kill them...*mortar a los bastardos!*"

The two captive *Hacha hatuks,* their eyes wide with fear were grasped by the men around them and roughly treated. Some hit them with their bare fists, others spat on them.

"Enough!" It was Narvaez. "We will hold them through the night. They may be of some value should the *Indios* return. We will wait here until morning before we proceed any further. We can only hope that our compatriots...and water will be returned to us."

The sun had disappeared from view and the bay was bathed in the afterglow of sunset. A gray mist began to rise from the water. The outline of the shore had all faded in the encroaching blackness.

"There is a canoe approaching!" It was friar Xuarez. The men on the boats strained to see as the vague shape of the *Indian* canoe materialized in the haze.

"It is them! They have returned! We will have water. Praise God."

The somberness of the past hours evaporated as the canoe drew nearer, its inhabitants still obscured in the darkness. Approaching Narvaez's boat, it wasn't until the canoe was very close that it became apparent that Teodoro and Loannes were not on board. The news spread quickly.

Even before Narvaez had instructed him to do so Estevan called out to the *Hacha hatuks.* "Did you bring water, and where are the *Christians* that we sent with you?"

The *Indians* acted as if they did not understand. Their canoe stayed just out of reach.

Estevan repeated again and again his question. "Where are the *Christians?*"

The *Indians* would not speak to the *Spanish,* but instead addressed the two captives. Both of them rose as if to dive from the boats and swim to safety, but Castillo had anticipated this and held them tightly.

The *Indians,* seeing their men held by the *Spanish,* backed further away from the boats and then, turning their canoe, returned from where they had come. The *Spaniards* were much despondent and saddened. Many stood up in the boats and called out to the retreating canoe.

"Come back you bastards and we will kill you!"

"Bastards!"

Castillo called out to Narvaez, "*Adelantado,* can I kill these assholes...*agujeros culo!*"

Narvaez was quick in answering. "Desist for now *capitan* Castillo, we may need them yet."

The captives, still squirming to free themselves, were being held tightly by those around them. Their movement, however, was upsetting the boat. Castillo, drawing his sword, brought the hilt down sharply against each of the captives' skulls, knocking both unconscious. The squirming stopped.

The last traces of the sunset disappeared. The five-boat flotilla, now so long at anchor, stayed in place, hoping that in the morning Teodoro and Loannes would be returned. The night was long and fretful. A clear sky allowed the temperature to drop just above freezing and the *Spaniards* suffered immeasurably.

The first rays of sunrise, unfettered by clouds, burst across the water. Alvar felt the subtle warmth as the shafts of light touched his exposed arm. He had slept only fleetingly all night, constantly awakened by the cold and his own shaking.

Suddenly, from boat two came the call, "*Idios, Indios*, to arms!"

Rising up and looking shoreward Alvar saw them. The long war canoe of the previous day was rapidly moving toward them, but behind it, in the distance, several other canoes were moving toward the mouth of the bay.

Alvar called out to Narvaez. "*Adelantado*, the other canoes are moving to block the inlet."

Narvaez scanned the horizon with his one good eye and agreed. "Pull in the anchors and set the sails."

 There was much commotion among the boats as the long anchor ropes were hauled in and the makeshift sails were attached to the booms. They had not finished the process before the large war canoe had pulled alongside. There were several *caciques* aboard, immediately identifiable by their clothing and regal bearing. In the morning chill, each wore robes of martin skins much like the one Estevan had liberated from the *Indio* village only days before. Their hair was very long and untied. Their gestures were demanding. Each of the *caciques* held a long spear in their right hand, its butt resting on the floor of the canoe, the spear point, adorned with feathers, high above their heads. They called out for the immediate release of their men.

The two *Indio* captives, now conscious, were tightly bound with ropes around their wrists and ankles. Wide-eyed, they followed the proceedings intently.

Using hand talk and the limited amount of vocabulary that they had learned, Estevan and Carmona quickly demanded the return of the *Christians*. The *Hacha hatuk* seemed evasive and instead indicated for the *Spanish* to follow them back to their village where they would return the *Christians* and provide water. Narvaez had fallen into a fit of coughing and Alvar took up the negotiations. Nervously looking at the other canoes moving toward the mouth of the bay he looked to Estevan.

"Tell them that the *Christians* must be returned before we will return their men."

There was much talk between the *Indian* chiefs as they seemed to argue with each other, gesturing wildly. All the while their canoe pulled back from the cluster of *Spanish* boats. Another smaller canoe joined them.

From boat four Captain Penalosa called out. "It is treachery, they are fitting their bows to attack us."

Several *Indians* rose to their feet in the smaller canoe and loosed several arrows at the *Spaniards*. Those aboard the boats, who still had their bucklers, held them up to shield those around them. Most passed harmlessly overhead, but two arrows embedded in the side of Narvaez's boat.

Alvar called out, "Drop the sails and make for the inlet."

Luckily the wind was blowing off shore and the overloaded *Spanish* boats slowly began to move toward the open sea. As they came to the inlet the other *Indian* canoes came up. Each would take turns running close enough to the *Spaniards* to pelt them with rocks and arrows. Several *Spaniards* were hit, the rocks leaving painful bruises. There only appeared to be three or four bows amongst the *Indians* and their supply of arrows was soon exhausted. None of the arrows had found their marks.

In one brazen attack, the large war canoe pulled alongside boat three. Two of the *caciques* stood and threw their long spears. One fouled in the rigging ropes and passed harmlessly overhead. The other found its mark...in the leg of one of the captives. The *Indian* began to scream and writhe about. Castillo grabbed the spear and pulled it from the man's leg. A fountain of blood spurted out, the femoral artery having been pierced.

"Throw the captive overboard, he is a dead man anyway!" It was Captain Dorantes.

Several of the *Spaniards* rolled the screaming captive over the gunnel and into the water. Trying desperately to stay afloat, the still bound *Indian* resembled a dolphin as he bent at the waist in a futile attempt to kick his feet. He soon disappeared under the waves, a red smear of blood coloring the waters where he had been.

On board boat three Castillo pulled his dagger and quickly slit the throat of the other captive. As they were lifting him up Dorantes called out, "Remove his binding first, for we are in need of the rope."

The offshore wind had increased and by noon the *Indians* who had been following them finally turned around and proceeded back from where they had come. The five boats, running before the wind to escape their pursuers, now turned westward as they passed through the inlet. That evening the wind abated somewhat and the boats moved shoreward once again where they anchored for the night. In the morning, to their astonishment, they had been following a line of barrier islands. Looking north from the islands rose the unbroken silhouette of the mainland. Each of these barrier islands was different. Some were covered in grasses that waved like the ocean itself from the incoming sea breezes. Others had a smattering of scrub cedars and bush palmettos. On the larger islands, live oaks, pines, and cedars abounded, some of the oaks so large that their horizontal limbs grew from the trunk almost parallel to the ground. On each of the islands, signs of recent habitation were everywhere. Piles of oyster shells littered the shore areas and well-worn footpaths crisscrossed the area. Fearful of attack they continued on.

A decision was made to cross to the more protected inland waters north of the islands. Here also, the chance of finding a fresh water source was much better for surely, there were streams and rivers that emptied into the bay. The day was clear and instead of anchoring, they sailed on until the hour of vespers.

16 November, 1528

Off the Coast of Mississippi

Evening was approaching fast and they moved closer to the mainland looking for the tell-tale sign of a river delta and fresh water. Boat five, Alvar's boat, was far ahead of the other four when a promontory was sighted that extended into the channel. Alvar, squinting as he looked into the setting sun instructed the helmsman to steer toward a small island just off the point.

There was barely an hour of daylight left as the bow crunched into the soft sand surrounding the island. From this vantage point, all could see that the promontory marked the beginnings of a river delta. For sure this was a fresh water river they had encountered. Jumping from the boat, Alvar stood in the knee-deep water. It felt good to stand. Cupping his hand, he reached down and scooped up some water. Tentatively he tasted it. It was brackish but drinkable. Driven by thirst he dropped to his knees and drank. Others aboard, those that were able, crawled over the side and drank as well, for their thirst was great.

Unable to control himself, Alvar drank too much. His head pounded and dizziness seemed to overwhelm him. His stomach muscles tightened and the water he had just drank exited his body like a geyser. He remained there on his knees retching until nothing came out anymore.

Rising to his feet Alvar instructed the others, "Only drink sparingly."

Others around him, however, were having the same reaction such that the immediate area around the boat was replete with men in various stages of discomfort. Still many continued to drink, unable to control themselves from their great thirst.

Alvar moved further down the beach and looked back to check on the other boats. Although somewhat spread out, they were converging on the island. The sickness had left him and he gingerly bent over and took another sip of the water, controlling his urge to drink deeply.

Boats three and four slid up onto the beach, but Narvaez, in boat one, chose to continue on into the river bay where there were numerous small islands. Boat two hesitated and then followed Narvaez into the bay.

"*Alguicil*, it looks as if the *Adelantado* is gesturing for us to join them." It was Captain Tellez from boat four.

Looking across the straight, Alvar could make out the men aboard the two boats in the bay waving at them. Helping to push his boat into deeper water Alvar called out, "Let us go to the *Adelantado* for they are gesturing for us to join him."

The men were forced to row to the bay as the evening breezes had abated. In a short time, they pulled alongside the governor. Here the current was slack but Alvar noticed the water was becoming stained and muddy. More islands were seen up ahead. They continued on.

Looking north, the mainland had dissolved into multitudes of bays, bayous, channels, and small estuaries. Islands were everywhere, some small some large, others just mud banks formed with the current.

The nearest island, was covered in grass and was somewhat isolated from the other islands This was desirable to Narvaez who was now very leery of attack. As Alvar's boat crunched ashore others were already fanning out gathering driftwood from the upstream end of the island. Now a proper fire could be built to warm themselves and roast their meager supply of corn. They would spend the night here.

In the morning Narvaez demanded that the boats disembark from the small river island before first light. As the sun was casting its first rays across the water's surface the five boats were well underway, being pushed by the river current into the bay. Again turning west they sailed for three leagues before the coastline turned abruptly to the south. Here they paralleled a long sliver of islands. These islands were narrow and wind-blown with an abundance of mangroves, grasses, and multitudes of sea birds. Finally, at the hour of Vespers, they hauled ashore on one of these narrow beaches to spend the night.

Morning broke clear and bright, the sun exploding on the horizon in a cloudless sky. Teeth chattering from the coldness of the night, the warming rays of the sun brought some relief to the *Spaniards* aboard the five boats. As morning extended into afternoon the offshore wind shifted slightly to the east and increased in intensity. White caps dotted the channel and spray from the roughening sea conditions soaked the men. Their clothes, worn, tattered, and rotting offered little protection from the elements. Except for the long beards, the dark amber of their sunburned skin made the *Spaniards* almost indistinguishable from the native *Indians*. Dried sea salt covered their bodies, chaffing underarms and genital areas. Lips, exposed to the unrelenting sun, split open in painful cracks that were further agitated by the salt spray.

The flotilla was again underway. The northeast wind sped them along until, at the noon hour, the river delta they had been traveling through became a labyrinth of mud flats and small islands. The water was murky, its surface a brown turbulent hue. Alvar, reaching over the side, scooped up some of the water and tasted it. It was brackish and gritty. He stood up and gazed to the north.

"This big muddy river is nothing like I have ever seen! The land that it flows through must be immense."

Already the effects of the current were slowing the boat's forward movement and pushing them seaward. The wind, which was now offshore, was of no help.

Alvar instructed his helmsman, "Try to steer close to shore, for there the effects of the current will not be as strong."

But it was of no avail. They pulled hard at the oars but the current became increasingly stronger. After a league it overcame them and the men, weak as they were, could no longer maintain forward movement. From Alvar's position, he watched as the boats became separated and veered further out to sea. As darkness came, each boat was now at the mercy of the unrelenting current and offshore wind.

CHAPTER 04

The Road To Santiago

El Camino de Santiago

He let his gaze drift across the heavens to the brilliant band of stars that stretched from horizon to horizon. This was called in Christian Spain, El Camino de Santiago...The Road to Santiago. Santiago...Saint James, of course, was the patron saint of Spain who appeared before the armies of Christendom and led them to victory against the Moors. A Spaniard who was just, honorable and fearless in life would ultimately walk this starry path at the time of his death to join the eternal army of Saint James.

19 November, 1528

Half a League off the Coast of Louisiana

Balanced precariously, Alvar struggled to keep his balance. Holding the coiled rope in his hands, he swung the heavy lead weight in a circle before letting it go. Standing in the crowded boat was not easy and those nearest held him tightly. The weight splashed into the water about twenty feet in front of the bow and sank rapidly. Alvar let the rope play out deftly, guiding it as it ran lightly through his fingers. Every five fathoms a knot of rawhide, tied to the line, indicated the depth. Down the weight went, still pulling strongly until the length of rope was exhausted.

"The line has played out, we are still in very deep water."

Alvar began to haul the length of rope back up, coiling it carefully for the next sounding. Looking to the north he could just make out the the dark line of the mainland in the weak glow of the predawn. Eastward, a thin wisp of cloud hung low on the horizon, iridescent against the darkness. Sunrise was still two hours away, but it would be a clear day, and for this Alvar was thankful.Alvar thought about the size of the great river they had passed. Surely it was many times bigger than *Spain's Guadalaquiver* of which he was most familiar. Even the river *Tagus, Spain's* largest, failed in comparison. He thought of the unknown lands that it traveled through, this land they called *Amichel,* and the mysteries that it must hold.

Next to Alvar, Alonso de Solis was staring at the mainland. "*Alguacil,* it is difficult to make out in this half light of morning, but there appears to be a great quantity of smoke in the sky."

Alvar turned his attention toward the mainland. He had to look long and hard, for the coast was still bathed in darkness. Above it, in the somewhat lighter sky, he could just make out several columns rising into the predawn. The offshore breezes had subsided, somewhat. The dark columns drifted slowly to the southwest merging into a dark smudge that was indistinguishable from the aphotic horizon.

"Let us try and make for the mainland where the smoke is rising."

For a day they had been driven far offshore by the relentless current of the river and the offshore winds. They had fought it, but the wind and overpowering flow of water made it impossible to overcome. Again, they had used up their supply of fresh water and the meager amount of dried corn was almost gone.

The boats had become widely separated such that it wasn't until now that three of the five had managed to regroup. Two, however, the one containing governor Narvaez and the other captained by Alejandro Tellez, were no where to be seen.Now, they sailed toward the coast and Alvar again threw the sounding line. This time the rope uncoiled for only a moment before the heavy weight contacted the bottom."Three fathoms!"

To be sure Alvar hauled in the line and threw it again. The results were the same.

Shoreward, the smoke continued to rise. Through the thick cover of trees an occasional flash of flames could be seen. This caused great consternation among the three boats.From boat two Alonso Enriquez called out across the water. "*Aguacil,* what should we do, I fear that there will be great danger if we go ashore."

Some favored going ashore while others were hesitant as to which measures to take. Fearing that enemies may be lying in wait for them it was decided to wait until the full morning light.

Far out to sea lightening lit up the sky. Each flash illuminated a sinister line of spiraling thunderheads. The storm had been visible most of the night as it slowly slid eastward. Although untouched by the storm, the three boats felt the effects of its ferocity; huge swells, spawned far at sea, rolled under them. As dawn illuminated them, the three boats, each still visible to the other, had once again moved apart.

The thick columns of smoke, observed earlier, had disappeared from the horizon. At about the noon hour Alvar's boat had fallen into a deep lethargy, most of those aboard sleeping or just staring out at the horizon. Julio Alves, asleep on the larboard side, had used the gunnel for a pillow, his left arm hung over the side. Suddenly, there was a loud bang that startled all aboard.

"Ohhh, Ohhh, my arm...it is gone! I am bleeding to death...mother of God...*Madre de Dios!*"

Alvar, startled like the rest, stared in disbelief at the ragged stump that once was Alves' arm. Nothing remained below the elbow. Arterial blood spurted out, spreading across the water in a red film.

There was another thump on the side of the boat. Alvar looked down and what he saw made his blood run cold.

"*Tiburones, Tiburones*...Sharks!" Several on the boat called out in warning.

A enormous hammerhead shark, crazed by the blood, lifted its oblong snout, its cephalofoil, out of the water next to the boat.

Thwack! Diego de Huelva, sitting near the center of the boat, brought one of the oars down on top of the beasts head. An explosion of spray erupted as the startled animal dove, its tail banging against the hull. To the consternation of all aboard, other sharks could be seen entering the area, their dorsal and caudal fins breaking the surface. Dark ominous shadows slid just under the keel and the whole area was suddenly alive with movement.

De Huelva attacked anything that got close but his movement was rocking the boat. Others aboard began to cry out.

"Enough Diego, or we will all be in the water...sit down!"

In the bow Alvar used the sounding line to stop the flow of blood from Julio Alves' arm. Underneath a loose loop of line around the man's bicep he slid his dagger. Using it as a handle he began twisting the line tight. The cord cut deeply into the flesh as it tightened. Alves groaned with the pain as the flow slowed and then stopped. The loss of blood, however, was already affecting him.Slurring his words Alves mumbled. "Senor de Vaca, I am loosing my sight, everything is turning dark. Help me."

Alvar had seen this before on the battlefield. When large amounts of blood are lost, eyesight many times was the first thing affected. The blood flow had been stanched but there was nothing else he could do. If ashore they could build a fire and cauterize the wound but here in the boat it was not at option.

"You will be fine *Senor* Alves, it takes more than the loss of an arm to kill a *caballista*."

Alvar lied. Already the cavalryman was beginning to shake as his body slid into shock.

On the starboard side of the boat, Julio's friend and compatriot, Rodriquez Arguello, had drawn his sword and was thrusting it into the water. Others were doing the same. Already they had skewered several, but these injured animals only added to the turmoil. Other sharks attacked them in a feeding frenzy. The waters began to boil, and overhead hungry gulls circled in ever increasing numbers.

"*Senor* Arguello...all of you, you must stop! You are only making matters worse."

Turning now to the men closest to the oarlocks Alvar called out, "We must leave this area as quickly as possible. Row with all your might!"With that he moved into the position held by Alves and began rowing himself. So thick was the ocean with sharks that they attacked the oars as they struck the water.

"Hoist the sail." It was de Solis.

Slowly, ever so slowly, the boat began to move away from the area until, finally there were no sharks visible. Only then did they ship oars and take down the sail. The escape from the sharks had taken them further out to sea. The other boats, two and three, had disappeared. It was now about the hour of Vespers and the sun was getting low in the western sky.

Alvar took another sounding.

"Thirty fathoms."

"*Alguacil*, two boats have reappeared off our bow." It was Lope de Oviedo.

Alvar turned quickly and squinted to see. Sure enough, there were two boats, one was but a speck on the horizon, the other was slowly moving closer.

"Can anyone make out which boat is approaching us?" Alvar strained to see.

Several minutes passed before Oviedo spoke once again. "It looks like the *Adelantado* has once again joined us."Alvar felt relief, for it was feared his boat had somehow been lost after being driven out to sea. "The other boat must be that of Captain Tellez."

"*Alguacil*, I agree but he is very far out and I cannot yet say for sure."

An hour passed as the boat containing Narvaez drew closer. Finally, it was in hailing range.

"Greetings *Adelantado*, we prayed to God that you would return to us and today our prayers have been answered." Alvar was standing, holding to the mast to steady himself, for the sea was becoming heavier. Narvaez was sitting in the bow of the approaching boat. Campo was attending to him. The *Adelantado* was pale and sickly looking, still, his voice carried across the waves.

"Only by the grace of God have we survived, for we were caught in a storm, the likes of which I have never encountered."

"We watched that maelstrom from our position here *Adelantado*. Praise God that you are safe! "Is that the boat of *Capitans* Tellez and Penalosa I see on the horizon?"

"*Si,* we were separated in last night's storm. It has only been in the last hour that they came into view. What of the other two boats?"

"We were together this morning but have since become separated. I am sure that they are not too far off."

"*Senor* De Vaca, what are your thoughts on what we should do?"

"Your excellency, I suggest we row out to join *Capitans* Tellez and Penalosa for we are much stronger together than apart. After that we can continue on to wherever God might take us."

Captain Alonso Pantoja, who was with Narvaez, leaned over and whispered something into his ear. Narvaez thought a moment before answering.

"*Alguacil* De Vaca, the boat with *Capitan* Tellez is still far out to sea and we are wanting to continue ashore. To expend our energy to join him means we will be at sea that much longer. We are all starving and cannot last much longer. Only through the strength of our arms can we land so that we may save ourselves."

Seeing the determination of Narvaez, Alvar agreed. Stepping down from the mast, he grabbed an oar and instructed the men on his boat to make for land. They would follow the *Adelantado*.

They rowed desperately, but the exertion of rowing the boats at such a pace was tremendous. De Vaca's boat soon began to fall behind. It was nearing sunset and the offshore wind, though not strong, tested the men severely. In choosing men for his boat, the governor had picked the healthiest and strongest. There was no way in which Alvar's boat could keep up.

So far ahead had the governor's boat progressed, that when Alvar called out it was several times before he made himself heard.

"*Adelantado*, we cannot keep up with you as your men are fit and healthy, ours are not. Send us a rope so that we may stay together."

Narvaez answered, "*Senor* De Vaca, it will take no small effort on our part to reach the shore before nightfall. If we tow your boat we will all be left adrift. We must continue on without you."

Alvar, surprised at such an answer, then asked, "*Adelantado*, if you cannot assist us we will surely not make shore. What are your commands for us?"

Narvaez, somewhat annoyed and wanting to proceed toward the coast, called out, "This is no time for orders. Each of us should do whatever it takes to save themselves. This is what we intend to do."

With this Narvaez turned away and ordered his men to continue rowing.

Stunned, Alvar stared at the boat as it pulled off. The seriousness of their circumstance was now all too clear. They were on their own. He looked past Narvaez's boat to the shore and tried to make a mental calculation as to the distance. His men were already spent and the offshore wind had increased. Even as they sat idle in the water the boat drifted to the southwest. Now, not only was Narvaez's boat growing smaller in the distance it was becoming further to the east of their position. He determined there was no way they could make shore now. Taking one more furtive look shoreward, Alvar ordered his men to turn about and join up with boat four which had drawn somewhat closer. It appeared to be waiting for them.

23 November, 1528

Somewhere in the Gulf of Mexico off the Coast of

Amichel

For four days the two boats captained by Cabeza De Vaca and Alejandro Tellez had stayed together, their dilapidated and rotting sails propelling them slowly westward. The offshore wind continued, becoming, at times, quite brisk during the daylight hours. At night the wind would fall to a mere breeze as the temperature dropped near freezing. At the end of the third day the supply of fresh water ran out and all were rationed to only a half handful of corn. It was during this time that Julio Alves died quietly after having slipped into a coma. Carefully, they had rolled his body over the side, but the corpse would not sink and drifted alongside the boat to their great consternation. After several hours, however, the body had moved several yards astern. That evening, in the darkness, they could hear the sharks attacking the now bloated remains. By morning of the fourth day, there was no sign of Julio Alves or the sharks. This day the sunrise had a brilliant red hue that spread across the eastern sky in a most wondrous display. All aboard said it was a bad omen. To the west a darkness hung on the horizon that contrasted markedly with the brilliant sunrise. As the day progressed, the wind increased and turned more westerly. The darkness of the approaching storm filled the sky. Wind streaks and frothy white caps soon punctuated the seascape.

As the sea continued to worsen, the two boats had come very close and for a time they were lashed together. Captain Tellez reported that two of his men had died. One, a slave of Pedro Lunel, named Caesar, had become quite incoherent, screaming in his native tongue of things that no one understood. He had ranted throughout the previous day and into the night. Sometime around midnight his ranting suddenly stopped to the relief of everyone aboard. In the morning, however, he was found strangled, by whom...no one knew. The other was *Caballista* Floriano Bras. He had succumbed to the dysentery...*las merdes*, his emaciated and shriveled body looking nothing like the fearless cavalryman that had accompanied Alvar along the road to *Aute*.

By noon the sea was becoming very rough and the two boats cast away from each other. The storm, building in the west, was now almost upon them. The sails, what was left of them, were lowered. By evening the storm had intensified even more. Wind streaks tore across the water and frothy, foamed-topped waves pounded the vessels. The wind, now a full northerly, was unrelenting. The sting of the rain upon bare skin was excruciating.

Alvar had deployed the sea anchor, no more than a length of rope tied to several heavy stones. Crude as it was, it kept the bow of the boat to the windward. The two boats were now far apart. Alvar caught sight of boat four in the distance, but when he looked back a few moments later it was gone, swallowed by the sea spray and haze. He would not see them again. As darkness fell, the full force of the storm was upon them. It raged through the night, buffeting the boat with towering waves and punishing wind. The temperature dropped. Rain turned to sleet and rattled against the boat like a thousand needles. Those that could frantically bailed water from the leaking craft, most using their cupped hands.

As one particularly strong wave came upon them, the bow raised high into the air and then fell rapidly into the ensuing trough. All aboard were thrown from their seats. Alvar watched in disbelief as Carlos Fenez, a musketeer, seemed to levitate above the boat, his arms and legs splayed in all directions. He came down hard and managed to grab hold of the gunnel, but his body was outside the boat and the next ferocious wave whisked him away in an instant. With no time to even react, Alvar scanned the angry, watery cauldron but there was no sign of the man. Fenez had been one of the weakest on board, suffering from multiple wounds and sickness that made it hard for him to even raise his head. Alvar was sure, that once in the water, he had sunk like a stone. Those still aboard, struggled to regain their seats, Many stayed where they had been thrown.

By morning the storm had passed, rapidly fading in the southeast. Again, the *Spaniards* were greeted with another startling sunrise. The beauty of the moment was lost, however, for the temperature hovered below freezing and the wind gusting heavily from the southeast. Rainwater from the night before had turned to ice on the mast. On de Vaca's boat only five were able to move about, the others, so weak and broken down that they lay in a jumbled heap. Many were unconscious, some seemed near death. The day lingered on. At noon both Alonso de Solis and Alvar struggled to set the sail while one of the *ballesteros*, Jorge Ramos, worked the tiller. Ever since leaving the Bay of Horses Ramos had insisted on this helmsman position. It had become a joke and he was soon nicknamed *El Timonel*...the skipper.

All day the wind remained strong, generally moving the boat along a west southwest track. They saw no land, for the storm had blown the craft far out to sea. Like the rest, Alvar was exhausted and with the featureless seascape before him he fell into a fitful sleep, his head resting against the shoulder of de Solis. At sunset the wind abruptly fell off to a slight breeze now blowing south southeast. Alvar, feeling the change, roused himself with difficulty and stepped over the sleeping bodies of his men to adjust the sail. It seemed that only Ramos, slumped over the tiller, was awake.

"Do you have anything to report *Senor* Ramos."

"Nothing Alguacil. Like yourself I have spent more time asleep than awake."

Alvar finished adjusting the single sail, amazed at how much this simple exertion had fatigued him. Looking around in the fading light there was nothing but the endless horizon, no land no boats, just water. A feeling of panic gripped him and he felt dizzy. Holding the mast to steady himself, he realized he had eaten nothing all day. Reaching for the container of corn, he scooped out half a handful. These he ate slowly, popping the kernels, one by one, into his mouth. Crunching them down hurt his teeth and he detected the faint taste of blood in his mouth. His gums were bleeding. So little moisture was in his mouth, that the act of swallowing had to be exaggerated. After consuming this meager ration, the dizziness seemed to pass. By now the sun had set and the crystal clear sky began to fill with stars and constellations. Alvar looked to find *Orso Mayor* and the pole star...*Estrella Polar*. He knew that following an imaginary line from the two outside stars of *Orso Mayor* would locate it. He had been taught this by his friend, Bartolome Valdez, who had died so tragically during the hurricane at *Trinidad*.

"There it is!" Alvar spoke the words aloud but no one heard or cared. The pole star was on the starboard side. This had to mean that they were moving almost directly west. He let his gaze drift across the heavens to the brilliant band of stars that stretched from horizon to horizon. This was called in *Christian Spain, El Camino de Santiago*...The Road to Santiago. Santiago...Saint James, of course, was the patron saint of *Spain* who appeared before the armies of *Christendom* and led them to victory against the *Moors*. A *Spaniard* who was just, honorable and fearless in life would ultimately walk this starry path at the time of his death to join the eternal army of Saint James. This evening, it seemed especially bright.

Looking again toward Ramos, he saw him still slumped over the tiller, the look of death in his eyes.

Ramos caught his gaze. " Alguacil, I would ask that you take the tiller for I feel my life slipping away this night and I don't think I will live to see the dawn."

"Surely not, friend Ramos, for we are in desperate need of your guidance at the tiller."

"It is true Alguacil, forgive me for I cannot bare to go on."

Alvar stumbled his way to the back of the boat. Ramos slid away from the tiller and lay down as best he could.

Alvar grasped the tiller and maintained a heading that kept the pole star amidships. He looked down at Ramos, now instantly asleep or unconscious, he did not know which. He crossed himself and said a short prayer for *El Timonel*.

25 November, 1528

The Dorantes/Castillo Boat in the Gulf of Mexico, off Galveston Bay

The shrill screeching of gulls awoke him from an exhausted sleep. Captain Andres Dorantes lay there a moment. He tried to gather his senses. Last night's storm had come close to killing them all. More than once he had accepted that he and his companions would die. So high were the waves that upon reaching the crest, the boat careened down the wall, gaining such speed that all aboard were terrorized. Men cried out in fear and lamented their sins. This torment remained with them through most of the night, only abating in the early hours just before dawn.

Now, his mouth was dry as a bucket of sand. It was daylight, but from where he was laying all that was visible were the men slumped around him and the sides of the boat. Overhead, the gulls seemed to orbit the boat, hundreds of them. He pulled himself upright. The water around the boat churned with a life of its own. The gulls folded their wings and sliced into the water, their splashes like hailstones across the surface of a pond. In the water, hundreds, no...thousands, of fish, no longer than his hand, crowded the surface, darting in all directions. Other birds arrived. Pelicans, terns and cormorants all joined the fray. For a moment Dorantes forgot his plight and reveled in the action before him. Then, something caught his eye, a patch of white on the distant horizon that he hadn't seen before.

Carefully, he stood up and strained to see. The morning sun was still low in the eastern sky. Its light, spreading across the water, accentuated each wave and reflected off the object he was seeing.

"It is a beach...I see land!"

Dorantes looked down into the boat but everyone was either asleep or unconscious. He knew not which. The fury of the storm which they had endured during the night had exhausted everyone. Hardly a body moved.

In the bow he saw the slave Estevan roused himself ever so slightly.

"Estevan! rouse yourself, I see land. Estevan *despertar*!"

The black slave rubbed his eyes and sat up, blankly looking around. His eyes finally fixed on Dorantes who was pointing to the west.

"Estevan, over there, tell me what you see."

Estevan turned and squinted, not knowing what he was looking for. The seabirds distracted him briefly as he watched one splash into the water not ten feet from the boat. Then he caught it, the undeniable sight of land on the horizon. He looked back at

Dorantes, but in doing so picked up another spit of land further to the south.

"*Capitan*, behind you, there is land behind you!"

Dorantes turned and saw land in this direction as well. "Estevan, we must wake the men and row to shore."

"But *capitan*, which shore?"

Dorantes thought for a moment. The wind was blowing east southeast. "We will take advantage of the wind and current and row in that direction." He pointed to the west northwest.

The strongest men aboard were Alvaro Fernandez, Natalo Figueroa, Xavier Mendez and Francisco Estudillo. These Dorantes assigned to the oars while he would man the tiller. Estevan would tend the sail.

It was late morning when the boat neared the beach first sighted by Dorantes. All the men on board were now awake. Captain Alonzo Castillo stood at the mast, scanning the coast. They were now only a few hundred yards from the breakers that broke lightly on the shore. The seas were calm with no obstructions between them and the beach. Looking to the south, the coastline continued unabated far into the distance. To the north a point of land maybe half a league from their position indicated that this was either an island or a peninsula. It seemed uninhabited for Castillo could see no movement on shore. He called to his friend.

"Captain Dorantes, I see no obstructions and a fair beach ahead of us."

"I agree, Alonzo, we will come ashore here."

By the time Estevan had lowered the sail, the bow of the boat slid easily onto the sand. Captain Castillo dropped over the side into knee deep water. His knees were so weak he stumbled in the surf.

Those in the bow handed him the anchor rope and he splashed ashore keeping a wary eye on the line of grassy dunes just off the beach.

All was quiet. The boat began to empty of men. Those that couldn't walk were helped to the beach. One of these was Pietro, the young bondsman of Captain Castillo. So emaciated and sick was he that Castillo carried the boy and placed him tenderly on the ground. Pietro himself was only vaguely aware as his eyes fluttered open for just a moment.

Those that could, collected drift wood from the beach. Captain Dorantes and Natalo Figueroa took it on their own to proceed further inland in hopes of finding water. After crossing the dunes, they had gone only a short distance before coming across a beaten path covered with human foot prints. They turned southwest, for the trail seemed to end on the rounded point just north of their position. The day had cleared considerably and, climbing a high dune, Dorantes could clearly see a broad bay just to their north. It looked like they had come ashore on an island. Here at its northern tip it appeared to narrow, but looking to the southwest, the island widened considerably. From his vantage point he could not see the other end, but instead, an undulating grassland of very tall grass punctuated with an occasional grove of trees. More important, he spied a low swale that seemed to contain water.

Pointing, Dorantes said simply, "Water!"

Quickly, they proceeded forward and gained a marshy area surrounded with cattails and reeds. Here the trail opened considerably so that it appeared to be a gathering place. Dorantes and Figueroa took notice, but so dehydrated were they that they fell on their hands and knees and drank deeply.

Back at the landing sight Castillo and the men had managed to gather enough wood for a fire. All gathered around as the flames, fed by bundles of dry grass, leaped high into the air. What little corn that remained was brought from the boat and roasted in the one remaining cooking pot that remained. The warmth of the fire and the meager food revived many.

There was a commotion. "*Capitan* Dorantes has returned!"

"*El tiene agua*...He has water."

Dorantes and Figueroa each emerged from the grassy dune, each carrying a vessel briming with water. As they stepped onto the beach, however, there was movement behind them.

"*Indios*! There are *Indios* with him!"

Those that were able reached for their swords, but Dorantes quickly called out. "*Alta*...Stop! They mean us no harm, put away your weapons."

The *Indians*, about 22 of them, stopped at the grass line and peered at the assemblage of strange emaciated and bearded men before them. They tentatively came forward onto the beach and squatted down. All male, they were tall and well built like all of the natives that the *Spaniards* had encountered. Seemingly oblivious to the cold, most wore nothing but a breech cloth and perhaps a skin over their shoulders with the fur side in. Many carried bows. A few had in their possession short wooden stakes for digging roots. All were tattooed on their chests, legs, face and arms. Most distressing to the *Spaniards* was the practice of inserting lengths of reed through their nipples. These reeds hung out as much as two and a half spans and bobbed up and down as they walked. Additionally, they inserted a piece of cane through slits in the lower lip which drooped down and exposed their teeth. This gave the *Indians* a particularly fearsome look. Their hair, jet black, was cut off just below their ears.

Dorantes called out, "Estevan, bring the bag of beads and bells...quickly."

Estevan hurried to the boat which was still close at hand. Finding the bag, he trudged through the sand up to where Dorantes was standing. The *Indians*, seeing this strange black man, began pointing and talking amongst themselves. Estevan passed the bag to Dorantes and tried several of the hand talk gestures. One of the *Indians* stood and returned the gestures.

"Estevan, tell them that I wish to give them presents."

Estevan uttered a few words in the language of the *Appalachees*, but was greeted with only blank looks. He tried the few words he had picked up from other *Indians*. Again, blank stares, except for one that seemed to understand. This man stood and talked with what appeared to be the leader and then approached Estevan. Together, the black man and the Indian worked at understanding each other.

Impatiently, Dorantes interrupted the discourse. "Estevan, what does he say?"

"*Capitan*, their language is much different than any I have yet heard, but they call themselves *Han*. This man, who calls himself Wyondi, I can understand...sort of. He was a fisherman but like us, a great storm blew him out to sea and deposited him here long ago. He hasn't spoken his native language for many years."

"Ask them if they have food that they could share with us, for we are starving."

Estevan conveyed this message as best he could, struggling with the hand talk and his rudimentary knowledge of the fisherman's language.

Wyondi turned and talked excitedly with the leader who directed all of his compatriots to gather food for the starving *Christians*. As quickly as they had appeared, the *Indians* disappeared back into the tall grass, leaving Wyondi alone with Estevan.

"Estevan, where have they gone, what did they say?" Dorantes was concerned.

"*Capitan*, this Wyondi says that they will return with food and that they will show us a better place to make our camp."

Estevan and Wyondi then sat in place and soon became very animated in trying to better learn the others language. There was much hand talking and some laughing as they struggled with the language nuances of each. Wyondi found it particularly difficult to pronounce the word "*Christians*" after Estevan used it to describe the *Spanish*.

Dorantes passed the water he had gathered to the other men of the boat. It was quickly consumed and two additional trips to the marsh were needed before the thirst of all was slaked. The fire had begun to die down and the shadows were growing long when the *Han* finally returned. This time there were several women and a few children among the group. The men came forward with fish and roots and distributed them among the *Spanish* who, almost crazy with hunger, consumed them immediately. The women and children of the group remained by the sand dune watching the proceedings with wide eyed wonder.

As evening fell, Wyondi took his leave from Estevan, telling him they would return the next morning and lead the *Christians* to a more suitable campsite. It was this evening that Pietro, burning with fever, died in his sleep. His patron, Captain Alonzo Del Castillo Maldonado was inconsolable.

November 26, 1528

The De Vaca Boat in the Gulf of Mexico, off

Galveston Bay

Throughout the night Alvar kept himself awake identifying the constellations that Valdez and his assistant, Angel Jiminez, had taught him. Most prominent was Orion or what Jiminez had called *El Cazador*...The Hunter. He wondered if Jiminez, at this moment in the caravels was also looking at *El Cazador* as he searched for the men of the expedition. Alvar hoped this was so, but it had been seven months since they had left the ships and wondered inland. Surely by now they had given up...but...maybe not. There was always hope.

Somewhat after midnight Alvar reached down and shook Jorge Ramos to see if there was any sign of life. He moved!

"*Senor* Ramos, you are still with us. How do you feel?"

Ramos sat up rubbing his eyes. "I cannot believe it, *Alguacil*. I feel much improved. The angel of death has surely passed me by this night. Let me take the helm once again so that you can get some rest."

Alvar moved aside and tried to rest, but sleep would not come to him. He thought of the dead and dying, and the failure of the expedition. If it had been at all possible he would have surely forfeited his own life rather than see so many in this condition. These thoughts swirled in his head and gave him no respite.

Near dawn Alvar lay in that nether world between awareness and sleep. There was a sound, he tried to ignore it as his body craved sleep. But there it was again and he began to pull back into consciousness. He raised his head.

"Could that be the sound of surf?" He cupped his hands behind his ears.

"It is!" He could distinctly hear the rise and fall of waves in the darkness.

"Ramos do you hear that?"

Jorge answered in the affirmative. "*Si Alguacil*, I think we are near land."

Alvar rushed to the front of the boat to take a sounding. Deftly holding the line he let it slide through his fingers. It stopped dropping just after the 15 fathom knot.

"Fifteen fathoms Ramos, we are moving to shallow water."

"It appears that way, *Alguacil*, but let us stay away from shore until daybreak for we know nothing of this coast."

Alvar rushed to lower the sail and then took an oar on the starboard side so that the boat turned away from the sound of the waves. By now, Alonso de Solis had awoken and also grabbed an oar. By sunrise, four men were at the oars holding the boat just off the shoreline. What they saw at first light was encouraging, a sand beach with no apparent obstructions. The distant coast line disappeared as it faded into a morning fog. From their vantage point there didn't seem to be any sign of habitation.

The sea, however, was running high and the waves were shoaling as they closed on the shoreline, becoming higher and closer together. Breaking near the beach, the foam extended well onto the sand.

Alvar instructed the other oarsman, "Let us go ashore here, for the beach seems to be without hazards, but we must turn the bow seaward and endeavor with all our strength to not let our vessel broach against these waves."

Slowly, at first, the craft closed on the beach, its bow rising high, as each incoming swell pushed it backward. Their speed increased and the chores of the oarsman multiplied. They labored desperately to keep the bow pointed seaward but their efforts were futile. One hundred yards from shore the boat broached to starboard and was lifted up like a toy. They sped toward the beach. With wide eyed terror the oarsmen and the skipper held tightly to whatever was close at hand. When the wave broke, boat five fell like it was dropped from a tree. There was a loud crash, the splintering of wood and the rush of cold seawater. Men tumbled in all directions. Those that had seemed near death were suddenly revived. The boat had been deposited a horse shoes throw onto the beach. It now lay on its larboard side, its contents of men and material thrown out in a wide arc. Men struggled to get ashore, some crawling, some on hands and knees and others staggering.

Alvar, unhurt, had landed face first in the sand and frothy foam. He came up sputtering and spitting. Another wave came in, washed up around him and then quickly receded. He was cold. Cold to the bone.

To no one in particular, Alvar called out, "We must get off this beach and light a fire so we can warm ourselves."

Some, still able to walk, moved down the broad beach looking for driftwood, others moved tentatively up past the dunes and onto the grassland beyond. Alvar and several others found a rocky area that was protected from the sea breezes by a high dune.

"We will build our fire here."

Most of the men carried flint and steel, and with the dry grass for tinder a roaring fire was soon burning brightly. The meager bag of corn was salvaged from the boat and some of it was roasted. Many who had been so desperately ill seemed to revive. Lope de Oviedo had found a marshy area some distance from the beach that still held fresh water from a recent rain. Everyone drank their fill. The men of boat five clustered around the fire in kind of a stupor. For now they were safe, and most importantly, warm.

Here and there clumps of oak trees broke the monotony of the grassland. Alvar, seeing this, called to Oviedo who seemed to be the strongest and heartiest of all the men.

"Senor Oviedo, if you are able, climb as high as you can and tell us what you see."

Oviedo made his way through the tall grass to a nearby copse of trees. One in particular was most advantageous for climbing, and he carefully moved higher and higher into the branches. Finally, well above the camp, he stuck his head through the branches and called out.

"*Alguacil*, we are on the tip of a long sliver of island. It seems to stretch far to the north, but I can plainly see water on all sides. Far in the distance I can see what appears to be the mainland." Turning and looking to the east, he again called out. "There is another spit of land northeastward from here that is either an island or a peninsula for I can not see the other side."

All were quiet as they strained to hear Oviedo's voice over the sound of the surf.

Alguacil!

"What is it, what do you see?"

"*Alguacil*, this island appears to to have hollows and trails in all directions as if cattle had been here...Ohhhhh!"

Oveido had been balancing precariously on a limb when it suddenly snapped. Still holding to the main trunk he struggled to keep from falling, his legs thrashed the air. There was a gasp from those below, but he managed to finally get a foothold.

"*Senor* Oviedo, are you hurt?"

"No *Alguacil*, but I think I will come down now."

In a moment an excited Oveido returned to the fire. "*Alguacil* if there are cattle on this Island I am sure there must be *Christians* about. We may even be close to *Panuco*."

Alvar asked him. "Did you see cattle?"

"Well, no, *Alguacil*, but the paths are wide and well beaten down like only cattle would do. This could only mean that we are near *Panuco* and *Christians are...*"

"*Senor* Oveido, calm yourself. If there are *Christians* about we will find out soon enough. Since you are the strongest, go out and follow one of these trails and see where it leads, but don't go too far and stay out of danger. There was much excitement among the men at the mention of *Panuco*. Many had lost all hope, and to hear that they may be delivered from this ordeal brought a new excitement.

Oviedo moved past the trees and quickly found one of the paths he had seen from the treetop. He studied the ground. There were no hoof prints or manure such that cattle would leave, only human footprints. This was a man trail. He followed it, carefully stopping every few yards to look around. He felt very much alone and vulnerable. The hollows he had seen were only natural swales formed by the shifting sand of the island. He continued on for a half league or more. Coming to a small rise in the trail, he suddenly caught sight of several huts. He dropped down. Cautiously he peered through the grass. There was no movement. Turning around he could just see the copse of trees far in the distance where the *Spaniards* had come ashore, a thin trail of smoke snaking into the air from their campfire.

He crept closer. There were five huts roughly laid out in a circle. There was no one around. He raised up and approached the encampment. As Oviedo neared the first hut, a little dog rushed out and came to him. Startled, he stood there a moment. His heart was racing. Next to the first hut was a cooking pot and some fish, drying in the sun. He gathered up the fish, the cooking pot and the small dog and hurried back down the trail, gnawing on one of the fish as he moved along.

Alvar had become concerned. Oviedo had been gone too long. He had instructed him to investigate the countryside, but that had been almost an hour ago and now there was still no sign of him. He turned to Lieutenant Palacios who was helping with the fire.

"*Teneinte* Palacios, take a man and see what has become of *Senor* Oviedo. He should have returned by now.

"*Si Algaucil.*" Palacios scanned the group of emaciated *Spaniards* now lounging by the fire.

"Ruiz. Come with me!"

Together Palacios and Gonzalo Ruiz headed in the direction that they had last seen Oviedo. Both were armed with a sword, but their appearance was most comical. They were barefoot with pantaloons that were frayed above the knees and a threadbare blouse that barely covered their upper body. Both were heavily bearded with long scraggly hair that hung past their shoulders.

They quickly found the trail that Oviedo had taken and carefully followed it. It wasn't long before Oviedo was spotted moving toward them.

"There he is *teneinte.* " It was Ruiz who had seen him first.

They could clearly see Oviedo moving along the trail, but he was turning as if talking to someone.

"He is being followed *teneinte*!"

Peering further down the trail, Palacios saw four Indians, armed with bows and arrows, following him. They were calling out, and he, in turn, was calling out to them.

Oviedo was coming closer. Palacios called out to ho him. "*Senor* Oviedo are you alright?"

The *Indians* stopped abruptly.

Startled, Oviedo turned toward the two *Spaniards*. A look of relief came over his face. "*Si teneinte*, but, as you can see, I am being followed."

Oviedo continued to walk forward, joining the other two. Once again he turned and motioned for the *Indians* to join him but they remained in place, watching intently.

Palacios saw movement inside the large cooking pot that Oviedo was carrying. "What have you there?"Peering over the edge of the clay pot was the small dog that Oviedo had picked up in the village. "I came across several huts that were deserted. When I entered them I found this cooking pot, the dog and some mullet drying in the sun." Oviedo pulled the dog out of the pot by the scruff and showed the slabs of fish resting in the bottom.

"Did you see any more *Indio*?"

"No *teneinte*, only these four."

Ruiz had been watching the *Indians*. "There are only three now. My guess is that one has returned to bring up the rest of their band."

Again, the three *Spaniards* motioned for the *Indians* to join them. They were ignored.

Palacios pushed Oviedo and Ruiz in the direction from which they came. "Let us hurry back to the camp so that we can tell them of what you found."

"*Alguacil*, they have returned!" It was the inspector, Alonso de Solis and he was pointing toward the beach.

Alvar looked to see the three men trudging through the sand.

"*Senor* Palacios, why did you return by a different route?"

"*Alguacil,* we hurried back by the quickest route. We have three *Indios* following us."

Alvar looked further down the beach, and there three armed warriors had stopped to study the strange gathering of bearded men that now appeared before them.

"They have stopped, *Alguacil*, and they ignore my greeting to join us."

"You have stolen what belongs to them, *Senor* Oviedo. I think it is best if you take the pot, the dog...and...whatever remains of the fish and walk it out to them."

With an audible gulp Oviedo gathered up the pot and dog. "*Alguacil*, I have eaten all of the fish."

Alvar shook his head. "No matter, take the dog and the pot out to them and lay it in the sand so they know you are returning it."

Oviedo trudged off in the direction of the three *Indians*. The had been lounging in the sand while keeping a wary eye on the newcomers. As Oviedo moved closer they stood. Somewhat intimidated, Oviedo stopped about 50 feet in front of them and set the pot, dog inside it, on the sand. He turned and began walking back. After going no more than a few yards the small dog bounded after him. Perplexed, Oviedo picked up the dog and walked back to the pot. Putting the small animal in the pot he turned and began walking back. Again, the dog bounded after him.

There were some snickers from the *Spaniards* but, as of yet, the *Indians* remained stoic in their expressions. This time Oviedo put the dog in the pot and turned it upside down in the sand. Satisfied that the dog would not escape, he turned and began walking once again. But, as all watched, the pot rocked back and forth until the dog managed to get its nose under the edge and wiggle out. It was soon at Oviedo's side.Now there was open laughter by the *Spanish*, and the *Indians* were talking among themselves and pointing. Oviedo looked to de Vaca for help, but Alvar only shook his head and spread his arms in resignation.

Once again Oviedo gathered up the dog and took it back to the pot. He turned the pot upside down and pushed it further into the sand. Then, in a rush, he ran towards the *Spanish* camp, throwing up rooster tails of loose sand from his churning feet. No sooner had he covered half the distance when the dog freed itself and ran up, nipping at his heels and causing Oviedo to loose balance. He fell forward in the sand. The small dog came up and licked his face.

Now, there were guffaws of laughter from the *Spanish* as well as the three *Indians* who were laughing heartily. After a few moments one of the *Indians* came forward, picked up the pot and, walking over to where Oviedo was now sitting, offered it to him.

"*Gracias*," was all that Oviedo could say as the *Indian* returned to his compatriots.

The laughing, however, was not to last. Further up the beach, scores of *Indians* began filtering out of the dunes to join the three who had been observing Oviedo.

To the emaciated and sickly *Spaniards* these men all looked to be giants, well built and each over six feet in height. Alonso de Solis turned to Alvar, who was at his side.

"*Alguacil,* we can not even defend ourselves, there are barely three or four of us who can even walk."

Alvar picket up the bag of trinkets that had been brought from the boat. "*Senor* de Solis, you and I will step forward and call to them. Perhaps they will see our plight and assist us."

The two *Spaniards* moved closer. Using the rudimentary hand talk they gestured for the Indians to come closer displaying some trinkets they carried. The *Indians* moved closer, encircling them.

Alvar tried to hide the fear that was within him, for the Indians pressed so closely that he could not see past them. But, so enthralled were they with the hawk bells, beads and mirrors that each offered an arrow in trade. A few separated from the discussion and walked over to the fire where the other *Spaniards* were clustered. They seemed much disturbed by the condition of the men and returned to where Alvar and de Solis were standing with tears in their eyes. "*Alguacil*, these men seem to be crying after seeing the condition of our men."

"This is most unusual. Perhaps we can convince them to help us." Alvar pointed to himself, de Solis and the rest of the *Spaniards* and repeatedly uttered the word "*Christians*."

The *Indians* seemed to understand. Struggling with the pronunciation they repeated "*Kish-ton*," for in their language the soft "R" was not used. Pointing to themselves and all that were around they uttered the word "*Capoques*." Alvar repeated the word but stumbled on the last syllable. The Indians laughed and repeated it again while emphasizing the last syllable. De Solis tried it also. Soon both sides were mouthing "*Kish-ton*" and "*Cav-e-qua*" repeatedly.

Through a variety of signs and pantomiming gestures Alvar and de Solis asked the *Capoques* for food. This they seemed to understand quit well and indicated although they had nothing now, the would return in the morning with food. With this the *Capoques* left the *Spaniards*.

Watching the *Capoques* move down the beach and disappear into the tall grass de Vaca and de Solis breathed a sigh of relief.

"We are safe for now *Senor* de Solis, and let us hope they return in the morning with food."

De Vaca and de Solis returned to the campfire and repeated to the men what had transpired. The stew pot, filled with water, corn and...dog meat, was boiling next to the fire.

November 27, 1528

Island off the Gulf Coast of Texas

The sun was hardly up when a long line of *Indians* were spotted walking up the beach toward the *Spanish* camp. Alonso de Solis, the royal inspector, was the first to see them, for he had arisen early to search the beach and dunes for firewood. The wind had picked up in the night. Blowing offshore, it made the bite of the low temperature even more uncomfortable. The bonfire, so welcome the day before, had now dwindled to a few embers.

"*Despertar*...awaken, the *Indios* have returned!"

Slowly the camp came to life. The few that could stood up to receive them. It was apparent that they had returned as promised, laden with food, water and firewood. They had even brought their women and children to observe the strange newcomers, but the women stayed well away, content to sit on the distant dunes to watch the proceedings.

The fire was soon blazing, its flames leaping high into the air. The *Cavaques* passed out morsels of roots and fish to the emaciated *Spanish* who gobbled them up as soon as they were received. Hesitant at first, Alvar tasted the odd shaped roots, some large, some small. Crunching down, the taste was similar to walnuts. He immediately consumed three in quick order and was sorry for it, because his stomach rumbled in protest.

Alonso de Solis had already entered into discussion with the head men of the *Cavaques* but he appeared quite frustrated in his attempts to communicate. Alvar stepped up and warmly greeted the leaders as best he could. The lead talker of the *Capoques* kept pointing to one of the silver bells that the *Spaniards* had given him. He had attached it to a length of rawhide that hung around his neck. These trinkets, Alvar determined, were of great value to the Indians who now felt very rich. As the attempts at hand talk progressed, Alvar determined that the *Indians* would return the next day with more food. He again thanked them, but by now the pressure in his bowels was overwhelming. He rushed across the beach to find some solitude. Just reaching the safety of the dunes his stomach muscles contracted and rejected the quantities of water, nuts and fish that he had consumed. Squatting there, waves of nausea enveloped him and he struggled to stay upright. It soon passed, but he was covered in filth and needed to clean himself.

Feeling that someone was watching him, Alvar looked to his right and saw a passel of *Indian* children watching him in wide eyed wonder. Mortified, he lurched forward and crawled to a position where, unobserved, he rose up and shakily made his way to the beach. Wading into the surf, the water chilled him to the bone, but he continued on until it was over his waste. The coldness of the water seemed to clear his head but he began to shake violently. With difficulty he rubbed himself vigorously to clean off the vomit and feces. Turning blue he struggled to reach shore. The wind whisked away all body heat. He was so tired. Finally, stumbling and crawling, he reached the fire and collapsed in a heap. The warmth enveloped him and he fell into a deep sleep.

When Alvar awoke the *Capoques* were gone. The fire was burning brightly and many of the men, like himself, had fallen asleep in its warmth. Those that were awake talked quietly among themselves or tended to the sick and injured. The sun was low in the west and the onshore wind had cooled the side of his body furthest from the fire. He rolled over and stared up into the sky. Only a few clouds floated above. One seemed to take the shape of a horse, another a sailing ship. He lay there thinking of his home in *Spain* and Maria. Ah, his wife. What was she doing at this moment. Had she learned of the loss of the expedition, had she given him up for dead?

"Ah, you are awake *Alguacil*, I trust you slept well." It was the *veedor*...inspector, Alonso de Solis.

Still, sleep blurry, Alvar rubbed his eyes. "Like a dead man Alonso, I remember nothing after crawling to the fire. It looks as if I have slept the day away. Have the *Indios* left us?"

"A short time after you lay down they proceeded back from where they had come. Their language is most difficult but we determined from gestures that they would return tomorrow with more fish and roots."

Alvar nodded. "That is good. Some of the men look much improved already."

"Some, yes, but not all. I fear that a few will not make it much longer." De Solis hesitated and seemed to consider his next question. "What of *Panuco*, *Alguacil*? Surely we must be close."

As Alvar considered the question, Lope de Oviedo joined them. He had brought with him a few fish that the *Indians* had supplied. Skewered lengthwise on a stick, each had been gutted, scaled and roasted by the fire. He offered one to both men.

"Gracias." Alvar bit into the oily skin and tore off a piece of the white flesh underneath. It burned his tongue and he sucked in air to cool it as he chewed. Spitting out scales and bones he carefully chewed each piece before swallowing. It tasted sweet, and his mouth watered in anticipation.

"As to *Panuco*, Alonso, I can only guess as to its location. The coastline of which we have been following all these months, now appears to lay in a north to south direction. This would indicate to me that we have come near the same longitude as *New Spain*."

Oviedo interrupted. "Then we must be close!"Alvar took another bite and waited before he answered. "We are most likely far north of *Panuco*."

"But *Alguacil*, we have traveled so far...and so much suffering. Certainly we must be near."

"I hope you are right Lope, but we must make every effort to continue on, for the closer we get, the more chance we have of being rescued. After we rest here a bit let's resolve to repair the boat and continue our journey."

28 November, 1528

Island off the Gulf Coast of Texas

The *Capoques* greatly valued the gifts that had been given them. They felt rich. They continued to bring food, water and firewood to show their appreciation. The health of the *Spaniards* improved. So much so, that the next day Alvar picked the strongest and proceeded to the beach to repair the boat that now lay on its side, half submerged and covered in sand. The men removed their clothes and waded into the water. Not having shovels they used their hands and pieces of driftwood to scrape away the sand. The work was laborious and the water was cold. A fire was built on shore so that the workers could warm themselves, many shaking uncontrollably. Finally, at about the noon hour, the boat was up-righted and floated. The oars and other necessities that had been thrown clear were collected and loaded on board.

Alvar called for all of the men to come on board. Some, too sick to walk were carried. When all was ready the boat was turned and pushed bow first into the surf. Wading up to their shoulders four men walked the boat out as far as they could before crawling aboard. Alvar and three other rowers strained at the oars to get away from the surf line. Slowly the boat moved out to sea. Since the wind was blowing offshore Alonso de Solis set the sail in hopes that it would lessen the burden of the oarsmen. The boat had moved about two crossbow shots from shore when the wind abruptly turned north and forced the bow abeam of the incoming waves.

The rowers on the starboard side struggled to bring the boat back around while de Solis hurriedly dropped the sail. A huge wave exploded over the bow soaking everything below. Alvar pulled on his oar as hard as he could, but his strength was gone and his hands were numb from the cold. He dropped the oar. As the boat rose on the next wave he knew it was going over.

"Jump for your lives!" Alvar and the others catapulted over the side. Alonso de Solis, feeling the boat roll, didn't have time to jump but reached out to grab whatever he could. The light of day turned dark as the vessel rolled over and green seawater swirled up around him. The waterlogged boat, now upside down in the surf, sank quickly so that only its keel remained above the surface.

"I have to get out from under this boat." was the only thing that de Solis could think of. His lungs ached as he let go and swam downward. The surf was so turbulent, however, that when he tried to surface he again came up under the boat. Disoriented, he found a small air pocket and tried to fill his lungs. He inhaled deeply. Vaguely aware that others were with him he started to dive again. This time, however, someone, grabbed hold of his waist and held tightly. Even underwater he could hear the panicked cries of whoever it was. De Solis fought, kicking and punching as hard as he could before the attacker released his grip and floated off. Lungs burning from the added exertion, he again tried to reach the air pocket but whatever air had been trapped underneath had disappeared. In one last effort de Solis dove to free himself, but with the effort he felt cold seawater flow into his lungs. His body convulsed and tried to reject the water, but this only made it worse. Panicking, he clawed violently at the boat above. Darkness began to envelope him. His strength failed. The panic subsided and a wave of peacefulness seemed to wash over him. He was sinking. He thought of his home in Seville, childhood friends, his mother and then...nothing.

Above, the remainder of the *Spaniards* struggled to reach the beach. The currents had pushed the party further down the shore where it was rough and the waves higher. The surf was dotted with the bobbing heads of the survivors. They crawled ashore, some dragging their companions. Most were naked, having shed their heavy clothes to stay afloat. They had lost everything. The winds of late November now blew in from the sea and wicked away body heat from the skin. Many were turning blue. The emaciated men, half dead, shaking violently in the cold, trudged back up the beach to the campsite they had just left.

Alvar and Lope de Oviedo were among the first to reach the remnants of their former fire. Collapsing in the sand, others joined them. After recovering somewhat, a few were able to find wood with which they brought the embers back to life. Other fires were built close by, such that the men could warm both sides of their body at once.

It was a sorry sight. In deep despair, these *Christians* huddled around the flames. Some were staring blankly into the distance, others were sobbing with grief and desperation, beseeching God to show mercy and deliver them form this terrible ordeal. Further down the beach the bodies of two compatriots, both musketeers, had been pulled onto the sand. The Royal Inspector, de Solis, was missing and it was assumed that he had drowned as well.

At sunset the *Capoques* returned. Thinking nothing had changed, they had brought food, water and firewood. Nearing the campsite the Indians stopped abruptly. They stared at the disheveled condition of the *Christians,* for their appearance had changed much since the day before. The two drowned bodies were still on the beach and in their confusion the Indians began to leave.

"No! Do not leave us." Alvar rose and moved down the path after them. The *Indians* paused and talked among themselves.

Alvar moved closer. "I beseech you, stay with us for surely we will die if you leave."

Of course the *Capoques* understood not a word, but the man before them looked so pitiful that some started to return. Using his meager knowledge of hand talk Alvar tried to explain what had happened. He motioned for the *Indians* to accompany him to the wreck site where, even now, the overturned boat could be seen wallowing in the surf.

Slowly they began to understand what had happened and then, a strange thing happened. The *Indians* began to cry. They sat on the beach next to the *Christians* and wailed so loudly and so long that the men of the expedition were completely taken aback. The men, women and children all joined in the lament and their tears seemed heartfelt. The depression of the *Christians* deepened.

For half an hour the crying continued and then, slowly subsided and stopped altogether. The women and children rose and began moving back to the village. The men remained in place sitting on their haunches.

During this time Alvar spoke to his despondent men. "*Compatriotas*, if we stay here death is surely close. Our only hope is to beg these *Indios* to take us to their homes."

Miserable as they were, several spoke up. "*Alguacil*, I fear that once we surrender ourselves to these *paganos* we will be sacrificed to their idols and eaten." It was Stancio Mellado who had been with Cortes in New Spain. In the terrible fighting around *Tenochtitlan*, he had witnessed the human sacrifices performed by the *Aztecs*. The thought of a similar fate terrified him. Others in the group nodded their heads in agreement.

Alvar considered this, but seeing the condition of his men, took no heed to their concerns and approached the Indians. In particular he addressed the one called Wee-ah-te-noka for he seemed to be the leader of the group. Somewhat older, he appeared to assume a more regal posture than the others. Alvar had noticed too, that the other males seemed to confer with him before taking any action.

Weeahtenoka rose as Alvar advanced. He was at least a foot taller and wonderfully built. Covered with only one loose pelage he seemed oblivious to the cold wind that blew in from the sea. He seemed like a giant.

Using hand signs Alvar struggled to communicate his desire to be taken to the *Indians* homes. Weeahtenoka watched thoughtfully as Alvar mimed and gestured. He was joined in this by Lope de Oviedo and the discourse went on for several minutes. Finally with an expression that seemed to confirm his understanding, Weeahtenoka turned and addressed the throng of warriors that had clustered around him. To Alvar's amazement the *Capoques* seemed to show great pleasure in this. Weeahtenoka expressed to Alvar that it would take some time to prepare the way. After much talking among themselves, about thirty of the *Indians* spread out and began gathering firewood. When each had an arm load they disappeared down the path toward their lodges. While this was happening Weeahtenoka and a small group stayed with the *Christians* and continued to parlay.As darkness approached a cold north wind began to blow. Even huddled around the fire the cold was intense. Nearly naked as they were, the men shifted constantly to warm the exposed sides of their bodies. In the west the last vestige of sunlight had disappeared below the horizon when the *Indians* returned and spoke briefly with Weeahtenoka. With this he turned to Alvar and motioned for all to follow him. The Indians then spread amongst the *Christians*, assisting the weak to stand and even carrying, on their back, those that could not walk. The whole procession then moved slowly down the trail, for by now it was dark with only the slightest hint of afterglow in the western sky.

They had not gone far when the intense cold and wind began to affect the men of the expedition. Their suffering was great. Weeahtenoka seeing this, waved them along, pointing down the trail and uttering *"Kish-tons...Kish-tons."*

Just when he felt that the men could not go much further Alvar noticed a glow in the distance. Before long the assemblage stepped into a clearing that the Indians had prepared. A huge bonfire was burning brightly. The men collapsed around it, warming themselves and recovering from their fatigue. After a half hour Weeahtenoka urged them onward. Again, they were whisked along, now being joined by the men that were attending the fire.

Looking into the night Alvar could make out the glow of another bonfire in the distance, and beyond that, much dimmer, another. Walking with Diego de Huelva, Alvar expressed in amazement, "These *Indios* have prepared warming fires all along the trail!"

After two or three hours of this intermittent travel the *Spaniards* and their Indian hosts entered the village enclosure. All about, the *Capoques* had turned out to see this procession. Women and children pointed at the strange bearded men who, in their nakedness, attempted to cover themselves. Before them the *Indians* had hastily constructed a large dwelling into which they directed the *Spaniards*. Within, eight fires burned such that the men could warm themselves without constantly shifting position. The men from boat 5 of the Narvaez expedition, now forty two in number, fell exhausted on the ground. Many feared they would be sacrificed in the morning, but all were too tired to care.

CHAPTER 05

I Will See You Soon

Voya Verte Pronto

Grabbing up Campo he rocked back and forth, holding the dead youngster in his arms.

"Little Rata, I will see you soon."

November 27, 1528

In the Gulf off East Matagorda Bay, Texas

The boat was becoming un-seaworthy. Water poured in almost as fast as the men could bail it out. The gunnels were only slightly above water level and another storm would surely be the end for *Adelantado* Panfillo de Narvaez and all his men aboard. They had been out of sight of land for three days now and it was with great joy then that it was sighted at mid-morning.

The last they had seen of the other *Spaniards* was just after coming upon the great river. There the current was so strong that it pushed the boats seaward, separating them in all directions. The *Alguacil's* boat was the last one to be seen, but it too disappeared into the distance. The shoreline disappeared from view. With the strong current and an offshore wind, it was only with much effort that their boat finally made land. Not really land, but a broad sand bar just off the coast. Here the exhausted crew spent the night. The next morning they continued their journey along the coast and for many days followed the shoreline as much as possible Three days ago, however, a storm had come up. The wind and rain had enveloped them, and again pushed the small craft far out to sea.

Now with the shoreline once again in view, there was new hope.

Panfillo carefully stood in the bow to get a better view of the land mass that was emerging on the western horizon. Today the winds were on shore and the dilapidated sail was propelling them ever closer. A glistening white beach stretched in both directions and he could see the surf was breaking lightly on the shore. It looked like it would be an easy landing. Further from the beach, the sea grasses seemed to stretch far inland with only an occasional tree or shrub disrupting the conformity. Overhead the sea birds filled the skies, their cries becoming louder as the boat came ever closer.

Panfillo looked down at his feet which were awash in seawater. He spoke softly to Campo who was by his side, "It is by God's grace that we have found land because another day in this leaking hulk and we would have sunk for sure."

Campo, his lips blistered by the sun and seawater, found it difficult to talk.

"My *capitain*, let's hope we can find water close by because of the few remaining canteens only two have anything left."

Panfillo scanned the beach again. "I see no signs of habitation, but to be safe let's prepare ourselves for battle"

The few remaining swords were gathered up and given to the strongest men. Panfillo still carried his *montante*, but in his weakened state he found it difficult to wield. Still, it had always been with him and he would not give it up.

"*Capitan* Pantoja, take five of the best men and scout the beach as soon as we come aground."

It was near the noon hour when the keel of the boat finally ground to a halt in the sand. People were already in the water. A few had jumped out in the surf to help guide the boat in the waist-deep water. The swordsmen were the next out. There were five of them, and their appearance was almost comical...five ragged, bearded, scarecrows holding rusted swords. After so many days at sea, they all walked like drunkards, swaying to and fro on weakened legs. Looking left and right, up and down the beach, no human form, or anything else, disturbed the view. They moved to the edge of the grass because if an *Indio* attack was to come it would be from this direction.

Still nothing.

They were all alone.

Glad to be off the boat, the men scoured the immediate area for a source of fresh water and anything to eat. Moving further into the grassy interior they came upon a marshy area. Here the water was drinkable, but just barely. Still, they filled their canteens and gave thanks to God

Narvaez instructed the men to pull the boat high onto the beach and overturn it. This would let the seawater drain out and the sun's heat would help dry the hull. They would spend the night here and then continue along the coast in the morning. After taking a drink of water offered by Campo, Panfillo sat in the sand next to the boat and fell into an uneasy sleep.

At about dusk, there was a commotion in the camp. Panfillo's good eye fluttered open and through the sleep-induced fog, he tried to understand what was happening.

"Capitan, Capitan!" It was Campo trying to rouse him.

"Capitan, there are men on the beach coming toward us!"

Reaching for his *montante,* Narvaez struggled to his feet, He couldn't help but think to himself., "Perhaps this is the day of my death at the hands of the *Indios."* He joined the crowd of his men staring at the beach.

"Who are they *capitan* Pantoja?"

Captain Pantoja squinted into the distance but could only answer, "They are still too far away, *Adelantado,* but there looks to be 30 or more."

The wind was now blowing in from the sea and the evening took on a deep haze. Wind-blown spray and sand particles helped to further obscure the approaching strangers. It had become quiet in the Narvaez camp. Perhaps each man, like Panfillo, was contemplating if this would be their last battle. The somber mood continued until, quite suddenly, Campo cried out.

"Friar Xuarez! The one in front is Friar Xuarez, I can tell by his walk. It is the men of the Purser's boat."

"Praise God," was all that Narvaez could say. He dropped his sword and sat in the sand.

Sure enough, as the approaching men became recognizable, some began to call out their names.

"Fray de Palas...yes, that's him just behind Xuarez!"

"And...in the back there, I see the Purser himself, Enriquez being helped along by friar Alaniz."

"Esquivel survives...I see him there on the left."

It was a joyous reunion as the two parties shook hands and embraced. From this boat, all of the pious friars had survived, but of the forty nine men who had left the Isle of Horses only 38 remained. Eight had died of thirst and disease, two had been washed overboard in a storm and one had taken his own life by cutting his wrists. All of the group were thin and emaciated. The purser himself, Alonso Enriquez, suffered from a worsening cough that sapped his strength and made it difficult for him even to walk.

Their boat, leaking badly, and almost uncontrollably, had come aground between two rivers that emptied into the sea. The first river was just to the north of their landfall, its abrupt entry into the sea marked by numerous marshes and a rapid current. The second river, no more than two leagues to the south, was also surrounded by marshes and mangroves. Its entry in the sea was more benign than the first and the *Spaniards,* moving further inland where the river narrowed, crossed its breadth with relative ease.

The men separated into small groups, all talking at once and sharing their experiences. As darkness fell on the beach the men of the two boats gathered around a large fire. The temperatures during the day had been quite moderate, but now the sea breezes cooled and they huddled together. Some dug little berms in the sand to shield themselves from the wind and to concentrate the fire's heat. Most of the *Spaniards* located themselves on the leeward side of the fire where the smoke gave some protection from the ever-present, voracious mosquitoes.

During the night the purser's condition worsened and by morning he was coughing up blood. In the morning Narvaez, who had remained in the boat during the night, addressed the group. He stood there by the fire embers, shaking in the coolness of the morning. It seemed as though he had trouble standing and many times Campo would help support him. His face and body were covered in sores such that he looked like a leper...a mere shell of the great captain that had begun this journey.

"*Compatriotas*, by the grace of God we have survived to this point. We have all suffered and many of our friends are not with us. Many have died terrible deaths. We now number 79 souls, 38 from the Purser's boat and 41 from mine."

Here he stopped and looked at the ground trying to compose himself.

"Today we travel toward *Panuco* to be rescued by our *Spanish* brethren. We must continue on at all costs. My *teniente* Alonso Enriquez from boat two...our friend and brother...suffers now from a sickness to which we all hope for a speedy recovery. But, in this capacity, he is not able to lead and so, until such time that he is able, I am appointing *Capitan* Pantoja to take his place."

There were nods and some grunts all around. Narvaez's reasoning seemed good, for Enriquez was obviously not well enough to lead. and Pantoja, although emaciated like the rest, was relatively healthy.

Pepillo Sotomayor, however, was not happy with the *Adelentado's* choice. He was well aware that Pantoja was Narvaez's friend and confident. Together they campaigned in Cuba. Sotomayor felt that he, as camp master ever since the expedition began, was more qualified. More than that, Pantoja was arrogant and not well-liked by the men.

"We will continue on in our quest for *Panuco*. Our boat is almost spent and for this reason, we will continue down the coast with only the necessary oarsmen aboard. All others will walk along the beach as we go. I do this so the boat will be available for crossing over the numerous inlets and estuaries that undoubtedly lie ahead. Besides the oarsmen, the boat will carry *teninte* Enriquez, myself, pilot Anton Perez, and my page Campo."

After a short blessing by Fray de Palas, the meeting broke up. Narvaez chose four

oarsmen and proceeded to the boat. Among those on shore, there was some grumbling about their being forced to walk while the governor stayed aboard the boat, but it subsided as they began the march southward. The group was careful to stay in the wet sand just above the water line. Here it was easier walking and their footprints were rapidly erased by the incoming waves, a precaution to any marauding *Indians* that may be about. A hundred *yara* off shore Narvaez's boat paralleled the progress of those on shore.

30 November, 1528

Near Cavallo Inlet on Matagorda Penninsula, Texas

It was the morning of the third day since they had made landfall. Narvaez estimated they had traveled about 14 leagues. Ahead was a broad inlet, and beyond that another beach line could be seen disappearing into the haze. About half a league to the north and northwest there was a heavy accumulation of mangrove islands with vegetation so thick that it was hard to tell one from the other. Further south still the mainland seemed to come to a point. Looking back at the inlet he could see that the current was moving rapidly...the tide was going out.

The oarsmen had beached the boat and had climbed out to rest in the sand. Campo and the pilot Anton Perez were hefting the large rock that was used as an anchor. Once past the gunnel, they let it go and it made a towering splash as it hit the shallow water. Both climbed out and tugged the rock further up the beach until the rope attaching it to the hull was tight. Then they sat in the sand to catch their breath. Campo seemed more distressed than usual.

Narvaez straddled the gunnel and painfully lowered himself into the water. The seawater stung his legs which were now covered in sores and mosquito bites. He bent down, splashed some water onto his face, and then slowly made his way to shore. Enriquez remained on the boat, his strength in decline and his breathing labored. Perez, grabbing a canteen, climbed back into the boat and offered the *teniente* a drink.

Enriquez could only mumble, *"Gracios."* He lay back and fell into a labored sleep. Perez looked up at Narvaez who only shook his head.

Further up the beach the rest of the men were trudging toward the boat. The three days of walking along the shore had taken its toll. There had been almost no food and the men subsisted mainly by eating the seaweed that washed ashore. On day two, however, they had come upon a pod of dolphins feeding close to the beach. The animals had cornered a large school of mullet and in their frenzy to escape, many of the mullet had beached themselves on the sand or little tidal pools at the water's edge. The men scrambled in a frenzy to collect the fish. Many ate them raw where they stood. Others collected driftwood and started a small fire. Sticks were passed through the fish's mouth and they were roasted over the open flame. It had been a blessing from heaven and Fray Xuarez had led them in a prayer of thanks.

Today during their trek down the beach one of the marchers, Antonio Remerez, had fallen down and was unable to get up. He had been carried along for the last league. Now writhing in the sand and almost delirious, Narvaez consented for him to ride in the boat.

Looking again at the inlet Narvaez noted that the current had subsided substantially...it was almost low tide. There were still two or three hours of daylight left and if loaded now he could get his men across and return for the men from the Purser's boat. He suspected that the window of opportunity for low tide was narrow and the condition of the oarsmen would not let them fight a strong current.

"*Compatriotas*, the tide is right and we must take this opportunity to begin ferrying our men across this inlet. It will take at least two...maybe three trips."

He turned and looked at his page. "Campo, get the boat pushed out to deeper water so that we can begin loading." Campo, however, continued to lay in the sand holding his stomach.

Narvaez looked at his young page with some concern. "What is it, Campo?"

"I am sorry my *capitan* but I am having terrible pains and when I get up I cannot hold my bowels." Just then he was seized with a spasm and shook all over. Fray Xuarez went over and felt the boy's head.

"*Adelantado*, he is burning up!"

Narvaez ordered several men to move Campo closer to the fire. Here he laid a heated rock on the youngster's stomach. "My little *Rata*, sometimes while we were on campaign in *Cuba* we would have similar symptoms...a warm rock always seemed to ease the pain."

"Now we must begin loading the boat if we are to take advantage of the tide."

Narvaez looked into the crowd. "Pilot Perez, you will assist me while my page is laid up."

"*Si Adelantado.*"

"Have the men from my boat board first. We will return for those men from the Purser's boat."

There was some grumbling, but Narvaez's men waded into the water and clambered aboard. Some were so weak they had to be helped into the boat by the others, but within an hour they had pushed off.

Capitan Pantoja called from the shore, "*Adelantado*, do not forget to return for us!"

Narvaez waved his reply but made no comment as he concentrated on the way ahead.

They had caught the tide at just the right moment. A few little swirls of current were all they had to deal with. An off shore breeze blew the boat slightly to port, but they landed on the opposite beach in good order.

"Everyone out!" Narvaez's voice boomed across the bay.

"I need four fresh oarsmen." Narvaez wanted to make the return trip as quickly as possible before the tide turned.

All made it out including Alonso Enriquez, the delirious marcher Remerez, and Campo. Each was gently laid in the sand. Enriquez was only semi-conscious now but was able to murmur, "*gracios, gracios.*"

Only Narvaez, Perez, and four oarsmen made the trip back. The lightened boat moved rapidly in the water and they were able to bring the boat back to their original starting point. The tide, however, looked like it was turning. Small swirls of current started to make their presence known.

"*Capitan* Pantoja, get your men aboard quickly!"

Those that were strongest literally threw the weakest aboard, depositing them over the gunnel like sacks of flour. Still, it took a half hour until the boat was ready to depart. Out in the inlet, the current had increased substantially and the oarsmen struggled to keep the bow pointed at their compatriots on the opposite shore. Try as they might the current was too much and the boat and its occupants were carried far to the east on the leeward side of the inlet. Still, the boat made it ashore and, led by the friars, all aboard offered up a prayer of thanks.

The occupants off loaded and began the trudge through the sand to join their comrades. The four oarsmen and five others "walked" the boat around the inlet, guiding it by hand in the shallow water. Finally, just as the sun was setting, the boat and all of the men from the Purser's boat reunited on the beach.

Anton Perez threw the rock anchor overboard and then jumped into the shallow water next to the boat to retrieve it. Struggling with the weight, he carried it just above the tidal line and dropped the rock in the sand. He checked the rope which was wrapped several times around the oblong rock...it appeared secure.

30 November, 1528

Just South of Cavallo Inlet on Matagorda Island, Texas

The temperature began to drop. The clear sky that had been with them all day rapidly clouded over and all the stars disappeared from view. The winds, light during the early evening, now shifted to the west and became exceedingly strong. Larger waves began to hammer the beach and the men suffered terribly from the cold. They moved off the beach and started a new fire in the shelter of a sand berm. As the weather deteriorated the heat from the fire was rapidly dissipated in the stinging wind, the smoke and embers being carried horizontally across the bay. In the early evening the friars, de Palas, Austriano, Alaniz, and Xaurez offered up prayers of forgiveness and hope, but these tapered off as they too fell into a huddled stupor.

Panfillo Narvaez was miserable, the most miserable he had ever been. More than that, however, he was concerned about his page Campo, the young urchin he had taken in at the port of *San Lucar*. Rising from his position by the fire, he gathered up Campo in his arms and moved toward the beach.

He called out, "*Senor* Perez, come with us."

Anton Perez reluctantly gave up his position by the fire and followed.

"*Adelantado,* where are we going?"

In his weakened state, Panfillo was struggling to carry the young page. The great strength that he had once had was gone. What remained was a deteriorating body covered in sores and racked with pain. Still, he found the strength to carry Campo for whom he felt great affection and responsibility.

"To the boat, we go to the boat. The gunnels will provide some protection from this damnable wind and I can wrap young Campo in the sail to keep him warm."

The boat, grounded on the sand, had turned sideways to the shore. It rocked back and forth with each oncoming wave. Upon reaching it Panfillo deposited Campo over the side and then climbed in. He grabbed the sail which was crumpled up in the bow and spread it out as best he could.

"Help me, *Senor* Perez."

Anton Perez, now in the boat, helped Narvaez lay Campo on the outstretched sail, and then, together, they rolled it around him. Even in the unrelenting wind, Perez could smell the unmistakable odor of feces emanating from Campo. The sick page had totally lost control of his bowels. Too sick now to even speak he lay there with closed eyes only emitting an occasional groan. Narvaez lay next to him and Perez next to the *Adelantado*. The gunnel did provide some protection from the wind, but not much. Together they tried to conserve body heat and drifted off into an exhausted sleep.

The winds, which had been blowing on shore, began to shift. The cold front which had passed over was followed by a broad band of light precipitation. Intermixed with the rain, sleet, and flakes of snow swirled in the air. Around the dying fire, the former inhabitants of boats one and two were huddled together in four scrums of humanity. They had each dug several feet into the sand for protection from the wind. All were oblivious to what was happening on the shore.

The boat, once pushed parallel with the beach, now had its stern in the water. The off shore winds pushed at its bulk and with each incoming wave, the keel slid ever slowly seaward. Still, the sand held the vessel in its grasp. Sometime in the very early morning hours, the keel had slipped far enough seaward that the anchor rope, once laying loosely in the sand, was now taut. With each wave, the friction between the keel and the sand was reduced. The boat moved backward, dragging the rock anchor ever so slowly with it.

Still, Narvaez, Perez, and Campo slept in their exhaustion.

The rock anchor was now in the surf being pulled slowly seaward across the sandy bottom which offered no obstructions to halt the movement. Worse still, the saturated rope knot began to loosen. Sliding along the sand, the rock anchor was suddenly impeded by the grass beds that grew just offshore. The anchor stopped abruptly but the rope didn't. The oblong rock turned sideways and the rope knot easily slid off.

Boat one, with the *Adelantado*, Campo, and Anton Perez aboard, was now adrift and being blown out to sea.

Still, they slept.

01 December, 1528

Just South of Cavallo Inlet on Matagorda Island

Texas

Alonso Pantoja awoke shivering uncontrollably. His back hurt and he was sore all over. He struggled to a sitting position and rubbed his arms and legs vigorously to warm up. He was hungry, no, "hungry" didn't describe it, "ravenous" would be a better description. Hungry and thirsty. He rose to his feet. Around him, others were also stirring. He noticed that many were coughing painfully while holding their ribs. The fire that they had started last night was now a bed of white ash, coals, and only a thin wisp of smoke trailing straight up into the sky. This morning not a cloud could be seen in the sky and it was dead calm...calm and very cold.

"*Capitan* Pantoja!" It was Fray Xuarez.

Pantoja turned, "Yes, what is it?"

"Both the Purser and Ramerez are dead. I came to check on both of them this morning. They are both very stiff."

Pantoja could only shake his head.

Fray Xuarez kneeled next to the two corpses and began to perform the last right ritual. He was joined by Frays Alaniz and de Palas.

Pantoja moved up the sand berm to get a better view of their surroundings and to look for any source of water. He scanned the area. The sea this morning was very placid. Turning, he saw in the distance what seemed to be a depression with a copse of small trees growing in and around it. Possibly that might be a good location to look for water. He started down from the dune but then stopped...something wasn't right. He looked back at the beach.

"The boat is gone!" Talking to himself he said it again, "The boat is gone!" Then turning to his compatriots he hollered aloud "The boat is gone!"

The men below looked up at him uncomprehending. He had to repeat it again, "The boat is gone!"

Only then did several climb the berm to see for themselves.

Fray Xuarez was the first to speak. "Did the *Adelantado* leave us to our fate?"

Pantoja turned and surveyed the men in the camp. "No, at least not intentionally, all of the oarsmen are in camp with us, only the *Adelantado*, Campo, and Pilot Perez are missing. The *Adelantado* could not handle the boat by himself even if he was healthy...the storm must have blown them to sea."

Fray Alaniz spoke up. "I saw the *Adelantado* carry Campo out of camp last night and as he left he called for Pilot Perez.

Together Captain Pantoja and several others made their way to the beach. There was nothing to indicate that the boat had ever been there. No rope, no anchor, and no marks on the tide-scrubbed sand.

Pantoja scanned the horizon thoughtfully. "The boat had been pulled out of the water and the anchor was set well onto the beach. I fear that last night's storm pushed the water much higher and floated the boat. Had their anchor been a grapnel and not a rock, it may have held. Now they are gone."

"God be with them." was all that Fray Xuarez could say.

01 December, 1528

Somewhere in the Gulf of Mexico off the Coast of Texas

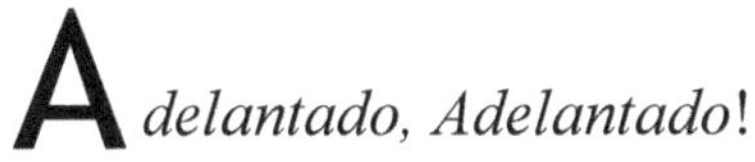

Adelantado, Adelantado!

Narvaez heard the words as if they came from afar. He tried to ignore it.

"*Adelantado*, please wake!"

Narvaez felt his body being shaken. He thought to himself, "Why would Campo be awakening me?" He started to drift off again.

"*Adelantado*, we are in trouble!"

"Why was he so persistent?" With effort, Narvaez roused himself to answer, "Campo, go away, leave me alone!"

"*Adelantado*, it is not Campo, it is me, Anton Perez, your pilot...Campo is dead."

The fog in his head began to clear. Narvaez opened his one good eye and saw Perez staring down at him. Suddenly realizing where he was he turned to where Campo was lying. Still wrapped in the rotten sail, the youngster's eyes were open and lifeless.

"Oh no, sweet Jesus, why have you taken this young man, why not me in his stead, Oh No."

The emaciated conquistador, a veteran of so many battles and so many deaths began to sob. His once great shoulders shook with emotion as he closed Campo's eyes and stroked his hair.

Behind him, Perez continued, "*Adelantado* we are adrift and there is no land in sight."

His eyes blurred with tears Narvaez finally raised up and looked around him.

Nothing. Only the endless sea in all directions.

"*Adelantado*, I have searched the boat and there is no water or food aboard. We need to set the sail and try to reach land" The pilot's voice was on the edge of hysteria as he roughly began to pull the sail away from Campo's body.

"No, no!"

Filled with rage at seeing his beloved Campo being treated so roughly, Narvaez swung at Perez with all his might. He caught him square on the left temple. The pilot crumpled into the back of the boat. In his prime, a blow such as this, delivered by Narvaez, would have killed a man, but in his weakened state, it merely dazed Perez. He jumped back up, dagger in hand, and attacked. Narvaez parried the first thrust and reached for his *montante* which was stored close by. A second thrust by Perez was only partially parried and the knife found its way into Narvaez's upper thigh, nicking his femoral artery. Narvaez kicked at Perez and spun him around such that his back was to the *Adelantado*. When the pilot turned, Narvaez, swinging the *montante* with two hands, cleaved him in half from his head to his breast bone. He then kicked the twitching body overboard.

The bottom of the boat was awash with seawater and blood. Narvaez knew he was bleeding to death and he didn't have long to live. He knew he would never see Maria again or his beloved *ranchero* in *Botobano*. But, Panfilo Narvaez with all his many faults, was no coward and he faced his death like the brave man he was. One of his last thoughts was of Rita la Salvaje and her story of the *Moorish bruja*.

Her predictions had been unerring. "How could she have known?"

Grabbing up Campo he rocked back and forth, holding the dead youngster in his arms.

"Little *Rata*, I will see you soon."

CHAPTER 06

Easy To Kill

Fácil de matar

*S*o-tu-han turned to his comrades, "These bearded ones, they are easy to kill!" He then reached down and took the morion from the dead Spaniard's head and put it on his own.

28 November, 1528

The Beach Present-Day Padre Island Near Baffin

Bay, Texas

So-tu-han had been walking the beach for some time and he was desperately hungry. It was that time of year called the big blow when the sea winds were unrelenting. Today the wind was cold and it made his eyes water. He pulled his deerskin cape closer to his body. Most everyone from his village avoided the beach at this time of year because of the cold and windblown sand, but by walking on the tidal line where the sand was hard packed he could avoid the stinging particles and, most importantly, search the shoreline for any editable detritus that may have blown ashore. Only two days ago he had come upon a conch shell inhabited by a hermit crab. This crab his people called *looma-tanti*, for it was the "naked crab" that inhabited the shells of other creatures. He had smashed the conch shell with a rock and ate the squirming creature inside. He savored each bite but it was hardly enough to satisfy the rumbling in his stomach. Since then he had found nothing else except for an occasional strand of seaweed to consume.

So-tu-han's people were called *Camone-li-tana* or "sand walkers," a name that had been shortened over the years to only *"Camone."* They inhabited the large bay and shared the many islands with their cousins the *Quitoles* who lived to the north and the *Chigo* who lived further to the south. For the most part, the three groups lived peaceably and shared territories. Occasionally disputes occurred, usually over scarce food sources, but these were quickly resolved. The *Camone's* real enemy was the *Maliacones*, a group that lived inland and made occasional forays to the coast in search of food or women. Pitched battles usually occurred when the two groups met and for this, all *Camone* men carried weapons and were trained to fight.

Up ahead was a shallow tide pool that had been productive in the past. He was disappointed, for on reaching it there were three horseshoe crabs swimming about. These were called *puna-tang-tanti,* meaning *"spear-tailed crab."* It was long past the time when they would be carrying eggs, the only thing edible on them, but still, he would check. Sometimes, they held their eggs late into the year.

So-tu-han laid his deerskin cape on the beach and stepped into the ankle-deep pool. They were not easy to catch and rapidly skittered away, surprisingly fast for their awkward appearance. Finally, after much splashing about, he was able to pounce on one. He rose to his feet and turned the animal over.

No eggs.

Disgusted, he threw the crab onto the beach where it landed upside down. The next two were also without eggs and these he also cast onto the beach. He stood there in the sand watching the three creatures attempt to right themselves with their long pointed tail. He knew that these *puna-tang-tantis* could live for long periods out of the water. If they were successful in righting themselves. they would rapidly crawl back into the surf.

Then, something else caught his eye in the tidal pool. It was a large fish, the kind with a black spot on its tail and highly valued by his people for food. It had been hiding under some seaweed and just now made its presence known. So-tu-han jumped back into the pool and tried to corner it. Back and forth they went, each time the elusive fish darting past him just out of reach. Time and time again he missed it. Grabbing his deerskin vest from the beach he again stepped into the tidal pool and maneuvered the fish into another corner. This time he wadded up the vest and threw it just to the right of the wary animal. It darted to the left and into So-tu-han's waiting hands. He had trouble holding it and several times the wriggling creature almost escaped his grasp. Finally, with a great effort, he threw it up on the beach.

Exhausted, So-tu-han stepped out of the tidal pool. Breaking off a piece of cane he ran it through the fish's lips. Holding onto the cane, he threw the fish over his shoulder and began the walk back to his village. This prize he would roast over a fire.

The fish was wet and So-hu-han shivered in the stiff wind. He knew, however, that soon he would be back at the village sitting in front of a fire. Just before turning from the beach, he stopped to adjust his load. The fish, still alive, gave a flip of its tail. He switched the load to his other shoulder.

Something caught his eye!

Here on the seashore, the barren view remained almost unchanging...long stretches of barren beach bordered by sea-grasses on the inland side and the endless sea on the other. Changes occurring in this landscape are noticed rapidly. What So-tu-han noticed was a dark object far out in the water. It was strange looking.

Always careful, the young Indian moved to a high dune with a heavy stand of sea grass growing on it. He parted the grass and watched intently.

It was coming closer.

It looked like some sort of large canoe, but nothing like one he had ever seen. A single pole stuck straight into the air and from it, a piece of hide flapped in the wind. He could see people aboard. For a moment he thought that he should run, but his curiosity was great and he stayed.

The craft approached the beach sideways, broaching heavily in the surf. It did not seem to be under control and So-tu-han could see no paddles. Carried rapidly by one particularly strong wave it rushed ashore and then came to an abrupt stop as it grounded on the sand. The force of the grounding tipped the craft sideways and from within men and equipment spilled into the surf and sand.

So-tu-han had never seen men like this.

They were no more than skeletons, many so weak they could only crawl toward shore. Some didn't move at all. All were almost naked and their faces were covered in hair. Three of the men had black skins. A few wore strange metal hats and others had long metal knives. So-tu-han looked at these closely for they were a weapon of a design that he had never seen. In their dilapidated state, he doubted that the bearded ones could even wield these fearsome weapons.

What kind of people were these?

He watched in disbelief as some struggled ashore and then lay in the sand unable to go any further. Others, dead or dying, bobbed in the water and slowly drifted out on the tide.

Gathering his fish, So-Tu-han carefully made his way down the dune and sprinted back to his village.

28 November, 1528

The Tellez/Penalosa Boat Present Day Padre Island

Near Baffin Bay, Texas

Alejandro Tellez was a man of strong will. Even after the multitude of hardships endured in prior months he still was an imposing figure. Larger than most *Spaniards* of the time with an unprecedented drive to succeed in every thing he did. But today, the challenges he faced were beyond anything that had ever happened before. Aboard that terrible boat, he had watched his body deteriorate from hunger and thirst. He had watched his friends and compatriots sicken and die and commit repugnant acts that only a few months ago would have been unimaginable. And now, at last, he was off it. He looked back at the crumbling hulk laying on its side in the surf, the lone mast, with its dilapidated sail, dragging in the sand. In the bow he could see the crude seat were he had sat and suffered, his knees and back aching from the lack of movement. Behind him had been the rest of the forty seven-man contingent, now reduced to thirty-eight at last count. He looked about him. Some, like himself, had dragged themselves onto the sand, others were still in the surf feebly trying to extract themselves from the cold water. Beyond the boat he glimpsed several bodies floating face down...men that had been so weak thy couldn't even make it to shore. They were dead, perhaps mercifully, for now, their suffering had ended.

Suddenly, he thought of his co-captain, Enrique Penalosa, who had become so feverish the night before. Unable to sit, Penalosa had collapsed onto the floor of the boat wedging himself under the seats.

"Where was he now? Where was his friend and fellow captain?"

Mustering as much strength as he could, Alejandro pushed himself upright and, kneeling there in the sand, looked about him. His eyes played around the terrible scene. He counted 27 that had made it ashore. He looked hard at each one, but could not see Penalosa.

"Was he still in the boat?"

Alejandro pushed himself to his feet and for a moment tried to steady himself as the world spun around him. He had to kneel down again. He breathed deeply and then, pushing off with his right arm, stood erect once more, this time a little more steady. He shuffled toward the boat. Beside him his sword, still in its scabbard and attached at his waist, drug in the sand. Splashing into the surf, the water was cold and getting deeper as he came up to the bow of the boat.

Nothing here.

Holding on to the overturned gunnel for support, he moved toward the stern which was almost underwater. Now almost waist deep he struggled to remain upright in the current, each incoming wave rocked the hull and sucked at the sand under his feet. One particularly strong breaker tore at him and he slid underwater. Thrashing about for any handhold, Tellez finally surfaced. The current had pushed him all the way back to the stern and there in the frothing water was the face of Enrique Penalosa staring at him with lifeless eyes.

"Mother of God!"

For a moment the two men stared at each other, one alive, one dead. Slowly Tellez lifted his hand and closed the eyes of his friend. *"Ve con Dios mi amigo."*

Tellez slowly began to make his way back along the overturned hull. He found it easier to pick his way hand over hand, letting his legs float free. High on the beach, he could see seven or eight men clustered together trying to start a fire. Others were tearing at the grass growing on the dunes and collecting driftwood...anything that would burn.

Something caught his eye.

Further up the beach shapes were emerging from the dunes. Tellez rubbed the seawater from his eyes and squinted at the distance.

"*Indios*!"

There were 20 or 30 of them and they were cautiously moving toward the *Spaniards*. Tellez could see they were armed, some with spears, others with bows, still others with wooden clubs.

He needed to warn his compatriots, but he was too far out in the surf.

28 November, 1528

The Beach Present-Day Padre Island Near Baffin Bay, Texas

Walking and talking, So-tu-han pointed at the strange bearded men, many of whom were now on shore.

"It is as I said, these bearded ones arrived in that strange craft. They are fools for it overturned in the surf and threw them all about."

So-tu-han looked across the beach to the grassy dunes. Here the women and children were watching them from a safe distance. The whole tribe had turned out to see this thing that he had discovered.

They silently approached one of the *bearded ones* who was struggling with a piece of driftwood in the sand. He had not seen them. Breathing hard, he had dropped to his knees to catch his breath.

They watched him.

He was barefoot and clad only with frayed pantaloons and a vest-like garment that just covered his shoulders. On his head was a strange metal hat pointed front and back. The skin on his arms and legs was covered in sores and his ribs and back bone protruded from the weathered skin. Attached to his waist was one of the weapons So-tu-han had described. It also was metal and like nothing they had ever seen.

Still breathing heavily the bearded one raised up and again struggled with the piece of driftwood. This time, however, he stopped and slowly looked around. He had felt their presence. Seeing the band of men so close behind him his eyes widened in fear. Dropping the driftwood the bearded one grasped his sword and slowly began to back up. He cried out in a strange language that no one understood.

"Indios, Indios, a las armas!"

Two of the young men in the group raised their bows and released arrows into the bearded ones' chest. Both passed completely through and buried themselves in the sand a short distance behind him. They had been lung shots and frothy blood oozed out of his chest, nose, and mouth. He fell heavily to the ground.

So-tu-han rushed forward and grabbed the metal weapon, prying it from the bearded one's grasp. The man was still alive but wheezing heavily and coughing on his own blood. So-tu-han raised the weapon to show the others in the group and then, holding it with both hands, he plunged it into the dying man's heart. Only a feeble croak emanated from the *Spaniard's* mouth as he passed into eternity.

So-tu-han turned to his comrades, "These bearded ones, they are easy to kill!" He then reached down and took the morion from the dead Spaniard's head and put it on his own.

Caught up in the moment the other *Indios* rushed forward, each to acquire booty of their own and to feel the thrill of killing these almost defenseless bearded ones.

28 November, 1528

The Tellez/Penalosa Boat Present Day Padre Island Near Baffin Bay, Texas

From his vantage point behind the boat, Tellez watched in horror as the mass of *Indios* rushed forward. Although alerted, many of the *Spaniard's* could not even stand to face their attackers. Those who had weapons tried to stand their ground, but their ineffective thrusts were easily parried by the *Indios*. Some of the *Spaniards* made no attempt to resist, instead, they hung their head or looked the other way knowing that a killing blow was just moments away.

The only *Spanish* resistance seemed to center around the fire pit and for just a moment the attackers were held at bay. Tellez saw at least one of the *Camones* fall to the ground. A barrage of arrows, however, put an end to the resistance and the *Indios* quickly dispatched those that were left. Even the women and children came out of the dunes to join in the slaughter. It became almost a carnival atmosphere as the victorious *Camones* held up the booty that they had collected. Swords, bucklers, morions, rosaries, crosses...everything was taken. One *Camone* even flailed the skin off a *Spaniard* to save the tattoo.

Tellez kept himself low in the water and from the shore, he looked like just another body floating in the surf. Tears welled up in his eyes as he thought about his friends and compatriots who had met violent deaths on the beach. But, behind the sorrow, something else had welled up inside...rage! He knew that he would not survive this day, but he would make them pay for their actions.

28 November, 1528

The Tellez/Penalosa Boat Present Day Padre Island

Near Baffin Bay, Texas

So-tu-han's family had joined him now and together they rummaged through the dead bodies. Most had been picked clean. He was still holding the blood-soaked sword that he had taken off the first bearded one. He had used it to kill several more. There were other bodies floating in the surf. No one had checked them yet. Nodding to his wife, they trudged out toward the beach together, children in tow.

There in the shallows, they came to the first body, floating face down. Each time a wave would roll in the body would turn sideways causing the arm to appear as if it were alive. The children held back but So-tu-han rolled the corpse over...this one was very dead. He removed a ring from the dead man's finger and showed it to his wife.

Another body floated nearby. Together they made their way out to it. There were no weapons or rings on this one, nothing but a rotten feces-stained garment that half covered him at the waste. They moved away.

Looking out toward the boat So-tu-han saw another body, this one in deeper water by the overturned vessel. He handed the sword to his wife and began making his way toward it. The water here was deeper and soon it was almost to his waist. As he neared the deserted hull he noticed a piece of knotted rope that banged against the hull with every wave.

"Thump, thump."

The sound it made was eerie and he stopped to survey the inside of the vessel.

"What is it, husband? His wife called out to him.

He ran his hand over the crude boards that formed the hull. It was made like nothing he had ever seen but nothing remained that was salvageable. He was uncomfortable.

"Wife, I think the spirits of the dead are on this strange boat."

So-tu-han looked at the body floating just an arm's length from him, but decided not to disturb it. He turned to leave. Looking back toward the beach he saw his wife and, behind her, his two children.

"We will return to the village." It was the last thing that So-tu-han would ever speak.

Behind him Tellez rose out of the water and grasped the deerskin cape, pulling the *Indio* backward and off balance. With a single swipe of his sword, Tellez cut the *Indio's* throat all the way to the spinal column.

The wife stood transfixed as the crazed *Spaniard* thrashed toward her in the water. She called out to the children to run, but they just stood in the ankle-deep water and stared. Another swipe of the sword ended her life as she fell into the surf. Gaining speed in the shallower water, Tellez caught up to the children and decapitated each in turn as he ran.

Two *Camones* at the water's edge rose up and called out to the rest. Tellez, charged up with adrenaline, headed toward them. Neither ran. Instead, they picked up the spears they had laid down and faced their advisory. Tellez easily parried the first *Camone's* thrust and then buried his blade into the man's abdomen. He had to yank the blade free, however, and in that time the other man sunk his spear into the Spaniard's shoulder. Hardly noticing the pain, Tellez swung at the shaft and splintered it. Holding the broken shaft the *Indio* tried to protect himself. He made a roundhouse swing at the bearded one but the momentum exposed his right side to the sword thrust that ended his life.

Standing in the surf Tellez turned toward those on the beach and started toward them, the broken spear dangling from his left shoulder. By now the *Camones* had recovered their senses and those with bows began sending their shafts into the bearded one. Arrow after arrow punctured his torso, arms and legs. Still, to the *Indios'* amazement, he kept coming.

They heard him clearly repeating, "*Bastardos, bastardos!*"

Tellez stopped there in the sand, still standing, and dropped his sword. One of the *Indians* approached him to no more than a few inches and looked into the bearded one's dying eyes. Mortally wounded, Tellez growled at the man like a caged animal. Stooping down the *Camone* picked up the sword. Raising it above his head he brought it down, cleaving the *Spaniard's* skull into two halves. Only then did Tellez's body fall to the ground.

The *Indio* who had dispatched the bearded one turned to his compatriots.

"This one was not so easy to kill."

CHAPTER 07

Season Of Death

Temporada de Muerte

*C*rossing the bay it was then that Hernando de Esquivel realized that he had survived this season of death. What lay ahead was probably a life of servitude, but of the 75 men who had entered the Indian camp, only he was left.

24 November, 1528

Matagorda Island

The *Spaniards* were in disarray. With the *Adelantado* lost at sea, no one was quite sure what to do next. Now that the expedition comptroller, Alonso Enriquez, was gone captain Alonso Pantoja was clearly in charge. He called a meeting of all the men now surviving. A count of all present totaled 74 souls. Most were in bad shape.

Pantoja began, "By decree of the *Adelentado,* I am now in charge and my orders will be followed."

A few of the men looked at each other as if to say, "What is this?"

Pantoja continued, "It is mid-November and the weather grows worse with each day. Our last boat is lost, so all travel will be on foot. What little strength we have must be used to go forward and find a suitable place to hold up for the winter."

Hernando de Esquivel was next to speak. "I am not convinced that the way to *Panuco* is *adelante*...forward," He pointed to the south.

"The friars and I have talked much about this and we are all in agreement that *Panuco* lies *atros*...behind." He pointed again, this time to the north.

"Hernando, why would you believe this?' Pantoja was incredulous.

Instead, Juan Xuarez spoke up. "Father de Palas and I were in *New Spain* with Cortez in 1524. We landed first at *Vera Cruz* and then made the long overland trip to *Tenochtitlan*. The distances there are vast. I talked with many *Christians* who spoke of the settlement at *Panuco*. They would tell me it was a long six or seven-day sail up the coast...at least 80 leagues or more. They also said that the way was marked by many inlets, beaches, marshes, and lagoons. They also spoke of four or five large rivers that flowed into the ocean. Indeed, on leaving New Spain we sailed up the coast for a day before turning east towards *Hispaniola*. The similarities we saw have convinced father de Palas and I that the area that we are now at is the same and that we have passed by the settlement of *Santisteban del Puerto*."

There were nods of agreement all around.

At this point, the gathering deteriorated into individual arguments between the men and the friars. Finally, it was Pantoja that quieted everyone.

"Enough! I do not agree with the idea that we are south of the settlement at the river *Panuco*. If we were, then we would have seen signs of other *Christians*...horse trails, mounted *cabelleros,* and even ships at sea bringing supplies to the settlement."

There were nods of agreement from many, but the friars were steadfast in their belief.

Frustrated, Pantoja continued, "If indeed we are south of *Santisteban del Puerto* then we are that much closer to *Vera Cruz!*" Pantoja let out a cynical laugh. "There will be no more talk of turning around and proceeding *atro*. I will not allow it."

Pepilo Sotomayor, the camp master, seethed inside, for he harbored a hatred for Pantoja and his haughty attitude.

"And what if you are wrong *capitan* Pantoja."

Pantoja felt Sotomayor's disdain. "What would you have us do, camp master...proceed back the way we came and re-experience all the hardships we have undergone. The weather grows colder and more unsettled every day and you want us to proceed *atro*...to the north? I think not."

Sotomayor made a step toward Pantoja but *Padre* Juan stepped between them. "Let us put aside our differences and, for now, seek shelter for on this barren beach we will all die.

Sotomayor turned and walked away shaking his head.

So the motley collection of *Spaniards* proceeded *adelante*...forward. Those who had trouble walking leaned heavily on their comrades. Progress was slow, but they marched steadily southward along the narrow island. They stayed close to the water where the wet sand was packed and made for easier walking. At night they huddled in the dunes protecting themselves as much as possible from the unrelenting on-shore winds. Along the route everyone kept their eye on the sea hoping to catch sight of a sail on the horizon but, of course, it never came.

27 November, 1528

St. Joseph Island

What lay before them was a strange morass of swamp, small islets, and sandbars. Two meandering waterways snaked through this marsh and converged just before reaching the ocean. When they arrived the tide was receding and the water at the confluence of these two arms was boiling. The channel formed by this rush of water was deep and about 400 *yara* wide. On either side of the channel, a broad fan of sand extended far out to sea.

This *brazo pantanoso*...bayou, linked the large bay to the west with the ocean to the east. Across the bayou Pantoja could see that the narrow peninsula continued on into the distance.

"To cross this inlet we will have to proceed into the marsh where the water is shallow and slower moving. At *marea baja*...low tide, we should be able to cross. Gather whatever drift wood is available so that those who cannot swim may hold on."

There was an assortment of driftwood scattered about in the sand and after an hour of searching the beach, a sizable pile of it had been accumulated.

Pantoja spoke up again, "Grab whatever wood you can, and let's proceed further into this bayou and find a suitable place to cross over."

Together they trudged into the tangle of wetlands, bogs, sandbars, and grassy islets. All manner of wildlife skittered around them. Waterfowl, armies of crabs, snakes, lizards, turtles, and small mammals. In the deeper water sting rays exploded out of their sandy hideouts and armies of small fish and juvenile sharks glided everywhere. These waters were an aquatic nursery for all manner of marine life. In the deeper cuts, the water was seldom over their heads, still, the driftwood was piled and interwoven into a crude raft to which the *Spaniards* clung.

After crossing the second deep channel channel the land became less forbidding. Now the men slogged through water that was only ankle-deep. At this point, Pantoja made a decision to turn towards the beach. The sun was getting low in the western sky and already the temperature was starting to drop. Overhead was a cloudless sky and the evening promised to grow even colder.

They clambered back onto solid ground marked with dunes, sea grass, and small shrubs. At a particularly high dune, they stopped at its base and used the driftwood to start a fire. All of the men were chilled from the crossings and suffering from exertion. As the fire took hold they huddled around it trying to absorb the warmth and protect themselves from the ever-present mosquitoes.

Concerned that the smoke might get the attention of any *Indians* in the area, Pantoja climbed the large dune for a look around. From its top, he could see far down the beach and across the bay. There was no sign of any other inhabitants and far into the distance, the peninsula appeared to widen and become increasingly forested. This is the direction they would take in the morning.

28 November, 1528

St. Joseph Island

Crossing the swampy inlet had been hard on the men. Their clothes had become soaked in the crossing and the November winds had chilled them to the bone. The fire had helped dry everything out but temperatures had plummeted during the night and the wind had blown out of the west relentlessly. Just getting the men up and moving the next morning had been a chore. Pantoja estimated that their trek down the beach had been limited to only 2 leagues. Again, they camped behind a large sheltering dune and gathered firewood. The day had been cool and clear but as evening progressed, a sullen grayness settled over them. The wind, still blowing strongly, had shifted to the north. As darkness settled in a light rain began to fall. The fire, started earlier, burned brightly but the gusty north winds licked the flames to and fro blowing much of the heat away.

During the night one of the men died. Papilo Sanchez, a member of the friar's boat, failed to answer the Campmaster's morning call to arise. They had shaken him only to find the body cold and his eyes staring lifelessly back at them. Sanchez hadn't complained of any sickness and, indeed, seemed to be one of the most fit of the group. Pantoja could only guess that the stress of all that had happened had been too much and he had died of a heart attack. Together the men scooped out a shallow grave in the side of the sand dune and covered it with the remaining drift wood from the fire. A small wooden cross was lashed together and set in the sand.

The rain had stopped, but the wind continued to blow strongly out of the north. Delayed by the burial, the remainder of the men proceeded down the beach, heads down to protect their eyes from the swirling sand.

The island was becoming increasingly forested. At first, only an occasional stunted tree grew amongst the grasses that spread inland from the beach. Now, groves of trees began to appear and up ahead a woodland canopy outlined the horizon. The bay that was on their right was narrowing and the mainland had closed to within a league of the island. At about noon the skies had cleared and the wind had finally abated. They had made good time today, Pantoja estimated 3 leagues.

As they neared the treeline they became aware that an *Indian* camp must be somewhere ahead. It was obvious that they had seen the *Spaniards* as well because *Indian* scouts were now sighted watching them. Pantoja ordered the column to move inland to investigate. Finally, at some distance and interspersed among the trees the *Indian* camp came into view. At first, the men of the camp put on a show of strength by lining up and displaying their weapons. Neither side knew what to expect from the other.

Pantoja called a halt and ordered those who were most able to prepare themselves for battle to place themselves at the front of the group.

"At no time display your weapon, for they outnumber us. We want them to think we are peaceful."

For an hour the standoff continued with both sides eyeing the other. At one time frays Xuarez, Alanis, and de Palas tried to approach the camp but were stopped short by threatening gestures from the *Indians*.

It was shortly after this incident that the *Spaniards* noticed activity in their camp. The women of the group were dismantling some of the crude huts and loading them into canoes that were pulled up on shore at the bay side of the island. The operation took several hours and it wasn't until dusk that most of the *Indians* had vacated their campsite. The armed men of the group were the last to leave as they wearily boarded the empty canoes that had been sent back for them.

Pantoja turned to Sotomayor, "Campmaster, prepare the men, we will move forward into the *Indio* encampment."

The weary *Spaniards* trudged off the beach and into the woodland clearing that had been inhabited by the *Indians*. Looking across the bay, Pantoja watched the *Indian* canoes as they disappeared into the distance.

In their hurry to vacate the area, the *Indians* had left a few unfinished huts. Here and there campfires still smoldered. The clearing was surrounded by thick woodland that offered material for cover and fuel. Most importantly, a small freshwater spring gurgled up nearby, its overflow forming a marshy pond surrounded by reeds.

From this position, they could make the short trek to the seaward side of the island to check for *Spanish* sails on the horizon. On the mainland side schools of fish could be seen swimming in the shallows.

Calling a meeting, Pantoja addressed the men. "The weather grows colder every day and here we have water to drink, wood to burn, and protection from the cold and wind. I propose we remain here until spring when we will again continue our travels to the south."

Most agreed, but Sotomayor disagreed. Standing up, he spoke directly to Pantoja. "I feel that on this island we are too exposed and will suffer from the extremes. I suggest we continue across the bay to the mainland and continue moving *adelante*...to the south. Although I agree with the friars in that the settlement of *Santisteban del Puerto* is *atro*...behind us, we are sure to encounter a *Spanish* patrol at some point in our travels."

There were some nods of agreement and for a moment the meeting broke up into many individual discussions, some advocating for continuing on, most for staying. Finally, Pantoja called for silence.

"Look around, all of us are weak, barefoot, and without winter clothing. To continue on is madness. We just saw the *Indios* proceed to the mainland. If we cross over we will have to deal with them. We are in no condition for battle."

Pantoja paused to take a breath. No one spoke up. Even Sotomayor was quiet but he eyed Pantoja with an evil glare.

Pantoja continued, "We have this island to ourselves so while we still have some energy left in our bodies let's strive to gather food and build more huts to protect us from the winter winds."

Sotomayor walked off, but the majority of the men agreed or said nothing at all.

"It is settled, we will stay here until spring and then continue on. Make yourselves as comfortable as possible tonight. Tomorrow I will assign work parties to gather firewood, build huts, and procure food."

As evening approached the clear skies that had been with them all day deteriorated into a hazy overcast. The temperature began to drop and the darkness came early. A large fire burned in the *Spanish* camp, its dancing light reflecting eerily off the tree trunks and canopy overhead. Just before midnight, a thick fog blew in from the bay, the air heavy with moisture. Here on a barrier island off the coast of *Amichel,* the remnants of the two wrecked boats of the *Adelantado* and the friars huddled.

21 December, 1528

St. Joseph Island

It was late December and the worst weather of winter had descended on the *Spanish* camp. The marsh where they had gathered crayfish was now covered with a thin sheet of ice. The small crustaceans had become increasingly more difficult to find. Breaking through the ice and wading in the freezing water was torturous to the bare-footed *Spaniards*. The men that could, walked the beach on both sides of the island, hoping for anything edible that may have washed up on the sand. Some carried long sharpened sticks to skewer fish in the shallows while others searched for oysters and clams. The rough huts that they had constructed leaked badly and were filled with vermin and filth. Those who were critically sick and incapacitated were moved to a separate hut where the conditions inside were unspeakable. Dry firewood became increasingly harder to find.

During a winter storm, the temperature dropped to just above freezing and the rain fell in torrents for two days. All of the fires were extinguished. The wind blew so hard that one of the huts collapsed. Those who could, struggled to reconstruct the structure. Others, incapable of any physical activity huddled under the trees, shaking violently in the cold.

Pantoja, Sotomayor, Hernando de Esquivel, and two of the friars labored on the collapsed hut. The frame of sticks had been set upright and lashed together. Now what remained was to intertwine smaller sticks and then cover this framework with grass. The camp master, Pepilo Sotomayor, had just returned from the marsh with an armload of grass. Setting it down beside the structure he began to weave the canes into the hut's framework.

Pantoja, working nearby, called out, "Camp master Sotomayor, we are not ready for the grass yet. The framework is incomplete and we need to weave more small sticks into the structure so the grass will be held more firmly and not blow away."

Sotomayor remained silent and continued to sullenly weave the grass into the structure.

Pantoja again, "Camp master, did you not hear me?"

Sotomayor sat completely still, and then under his breath he murmured, be*same mi culo*...kiss my ass!"

Pantoja and both friars heard his response. All worked stopped. Pantoja stood and faced Sotomayor who also slowly raised up while clenching his fists.

"I am your commander, you will not talk to me this way."

Sotomayor took a step toward him. "You are not fit to be commander of anything. You kissed the *Adelantado's* ass to get where you are."

At this moment Esquivel stepped into the clearing carrying an armload of sticks.

"What is going on here?"

Pantoja, distracted, turned to face Esquivel.

Sotomayor, seeing an opportunity, grabbed one of the large rocks that was anchoring the hut.

Pantoja, sensing the Sotomayor had come up behind him started to turn. He was too late.

Raising the rock high over his head, Sotomayor brought it down on Pantoja's skull with all his strength. The sound it made was like a melon being thrown against a tree. Pantoja's scream was cut off as the rock crushed his frontal lobe just above his right eye. Blood and brain matter sprayed out from the force of the blow as his body collapsed onto the wet ground. The friars and Esquivel stood in stunned silence. Others who had seen what had happened stared in disbelief. Fray Juan Xuarez, who was standing close by, saw the whole thing.

"Mother of God!"

Sotomayor stood over Pantoja's body as it lay twitching in the mud. He was still alive, but just barely. Seeing this, Sotomayor stomped on the man's head, breaking his neck and killing him instantly.

He turned to the stunned friars, Esquivel, and then to all that had gathered around.

 "There, we will not be dealing with *Senor* Pantoja anymore. I am the camp master and I am now in charge."

There would be no retribution. Sotomayor was a large man and still one of the strongest in camp.

Esquivel and the friars dragged Pantoja's body out to the beach and covered it as best they could in the loose sand. When they returned Sotomayor was busily weaving the grass into the hut's framework as if nothing had happened. The four of them completed the structure before nightfall and then, as the light faded, helped those who couldn't walk into the structure.

It continued to rain.

11 January, 1529

St. Joseph Island

Over the next three weeks, five more *Spaniards* died of disease and exposure. Food was extremely scarce, limited to whatever mollusks could be dug out of the ground, crabs, acorns, pine nuts, and a few fish. Some chewed on the bark cambium layer of the pine trees in the area. It was unappealing but seemed to somewhat satisfy the horrible feeling of emptiness that gnawed at the stomach. Tasting like sawdust and very bitter many of the *Spaniards* would not eat it. Consuming the material had an undesirable side effect. High in fiber it passed rapidly through the gut causing explosive diarrhea. Most of the survivors already suffering from dysentery refused to compound their misery. Still, some like Hernando de Esquivel didn't seem to be affected by its deleterious effects.

Most critical was the weather. Originating from the northernmost climes of *Amichel* an advancing trough of cold air had extended itself far to the south. January temperatures dropped below freezing during the day and well into the teens at night. The marsh where the *Spaniards* obtained their fresh water took on a thin sheet of ice. The wind blew incessantly with a ferocity that kept the men huddled in their filthy, vermin-infested huts. Huts such as these needed constant repair and upkeep to remain waterproof. The strong winds and moisture deteriorated the covering and they began to leak badly. The men, now severely weakened, wouldn't or couldn't venture outside the enclosures to repair the damage.

Today, two of the friars, Juan de Palas and Agusto Alaniz died. De Palas died quietly in the night but Alaniz lapsed into a rage screaming out *Latin* idioms that made no sense. Quite unexpectedly he lurched out of the hut and ran into the night, his vocalizations fading in the freezing air. De Salas' body was found outside of the hut in which he resided and remained there for several days until Esquivel drug the shriveled corpse out to the beach. Here Esquivel found the body of friar de Palas floating in the surf, already partially consumed by sea creatures.

The temperature continued to plummet and the wind blew relentlessly. So cold was it that the *Spaniards* remained in their huts for days on end, only dragging themselves out to drink at the nearby marsh. Even this effort was curtailed if the depressions around the camp held rainwater. The huts became mephitic structures of death and dying.

On a day in late January, the wind subsided and the skies cleared.

Driven by thirst, Esquivel crawled out into the sunlight and rose to his feet. He was lightheaded and had to pause to maintain his balance. Looking from hut to hut he counted eight bodies lying on the ground, pitiful reminders of the proud *hildagos* who had left *Spain* a little more than a year ago. He turned and staggered toward the marsh. Dropping to his knees, he broke through the thin skin of ice and drank deeply. Pausing, he sat back on his haunches. He could feel the cold water entering his stomach and it chilled him from within. The bile rose in his throat. Nausea overwhelmed him as his stomach muscles contracted. The water left him in violent spasms of projectile vomiting.

Finally purged, Esquivel lay on his side and shivered uncontrollably. He was still thirsty. Finally, he found the strength to drink again, only this time more sparingly. He clenched his teeth while sucking up the water to help strain out the detritus. This time the water stayed down and gradually the shaking subsided. Half crawling, half walking, he made his way back to the camp.

At the camp, Sotomayor and two others had managed to start a fire. Gradually the men in the huts began to appear, crawling out to warm themselves. Two more bodies appeared. It was then that Esquivel noticed that Sotomayor and the two men were working over one of the corpses. They had flayed the skin off the thighs and buttocks and were removing the muscle tissue. One of the men helping Sotomayor was Fray Xaurez. He looked up and met the gaze of Esquivel for only an instant before turning away.

The chunks of meat were sliced thinly and hung on hastily constructed racks to be dried and smoked over the fire. As the meat heated the smell of cooking flesh permeated the camp. Crazed by hunger the men moved toward the fire.

Sotomayor held them back. "We will eat well tonight but first gather up the other bodies and help us build more racks and maintain the fire.

From behind him, Fray Xuarez muttered, *"Dios nos perdone...*God forgive us."

The first body had been harvested and been drug to the side. Esquivel looked into the lifeless eyes and recognized him as Marino Carmona, one of the men of his boat. He tried to think of how this man, now lying dismembered in the dirt, looked in life. He felt the bile rising in his throat once again, and turned away. Still, the smell of the cooking meat that wafted through camp made his mouth water in anticipation.

15 February, 1529

St. Joseph Island

A month had passed and now the 16 *Spaniards* that remained alive in the camp no longer appeared human. Their clothes had been reduced to tatters. Individually, each appeared as walking skeletons draped with a loose covering of skin. Joints were swollen and painful. Scraggly hair and beards, infested with all matter of vermin, hung to their waists. Teeth were loose in bleeding gums and just the act of chewing and swallowing was excruciating.

No longer were the dead and mutilated corpses removed from the camp area. Instead, bones and body parts littered the camp. Skulls of the dead had been broken open for the nutritious brain matter. In most cases, the skull and spinal columns remained in-tact but the extremities, legs, and arms, had been removed. The stench of death and decay drifted far out into the bay when the wind was right.

Of the men now alive, seven were breathing their last. Unable to move, and burning with fever they lay in their own filth with no one to care for them. By morning most of these would be dead.

Pepilo Sotomayor was growing impatient. He was hungry and Fray Juan Xuarez, suffering beside him, refused to die. The priest had laid in agony for three days lapsing in and out of consciousness.

Now he just lay there murmuring words that made no sense at all to the Campmaster. Picking up a rock that lay near the entrance to the hut Sotomayor shuffled over to the dying holy man and crushed his skull. He continued to bring the rock down until the brain matter oozed out of the bloody mass. Laying the rock aside he greedily scooped up the viscous pulp and consumed it. All traces of humanity in the Campmaster had disappeared. He felt no remorse.

28 February, 1529

St. Joseph Island

The weather was changing. The days were growing longer. The biting wind that blew across the bay had now been replaced with a more southerly flow. Migratory birds filled the skies. Trees were budded out and a soft fragrance drifted in the air. In the camp only two *Spaniards* remained alive, Pepilo Sotomayor and Hernando de Esquivel. Each, barely alive, stared across the short distance between their two huts. Both knew that the one who died first would be eaten by the other. Of the two Sotomayor was the larger and more powerful, but powerful was a relative term, for both men were so weakened by hunger and disease that just crawling to the swamp for water was exhausting. Hernando de Esquivel knew that in a one-on-one struggle, he would probably lose. Each night he slept fitfully at the back of the squalid hut, sword by his side and a camp knife in his hand.

But, Pepilo Sotomayor had a problem. It started off as an irritation in his throat and an occasional cough. It had rapidly grown worse, however, and now he felt an uncomfortable tightness in his chest. The cough was now rasping and deep. What was left of his strength was ebbing away hour by hour. In one particularly bad coughing spree, Sotomayor, on hands and knees, convulsed at the front of his hut. His sputum, thick and yellow, slavered from his mouth. Looking up, he saw Esquivel intently watching him from his own hut. He saw the camp knife in his hand. It was then that Pepilo Sotomayor knew that he would be the loser in this contest of life.

The two stared at each other for a moment and then Sotomayor did a strange thing. For a moment a piece of humanity crawled back into his tortured brain. He crossed himself before crawling back into the recesses of his hut.

The next morning the remains of Pepilo Sotomayor lay dismembered by the fire pit. Esquivel had crawled to the campmaster's hut during the night. On entering Sotomayor had tried to resist but his weakness overwhelmed him and he collapsed to the ground sobbing. Esquivel grabbed a handful of hair and lifted the man's head so that his neck was exposed. Looking down, Esquivel muttered *"Dios perdoname*...God forgive me" before slitting the Campmaster's throat from ear to ear.

The emaciated body of Pepilo Sotomayor had not yielded much. Esquivel had immediately cut out the liver and consumed it raw. The heart he had skewered on a stick and placed over the coals to roast. The muscle tissue from the buttocks and thighs he sliced into strips and hung on a rack above the fire. The body was completely devoid of fat and only a minimal amount of meat could be harvested from the other body extremities.

Sitting there watching the heart tissue sizzle in the heat of the coals, Esquivel still felt a degree of remorse but, more than that, he felt...nothing.

07 March, 1529

St. Joseph Island

Quana-santa was a member of the tribe that called themselves *Quevenes*. He had been on the island months ago when the intruders had first appeared. Now, driven by curiosity he guided his lone canoe across the bay. This day was particularly beautiful with a clear sky and almost no wind blowing. The surface of the bay exhibited only a small ripple that gently lapped against the hull of his small canoe as he glided along. Up ahead the island loomed closer. Still too far away to pick out individual characteristics, he did notice that there was no trace of a cooking fire. Above the trees, the air was clear with only an occasional flock of pelicans to disturb the serenity.

He remembered the day that the hairy ones had appeared on the beach.

He and several others had scouted them, watching from the safety of the tall grasses. The hairy ones had not seen them. Quana-santa had stared in bewilderment. Most wore strange hats made of a material he had never seen. On their wastes hung long knives that looked particularly formidable. Both their hats and their weapons reflected the rays of the sun and appeared as the color on the inside of an oyster shell. Several of the hairy ones had worn long blankets and seemed to stand apart from the others. Once when the wind changed direction Quana-santa could even smell them, an odor that was disagreeable and one that he had not experienced before.

There had been rumors from the surrounding clans of a strange group of men who had come from the sea but he had largely discounted them until now. As they moved along these men spread out and scoured the beach for anything edible. At the forefront of the column, several well-armed men seemed to scout the area ahead. Quana-santa remembered that one of these scouts was the first to become aware of his village. The village wasn't visible from the beach, but a line of smoke rising from the cooking fires had hung like a blanket over the trees. It was then that the intruders had turned inland. Quana-santa and the other scouts rushed back towards the village. Rapidly moving through the brush they had been observed by the hairy ones who now advanced on the village.

The two cultures stood apart, each observing the other. When Quana-santa and the other scouts described the weapons that these intruders carried a decision was made to leave the island and not risk a confrontation. Immediately the women and children were ferried across the bay. On the return trip, the men quickly slipped into the canoes and moved out into the safety of the bay. Quana-santa was one of the last to leave and remembered seeing the hairy ones cautiously enter the camp. He watched as they tore apart each hut looking for anything edible. Several walked to the edge of the bay and exchanged looks with Quana-santa who stood at a safe distance off shore.

Now he was returning to see what had become of these intruders.

Again Quana-santa suddenly smelled the disagreeable odor of the hairy ones, only this time it was more pungent...almost sickening. He also smelled the odor of death. For a moment he hesitated, back paddling the canoe in the light surf. The wind shifted and the smell abated. Still not seeing any movement on the island he continued forward. The canoe slid ashore in the soft sand and came to a stop. Quana-santa climbed out and dragged it further on shore. The huts would be further ahead past the tree line. He moved cautiously through the salt grass, stopping frequently to listen and scan the area. The stench of decay and death grew stronger. He tightened his grip on the spear that he carried.

Further inland the vegetation changed and Quana-santa picked his way amongst the shrubs and young trees, careful to stay off the trail. Ahead was the thick grove of tall oak trees where the village was located. Staring intently ahead Quana-santa stumbled on something at his feet. Quickly recovering his balance he looked down at a mostly decomposed body. He recoiled backward, for in his culture the spirits of the dead were something to be avoided.

Moving slowly, Quana-santa came to the edge of the clearing and stared in disbelief. Scattered all about were the dismembered parts of bodies. Skulls smashed open, rib cages scattered about, and individual sections of arms and legs tossed haphazardly here and there, many with meat and sinew still hanging on them. It was immediately obvious that these hairy ones had turned to cannibalism to survive. The smell was overpowering.

This was a place of death and bad spirits.

Quana-santa turned to leave, but something caught his eye. There was movement in one of the remaining huts. A face appeared in the doorway. It looked more like an animal than a man. Slowly the creature crawled out of the enclosure. He looked more dead than alive. The hairy one struggled to his feet and began moving toward the swamp. Quana-santa then understood that the hairy one was going for water. He waited until the man had passed from view and then moved into the camp. He checked each hut only to find more macabre scenes of disease and death.

There was no one else alive.

Esquivel moved slowly along the well-beaten path. He had drunk his fill and he moved along as if in a daze. All of his joints hurt and the pain in his teeth was overpowering. The sudden rush of water into his system had made him light-headed and he was sweating profusely. He kept his head down, carefully placing each step so he wouldn't stumble and fall. On reaching the clearing he felt a presence. Looking up he stared into the face of an *Indian*, much taller than he and hideously covered with tattoos. The *Indian* held a spear only inches from his chest.

Esquivel was prepared for death. Many times he had contemplated taking his own life, but somehow wasn't able to do it. Now death was directly in front of him and he felt a strange acceptance, almost a relief from the hell that he had been living.

For a moment the two men stared at each other. Then, quite unexpectedly, Quana-santa motioned for Esquivel to move down the trail toward the beach.

"Why didn't he kill me!" Esquivel's thoughts were spinning.

They moved along without talking except for an occasional grunt by Quana-santa and a prod of the spear when Esquivel needed to change direction.

When they reached the water Esquivel saw the canoe and started to get in. Quana-santa, however, placed a foot on the Spaniard's *b*ackside and propelled him into the water. The water was cold and the salt was painful on the sores that covered his body. When Esquivel surfaced Quana-santa indicated by gestures to clean himself and scrub with sand to remove the stench that permeated him. Shaking violently from the cold, Esquivel did as he was told and then climbed into the canoe.

Crossing the bay it was then that Hernando de Esquivel realized that he had survived this season of death. What lay ahead was probably a life of servitude, but of the 75 men who had entered the *Indian* camp, only he was left.

CHAPTER 08

Isle Of Ill Fate

Isla de Malhado

Halfway across the bay, the paddlers stopped briefly to rest. Alvar looked back at the island where so much grief and hardship had confronted them. He thought of the friends he had lost and those that were still missing. To no one in particular he said, "This has truly been the island of our suffering and ill fate, our isla de mal hado!

30 November, 1528

Indian Camp on Present Day Galveston Island

He had slept fitfully. The *Indians* outside the enclosure had carried on in a strange rhythmic dance all night, interrupted periodically with wild whoops and hollers that were unnerving. After warming himself by the fires, Alvar had stood and moved closer to the dancers. The night was cold, and yet the Indians were bathed in sweat from their exertions. Head down, they followed each other in a circular route, marching with a heel-and-toe step. Then, suddenly, one of the revelers would dash into the middle of the circle and throw himself about in the wildest of gyrations imitating, what Alvar guessed, was some kind of animal. Some would flap their arms like a bird, others would paw the ground like a bull. A few would drop down on the ground and slither about like snakes, all the while accompanied by loud yells that accented the movements. The women stayed mostly on the outside of the circle shaking rattles and talking amongst themselves. Occasionally, one would join in the line but never enter the circle. At this point, a performer would grab her from the line and dash off into the shadows. Alvar watched them there, still not completely out of sight, having sex, the woman on her hands and knees, the man thrusting from behind. So quickly was it over that Alvar could scarcely believe it. The man would jump up and immediately rejoin the line of dancers, the woman would dust herself off and resume her place with the other women. Both acted as if nothing had occurred.

This had gone on until just before dawn when the celebration abruptly ceased, the men and women drifting off to their lodges. Several younger men, however, continued to tend the fires within the enclosure where the *Spaniards* slept and talked among themselves. There was much fear that the Indians would continue their celebration in the morning and feast upon them. Stancio Mellado, a former soldier with Cortes, was the most vocal and his fears spread quickly among the men.

"I tell you, this is the end, for in the morning they will slay us and roast our bodies on their *barbacoa*."

Now with the first light of dawn lighting the eastern sky the village was eerily quiet. In the cold air, a slight ground fog wafted through the village giving it a ghostly appearance. A feeling of complete helplessness overwhelmed Alvar. He stood there in the damp morning air with only the rag of a rotted tunic to cover his shoulders and a loincloth fashioned from other scraps of cloth. And yet, because of these *Indians* he was warm for the first time in days The *Indians* had maintained the fires throughout the night. There were no guards posted to restrain them and they were free to move about. Of course, where would they go? This was an island.

As Alvar mulled over all of this in his head he detected movement in the village.

"They will be coming for us soon!" It was Mellado.

"I tell you, I won't be taken without a fight." Alvar turned to see who had spoken. Diego Lopez stood defiantly holding a stick of firewood as a weapon.

Alvar looked about him at the pathetic assembly of men. "Of course, we will defend ourselves with whatever means we have, but let us first see what are the intentions of these *Capoques* before we unnecessarily provoke them. Put down the stick *Senor* Lopez."

"Here they come!"

Alvar turned to see a large assembly of the *Capoques* approaching their enclosure. Feeling that this was the end, even the sick and wounded struggled to raise themselves to their feet. They would offer whatever resistance they could.

"We will die as *Christians*!"

As the *Capoques* drew nearer Alvar could clearly see that they were carrying platters of food...dried fish and roots.

"The *Indios*, they are bringing us food! Praise God." Alvar relaxed and prepared to welcome their hosts. The apprehensions of only a moment before had all but evaporated. The men tore into the food, gladly shaking hands with the *Indians* who smiled and nodded but didn't understand this strange custom.

Alvar looked to Stancio Mellado who had just torn off a bite of the dried fish. Mellado caught his stare. With his mouth full of the masticated fish he called out, "They are just fattening us up."

The *casique* of this village, whose name was Wee-ah-le-nok, sat next to Alvar and together they attempted to communicate. They were joined by Lope de Oviedo. Using the hand talk of which he now had an elementary knowledge, Alvar thanked the *casique* for his generosity. As the pleasantries continued he attempted to learn more about the *Capoques* and their surroundings. Other *Indians* joined them.

The necklace of one of the newcomers caught the eye of Lope Oviedo who nudged Alvar and nodded toward the ornament. It was a copper hawks bell, a trinket that only could have been obtained from a *European*. It was of the same design that the expedition had brought with them.

Alvar pointed at the hawk's bell and attempted to ask from where the man had obtained it. Weeahlenok misunderstood and commanded the man to give up the ornament. Alvar immediately gestured in the negative and tried again to determine its origins. After a lengthy discourse Weeahlenok at last seemed to understand and pointed to the north. The *Indian* had received this gift from bearded men who had landed on the other side of the island. There, a neighboring tribe, the *Han*, had taken them in, fed and cared for them.

Excited, Alvar asked the *casique* if they would lead two of his men, Lope Oviedo and Stancio Mellado, to these bearded men, for he was sure it was one of the other boats. Weeahlenok agreed and assigned two of his men to show the way.

The news of other *Christians* on the island spread quickly among the *Spaniards*. "Who could it be?" Everyone speculated.

"It has to be the men of the *Adelantado's* boat, for they were the strongest and most fit."

"No, it must be boat 2, the one with the friars, because they were the closest to God."

"Perhaps it isn't any of our men, but a rescue party from *Cuba*."

As to his thoughts, Alvar was glad to rid himself of Mellado, at least for a while, for his constant talk of being sacrificed was scaring the men.

30 November, 1528

Indian Camp on Present-Day Galveston Island

It had been an hour since Lope Oviedo and Stancio Mellado had left the village in search of the other *Christians*. Alvar had ordered the men to stay within the confines of the enclosure while they waited. The last thing he needed now was for one of his men to become embroiled in an argument with the natives. Worse yet, there were women about, and even in their pathetic state, he could see the lust in the eyes of some of the *Spaniards*.

Alvar accompanied Weeahlenok on a walk through the village. They were a poor people with very few permanent possessions. Necklaces of sea shells, colored rocks, and effigies carved into pieces of driftwood were the extent of their valuables. Their weapons consisted of clubs, spears, bows, and arrows. With these they hunted a variety of animals, but their principal source of food while on the island was the roots that they dug, fish, and mollusks. The women were attractive or could have been if not covered with a mosaic of tattoos and piercings. They kept their black hair long so that it hung to their waist. Besides providing for the care of the children, the women seemed to be the most industrious, preparing food, caring for the fires, hauling water. and maintaining the structures. Like the men, they seemed oblivious to the cold and wore only a loose animal skin shawl over their shoulders and a deerskin skirt that hung just below the knees. Underneath the skirt, they wore nothing, which Alvar all too quickly noticed. Both sexes seemed to stay apart, the women in their small groups and the men in theirs. Periodically the men, in groups of three or four, would filter in and out of the village bringing caches of roots, fish, or small animals. To Alvar's surprise one party brought in a small shark about three feet in length which had been speared in shallow water. In no time at all the women had cut it up into small chunks and added it to a communal stew pot. The eyeballs and liver of the animal were presented to the hunter who consumed them immediately.

A disturbance in the village indicated that Oviedo and Mellado were returning. Alvar walked to the path by which they had left. Trudging toward him was a crowd of *Spaniards* with Indian guides in the lead. Still too far to see who it was, Alvar rushed toward them. Just behind the guides he first recognized Captain Castillo and then Captain Dorantes...and there was the slave Estevan...and Mendez...it was the crew of boat 3! Also among them were twenty Indians from another clan, the ones that had first come upon the survivors of boat 3. They called themselves, the Han.

The two groups of Indians, the *Capoques* and the *Han*, on seeing each other began to weep uncontrollably, a most strange reaction that the *Spaniards* did not understand. This continued for a considerable length of time and then abruptly stopped.

Castillo and Dorantes upon seeing De Vaca looked in disbelief, for clothed only in rags his appearance was most disturbing. They embraced and then Alvar shook their hands vigorously.

"*Alguacil*, your appearance is frightening, what has happened to you?" It was Castillo.

Alvar noticed he still carried his sword as did some of the men accompanying him. Alvar passed amongst the men shaking the hand of each as others came out to greet the newcomers. He began counting.

"*Cuarenta y dos*...forty two. *Capitan* Castillo, is this all of your crew?"

"*Si Alguacil*, we have lost six *Christians*." At that point, Castillo began to name them and recount the circumstances of each death. Alvar could only shake his head and mutter "God be with him" at the naming of each of the deceased.

The procession moved into the village and to the structure that held the remainder of Alvar's crew, those who were too sick or too injured to walk. Again, Castillo and Dorantes looked in disbelief, for the wretched men before them were in a sorry state. Alvar related how his men had suffered and spoke of the deaths that had occurred on his boat.

Alvar then took the two captains to meet Weeahlenok. They had brought their bag of trinkets and liberally passed the beads, hawk bells, and mirrors to the men of the village. The *Capoques* were delighted. They strutted about, talking among themselves while comparing their new possessions.

Weeahlenok ordered up a feast, for not only had the two groups of Christians been united, but the twenty Indians that had brought them here were of a neighboring tribe, the *Han*. The *Han* did not speak the same language as the *Capoques,* but together they managed to communicate with hand talk and a strange pidgin dialect, some even spoke both languages. In appearance, they were much the same. Men and women covered their bodies with tattoos; predominately line patterns and squiggles, with a few having crude likenesses of fish or other animals. The men would pierce one or both their nipples and extend a thick piece of reed, a span or more in length, through them. Men and women also pierced their lower lip, inserting a thinner section of cane that extended out on either side of their face. The *Han* men, however, wore their hair long, unlike the *Cavoque*, who bobbed theirs off just above the ears. The women of both tribes kept their hair long.

While they ate, the captains related to Alvar the circumstances that had brought them to this island. They had run aground and capsized on the northeastern side of the island, what Dorantes called *atras*...back. Alvar was confused by this description at first but came to understand that it meant the direction from which they had started their journey. The side of the island on which Alvar's boat had been wrecked was called *adelante*...forward.

"What of the other boats, when last did you see them?"

226

"Andres Dorantes thought a moment and then described how they had lost sight of Alvar's boat when they had just passed *El Poneroso Rio*. Alonzo Castillo further related that it was just after sighting the fires on shore.

"We were so distracted that no one noticed your disappearance until later in the day. After that, we stayed with the boat containing the priests until a storm separated us. That was the last we saw of them until landing here."

Alvar described the shark attack and the loss of Julio Alves. Then he related the last meeting with Narvaez and the insinuation by the *Adelantado* that it was now every man for themselves. After that, they continued on with Captain Tellez's boat until being separated in the storm.

There was quiet as each man contemplated the fate of the other boats. Finally Alonzo Castillo spoke.

"*Alguacil*, our boat is overturned and will need some repair. Perhaps with the help of the *Indios*, we can refloat it again."

"A good idea *capitan*, but our combined crews number far too many to fit in the boat."

Castillo had considered this and now put forth his plan. "We should man the repaired boat with only the fittest among us so that they can proceed to *Panuco* as quickly as possible. The rest of us will stay here until recovered sufficiently to move along the coast."

Everyone nodded in agreement. Captain Andres Dorantes added, "With the blessing of God, He will direct our mariners to the land of the *Christians* so that we may all be rescued."

01 December, 1528

On Present-Day Galveston Island

The very next day a party of eighteen *Christians, and* twelve *Capoques* proceeded back up the trail to begin work on the boat. The twenty *Han* accompanied them. Upon reaching the site they were met by the remainder of the *Han*, a group of about 120 men and women. Today the weather was mild and four dugout canoes were relaying some of these people and their possessions across the bay. They would overwinter on the mainland. A contingent of 40 *Han* would remain on the island with the *Capoques* residing in their shelters just a short distance from the *Capoque* encampment.

For the boat repair, there were almost no tools save a rusty chisel, two hatchets, a saw, a hammer, and an adze salvaged from the boat of Dorantes and Castillo. The work was hard and several trips were made back to the *Cavoque* village to gather additional men, food, water, and wood. The boat was pulled higher onto the beach using logs as rollers. The weather, although somewhat cool, remained mild and the work continued for two days without much discomfort. The long trek back to the village necessitated setting up a small camp in a sheltered sand dune just inland from the boat. Indians from the villages assisted the *Spaniards* in constructing a small hut from which they could be sheltered from the wind and rain. This sheltered area became quite comfortable and several of the *Christians* elected to stay rather than return to the Indian village. One of these was Santo Corral who was forcibly sent there by de Vaca for his actions against one of the *Cavoque* women.

Corral had attempted to pull the woman into the bushes to seduce her. The woman, however, had used a scrapper, that she was carrying, to inflict a nasty cut along Corral's forearm before running off. The whole affair would have gone unnoticed except that it had been witnessed by Stancio Mellado who had been relieving himself a short distance away. Mellado, always fearful of betrayal by the Indians, had reported the incident to de Vaca.

Shortly after this occurrence, a man of Alvar's company died. It was Carlos Tavera, a man of gentle birth who had been well-liked by all. His passing was a grievous event. Racked by *la mierda,* he had grown progressively weaker. Not even able to move away from where he lay, he had been dependent on others to feed and clean him. This his companions had done, but he had regressed rapidly, eventually refusing food and drink. Reduced to a mere skeleton of a man he had passed quietly in the night.

After extolling his virtues, all that Alvar could say as they covered his emaciated body in a shallow sand grave was, "At least now, he is out of pain and with God."

The next day Alvar and Castillo left the village early in the morning and arrived at the boat site in the afternoon. The boat was ready to launch. Alvaro Fernandez, the carpenter, approached Alvar.

"*Alguacil,* we have worked hard but I fear in vain. We have had no suitable caulking material and are without the necessary tools to construct new timbers and sheathing. The wood is waterlogged and wormy."

"Do you think it will float *Senor* Fernandez?"

"Our only hope is that the seawater will swell the wood such that the leaks will heal themselves, but I am fearful it is no longer seaworthy."

"Well, let us see."

Those that would proceed aboard the boat had already been selected. Alonzo Castillo, the most fit of the captains, would accompany a crew of seven.

With the help of the *Indians,* the boat was pushed back into the surf. Waterlogged as it was, progress was slow. With each incoming wave, the vessel rose just enough to be slid further out. It remained on its side until reaching deeper water when, at last, it floated free. Now in waist-deep water, the men, both *Indian* and *Spaniard*, were thoroughly chilled as they pushed it into yet deeper water. When the water depth was up to their shoulders Castillo gave the command to board the vessel. The seven men scrambled aboard while those in the water gave it a final push before returning to shore. Four men set the oars in their locks and rowed the vessel into deeper water just past the breaker line. Here they threw the bow anchor out.

During its time on the beach, the wood had dried and contracted. Now afloat, water gushed through the multitude of seams in the hull. This was expected, and the men aboard used whatever containers were available to bail the seawater over the side. They could only hope that the hull sheathing would, once again, swell. For an hour the men aboard continued their frantic efforts. Even in the cool air, their bodies glistened with sweat from the exertion. But the efforts were futile and the amount of water rushing into the boat began to overpower them. Finally, Castillo, breathing heavily, stood in the bow and called out to Alvar who was watching from ashore.

"Alguacil, it is of no use. The flow of seawater is too great and we cannot keep up with it."

Castillo turned to the men aboard. *"Campatriotas*, salvage whatever you can, and let us make our way back to the beach."

Grabbing the meager supply of roots, dried fish, and water that had been put aboard, the men slid into the water and abandoned the sinking vessel. On the beach, they warmed themselves by a fire and watched dejected as the boat sank to its gunnels in the surf, its mast, with a tatter of sail still attached, swayed back and forth with the incoming tide. Finally, the hulk disappeared below the surface leaving only the mast as a forlorn marker of what lay below.

Late in the afternoon, most of the crew and repair party began the long walk back to the village. Five men, however, elected to stay in the temporary camp. It provided shelter and for now, they had enough food and water. They were Alberto Sierra, Diego Lopez, Juan Palacios, Gonzalo Ruiz and, of course, Santo Corral.

04 December, 1528

Indian Camp on Present-Day Galveston Island

The boat sinking was met with bitter disappointment. All hope was lost. The captains, De Vaca, and those that could, huddled together to discuss what else could be done. At first, no one spoke, so great was their depression. Alvar looked up at the moon, now shining brightly in the night sky. He shared his thoughts with those around him.

"We are unarmed and almost naked, somewhere on an unknown island, off an uncharted land. All around us are savages that we don't understand and that we are beholding to for food and shelter. Our men are sick...some dying...and we are all weak and emaciated. We may as well be up there." Alvar nodded toward the moon.

It was Dorantes who spoke next. "*Alguacil,* we can only hope that with God's grace, He will bring us through this awful time, but we cannot give up."

Castillo was next. "I agree. Let us ask the *casique*, this Weeahlenok if they will allow us to stay with them until spring. After that we can cross to the mainland, those that can, and continue our journey *adelante*...towards *Panuco*."

Alvar turned to the others around him. "We are all in this together. What are your feelings?"

All nodded in agreement. It was the *Portuguese* carpenter, Alvaro Fernandez, who added. "There are several among us that are still able-bodied and excellent swimmers. If by chance the *River of Palms* and *Panuco* are not that far distant, it will be God's will to take us there such that we could relate the great hardships of those left behind."

The mood brightened at this suggestion while the captains and Alvar began evaluating who among them was the most fittest.

Fernandez spoke again. "*Alguacil*, those that are chosen must be *chripstianos nadadores...Christians* who know how to swim, for I am sure there will be many waterways, rivers, and swamps to pass over."

"*Senor* Fernandez, I will choose you as the first of this rescue party for you are as fit as anyone and a strong swimmer. Who else among us would you choose to accompany you?"

"*Gracis Alguacil*, it is an honor."

Looking around, Fernandez was quick to pick three others, Xavier Mendez, Natalo Figueroa, the soldier from *Toledo,* and Marco Astudillo from *Zafra*.

"All of these men assisted me with the repair of the captain's boat. They are still strong, and able and I have seen them swim. I would also ask if this *casique* would provide us with a guide."

Alvar called for Estevan who, even now was conferring with several men of the village. His ability to speak and understand these strange languages had amazed everyone since the beginning of the expedition.

Estevan rushed over. "*Si Alguacil*, how may I be of service."

"Estevan, we would like to ask the *casique* if we can remain here until spring. Also, these four men will soon be leaving to find *Panuco* and, God willing, to send help. They are in need of an *Indio* guide and canoes to take them to the mainland. I will need you to present these needs to Weeahlenok."

"Alguacil, it is customary with these people that a gift be given when requests such as these are asked."

"But, we have nothing!" De Vaca was frustrated by this request.

"*Alguacil*, I have heard that Weeahlenok is much desirous of a *Spanish* sword, of which our boat crew has several."

Alvar looked to Dorantes.

"It is true, *Alguacil*, we have 5."

"Then that is what we must do." Turning to Estevan, Alvar continued. "Request a meeting with the *cacique* such that we all will attend. If he fulfills our demands we will give him a sword. With the remaining four swords, we will keep two and provide the rescue party with two."

The two captains accented, but it was understood that *Castillo* would keep his weapon.

08 December, 1528

Indian Camp on Present-Day Galveston Island

Three days had passed since the rescue party had left the island. Weeahlenok had provided 3 canoes to transport the men to the mainland. Castillo had accompanied them. As they off-loaded he wished the four rescuers well. With tears in his eyes, he watched them disappear into the sand dunes. With them was a guide that Weeahlenok had provided, a man from a neighboring island called *Avia*. When he returned Castillo reported that the men seemed in good spirits as they set off.

The weather had been unusually mild and today was no different. A soft breeze blew out of the south. The bay between the island and the mainland, save for a few swells, was like a mill pond. But, change was in the air and the *Capoques* seemed uneasy. So much so, that Alvar asked Estevan to find out what was troubling them.

Estevan circulated about the village exchanging pleasantries and then accompanied a group of men to work their fishing weirs. It was only a short walk to the shoreline cane breaks. The weirs consisted of three circular enclosures, one behind the other, constructed of reeds pounded into the bottom of a shallow shoal. The reeds were inserted side by side such that a fish could not squeeze between them. The first enclosure was sizable with a wide opening at one end. At the other end a much smaller opening led into the next and smaller enclosure. It, in turn, had a rear opening leading to a smaller and final enclosure.

Four or five men would form a line in the knee-deep water and move toward the weir, beating sticks on the water's surface. Schools of fish would run before them and enter the first enclosure. Quickly the men would block the entrance and the fish would move through the smaller openings until they were in the final enclosure. Now trapped, the fish could be easily speared and collected.

On this day the catch was disappointing. Estevan helped them transfer the few fish into baskets. The mood among the Indians was glum and they related how they had seen this condition before. The weather, they said, would be changing rapidly, becoming much colder. This always caused the fish, in this case, the mullet, to move further out into the bay.

Backin the village, other fishermen were relating similar stories. The fish that had been collected were gutted, flayed lengthwise, and set on racks over a smoldering fire that was constantly tended by the women. Today the racks were noticeably empty.

Estevan related his story to Alvar and the captains. "We must do what we can to help our hosts collect food for if we don't we all will starve."

All able-bodied *Christians* were assigned to work with the natives as best they could. Collecting the nutritious roots from plants that grew in the marshes was the most difficult. The roots were deep and had to be dug by hand, sometimes using an oyster shell for a scoop. The water was cold and the work was back-breaking. After peeling, the roots could be eaten raw or dried and pounded into a kind of flour.

At low tide oysters and clams were collected along the beaches and in shallow water, but the oysters on this part of the island were playing out and the clams were difficult to find.

Worst of all, the weather did begin to turn. All noticed that the wind had shifted to the west. The mild breeze of just an hour before had become chilly. Dark threatening clouds obscured the sun. At sunset, the wind had increased in intensity and turned further to the north. It began to rain. Whitecaps formed in the bay, contrasting with the gray angry water. By morning the temperature had dropped substantially, hovering just above freezing. So strong were the winds blowing through the village that the warming fires under the open shelters provided little comfort. The rain became mixed with sleet that stung the bare skin of the *Indians* and *Spaniards* huddling around their fires. No one worked the fish weirs that day, no one collected oysters or dug roots. The suffering was intense.

All day the temperature dropped and the winds continued. Sleet gave way to flurries of snow that whipped through the air. Visibility across the bay dropped to a few hundred feet. By nightfall wood for the fires was depleted, but so naked and exposed were the men of the expedition that no one left the shelter...no one, that is, except Estevan who had retained the ermine robe taken from Ceontoadala at the village of *Quenecava* a few months before.

In the failing light Estevan, trudged barefoot to the beach in the hope of finding driftwood, for all other fuel immediately around the camp had been used up. Crossing the dunes he stopped short of the beach...or what once had been the beach. Now, angry breakers rolled across the landscape consuming everything in their path. The sand and salt spray whipped his face. The cold wind chilled his uncovered legs. His feet became so cold he couldn't feel his toes. Picking up a few small sticks he left the dune and returned to the shelter. Night fell as the storm continued. The temperature continued to drop. The men dug holes in the sand to get out of the wind. These they filled with grass or anything available that would protect them from the cold. Estevan, Dorantes, Castillo, and de Vaca shared a sand pit, taking advantage of the ermine coat and the warmth it provided.

15 December, 1528

Indian Camp on Present-Day Galveston Island

The storm continued unabated for a week. The fires had long burned out, the cold ashes swirling about in the wind. Three men, too sick and weak to even cover themselves died, their deaths undiscovered until the evening when the wind finally fell off. Dorantes, sore and cramped in his sand pit, left its relative protection to urinate and get a drink of water. The sun was just setting as he tried to stand. He was lightheaded and for a few moments stood there trying to regain his balance. His skin itched and sores covered his legs and torso. He lurched forward and made his way a short distance from the shelter. He relieved himself there and returned. He saw them then, three men huddled together in a death embrace, obviously dead, their eyes staring blankly back at him. He nudged each with his foot but their emaciated bodies were already stiff. All three were from the *Alguacil's* boat.

Returning to the pit he notified the others who were also now moving about. Alvar shook his head in despair.

"God be with them, for their suffering is now over."

Several *Cavique* men of the village entered the enclosure and distributed a meager amount of dried fish and roots. Conversing with Estevan, they apologized, saying that they were suffering as well and could barely feed their families. The cane fish weirs had been destroyed by the waves and no longer could they pull roots in the cold. The men helped drag the bodies of the dead *Christians* away from the shelter and then returned to their village.

The air was thick with moisture as the gray light of the day faded away. Across the bay, to the west, a powerful weather pattern extended far inland, storms stacked up like so many dominoes. Moving slowly to the east they struck the island with unprecedented fury. The tumult continued unabated, lashing the island with spates of rain, sleet, and snow. The sun did not shine. The *Spaniards*, crazy with hunger, ate whatever was available; leather shoes, lacings, belts,and scabbards, all were consumed. Men scoured the dunes for anything edible. Mice, when found, were eaten whole. Insects, grubs, and all manner of larvae were consumed immediately. Even the inner soft bark of trees was stripped and chewed on.

Suffering mightily from the harsh conditions, some ventured onto the beach for brief periods looking for anything that may have washed up. On these forays, Estevan would share his ermine coat as he worked his way along the shoreline. When the tide was out a variety of shells and debris littered the sand. Every shell was broken open and investigated for anything edible. So cold was the wind blowing across the bay that the time on the beach was limited. Alvar, after returning from one of these searches shook from the cold for an hour as he lay in the pit. Estevan, seeing his plight, brought over the ermine coat and lay next to him.

"*Gracias* Estevanico, I feel that I will never stop shaking."

Estevan, also shivering in the cold, looked thoughtful. "*Alguacil*, I fear we will not make it off this island."

Their eyes met and Estevan could see that de Vaca had the same fear.

"We must pray that God will deliver us from this terrible burden." Alvar thought a moment and then continued, "You were once a *Muslim*, to which god do you now pray?"

Alguacil, Christian or Muslim, it is all the same God, but in answer to your question, I have accepted the Christian faith long ago."

Alvar seemed pleased by the answer and pulled the coat tighter around him.

Estevan had lied. In the tightly controlled world of the *Spanish*, it was best for a slave to profess *Christianity*. Actually, Estevan was neither. To him religion was too restrictive, an impediment to free will. How could you pray to a god that kept you in bondage?

The temperature dropped precipitously that night. Gale force winds blew so strongly that sea spray and blowing sand obscured everything in the morning. Water froze in the containers so the men had to break the ice to drink. Two more died, consumed by disease and exposure. Felipe de Lome was from Alvar's boat, and Alberto Rayos was from boat three.

Finally, the weather offered a brief reprieve. After an intensely cold night, the morning dawned bright and clear. Throughout the day the temperatures continued to rise. Atmid-morning Alvar crawled out of the hole he had dug in the sand. Pushing aside the grass he had stuffed around him he stood on wobbly legs, stiff and cramping. The skin on his arms and legs was covered with red welts and his body itched all over. Others around him were also stirring.

"We must gather water and firewood." He said to no one in particular.

For the next few hours, the men moved about as if in a dream. Most made the short trek to the beach combing the sands for driftwood and anything edible. The small crabs that scurried across the sand were especially prized, their carapaces crunching as the men chewed them whole.

Alvar waded into the cold surf trying to get some relief from the incessant itching on his ankles and legs. The water was cold and the salt stung the open sores, but it seemed to help. He rubbed them vigorously

By afternoon a sizable pile of driftwood had been gathered and piled inside the shelter. The warmer temperatures had accelerated the decomposition of de Lome and Rayos whose cadavers still resided in their sand holes. Their bodies were drug from the shelter and deposited on the beach.

Towards evening Alvar, Dorantes, Castillo, and Estevan walked to the *Indian* encampment hoping to obtain some food, but what they found was most disturbing. The *Capoques* had become very protective of their food supplies. Those who went out after food were returning with very little. To them, the *Christians* were becoming a burden. Weeahlenok explained they could no longer support these sick and dying men. Those who were healthy and able to work, however, would be taken into the tribe and assigned to servitude roles.

Alvar was thunderstruck. Essentially they had become the slaves of the *Indians*. To resist was pointless. They agreed this was the only option available for them and it would be their duty to support the other men of the expedition. Returning to the camp, Alvar and the captains explained their plight. There were loud protests and discussions that lasted long into the night but in the end, all agreed that this was the only way.

As the leader of the *Christians*, Alvar was taken into Weeahlenok's family under the direct control of his son-in-law, a particularly fierce-looking man by the name of Sukta. Sukta had married the *casique's* daughter and lived in an adjoining hut with his wife and young son. At first, Alvar was provided with a few hides with which to cover himself and only the most meager of scraps, but as the relationship progressed, he was treated more like a family member. His days were spent collecting firewood and accompanying Sukta in hunting and gathering forays.

The other healthy *Christians* were distributed among the tribe. Because they were first discovered by the *Han*, Andre Dorantes, Alonzo Castillo, and the surviving crew of boat three were taken into the adjoining village. Andre Dorantes was taken in by a particularly large *Han* who towered above his charge. Castillo was taken in by a large family headed by two warrior brothers. Others were assigned to families throughout the Indian camps. Five *Spaniards* were kept as a kind of communal work-force, subservient to everyone but primarily responsible for camp maintenance...repairing huts, filling water pots, gathering firewood, drying fish, and scraping hides.

Of all the *Spaniards*, it was Estevan who received the best treatment. He was taken in by Weeahlenok himself, spending most of his time serving as an interpreter. Even after months on the island, his blackness was still revered by the *Indians,* so much so that Weeahlenok provided him with a woman. The woman, actually no more than a girl of fourteen or fifteen, had been taken into the tribe the previous summer. Found wandering alone on the mainland Weeahlenok's wife had persuaded him to adopt the child. Now, in the communal environment of the huts, it soon became the talk of the village as to the frequency and intensity of lovemaking between the black man and the young orphan.

Whenever possible, Alvar, the captains, and whoever else was able would take food and water to the sick and dying *Spaniards* left unattended in the shelter. It was a feeble attempt because food had become so scarce there was very little to share. All of the little dogs in the Indian camp were consumed and seabirds, generally avoided by the *Capoques,* were consumed whenever possible. As best he could Alvar tried to make the sick as comfortable as possible, but it was a losing effort. The sick got sicker and the death rate increased. The *Capoques* avoided the shelter completely calling it "the place of dying." Almost every day the few *Spaniards* that now visited the shelter would drag an emaciated corpse to the beach.

Starving, filthy, and diseased, the days stretched into weeks and months.

18 January, 1529

Isolated Spanish Camp on Present-Day Galveston Island

Alvar, like most of the *Christians*, was becoming more fluent in the strange language of the *Capoques*. On a day when the foul weather had relented somewhat, Alvar convinced Sukta and several others to accompany him to the other end of the island to see what had become of the five *Christians* that had quartered on the coast. With him were Diego Dorantes and Pedro de Valdivieso, both cousins of Andre Dorantes. Sukta brought with him three of his brothers. It was a long and miserable walk. Although the temperature had warmed somewhat, the onshore winds blew relentlessly, chilling the men. In many places, the trail had been obliterated by drifts of windblown sand. After a half hour into the journey, a rain squall blew across the island. The men took shelter under a small grove of trees which only provided minimal protection. The rain at times seemed to blow sideways with such intensity that visibility became severely limited. Huddled under the tree Alvar squinted as he looked out to sea. The driving rain and sand plummeted him. Water dripped off his nose and soaked the long straggly beard that now hung down to his chest.

Just as quickly as it came, the storm passed, now visible as an inky blackness in the north. Overhead, the skies lightened but remained overcast. The men resumed their journey. Intermittent flurries of snow now wafted through the air and the temperature began to drop.

Crossing a raised dune, Sukta pointed and called out, *"Yata lek!"*

Alvar understood these words to mean dwelling or house. He hurried up the side of the dune to see for himself. There in the distance was the makeshift hut that had been constructed during the attempt to repair boat 3 but, even from this distance, it seemed strangely deserted. There was no movement and no campfire smoke rising from the structure.

Sukta, standing beside him, seemed troubled, he squatted down in the sand never taking his eyes off the campsite.

"Dwa," was all he said. Alvar recognized this word too...bad!

They moved down from the dune and resumed the journey. The *Indians* seemed to hold back. Alvar noticed that all of them had fitted an arrow into their stout bows. To Diego Dorantes, who was leading the procession, he whispered, "The *Capoques* have armed themselves."

"I have noticed this, *Alguacil.*"

Pedro de Valdivieso, who was close by, also nodded but remained silent. The procession moved closer. When a hundred yards from the structure the onshore wind brought the unmistakable stench of rotting meat. Everyone stopped. The smell of death was in the air. Sukta and his brothers separated and moved off the trail. The *Christians* moved slowly ahead, now fearful of what they would find.

"Alguacil!" It was Valdivieso. He was pointing to something partially hidden in the dune grass. Alvar moved closer and for a moment couldn't comprehend what he was looking at. It was a pile of bones. As he parted the grass a partially decomposed human skull with the hair still attached leered back at him. Startled, he lurched backward almost falling over Valdiviesco.

"*Madre de Dios*!" The bones were obviously *Spaniard,* for the hair was blond and remnants of a beard were still attached to the lower jaw. Alberto Sierra was the only one of the five men with blond hair. What was even more obvious was that Sierra hadn't died here. The bones were piled haphazardly on top of each other. Someone had put them here.

The Indians joined them. Sukta poked at the bones with his bow and seemed to concentrate on one of the leg bones. Alvar looked closer. There were deep diagonal cuts on the surface. Many of the other bones had the same markings.

The horror and realization came slowly. Alvar stepped back. "This man has been butchered and eaten!"

His first thoughts were of the cannibalistic *Caribes* that he had encountered so many months before on the island of *Cuba*. But, this couldn't be them. What of the sister tribe of the *Capoques*...the *Hans,* who had helped the crew of boat 3? Who could have done this? All of these thoughts were swirling in his head when Diego Dorantes called out.

"*Alguacil*, there is another body!"

Alvar looked toward the hut. The *Indians* were advancing toward it slowly, their bows fitted with arrows and partially drawn. Diego Dorantes was pointing at an indistinguishable, small mound thirty yards from the hut. They approached slowly. Three crows noisily took to the air, their loud "caw-caw" startling everyone. They had been perched on a human rib cage and spinal column, picking at whatever morsels they could find. The head and other extremities were missing.

At the hut, Sukta pushed away the crude thatched door. It fell onto the ground with a loud "thump." Alvar, Valdivieso, and Dorantes moved toward the hut. The other two *Capoques* were poised a short distance away with their bows drawn.

Alvar tripped on something. He fell to his knees. It was an arm, severed at the shoulder, the forearm and fingers still attached. He felt the bile rising in his throat.

Along with Sukta, Valdiviesco and Dorantes entered the hut. Alvar rose and moved toward the door, but was immediately pushed aside by Dorantes who rushed out of the enclosure and vomited on the sand. Bent over with his hands on his knees, he continued to wretch uncontrollably.

Alvar entered the hut. What greeted him was beyond comprehension. Body parts littered the enclosure. Valdiviesco moved past him to join Dorantes outside. The smell was abominable. He gagged but managed to suppress his need to regurgitate. Sukta, apparently unaffected by the stench, moved about the hut poking at the multitude of bones and body parts that littered the floor. Huddled in the corner was the complete corpse of Santo Corral covered with filthy rags. Three skulls surrounded him, their craniums cracked with a rock that lay by his side.

That the five *Spaniards* had reverted to cannibalism was all too apparent. Corral's emaciated, almost unrecognizable body was untouched. He had been the final survivor. Alvar hurried outside and walked far upwind, almost to the shoreline. He sat there in the sand contemplating what he had seen. Valdiviesco joined him.

"How could Christians do this *Alguacil*?

Alvar looked at him and shook his head. He had no explanation. The thought of consuming another human was repulsive. He found some solace in the fact that at least one of the dead had not participated. The first to die...probably Alberto Sierra, whose bones had been deposited far from the shelter.

For a long time, only the sounds of the surf and the wind interrupted their thoughts. Diego Dorantes found them and stood there for a moment.

"What are we to do with them?"

Alvar rose to his feet and looked for a moment toward the sky.

"Burn them! Burn everything."

The three *Spaniards* collected all of the firewood they could find and placed it in the middle of the shelter along with armloads of dry beach grass. Alvar carried, what remained of Alberto Sierra, and added the bones to the pile. Then they collapsed the shelter onto itself. Dorantes was already working with flint and steel to ignite the grass. Strangely, the *Capoques* kept their distance. Perched atop a distant dune they seemed to glower at the three *Spaniards*.

The grass smoldered as *Dorantes* blew on it to entice a flame. It ignited with a rush. A steady onshore breeze quickly accelerated the blaze. Reaching down, Alvar grasped the rib cage that the crows had been feasting upon. Most of the bones stayed together, still held by pieces of sinew. He tossed it and the spinal column into the fire. Watching them being consumed by the flames, Alvar could only think that a few short months ago this had been a man, a proud *Spanish hildago* with hopes of making his fortune in the New World. He wondered, if would this be his fate as well.

The three men knelt in the sand and made a silent prayer. Alvar crossed himself and stood up. The *Capoques* were already moving down the trail. The *Spaniards* followed them. The *Indians* kept their distance, never stopping to talk. Only once did Alvar look back. A trail of gray smoke drifted across the island.

On returning to camp on that fateful day the *Capoques* had protested loudly, brandishing their weapons they caused an uproar that lasted for several days. Alvar and Estevan tried desperately to calm them. Weeahlenok shook his hand in front of Alvar's face and indicated that if they had seen what was happening in that camp they would have killed the men. Now, he was unsure whether to kill all of the *Christians* and be done with them. Sukta, Alvar's *padrone*, finally was able to talk the *casique* into sparing the Christians, *Cree-sans* as he called them, for in the *Cavique* dialect the letters "ST" was not used. He argued that the able-bodied *Cree-sans* aided his family in collecting food and firewood. Besides, so many of the *Cree sans* were already dead or dying there would soon be no need to kill them. Weeahlenok relented but refused any more help to the sick and starving *Spaniards* in the shelter.

01 February, 1529

Indian Camp on Prewentday Galveston Island

Now, it had been two weeks since the discovery of the cannibal *Spaniards*. The weather had once again turned for the worse. Freezing at night, the temperature only rose slightly during the day. Overcast skies blocked the sun and freezing rain lashed the island. Food had become so scarce that, even on their frequent forays to the shoreline, little could be found. On one foray Alvar stumbled across an injured mullet swimming upside down in the shallows, probably the victim of a thwarted dolphin attack. He snatched it up and consumed the fish there on the spot, swallowing scales, fins, and viscera. He carefully picked every morsel of meat off the bones before discarding it. His stomach growled in protest. Looking down at the fish skeleton he could only think that a few short months ago this kind of action would have disgusted him.

The *Capoques* were suffering as well. Many had a strange stomach ailment that caused them to double over in excruciating pain. Laying in the fetal position their moans could be heard throughout the camp. Languishing in this state for days on end, they began to die. So many of the *Capoques* succumbed to this disease that Weeahlenok and others of the village again blamed the *Spaniards*, saying that they were responsible. Weeahlenok and a group of warriors planned to kill the remaining survivors. As they moved out to execute their plan, however, Sukta and several others once again intervened, arguing that if the *Spaniards* had the power to cause the deaths why was it that so many of them had died as well? He further pointed out that not one of the *Cree-sans* had ever caused any harm or injury to the *Capoques*. After much argument Weeahlenok once again relented.

The shelter that had housed the sick and dying *Spaniards* had become a scene of incomparable wretchedness. On one particularly dark night, a party of *Capoques* had entered the structure and slit the throats of all who remained alive. They would have burned the shelter, but so desperate for firewood were they that the structure was dismantled and taken back to the lodges piece by piece.

Early the next morning Diego Dorantes was awakened by a disturbance in the village. Men were carrying armfuls of wood and depositing them by the communal fire. Curious, he inquired where such a vast quantity of wood was obtained. The *Capoques* avoided him, but he soon recognized that the wood was the remnants of the structure that housed the sick and dying *Spaniards*. He rushed down the trail passing other Indians carrying their loads. When he reached the site of the structure he stopped and stared in disbelief. It was gone, razed to the ground. Only a few sticks and logs remained and these were quickly being snatched up and carried away. The *Spaniards* that had been housed here were all dead, throats slit from ear to ear, still wrapped in their filthy rags. They lay there where they had huddled together for warmth or half buried in their sleeping holes. Dorantes walked among the corpses saying a silent prayer for each of the men, his comrades, the friends that he knew and had suffered with these many months. He was heartsick.

Dorantes was interrupted from his reverie by a push from behind. He turned to see one of the *Capoques* motioning for him to help pick up firewood. There was no arguing. Resigned to his fate he gathered what he could and joined the procession back to the village.

Of the eighty *Spaniards* who had accompanied both boats only fifteen now remained alive.

The *Capoques* had customs that mystified Alvar and the remaining *Christians*. If a child dies, that is, a youth under the age of 12, the parents, and relatives show their grief by wailing three times a day: At sunrise, at noon, and at dusk. They are joined in this by the rest of the tribe who still go about their business while weeping loudly. This weeping activity lasts for an entire year.

Should an older son or brother die, their death is also mourned by loud weeping, but in addition, the people of the household further mourn the death by not gathering food for a period of three months. In this, they depended on their relatives and neighbors to provide the necessary victuals to sustain them. Now, the families of those who died from the strange stomach ailment, died from starvation as well, for their relatives and friends, try as they might, were unable to help them. So strong was this belief that they preferred to starve rather than help themselves.

Soon, over half the village had succumbed.

In this dying time, the weeping continued unabated day after day. As was their custom, the *Capoques* buried their dead in the soft dune sand. Only the *fisicos*...medicine men, were burned, their bones gathered up and ground into powder. The *fisicos* were thought to be agents of what they called *Ye suni deo-cuk*. This name Estevan translated as "Great Provider." By burning the body, the *Capoques* were returning the medicine man's power so that it could be reused. At the end of the mourning period, the powdered bones were mixed with water and consumed by the relatives. By doing this, the soul of the *fisico* lived on in future generations.

Such was the fate of Weeahlenok who, along with his two wives contracted the disease. As the wives were the first to show signs, Weeahlenok administered to them as he did the others in the village. He placed heated rocks on their stomachs to ease the pain and cramping. He blew on the affected areas. When the cramping worsened he made small diagonal cuts in the skin and sucked out the blood around the incision. All of this was to no avail, and soon Weeahlenok himself had contracted the ailment.

As part of the household, Alvar did what he could to help the suffering *cacique* and his family. Their stomach cramping was followed by diarrhea and fever. They soon became so weak that they were unable to rise and leave the shelter to relieve themselves. Alvar enlisted the help of Estevan and together they did what they could to ease the pain and suffering of those around them. In three days Weeahlenok died suddenly, consumed with diarrhea and high fever. Strangely, both his wives survived. Each morning Alvar would tend to them, making the sign of the cross after offering up a short prayer. In this, he was closely watched by the others of the village. Very few of the *Indians* who contracted the ailment survived, and Alvar's successful ministrations to the wives were seen as a miracle. The people of the village now summoned Alvar to take up the responsibilities of curing the sick, in effect to become a medicine man. Indeed, they began to look on all of the *Christians* as having the power to heal after the woman provided to Estevan also survived the sickness.

Faced with the request of the Indians, the *Spaniards* conferred amongst themselves. At first, it was not taken seriously.

Andre Dorantes addressed Alvar. "*Alguacil*, they favor you and Estevanico amongst all of us to become *fisicos*...physicians."

Alvar laughed aloud, "Andre, you know as well as me that we have no training or diplomas for this."

"This I know, but they know nothing of our examinations and diplomas. They believe there is power in all things...even the rocks in the field. They have seen their people cured and this is all that matters to them."

Alvar laughed again, "I do not believe in the power of rocks, but I will talk with Sukta and relay that I have no special training or powers to do this."

Later that day the conversation with Sukta did not go well. Alvar tried to explain that he had no powers of healing and that the power of life and death resided in God almighty and his son Jesus Christ not in stones and things growing in the field.

Sukta responded, "I know nothing of your god or this one you call Jesus." He pronounced Jesus as "*Ya-seez*"

Sukta continued, "We have seen you and *Wee-ka-nah*...the black one...care for our people and we know that the Spirit Father has given you powers to cure our sufferings."

Alvar tried to explain. "We have no special powers. Neither I nor *Wekanah*, or indeed, any of the *Christians* know how to cure people. We can not accept the responsibilities of healers."

With this Sukta answered, "You do not know what you are talking about. The Spirit Father resides in all things. You as wiser men have great power."

Again Alvar refused.

Sukta, very much upset, turned and walked away.

For three days the *Indians* withheld food from the *Spaniards*. Alvar was denied meetings with Sukta. He was told only that should they agree to heal their people, to become *fisicos,* the food would again be distributed. It was the same with *Han* with whom the men of boat 3 resided, for both captains Castillo and Dorantes had been asked to perform similar functions.

Finding themselves in dire straits Alvar at last called for another meeting with Sukta, who as Weeahlenok's son, was now the unofficial leader of the *Capoques.*

Summoned at last, Alvar entered the lodge and sat cross-legged in front of Sukta who remained stoic. The uncomfortable silence continued until, at last, he indicated that Alvar should speak.

"Sukta, I congratulate you as the new leader of the *Capoques.*"

Sukta unimpressed, remained silent.

Alvar continued, "I have talked with my people and we have agreed to serve as *fisicos*...your medicine men.

Sukta's mood immediately brightened. He rose and clapped Alvar on the back saying, "This is good, this is good."

And so, the process of becoming physicians to the *Capoques* and *Hans* began. Together, Alvar, the captains Castillo and Dorantes, and the black slave Estevan agreed on their manner of treatment. They would make their patients as comfortable as possible and recite a Pater Noster and Ave Maia over them while making the sign of the cross. Many times they would duplicate the treatment of the native medicine men, placing hot rocks on the affected areas and appearing to blow away the disease with their breath. At all times, however, they placed their faith in God and credited Him with the cures that, somehow, were amazingly successful.

24 February, 1529

Indian Camp on Present-Day Galveston Island

By Alvar's best guess, it was the month of *February*. Although the weather was raw and unyielding, the days grew longer. The roots that the Indians had dug in the shallow water were now beginning to sprout and were no longer fit to eat. On a day when the weather was unusually calm, the *Capoques* whom Alvar lived with, gathered their belongings and made their way to the beach. Here, the four canoes that they possessed were made ready. Each canoe would hold five people. If all were adults, four would paddle, including the women, as they made their way across the bay. It was an agonizingly slow process. Alvar stood on the beach and watched as the canoes paddled off toward the mainland, becoming mere specs in the distance. After unloading, two paddlers would return the canoe to the island. Occasionally, with small children, a canoe would carry as many as eight people. Alvar and the older *Capoques* were the last group to leave the island.

The other *Spaniards,* accompanied by the *Han* had left the island the day before. Twelve had crossed to the mainland. Two, the notary Jeronimo Alaniz and Lope de Oviedo remained on the island, too sick to travel. Several *Capoques* and a few *Han* remained on the island as well.

As Alvar stepped into the narrow canoe he struggled to keep his balance. There were no cross members to sit on so each passenger squatted on their knees. Alvar was handed a paddle as two of the men pushed the canoe into deeper water. When they jumped aboard he dropped the paddle and hung on to each of the gunnels fearing the craft would overturn. Again, he was handed the paddle. Struggling to maintain balance, his first attempts at paddling were awkward. He was not coordinated with the other three men. Behind him, one of the other Indians smacked his paddle into the water sending a spray of water over Alvar that quite surprised him.

Sputtering Alvar turned around.

"*Cree-san,* you paddle like a woman!

The others in the canoe erupted in laughter each in turn using their paddles to spray Alvar with cold seawater. He tried harder and eventually was able to adapt to the rhythm of the other paddlers...sort of.

Halfway across the bay, the paddlers stopped briefly to rest. Alvar looked back at the island where so much grief and hardship had confronted them. He thought of the friends he had lost and those that were still missing. To no one in particular he said, "This has truly been the island of our suffering and ill fate, our *isle de mal hado!*

Rested, the paddlers renewed their efforts. Alvar turned his gaze from *Malhado* Island and looked toward the mainland.

CHAPTER 09

Spirit Bear Walker

Wasapi-tun-loki

From that moment on Alvar Nunez Cabeza de Vaca was known to the Charrucans and indeed, all other tribes that he would encounter, as Wasapi-tun-loki...Spirit Bear Walker.

01 April, 1529

The Mainland of Present-Day Texas Across From Galveston Island

For once he wasn't hungry. Captain Alonzo del Castillo Maldonado licked his fingers and lay back against the pile of shells that surrounded him. He let out a sigh. What he would give for a glass of wine from the *Madeira Islands*. Closing his eyes, he could almost taste the sweet bite of the wine as it touched his tongue. He was thirsty, but he resolved to tarry here, taking in the warmth of the morning sun and the quietness of the moment. Besides, the water was so bad on the mainland that he tried to drink only from the puddles left after a rain. The permeability of the sandy soil and the tidal surges of the bay left the streams and ponds brackish.

Today the air was stunningly clear with only a few wispy clouds hanging lazily in the sky. He looked across the bay and could just see the outline of the island he had left only two months ago. It saddened him to think of the friends and compatriots that had been lost on that spit of land. Of the two boats and eighty *Christians* that had shipwrecked there, only a few now survived. Most of the survivors of his boat now resided with those Indians that had first come upon them; they called themselves the *Han*. The survivors of *Alguacil* de Vaca's boat resided with another group who called themselves *Capoque*. Both groups lived in close proximity and although they spoke different languages, each was able to understand the other with common words, hand language, and a pidgin mix of both languages.

Although both groups had moved to the mainland, he had not seen the *Christians* residing with the *Capoques* since leaving the island. Only occasionally would he hear about them from chance meetings between the two groups. He estimated that it was now late March or early April. The weather was still in transition, but generally, the days and nights were warm. Quite a difference from their time on the island only a few months previous It was wet though, and afternoon thunderstorms became so frequent that everyone adjusted their activities around them. The wetness produced something else that was most uncomfortable...mosquitoes! Hordes of them. Here on the beach, the sea breezes kept them somewhat at bay, but without the sticky concoction spread over his body, he would be most uncomfortable. The women of the tribe contrived this potion that was a mixture of animal fat and herbs. The smell was atrocious, especially as the mixture became rancid. Bear grease seemed to give the most desirable results, but in its absence, the fat from other mammals and even *allegarto* were used interchangeably. For the relief that it provided, however, he could live with the smell, besides, the stronger the odor, the better it seemed to work. Alonzo looked down at his legs. They were covered with welts and scratches, especially where the skin was tightest around the ankles and feet. Strangely, what bothered him most were the tops of his ears which seemed to resist all effects of the potion.

Alonzo's position with the *Han* had changed dramatically. During the dying time on the island, they had accepted him only as a slave, subjecting him to the most menial work and offering only scraps to eat. He lived with a family of five individuals who were more or less responsible for him. The man was of enormous size standing well over a foot above Castillo. His name was Quala-ne-nok and he was said to be the strongest in the area. The woman...his wife...might have been attractive in a civilized world, but the profusion of tattoos and piercings left her quite unappealing to Castillo's tastes. Two young children captured her constant attention. The fifth member of the family, the woman's father, had lived with them while on the island, but the stomach ailment that had claimed so many of the Indians took him just before leaving for the mainland.

To Alonzo, the love and care that the *Han* gave to their children was like no other he had ever seen. They always seemed to have food to eat even at the expense of the mother and father. Alonzo had learned early that a way to gain favor with the parents was to dote on the children. This relationship had taken a strange turn while still on the island. One of the children, a girl, had been stricken with the same stomach ailment that had taken her grandfather and so many others. Assisting with the care of the youngster, Alonzo had tried to make her comfortable, smoothing her hair and wiping her feverish skin with wet moss. He had taken a moment to pray over the child before leaving the dwelling. His actions had not gone unnoticed, for not half an hour after leaving the little one's side the fever broke and the pain within her bowels began to subside. It was looked on by the parents and indeed, all of the *Han*, as a miracle. Others began to bring their sick to him and although not all survived, a greater number lived. Almost without knowing it, his status among the *Han* had risen to a medicine man. In fact, it became rumored among the Indians, both *Han* and *Capoque* alike, that all of the *Christians* possessed this power.

Alonzo dismissed this idea immediately and tried to explain to the *Indians* that he was not trained as a physician and had no special powers. The other *Christians* were of the same feeling and initially refused to participate fearing that they would be held accountable for all who died. However, the *Indians* were adamant and refused food to the *Christians* until they agreed.

"Now I am a *fisico*...a physician." Alonzo laughed to himself. "Where before my only concern was taking life in service to my king, now I save it."

Castillo was jolted from his reverie by a call from Quala-ne-nok who informed him that the *Han* would be proceeding back to the island this very day.

"Why must we do this?" he answered. "That island is a place of hardship and sorrow. Here we have food." Alonzo pointed to the mounds of oyster shells surrounding him.

"*Cash-e-lo,*" This was as close as Quala-ne-nok could get to pronouncing Castillo's name. He talked to Castillo as if addressing a child. "We gather the eggs when our ancestor, *Kena,* leaves them in the sand for us. *Kena,* Castillo knew, was the name the *Han* used for the sea turtle. They believed that their departed souls resided in this animal and that its yearly visits to the beach were made to reward them.

With that Quala-ne-nok began gathering his family for the trip back to the island. The wind was calm and the sea between the mainland and the island was featureless. The few canoes owned by the *Han* were collected and began making their round trips to the island. It wasn't until nightfall that all the people had been transported across the bay. Castillo and the rest of the *Christians* with him were the last to go.

The sun was setting over the mainland. Scores of seabirds crisscrossed the sky en- route to their evening roosts. The sky remained clear, and in the darkening east, the stars were just becoming visible. Further out there, Alonzo knew, there were *Spaniards* like himself and civilization, but that was another world and one that he may never see again. A feeling of melancholy overwhelmed him as the canoe crunched onto the sand of the Island.

01 April, 1529

The Mainland of Present-Day Texas Across From Galveston Island

Alvar stuffed a fist full of blackberries into his mouth. He tasted the tangy sweetness and crunched down on the seeds. The juice trickled out and ran down his chin and neck. He stood on a raised sandy hillock surrounded by the thorny plants with their clusters of berries. Others from the band of *Capoques* had joined him, and everyone was filling themselves to bursting. Naked like the rest, he looked down at his arms, legs, and torso. Cuts and red welts covered him and, indeed, his whole body seemed to be covered with the dark berry juice.

Something caught his eye. From his vantage point, he could look out at the bay and *Malhado Island* far in the distance. It was a bright, clear day and the bay was very calm. Moving across this expanse was a line of four canoes coming from a different part of the mainland and moving toward the island. Alvar stopped picking and watched their slow progress.

"It is our brothers the *Han*. They return to the island for the eggs that *Kena* will bring to them. They are taking your brothers, the *Cree-sans,* with them." It was Sukta.

Alvar turned to face the tall warrior, now *casique* of the band of *Capoques* that had taken him in. Like himself, Sukta was covered with berry juice stain and equally cut up from the sharp thorns.

"Who is *Kena?* I don't understand this word."

Sukta nodded. "*Kena* is their spirit grandfather who comes every year at this time to leave them eggs.

Confused even more, Alvar asked, "Where does this *Kena* come from and who is he?"

Sukta let out a long belly laugh and all those around turned to look. "*Kena* is not a man, Cree-san, is an animal in the sea with a shell on its back."

Sukta tried hard to pantomime a turtle. "Every year at this time it crawls on the beach to lay its eggs."

Everyone was laughing. Alvar, finally understanding that a *Kena* was a sea turtle, laughed as well.

"Now I understand the word, but why don't the *Capoque* go as well?"

"Many years ago we fought a war with the *Han* over the turtles. To them the turtles on this island are sacred...they are their grandfathers; to us, they are just turtles. After many deaths in battle, we agreed to let them visit the island alone during this time. Besides, there are many turtles here as well. Not only do we eat their eggs, but we roast the *Kena* over a fire, this the *Han* do NOT do!" Sukta smacked his lips.

Alvar and the *Capoque* continued to feast on the blackberries for another week. So busy were they gathering the sweet fruit that no other victuals were collected. In the evening the *Capoque* would begin dancing and celebrating far into the morning hours, for what reason Alvar was never able to fully understand.

After this period, the blackberries began to dry up and the *Capoque* looked to other food sources. It was amazing to Alvar all the strange plants, berries, nuts, and roots that were available. There were purple grapes that grew abundantly at the edge of the woods that burned your lips and tasted very tart, but when boiled and mixed with other plants were quite pleasing. There were also mushrooms that grew on dead trees and looked every bit like a human ear. The *Capoque* especially liked a plant that grew in moist areas and on the banks of streams and ponds. The root had tubers as large as hens' eggs which were especially prized, but they also ate the flowers and seed pods. Alvar acquired new tastes and learned to eat things he would never have touched only a year before, but life was still hard and the *Capoque* continued to treat him more like a slave than a member of the clan. Sukta's position in the tribe was threatened by another younger man, who criticized him for his preferential treatment of Alvar. In a strange conclave, it was decided that the newcomer would now lead the band and Sukta, along with his family, were left to join another clan further up the coast. Strangely, Alvar was left behind.

The new leader, Tob-e-sas, treated Alvar with contempt and he was made to work long hours gathering food and doing menial jobs. He was forced to labor from dawn until dusk digging roots among the rushes. The only implements to accomplish the digging were rough pieces of oyster shell. His fingers became so worn that the slightest touch caused them to bleed.

By now, all of the *Christians,* except Alvar, had either died or left the *Capoque* and taken up with the *Han* on *Malhado Island*. In mid-April Alvar contracted a sickness so severe that he was unable to even lift his head. In this condition, the *Capoques* avoided him completely. On the third day of his sickness, Alvar had resigned himself that he would die on this remote mainland among heathens and thousands of leagues from home. He thought of his beloved Maria and tried to picture what she was doing at that moment. Had she heard that he was missing, had she been told that in all likelihood he was dead, was she grieving, or was she in the arms of another lover? All of these things passed through his feverish mind.

While in his feverish stupor, Alvar received a strange visitor. He was vaguely aware of an old, spindly-legged *Indian* entering the crude shelter where he lay. The man's hair was matted and festooned with small bones, feathers, and sea shells. His face was a mass of tattoos such that it highlighted the strange piercing look of his eyes that seemed to be sunk deep in his skull. His teeth, the ones that remained, were darkly stained from the juice of the wad of leaves that he chewed. Spittle ran down the corners of his mouth. Around his neck hung four bags made of deerskin, each containing some potion. He spoke the language of the *Capoque* and indicated that he had come to free Alvar of the evil sickness. There was no doubt or hesitation in this statement. He was Wacch-on-a the spirit healer.

The next few days were a blur for Alvar as his feverish mind drifted in and out of consciousness. He remembered the large fan of eagle feathers that Wacchona continually passed over him. He felt the warmth from the heated rocks that spewed clouds of steam throughout the enclosure where he lay. Most of all he dreaded the foul mixtures that Wacchona made him swallow and the gobs of brown spittle rubbed on his neck, chest, and stomach. Between treatments Wacchona would sit on the floor and chant phrases in a language that Alvar did not understand.

After a week of these ministrations, Alvar felt himself improving. Slowly he began to eat, although sparingly. He was still weak and would remain so for some time, but the sickness had left him and upon waking one morning discovered that Wacchona had left.

The *Capoques* who had ignored Alvar now grudgingly supplied him with drink and one meal a day. It wasn't until many days after that Alvar learned more of Wacchona. He was a chimerical medicine man of legend. He was respected and feared by all. It was said that his spells could destroy people, and villages...even change the weather. Indeed, the fear of one of these spells is what compelled the *Capoque* to supply Alvar with food and drink. Wacchona traveled alone and was not aligned with any tribe. None knew of where he came from or where he dwelt. He would suddenly appear and then disappear. Many felt that Wacchona could change into an animal. On the day he disappeared from Alvar's hut, a young boy had seen a poisonous snake slithering away from the enclosure. Most importantly, all who were treated by Wacchona lived a long life and seemed immune from harm.

18 April, 1529

Malhado Island

With considerable effort, captains Alonso del Castillo and Andres Dorantes gathered the remaining *Christians,* for they were distributed throughout the island. The black slave Estaban and the *Asturian* cleric Pietre de Asturiano had been with other *Han* on a nearby island gathering turtle eggs. They were the last to arrive. Together there were fourteen in number. In the group were the cousins of Andres, *hildagos* Pedro de Valdivieso and Diego Dorantes, cavalry lieutenant Fernan Estrada, musketeers Jorge Tostado, Lope Chaves, Silvio Gutierrez, Diego de Huelva, Victor Benitez, expedition scribe Jeronimo Alaniz and Lope de Oviedo

With the *Christians* sitting cross-legged on the ground before him, Castillo scanned the group for a moment. No one looked like their previous self, all were gaunt, nearly naked, and heavily sunburned. They, of course, were distinguishable from the *Indians* by the thick beards that now covered their faces. Some had fared better than others. All were covered with the foul mosquito potion that always seemed to be available in large quantities. In the back, Jeronimo Alaniz and Lope de Oviedo lay on reed pallets both suffering from stomach sickness. A few of the *Han* invited by Castillo had also joined the gathering, seating themselves around the outskirts to observe the happenings.

Castillo spoke in the language of the *Han,* only occasionally mixing it with *Spanish.* He did this so as not to arouse the suspicions of the *Han.*

"*Companeros*, we are all that remain in this area except for the *Alguacil, Senor* de Vaca who still lives with the *Capoque* on the mainland. Our ranks have been decimated by starvation and sickness and it is now that we must pull together to survive this terrible ordeal.

Jorge Tostado called out. "*Capitan*, what of our rescue party?"

Andre Dorantes stepped forward for this question. "The brave men that ventured out last winter had a long and arduous journey to make. They were picked for their stamina and abilities. Indeed, some of them may make it to the settlement in *Panuco* and bring back rescuers, but we can't assume that this will happen. We must gather up the *Alguacil* and begin our own journey."

There were nods all around.

"But *capitan*, who will take us to the mainland to gather up *Senor* de Vaca."

Castillo took up the conversation. "I have talked this matter over with Quala-ne-nok and he will allow us to leave and begin our journey to the south. He said to me, '*Cash-e-lo,*' it is time for you to return to your own people." Everyone laughed as Castillo repeated the pronunciation of his name.

"All he asks in payment is the sable robe now in the possession of Estaban. For this, he will take us across the bay."

All heads turned toward Estaban. He was the only surviving negro of the expedition and his uniqueness was such that he had been allowed a woman and special privileges by the *Han*. His status as a slave to Andres Dorantes was no longer relevant, at least as long as they remained with the *Indians*. The decision to give up the robe would have to be his alone.

His life of slavery with Dorantes had not been particularly hard. The captain had treated him well and together they had a relationship more like companions. He had grown used to the easy life of *European* culture. True, there was freedom living with the *Indians* but also immense hardships. He also felt that eventually they would be rescued. Maintaining his loyalty would ensure his easy life with Dorantes would continue.

Estevan stood and addressed the gathering. "The coat of Ceotoadala has served me well, but I would gladly part of it such that it would help in our journey to *Panuco*."

The gathering of *Spaniards* applauded, for up until now they had all been unsure of what position Estevan would take. Now, he was still one of them.

Later that day Castillo, Dorantes, and Estevan promised the sable coat to Quala-ne-nok, and the journey to the mainland was scheduled for the next morning.

19 April 1529

Galveston Bay

Estevan looked back at the Isle as the flotilla of canoes made their way to the mainland. He actually looked forward to the journey ahead and what awaited him in this strange new land. Somehow, he knew that he would survive.

When the last canoe carrying Estevan scrapped against the mainland shore, there were only twelve *Spaniards* in total. Jeronimo Alaniz and Lope de Oviedo had been left behind. Both were so weakened by the stomach sickness that it would have been impossible for them to keep up, indeed, there was even concern that neither would survive. It had been difficult to leave the two, but the *Han* treated them well and promised to bring them over once the sickness had passed.

Once on the mainland, the *Christians* parted with the *Han*, the people who had taken them in for so many months. Estevan presented the sable coat to Quala-ne-nok with much fanfare. As was the custom, the *Indians* began to weep, and even as they pushed off and paddled back to *Malhado* their anguished sobs carried across the bay.

The little group of *Spaniards,* now alone on the Mainland, wanted desperately to make contact with Cabeza de Vaca, but there were no *Indians* to greet them and his exact whereabouts were unknown. They turned south and began their journey down the coast. It was an ill-prepared and haggard group that followed the shoreline. Some had covered themselves with loincloths salvaged from rotting clothing, most were naked, and all were barefoot. Their feet, like those of the *Indians,* were deeply calloused such that the hot sand along the seashore bothered them little. All of the *Spaniards* carried walking sticks or crude spears. Each man had his meager possessions in a deer hide pouch tied around the waist or strapped to their back. In this pouch were such things as stone knives, scrappers fashioned from oyster shells, dried fish, and personal items. Andres Dorantes carried a crude net with cords he had woven from the long leaves of water plants. He had learned this skill from the *Han* women to whom he had been assigned. The *Han* men, busy with hunting and food gathering, had not the time or interest to deal with such things. The women taught him how to cut and dry the leaves. The dried leaves were then sliced lengthwise and wetted. Using two strands of these leaf parts they would twist and splice them together in a pattern that Dorantes came to call *giro inverso*...reverse twist. When lengths of this cordage were completed they would knot several lengths together to form a net with square openings two finger widths apart.

After only a short time the party of *Spaniards* saw a lone figure walking along the beach toward them. Unsure of what to expect they stopped and waited. As the figure drew closer, they recognized it as another *Christian,* for, unlike the *Indians* he was short and heavily bearded. Fernan Estrada and Diego Dorantes ran toward him. When halfway there they turned and hollered back to the main party, " It is Francisco de Leon!"

Estrada and Dorantes embraced him as the others hurried up. There were a thousand questions and the men sat in the sand for an hour talking of their experiences.

De Leon was a member of Boat 5 and had come ashore with De Vaca. He had survived the terrible winter and traveled to the mainland with the others. On a hunting expedition with the *Capoque,* however, he had been traded to the people of the forest for three deer hides. These people called themselves *Charruco.*

Now numbering thirteen, the *Spaniards* fell into a discussion of how best to find Cabeza de Vaca. De Leon, being on the mainland, but with a different group of *Indians,* had heard rumors, but knew nothing of where to find him. The last he had heard of the *Alguacil* was that he was very sick and not expected to live. After much deliberation, they decided that to further interact with the *Indians* in search of de Vaca would put them all in jeopardy, and besides, de Vaca may already be dead. They would continue on, *adelante*...to the south, in the direction of *Panuco*.

September, 1529

The Texas Mainland

It was now early fall and Alvar labored in the cane fields. He had been put back to work soon after recovering from the sickness. During the summer he had suffered mightily. Sore and weak, it was all he could do to rise in the morning. The *Capoques* had treated him with contempt, kicking and pulling on his beard whenever he stopped to rest. Alvar had feared for his life. Threatened constantly, the *Capoques* would draw their bows and talk of how they would fill his body full of arrows. Many times they would release their arrows, missing him by only the width of a few fingers. But, strangely they never carried out their threats of death. Alvar learned much later that Wacchona, the spirit healer, had told the *Capoques* that if any harm came to the bearded one, a pestilence would consume the tribe. Uncomfortable as it was, Alvar became accustomed to the threats and was able to stare down his accusers. It was shortly after this that the threats stopped. The abuse, however, continued.

Few of the *Capoques* talked with de Vaca, but from those that did he learned the other *Spaniards* of *Malhado Island* had come ashore in the Spring and proceeded down the coast. They also related how two of the *Christians* had remained on the island, too sick to travel. He was saddened by the fact that he couldn't join the party on their way to *Panuco*.

The mornings were becoming cool and the days were growing shorter. It was time for the *Capoques* to cross over to the island, for now, was the time that the *wokasee-re-taka...*spotted tail fish, gathered to breed in abundance around *Malhado Island*. The trip across the bay had been uneventful. On the same day he arrived Alvar was put to work constructing fish weirs. Hundreds of poles had to be cut and set side by side in the soft mud and sand. These were loosely woven together to form an impenetrable barrier. Once constructed, the *Capoques* would gather in the water and drive *wokaseeretaka* toward the mouth of the weir. Once inside, the trapped fish thrashed about as Alvar closed the gate and proceeded to gather them into large baskets that the women had woven. Alvar's hands suffered a multitude of cuts from the spiny dorsal fins as he struggled to hand-catch the fish as they milled about.

When not tending the weirs, Alvar spent his time helping the women of the tribe in preparing the fish. Using a sharp oyster shell, he would scale each one and then slice the belly open to remove the entrails. The liver, heart, and roe were saved and thrown into a communal pot. The flayed fish was then laid on a lattice of poles over a smoky fire pit. The pit itself was surrounded by an enclosure similar in construction to the fish weirs, that is, to contain and channel the smoke.

The unusable entrails of *wokasee-re-taka* were also saved and used to attract crabs into another type of weir that was smaller and more compact. Of prominence was a large crab with a blue claw the *Capoques* called *keekee-aka...*blue claw. Also caught to a lesser degree were dark brown crabs with one black claw banded in red and yellow. These were *laka-aka*...black claw. Only the claw of *laka-aka* was collected, the live animal thrown back into the bay, minus the appendage.

The entrails were also used to attract another prey animal, this one they called *tanga-taka*...killer fish. Two or three canoes would proceed into the shallow bays where the viscera was thrown over the side to attract sharks. In addition, each canoe would tie off a butchered fish and suspend it just under the water. Positioning themselves in a loose circle, the canoes would wait for the sharks to congregate. When individual animals rose to take the suspended fish, a man stationed in the bow would plunge his spear deep into the animal's body.

What happened next was sheer mayhem, for the shark exploded in watery convulsions to free itself of the spear. Depending on the shark's size, there was a good chance that the canoe would be upset, sending both the spear thrower and the paddler into the water. This happened frequently and the other canoes would move quickly to rescue the capsized swimmers.

The position of spear thrower was highly regarded by the *Capoques* and many of these men carried the marks of previous hunts. Long serrated scars on arms and legs as well as missing appendages testified to the ferocity of the sharks in the bay; indeed, several had died. The shark most sought after was *laka-wa-tanga-taka*...black-finned killer fish, but more often than not others were also taken. One of these was a much larger shark that the *Capoques* called *kena-tanga-taka*...terrible killer fish. This shark was usually taken near the mouths of rivers and streams. *Kena-tanga-taka,* because of its size and aggressiveness, was responsible for most of the injuries.

Several times the hunters would come across pods of dolphins frolicking in the water, but they were never harmed. They were called *qua-taka*...smiling fish and the *Capoques* believed that these mammals were the personification of their dead ancestors. To harm one in any way would bring bad luck to the individual and the tribe.

Alvar participated in several of these hunts, but only in a follow-up role. His canoe would tow the dispatched sharks back to the beach where the women would butcher and dry the meat. Hard as his life among the *Capoques* was, he enjoyed these hunts and the excitement they initiated.

The days of Fall progressed into Winter. This year, however, the *Capoques* had prepared well and the bad months passed without incident. It was during this time that Alvar made contact with Jeronimo Alaniz and Lope de Oviedo who were still on the island. Both had accompanied a hunting party of *Hans* who visited the *Capoque* camp. Among the two groups of *Indians,* there was much weeping as was the custom. The three *Christians* greeted each other warmly. It was Alvar's first time in months to talk in his native tongue. While alone with his compatriots Alvar shared his plan to escape from the *Capoques* when they migrated back to the mainland in the spring to pick blackberries. He told them of his continued harsh treatment and his fear of dying here before he could return to *Panuco*. Oviedo listened intently but seemed strangely distantfrom the idea.

"*Alguacil*, the *Han* have treated me well and I fear venturing out among the unknown tribes on the mainland will result in our death."

Alvar considered this and answered, "*Senor* Oviedo, if you remain here with the *Han* there is a chance you will never see *Spain* again."

"I think that providence has already made that determination, *Alguacil*. My chances of surviving this ordeal that God has given us are probably better if I remain safe, here with the *Han*."

Alvar turned to the scribe. "And, *Senor* Alaniz, what are your thoughts on leaving this place?"

"*Alguacil*, it is true that the *Han* have treated us well, but I long to return to *Spain* and my countrymen. When the time is right I will gladly join you in your journey."

After the short visit, the two groups separated to go their respective ways.

April, 1530

Galveston Bay

It had been many months since Alvar had met with his companions on *Malhado Island* and more than a year that he had lived with the *Capoques*. Since that time he had made numerous trips across the bay and visited the many islands and estuaries that lined the coast. Once again the *Capoques* had moved to the mainland, where his treatment had remained harsh and he resolved, more than ever, to escape. It was the season for *Kena*...the turtle, and although the *Capoques* would not travel to *Malhado* during this time, they did visit the other smaller islands in search of the eggs. On this morning, Alvar accompanied two men from the village in a single canoe. The island they landed on was very narrow and no more than half a league in length. Dominated by a thick growth of chest-high grass, only a smattering of small trees dotted its surface. After coming ashore each traveled down the beach in search of the telltale signs of a nest. At midday, Alvar noticed that both of the men were a considerable distance down the beach and that he, in his meanderings, was only a short distance from the canoe. He resolved then and there to make his escape.

As the two *Indians* became involved with digging up a nest, Alvar hurriedly slid the canoe into the water and jumped in. The bay was calm and he paddled furiously. On the beach, one of the *Caoques* raised up and saw the canoe moving off. Alerting his companion he raced toward the water and dove in. The *Capoques* were magnificent swimmers and he stroked rapidly toward the canoe, but the distance was too great. As Alvar looked back for the last time the lone swimmer was treading water and shaking his fist at the receding canoe while his companion, standing in the surf, looked on.

When out of sight Alvar reversed his direction and turned south paralleling the mainland. He continued more than a league before turning shoreward. Carefully scanning the beach, he put ashore at an isolated spit of land surrounded by mangroves. He slid the canoe in amongst the branches, hiding it from view. Staying low, he made his way to a raised dune and gazed around him. There was no sign of humanity in any direction.

At some distance to the west the beach grass and sand dunes melted into a plain of low scrub; after that, and far in the distance, stretched a woodland. It was there that a tribe called the *Charrucans* resided. Alvar had become acquainted with these people in a few brief encounters while hunting with the *Capoques*. They were a warlike people that the *Capoques* tried to avoid but they were known for treating their slaves and captives well. It was with them that Alvar would seek refuge. Rising up, he cautiously made his way inland along a faint trail. Still wary of being pursued by the *Capoques*, he stopped every few yards to listen and check his surroundings.

As he walked along, an explosion of quail erupted from their hideout in the thick grass. Twenty or thirty birds rocketed skyward in a profusion of feathers and noise. Alvar, startled, dropped to the ground, his heart racing. Long after the covey had disappeared he lay there listening. Finally, raising his head above the vegetation he scanned the area. Other than a few sea birds and a pair of hawks circling high above, nothing seemed to be disturbing the tranquility of the place. He continued on.

The transition from grassland to forest was marked by mottes of live oaks. They seemed like islands in a sea of grass, but as he continued inland the trees became more numerous and the grasses gave way to leafy shrubs. Since landing on shore, Alvar had not drunk, and now the thirst was overwhelming. Ahead was a swale surrounded by cat tails. The trail at this point seemed more heavily traveled and he proceeded cautiously. Parting the thick reeds he stepped into a small pond of water and dropped to his knees. The water was brackish but fit to drink. After skimming off the top layer of insects and grass, he drank deeply. Raising up, Alvar caught his breath and then plunged his head into the water. The coolness felt good and he sat there rubbing his hair and face. The sting of the salt from his sweat trickled down into his eyes. He splashed more water on himself.

Distracted as he was, Alvar suddenly felt the presence of someone watching him. Turning slowly he saw them, five *Indians* peering through the reeds, their copper-colored bodies blending in perfectly with their surroundings. Slowly he stood and raised his arms out to the side to show that he had no weapons. They came forward and Alvar recognized one of them. Tall and wonderfully proportioned, this one had a distinctive scar that began at his left ear and terminated just below his lip. The lip was disfigured and Alvar remembered that he spoke with a lisp. It was this man that Alvar approached.

His name was Wa-ton-ta and he was *Charrucan.* This band of natives spoke a language somewhat different from either the *Capoques* or the *Han,* but like all the other tribes of the area, they could converse with each other through hand talk and a type of pidgin jargon. Alvar had learned some of this jargon on previous trips to the mainland and now struggled to explain that he had left the *Capoque* and wished to join the *Charrucan.*

Squatting down, Watonta and the others listened intently to what Alvar had to say, only occasionally answering with a grunt or a gesture that they understood. When finished, he also squatted down and waited for their decision. It was anti-climactic. Watonta nodded his head in the affirmative and signaled for Alvar to follow them. Rising up, the six men moved out as one. The *Charrucans* were hunters, and just down the path to the watering hole, the party stopped to pick up a deer. Tied feet first to a pole, the animal had already been gutted. Watonta signaled for Alvar to pick up one end of the pole as he picked up the other. The pole, now suspended between the two men was lopsided and the deer carcass slid down toward the much shorter Alvar. The *Charrucans* laughed heartily as Alvar struggled to support the load, now unevenly distributed to his side. Presently, one of the other *Charrucans* pushed Alvar aside and shouldered the other end of the pole.

As they proceeded further west the forest seemed to close in around them. As he had been since the start of the expedition, Alvar was fascinated by the size of the trees they encountered. Straight and tall, soaring seventy feet or more into the sky, the bases of the largest oaks could not be spanned by three men holding hands. The forest floor was amazingly clear with only low shrubs and ferns dominating the understory. At one point along the trail, the five *Charrucans* abruptly stopped and squatted down. Alvar mimicked their actions, not knowing what the reason was. All the Indians affixed arrows to their bows and stared intently ahead. Watonta nudged Alvar and pointed to a section of the forest. Alvar could see them now, a sow and two bear cubs. The sow was looking directly at them, sniffing the air. The cubs looked on from just behind her.

"The bear mother will defend her children," Watonta mumbled. He lifted his bow, drawing it back ever so slowly. The others did the same. This was a large black bear and Alvar was familiar with the ferocity of these beasts when protecting their young.

With a sudden rush, the sow charged forward directly at them. The ferociousness of the sow's attack was enhanced by the shrubbery and limbs she tore through. At this moment Alvar did something quite unexpected, even to himself. Screaming in *Spanish* and madly waving his arms he stood up and charged the bear. So unexpected were his actions that the charging sow abruptly stopped and turned in flight. Calling to her cubs, all three disappeared into the forest.

No longer concerned about the bear, the five *Charrucans* lowered their bows and looked strangely at Alvar. He was breathing hard, adrenaline pumping through his veins, and for the life of him, he could not fathom why he had done what he did. He just stood there staring into the forest in the direction in which the sow and two cubs had disappeared.

Watonta was the first to approach, lightly touching the white man's arm. Alvar turned a wild look still in his eye. The *Indian*, a good head taller than the *Spaniard*, actually took a step backward. Presently, the other *Charrucans* also gathered around. They talked among themselves, repeating stories of what they had just seen. Finally, Watonta turned again towards Alvar.

"Wasapi-tun-loki, we have never seen anything such as this."

Alvar, not knowing the meaning of this word, asked what it meant. Watonta, with some difficulty, tried to explain. Pointing toward the section of forest where the bear and her cubs had disappeared, he mouthed the word *Wasapi* over and over again. Next, he walked back and forth in front of Alvar, exaggerating each step. The other *Charrucans* howled with laughter as he did this. *"Tun, tun"* he repeated. Alvar was familiar with the word for "walk."

It was the final word, *"Loki"* that gave Alvar the most problem. Watonta became more subdued. He pointed at the sky and to all things around him and then touched his chest before repeating the word *"Loki."*

From that moment on Alvar Nunez Cabeza de Vaca was known to the *Charrucans* and indeed, all other tribes that he would encounter, as Wasapi-tun-loki...Spirit Bear Walker.

August, 1530

On the Brazos River Near Present-Day Freeport, Texas

The *Charrucans* readily accepted Alvar into their society, and the fact that he had already been given an Indian name for a noteworthy event immensely helped his position. On the mainland, most of the tribes were in a state of constant conflict. The groups fought constantly over territory, food, and women, in that order. Allies one week could be enemies the next. Many times the combat was ritualistic with few injuries to either side, other times the violence was brutal and many died.

Alvar was not considered a warrior, but because of his uniqueness, he became an emissary between the tribes. Already proficient in hand talk and conversant in at least two *Indian* languages, he quickly learned the parlance of the other local clans. At first, he participated in the more trivial disputes, but as his judgment became more respected, Wasapitunloki's fame began to spread.

During the late summer, a neighboring band called the *Kohani* had entered into a protracted conflict. They had been raided by an inland group called the *Cavas* who took many hostages. A counter-raid by the *Kohani* had likewise killed several *Cavas*. Now each side desired to end the conflict because the season of the *noch-tli*...paddle cactus, was close at hand. In this area along the coast, the paddle cactus grows in abundance. At the height of the summer months, the *noch-tli* emit buds that enlarge quickly into a fruit called *ton-a*. It is this fruit that is prized by all the tribes of the area and, in fact, becomes the sole source of nourishment during the months of September and October. At this season of plenty, all of the tribes put aside their disagreements and join together in the harvest. Both the *Kohani* and *Cavas* desired a quick resolution to their problem. As a result, both tribes requested Wasapi-tun-loki to act as an emissary in the negotiations.

This was a prestigious position and it helped to enhance Alvar's status. He would meet both tribes at a timber blow-down area known by both parties. It was early morning and as he prepared to leave, Watonta approached him with a deerskin containing a bundle of reeds and a bag of shells.

"What is this," asked Alvar.

"Wasapi, we desire many things that the *Cavas* have, and they, in turn, desire the things that we have. You will take these seashells and cockles to them, for they value them. In return you will bring back the rocks that we use for our tools and weapons, and the red powder that we use to color our bodies."

Alvar understood that the "rocks" were the flint pieces that were shaped and fitted to shafts for arrowheads, spear points, and scrapers. The red powder was ocher and in addition to coloring their bodies, it was used for ceremony and as a dye for clothing. Both of these resources were scarce or non-existent by the coast, but readily available further inland. Peering into the bag he saw a variety of seashells, some large and jagged, others like snail shells, very small and colorful.

Watonta, anticipating his next question explained, "The *Cavas* use the large shell pieces to make a knife which they use to cut the pods of certain plants. The small pieces and snail shells are bored and strung together and worn by their women. The reeds are much desired and are used in the construction of their arrow shafts."

Alvar gathered up the trade goods in a crude backpack, the bundle of reed extending out a foot on either side of him, and proceeded inland. Two guides accompanied him, both young men, not yet warriors. Alvar had been assured that because of his mission, he had special immunity and would be treated with respect by all that he met along the way.

The meeting place was five leagues inland. The land that they passed over became less timbered and increasingly dry. At the halfway point the guides altered their course to the west. It was noon when Alvar spotted a massive tree line on the horizon. In the dryness, he knew this was the mark of a large river. He could smell water, even at this distance. The guides quickened their pace and Alvar struggled to keep up. Two hours passed before they reached the water. Before them was a river of striking beauty. The main channel was no more than two hundred yards in width, but the wetlands extended out hundreds of yards on either side with massive cypress trees growing in abundance. In the drier areas, stands of enormous oaks, hickory, and willow trees skirted the perimeter.

What amazed Alvar was the transition between the dense forest and the dry land from which they had just come. Here they stopped briefly to drink before continuing on. A well-traveled path followed the river and walking was easy. Finally, as the shadows began to lengthen in the late afternoon sun, the three men entered an area of complete devastation. Huge trees lay twisted on the ground, their root balls torn from the earth. The path of ruin extended out for half a league. Near the water's edge was a clear area, scoured of all vegetation as if by a giant sickle. It was here that they came upon the delegations from both the *Kohani* and *Cavas*. Each was camped at opposite ends of the clearing. By mutual agreement neither party carried weapons. Alvar directed his guides to move to the center of the clearing. Here they laid down mats which had been brought for the occasion.

Alvar seated himself while the two guides remained standing. Motioning to the warring parties, he indicated that they should join him. Three men from each side came forward while the remainder drew closer, but at a respectable distance. Neither side spoke and the silence was overwhelming. Alvar stood and walked to the side of the clearing where he picked up two small sticks. Carefully he trimmed both so that each looked identical except for the length. Hiding his actions he held them tightly in his fist and walked back to the center.

Speaking in the combined pidgin language that both sides understood, Alvar said, "In my hand are two sticks, one shorter, one longer. Each side will draw one of the sticks. The side drawing the longest stick will speak first, and I will listen. When finished, the side drawing the shorter stick will speak and again, I will listen."

He extended his fist and a member from each side approached. They seemed perplexed, each closely studying the sticks whose length Alvar had carefully concealed. Finally, one of the *Kohanis* reached out and slowly drew one of the sticks from Alvar's outstretched fist. Alvar turned to the *Cavas* who did likewise. The *Cavas* stick was longest and the man beamed with pride as he turned and showed it to the others of his group. For a moment it looked as if the *Kohanis* would protest, but Alvar turned and pointed to the mats, indicating that they should sit.

They did.

In a lengthy discourse, the *Cavas* spelled out all their grievances. Their initial raid, according to them, was in response to the *Kohanis* encroaching on their territory. They were quick to point out that no lives had been taken and only a few women had been taken as hostages. The counter-raid by the *Kohanis* and the taking of lives had escalated the dispute. For a moment the assemblage looked as if it may break down as members from each side shouted, some shaking their fists. Once again Alvar controlled the situation. He stood and sternly indicated that the next one who spoke out of turn would be ejected from the discussion. Surprisingly, the sharp discourse ceased and the discussion continued. *Wasapitunloki's,* presence was indeed respected. While standing, Alvar addressed both sides.

"I will ask each of you to tell me what it is you want and what would bring peace between the *Kohani* and *Cavas*." He indicated for the *Kohani* to speak first. Their spokesman, a stocky and older member of the tribe, briefly conferred with his companions, then stood and responded. When through, he sat and Alvar turned to the *Cavas* delegation. Their spokesman, an extremely tall andfrightening-looking individual, made his requests.

And so it continued, with Alvar as intermediary they bantered back and forth until after an hour both sides agreed on the price of peace.

The *Cavas* would return their *Kohani* hostages. In addition, the *Kohani* would make amends for the lives taken with twenty deer skins.

The proceedings were over.

What happened next surprised Alvar. All of the Indians began to cry; *Kohani* and *Cavas* embraced as if they had not seen each other for years. The crying lasted for an hour. During this time Alvar spread the wares that Watonta had given him on the ground. With the help of the *Charrucan* guides he successfully bartered for everything he had carried with him. The bag that had contained shells and cockles now was loaded with pieces of flint and red ocher and a bale of deer skins replaced the bundle of reeds.

As he prepared to leave, each of the Indians of both tribes, fifty or more, embraced Alvar one by one until he thought his ribs would crack. They proceeded to cry and wail once again. Shouldering his pack, *Alvar* and his guides began their journey back. Behind them, the crying continued until muted by the distance and only the crunch of their footsteps broke the silence. Overhead a hawk, circling in a developing thermal, called out, "Creeee, Creeee."

September 1530

Inland, Near Present-Day La Grange, Texas

The journey back had been uneventful except for the sighting of four bison. Far in the distance, Alvar at first thought them to be cattle and for a moment entertained the thought that their *Spanish* owners would be near. As they drew closer, however, his hopes faded. He had never seen beasts such as these. Much larger than European cattle, their shaggy head and forefront seemed out of proportion with the rest of the body. Drawing closer, the two guides squatted down and carefully watched the animals. Alvar did the same. From behind a mass of brush, a fifth bison emerged, this one much larger than the other four. Testicles hanging to its knee, this was obviously a bull, and the one that the two guides were most concerned about. It was huge. While the others grazed, it seemed preoccupied with investigating its territory. The bull moved closer and then stopped. Its nostrils flaring, it picked up the scent of the three humans. The *Charrucans* remained absolutely motionless, Alvar did the same. He was terrified. This was the biggest animal he had ever seen. Still testing the wind, the breath from its nostrils left clouds of condensation in the cool air. Each exhale was accompanied by a loud "hoooooooph." Raising small clouds of dust, the animal pawed the ground with its front hoofs. It looked as if it would charge at any moment. Alvar's thoughts flashed to the bullfights he had attended in *Seville*. The moment seemed to last forever. Then, slowly...ever so slowly, the bull backed up, all the time keeping his eye on the three humans. Then, with a loud "whoof" it turned and cantered away, the four cows following in turn.

Still frozen in place, Alvar and the two guides watched the animals until they disappeared from view. Only then did he relax.

"What are these animals called?" He asked his two companions.

"*Yani-cee*," they both answered in unison, saying that seeing such animals was a good omen because, in these parts, they were scarce. Further north and west, however, they existed in numbers that could not be counted.

Returning to the village of the *Charrucans,* Alvar became increasingly more involved with the trading of goods to the other inhabitants of the area. Word of this strange, bearded white man began to spread. Many times as he entered other villages, the inhabitants would line the path to gaze at *Wasapitunloki* in wonder. Even among warring tribes, he was unharmed. Traveling freely through this rugged land he was greeted warmly by all with offerings of food and shelter.

A group of Indians known as the *Payaya* lived seven days travel inland. Their quality of red ochre was superior to all others, and for this Alvar undertook the long journey. Traveling alone with a large pack of trade goods strapped to his back, he was armed with only a knife and spear. For food, he carried dried fish and dug roots.

The journey had been long and arduous. For a time he had been trailed by wolves that eyed him from behind cover. As night fell he was forced to sleep in a tree to avoid the animals that circled his campfire, their eyes reflecting red in the distance. In the morning they were gone. Barefoot as he was, snakes were always a concern and he learned to always keep one eye on the ground as he walked, quickly becoming familiar with the fearsome buzz of the snakes that carried rattles on their tail. These were most fearsome but good to eat and he killed several on the journey.

The further west he traveled the more sparse the land became. The trees that existed were to be found only in lowlands and the streams that meandered through the country. Now, only a sea of grass greeted him, and the bison, the *Yani-cee*, became more numerous. He was careful to avoid them.

The village of the *Payaya* was situated next to a stream that cut through the vast grassland. First encountering a group of children playing just outside the camp, Alvar watched them run in terror at seeing him. He stopped there, not wanting to cause too much of a commotion. A group of armed men accompanied by their chief quickly came forward to investigate. These were rough-looking people. All of the men had wooden pegs inserted through slits in their chests and their faces were festooned with a fearsome array of tattoos. Not as tall as the coastal people, they were nevertheless well-muscled. Completely naked and barefoot, several carried fearsome-looking war clubs, and the others held bows fitted with arrows. The chief, an older man, but no less fearsome, stepped forward and spoke in a language unfamiliar to Alvar.

Raising his hand in greeting, Alvar spoke his name and thumped his chest. "I am Wasapi-tun-loki. "

The chief, recognizing the name, turned to the other men and explained. All lowered their weapons and nodded in understanding. The chief, whose name was Takoni-ak-ah came over and embraced Alvar, clapping him on the back at the same time. He followed the men back to the village and was assigned a place of honor in the chief's hut. These dwellings were constructed of willow saplings and covered with bison hides scraped clean of hair. Inside, the ground had been swept and covered with other hides, hair side up. Takoniakah's hut was somewhat larger than the others. Outside, his two wives were busily roasting what appeared to be several rabbits. The two women wore a single garment of deer hide that covered them to their knees. In each earlobe, a small wooden peg had been inserted and was adorned with feathers or shells attached by rawhide strips. Unlike the men, whose hair was bobbed off shoulder length, the women's hair, coal black, hung to their waists. Looking around, Alvar noted that most of the women had tattoos on their faces, hands, and arms. The young women were not unattractive to his *European* standards.

Before any trading began Alvar was offered water to drink and the rabbit to eat. Takoniakah joined him along with several of the tribe's elders. Communicating mostly with hand talk they were soon joined by a younger man that spoke the language of the coastal people. Through him, Alvar learned much about these people and they, in turn, were fascinated to learn of his story, his adventures, and the great lands to the east across the water. The talk lasted well into the night. Finally, Takoniakah announced that they would trade in the morning and motioned for Alvar to join him. Inside the hut, Alvar was joined by one of the chief's wives who shed her deerskin garment and lay down beside him. Taken aback, Alvar looked to Takoniakah who was already well into lovemaking with the other wife. Apparently, this was their custom, for it was a night of wild sex and the wife, her name was Soni-la-ke, was insatiable, continually waking an exhausted Alvar to perform again and again.

Alvar spent several days with the *Payaya* filling his backpack with flints, ocher, hides, tassels made from deer from deer hair, and a particular kind of glue that the *Payaya's* used to adhere their flint arrowheads to the shaft. Each night with Sonilake was a repeat of the last and it was with some relief that he took his leave. Loaded down with the trade items, Alvar left the village and proceeded eastward. Looking back he made a final wave to Takoniakah who, standing with his two wives, waved back. He couldn't help but chuckle to himself, for if he made it back to civilization, who would ever believe his stories?

Accompanied for several leagues by three members of the tribe, Alvar traveled east. When his companions finally took their leave, he was heavily loaded with the burdensome trade items such that his back-pack was piled high above his head. Watching them leave, Alvar noted the darkening of the western sky with some apprehension. Throughout the remainder of the day, the strengthening storm slowly approached as Alvar hurried along. His load, however, was heavy and he stopped frequently to rest.

By mid-afternoon, the landscape was bathed in an eerie darkness. The temperature dropped. Everything seemed to take on a strange greenish hue and the wind began to blow in gale force. Alvar looked for some kind of shelter, but there was none. The first giant drops began to fall just as he spotted a low depression in the ground. Hunkering down, he unrolled and spread one of the deer hides over his head. In the distance, he heard the roar of the deluge. He pulled the hide closer around him. The rain fell as if poured from a bucket and cascaded off the deerskin in torrents. The lightning and thunder were immediate, such that it seemed like one event. The smell of *azufre*...brimstone, filled his nostrils. So hard did it rain that the depression in which he lay began to fill with water. As he prepared to move something crashed into the small of his back. Uncomprehending, Alvar watched as a ball of ice as big as his fist rolled off the deerskin. Another hit him, and then another. He flinched painfully with each strike. Never had he seen hail of such size. Curled into a fetal position he protected his head with one of the heavy packs. Geysers of water exploded around him and the ground soon became covered with ice balls.

The deluge lasted for some time and then abruptly stopped. Lying in the icy water, Alvar threw back the deerskin and stood. For as far as he could see the ground was white, looking like a winter landscape. It was strangely quiet. He gathered up his trade items and once again began his trek. Walking on the ice balls was treacherous and painful as he moved slowly along, frequently stopping to rub his feet to warm them up.

The rain had stopped. Far ahead Alvar could see the diagonal lines of the torrent as it moved across the grasslands. Ribbons of lightening filled the sky. On a raised knoll that was clear of ice, Alvar stopped and rested. His arms and legs were still stung from the impact of the hailstones. Overhead the first patches of blue sky began to show. To the west and south, shafts of sunlight pierced the clouds and reflected off the icy ground. Pulling a piece of dried deer meat from his pack Alvar tore a piece off with his teeth and sat cross-legged on the ground.

Desperately alone, he spoke aloud in the language of the *Charrucan.*

"I am *Wasapitunloki* and, praise God, today I am alive!"

CHAPTER 10

Spirit Song Rock

Mira-ton-peechi

"It is called mira-ton-peechi...Spirit Song Rock. It was from here that our people first came into this world. It is very sacred. At night our ancestors call to us from its top and we can even see their campfires."

Sept 1530-April 1532

An Extended Period Where Cabeza De Vaca Traveled Throughout South Texas

And so, Cabeza de Vaca, the merchant, traveled extensively among the indigenous tribes of Texas. His fame as a trader and medicine man spread rapidly. Visits from Wasapi-tun-Laki were treated as a celebration. The people of the various villages would turn out with food and gifts when he arrived. Dancing would continue long into the night. Women would ask him to touch their newborns to ensure a long life. In the morning the sick and injured would be presented to him. Alvar would linger over these individuals, making the sign of the cross and breathing on them as he had seen Wacch-on-a do to him. He had learned that the more elaborate these ministrations were, the more in awe the *Indians* were of his services. In addition to his trading wares, Alvar now carried a small deerskin bag that he filled with potions and talismans. He would pass a large golden eagle feather over the bodies of the afflicted, all the time repeating a *Pater Noster* or *Ave Maria*. Secretly he prayed that God would not punish him for presuming that he had healing powers,

Many times Alvar would have to administer to individuals with broken bones. He learned to carefully probe the afflicted area with his fingers to establish the extent of the fracture. When in need of help in setting a broken arm or leg he would perform an elaborate ritual in which his assistants would be consecrated before being allowed to touch the victim. Together they would straighten the limb, deftly manipulating it until the bones felt aligned. Then using willow branches, moss, and hide straps he would bind the break tightly.

Snake bites were one of his most frequent maladies and one of the most difficult to treat. Depending on the snake, a strong male adult had a 50-50 chance of survival. Women's survival rate, surprisingly, was somewhat higher. It was the young and the old that had little or no chance. To explain the deaths Alvar revealed that snakes were the devil incarnate and in each case he would have to go through a life-and-death struggle that, in some cases, would last for days. Isolating himself with the victim he would emerge at the end of the struggle looking bedraggled. Only then would he talk of the victim, whether they had lived or died.

During his treatments, some died, but surprisingly, most of the people that Alvar treated survived and returned to health. For this, he had no explanation except for the tremendous healing powers of the *Indians* and the mercy of God looking after him.

For his services, Wasapi-tun-Laki was provided with food, shelter, trinkets, and women. He soon lost count of the women he had lain with. At one village visited the year before, a woman of the tribe presented him with a baby to bless. The male child was distinctly white-skinned and only then did he realize that it was his. For this Alvar was burdened with guilt thinking that his son would only know life as a savage in this forbidding land. He was partially placated by the fact that the child was held in great reverence by the rest of the tribe with the promise that he would grow to be a great warrior and chief. Before leaving he kissed his young son and prayed fervently that God would watch and protect the infant and, eventually, the man.

The days passed into weeks, the weeks to months, and the months to years. Alvar's trading forays took him further and further inland. News of his arrival preceded him and crowds would gather as he neared villages. Even local wars were postponed as he passed through their land. Each tribe that he encountered was unique in their own respect, each had their own language or, at least, variations of languages he had encountered before. He had become fluent in some of them and semi-fluent in most. For those he didn't understand, the hand talk seemed to be a universal form of communication. The goods that he brought were prized, but the healing and stories he related were most looked forward to. Long into the night, Alvar would talk about his travels and life in the civilized world. The great cities, strange animals, and military exploits of which he talked were listened to in quiet amazement. Many times there were no words to express that which he described; for these Alvar would draw pictures in the sand. These likenesses were revered and the *Indians* took great pains to preserve them, many times copying the artwork onto the smooth sides of stretched skins.

The vastness of the land at first scared and baffled him, but growing accustomed to its challenges he experienced a strange fondness for everything around him. His body had grown hard and he could walk barefoot for hours in the blazing sun. Sleeping on the ground he seldom covered himself, even in the coolness of the nights. Caught in the open in rain and hail he would hunker down in whatever protection he could find. Save for a breechcloth, his nakedness was complete. He carried a spear, that is, a long straight pole slit at one end to accept a flint blade held in place by deer hide strips wrapped tightly to hold it in place. The spear was most useful for removing snakes from the trail, stirring a camp-fire, and as a walking stick, although once he had used it to discourage a hungry mountain lion that had been stalking him. Hanging from a strap around his neck was a fine obsidian blade fitted to a carved mesquite handle, a gift from a *casique* whose son he had administered to. Carried on his back was a load of trade goods that at any time equaled half his body weight. Sea shells, reeds, obsidian, flint, ocher, and furs were his usual commodities, but other, more unusual items could also be found: porcupine quills, penis bones from the male raccoon, eagle feathers, bear claws, and bison horns. Completing his outfit, Alvar carried a bow and several arrows. Although nowhere near as proficient with it as the *Indios*, he was able to occasionally bring down a rabbit, grouse, or even a turkey.

The land to the west presented a never-ending variety of environments. There were hills, rock formations, limestone cliffs, caves, beautiful valleys of trees and lush grasses. In the dry areas, cactus and other drought-resistant plants flourished. Further to the west the land began to rise up and the hills turned into mountains. From these high places, he could look out at what lay before him, a vast plain interrupted by yet another ridge. Once at the top he would rest after the long climb and take in the panorama of everything below. Many times a *Torbellino*...dust devil, swirled across the plain, sending clouds of debris high into the air. Further on he might see a threatening storm, its darkness in contrast to the brightly lit hills and valleys in the foreground. He would watch the lightning streak across this blackness in magnificent displays. In the quietness of his lofty perch, the ensuing rumble would come to him mournfully as it echoed along the valley below. In the valleys, he would occasionally see small herds of the *vacas peludas*...shaggy cows, meandering along in search of grazing. The *Charrucans* had called them *Yani-cee,* but each of the tribes that Alvar had encountered had a different name for the huge beasts.

On the high ridges clusters of fleet-footed, goat-like animals, abounded. They looked somewhat like goats but it was their flat horns and two colored coats that defined them. Not really "goats," the animals stood nearly three feet tall, had two flattened horns, and their overall tan color was marked by a series of white bans that wrapped halfway around the neck. Because of the colorization, Alvar called them *barrendos*. These *barrendos* and the *conejo orejas largas*...long-eared rabbits, Alvar enjoyed watching the most. The speed of the *barrendos* and the jumping ability of the *conejos* fascinated him.

April, 1532

Traveling Inland From the Charrucan Village on the Mainland

Winter months were always brutal. Traveling in winter across such rugged land was not prudent and it was a time when the *Indios* remained in their dwellings and ventured out very little. After spending his third winter with the *Churacans* Alvar was happy to once again be traveling inland in good weather. He had picked his way northwest, stopping at several villages along the way. The route he took was through an extremely rolling and hilly country. He was in search of a people who called themselves *Sana* and lived at the confluence of two rivers. The *Sana* were in possession of flint and a particular kind of yellow ocher pigment which when mixed with copper resulted in shades of blue and green, much prized. The *Sana* were not popular, however, because it was said they ate human flesh. It wasn't until Alvar had received a runner who requested his presence that he decided to make the journey. The runner had related how a son of one of the *Sana* leaders was besieged by uncontrollable fits and had asked for the white medicine man known as Wasapi-tun-laki. The runner, a boy of perhaps 16, would lead him. His name was Peleowa and it wasn't until well into the journey that Alvar learned that he was the brother of the afflicted. After 11 days they came upon a large river that flowed from the northwest. Peleowa called this river *Pashohono*.

It was a word not familiar to Alvar.

When he asked Peleowa its meaning the youngster scratched his head and answered. "Wasapi, it has been called this name as long as I can remember, but it is just a word that means *Long River*."

From here they continued up the river until reaching another river, much shallower than the first, that flowed from west to east. This river Peleowa called *Tato-ato* and before Alvar could ask he explained it was so named because of the profusion of flat rocks along its course. They followed this river for 3 days before leaving it and proceeding to the north. As they traveled along, fields of blue flowers contrasted with the profusion of new spring growth that was everywhere. It was from one of these fields at the summit of a hill that Alvar first viewed a great mound of bare rock. It was a naked dome of exposed granite that seemed to overpower everything around it. A strange pinkish color, it seemed so out of place.

For a moment Alvar just stared at it before turning to Paleowa, who replied.

"It is called *mira-ton-peechi...*Spirit Song Rock. It was from here that our people first came into this world. It is very sacred. At night our ancestors call to us from its top and we can even see their campfires."

They traveled closer and as night fell camped at its base, the natural megalith towering high above them. It was a particularly clear night and the stars were shown with an eerie brilliance. Alvar bent to the task of gathering firewood, for the nights were still cold and Paleowa had killed a rabbit that needed cooking.

"Crack!" From somewhere above them the noise echoed across the expanse. Alvar jumped and dropped his load of sticks. He scanned the rock above him but could see nothing.

"What could that be?" He wondered to himself.

"Crack...Crack!" The two noises followed in quick succession. Alvar squatted down, not sure what these noises were or what they represented.

It was quiet for a moment. Not seeing any immediate threat, Alvar rose up and gathered the sticks that he had dropped. Reaching the campsite he had begun the process of starting a fire when a low groan emanated from the hill above. Paleowa had just returned from gathering firewood as well and Alvar looked questionably at him.

"What is this I am hearing from the hill?"

Looking up at the great white dome above them, Paleowa thought a moment before answering. "Wasapi-tun-Laki, it is as I said. This is spirit rock and the home of our ancestors. At night they call out to us. Sometimes, when the night is dark, we can see their campfires glowing far above."

Alvar looked up and studied the hill. White against the star-lit night, its presence seemed to dominate the sky. "I would like to climb it in the morning."

Paleowa looked horrified.

"Wasapi, it is very dangerous, only our holy men dare to go to the top. They talk of spirits and strange things inhabiting Spirit Rock. They say that once you reach the top you will become invisible."

"I am not afraid. In the morning I will climb to the top. You wait for me here and when I return we will resume our journey."

The noises continued through the night. In the early hours, Alvar arose to urinate. The sky had clouded over and in the darkness, the summit of Spirit Rock was no longer visible. Something caught his eye. High above a faint light materialized and then disappeared.

There it was again, this time lasting longer, its brightness just perceptible before it faded. At its brightest, a ghostly outline of the summit was just visible. The light seemed to dance about, much like watching the glow of a fire, but it was very faint.

Alvar rubbed the sleep from his eyes and then sat down on a rock to stare above. Only once more did he see the light and this time fleetingly. After that, the faint glow of dawn began to permeate the eastern sky. Stirring the fire and adding a handful of branches, he warmed a small piece of the rabbit and ate it. Paleowa was awake and Alvar related to him the sighting of the light on the summit. Once again, Paleowa warned him not to go to the top. The clouds that had blackened the sky were now dissipating and the white dome of spirit rock seemed to glow as the sun's rays illuminated it.

Alvar began his climb.

The journey upward was steep but relatively easy. The base of the hill was marked by many small rocks that, in preceding eons, had tumbled down from above. Cactus, brush, and mesquite trees extended upward for about half the way. Higher up, boulders the size of houses caused Alvar to pick his way carefully, jumping from one to the other as he moved along. Past the boulders the great mass of the granite dome predominated, its surface fractured into huge slabs of rock.

Alvar paused before reaching the top to take in the view that spread out before him. He thought of how an eagle must feel as it soared through the sky. In all directions, the hilly, dry country continued to the horizon with no sign of human habitation. He looked to the south. That was the direction of his salvation. That was the direction where he would find *Spanish* civilization and rescue. He wondered if that would ever happen. Turning, he continued his climb.

Not quite at the top yet, Alvar felt uneasy, as if he was being watched. He scanned the area around him.

Nothing.

He continued upward and upon reaching the top was surprised to see a small mass of vegetation present on this bare rock. What lay before him was a depression that had collected rain-water. Stunted grass and shrubs grew in the detritus deposited over millenniums.

He squatted down to drink and then noticed something else in the rocks to the left. A mountain lion was watching his every move. Armed only with the spear that he used for a walking stick and the knife that hung around his neck, he began backing up to a wall of boulders that lay just to his right. *El Puma* watched him intently. He had had encounters with these beasts before, all of them terrifying. Nearing the boulders he caught sight of a fissure that formed a small protected hollow in the rocks. It was a den. Inside three sets of blue eyes stared back at him...the lion's kittens.

Realizing his mistake, Alvar slowly began to move in the opposite direction, putting as much distance between the den and himself as possible. *El Puma* crept forward and slowly moved toward the den, never taking its piercing gaze off Alvar. At the den, the kittens came forward to greet their mother. For a moment she surveyed the kittens. Re-insured, the lion returned her gaze to the human interloper who now was moving rapidly away. This was the last Alvar saw of *El Puma* but the memory of her stare would stay with him.

As Alvar moved away from the lion's den he came across the remnants of a campfire. Reaching down, he determined that the ashes were still warm. Strangely, there were no footprints or any other signs that would show someone had been there. Continuing on, Alvar briefly surveyed the area and then picked his way back down to the campsite where Paleowa was waiting in wide-eyed astonishment.

"Wasapi, you must certainly be a great medicine man, for I did not expect you to return."

Alvar talked of his journey and the things that he had seen and, of course, his encounter with the mountain lion and the abandoned campfire. Paleowa listened intently with a new reverence for this strange bearded white man. His only explanation was that the spirit that resided on the rock had disguised himself as a mountain lion and only because of Wasapi-tun-laki's great powers, he had let him live.

May, 1532

South Texas

After leaving spirit rock Alvar and Paleowa continued their trek to the northwest. This was indeed a land of strange and miraculous things. They passed towering rock formations, exposed cliffs of rock that looked every bit like the walls of some huge castle. Caves were everywhere, some extending only a short way into the rock formations, others seemingly without end. These, Paleowa explained, were the habitats of bad spirits.

Three days journey from Spirit Rock and across land broken with rifts, dry valleys, and high mesas they came to the confluence of two rivers. The larger of the two flowed from the west, the other from the southwest, together they continued on to the northeast. Paleowa proudly recounted that the larger river was called *Sana-pana*, named after his people. The smaller of the two was called *Wa-cera-pana*...river of many cliffs.

From the banks of the two waterways, the greenness of the trees, shrubs, and grasses were in stark contrast to the unrelenting dryness they had encountered in the past few days. They traveled only a short journey up the larger of the two rivers before encountering Paleowa's village. It was very large and extended to both sides of the river. The huts were constructed of willow branches intricately woven together and faced with dried mud. Several larger structures were situated throughout the community...meeting houses from which the elders of the *Sana* would meet and conduct business. Smoke from numerous cooking fires spiraled up into the clear sky, children chased each other around the huts while women gathered water from the river.

The children were the first to notice their approach. Startled, they stopped and stared. One girl, however, recognized Paleowa and yelled to the others before rushing to him.

Paleowa laughed aloud and caught the on-rushing child. "It is my sister, Selotakah!"

The children surrounded Paleowa but avoided Alvar. They made a sideways look at this strange human with hair growing from his face.

"Wasapi, they have never seen anyone like you." Paleowa grasped his sister with both hands and instructed her to fetch his father and the town elders. She was to tell them that he had arrived safely with Wasapi-tun-Laki, the white trader and medicine man of the Charrucans.

Soon, the two travelers were led to one of the large meeting houses where Paleowa's father sat within a circle of elders. Women from the village were busily bringing good things to eat and laying them on large flat stones that lay just outside the circle. Paleowa led him to his father's side.

"Wasapi-tun-Laki, this is my father Chen-o-saquani, leader of the *Sana.*"

Alvar had been previously instructed to grasp both hands of the sachem as a sign of respect. This he did and then continued down the line of elders, grasping the hands of each in turn. After greeting the last elder Alvar turned to the chief and inquired as to the health of his son. Chen-o-saquani was a large man still well formed at an age Alvar estimated to be about 50. His stern face was creased by time but his eyes were clear and piercing. Sitting cross-legged on the ground, he didn't answer the question but motioned for Alvar to sit opposite him. At the mention of his son, Alvar thought he saw a look of sadness pass across the leader's face.

"We will eat now and trade afterward!" Chen-o-saquani said and motioned toward the flat stones now piled high with food of all kinds. A thick broth of vegetables and meat was offered to him by one of the women. In it, Alvar could see generous portions of meat floating in the broth. He didn't eat it.

Turning to Paleowa, who was seated beside him, he asked in a low voice. "I have heard that the *Sana* eat human flesh, is this true?"

Looking down at Alvar's bowl of soup, Paleowa seemed amused. "No Wasapi, it is only during times of war that our medicine men consume the hearts of our victims. This ensures our success in battle. The soup in your bowl contains only the flesh of fish and deer."

Alvar nodded, and a little sheepishly began to eat.

During the feast, the elders talked about many things. They asked Alvar to describe his journey. What animals did he see, where did they find water, what route did they take? When Paleowa talked of Spirit Rock and Alvar's journey to the top, all other talk fell silent. Everyone listened with rapt attention. They asked Alvar to tell them again and again about his affair with *El Puma*, and the finding of the deserted campfire. These stories Alvar embellished as much as possible hoping it would elevate him in the eyes of the *Sana*.

It did.

After the food was consumed Chen-o-saquani rose and asked for Alvar to accompany him. They walked only a short distance to one of the many huts that surrounded the meeting house. A fire burned within. On entering, Alvar's eyes fell on the most beautiful woman he had ever seen. He was taken aback and paused at the doorway. She sat cross-legged by the fire next to a small boy. Her luxuriant hair, long and black, cascaded to the floor, spreading out around her. Looking up at Alvar, her dark eyes flashed with a brilliance that seemed to sear his soul. Clad in a deer skin shawl that extended to mid-thigh, her long legs seemed to capture everything in the room. Her eyes, however, were rent with sadness for the small sick child she was next to was her son.

It was with difficulty that Alvar turned to the child. A boy of about five years old, he resembled his mother, but had the large bones and wide shoulders of his father, Chen-o-saquani. The boy was thin, hollow-eyed, and listless. The skin of his arms and legs seemed to be covered with the remnants of a red rash. To Alvar, he looked undernourished.

Chen-o-saquani introduced his wife, her name was Mea-tona, and again, Alvar had trouble taking his eyes off her. The boy was Seoquana the youngest of their three children.

"Wasapi-tun-Laki, my son suffers much. He eats only occasionally and then has stomach sickness. There are times when it is very hard for him to breathe and these marks upon his skin never seem to go away."

Observing the youngster, Alvar was struck by something he had witnessed as a child while living in *Spain*. One of his Aunts had been plagued by a similar condition. Her sickness was accompanied by hives, vomiting, and extreme diarrhea. At times her breathing had become labored. She had wasted away in much distress until a physician from *Salamanca* diagnosed her condition as fish poisoning. The effects of eliminating fish from her diet had been immediate. To Alvar, the boy sitting before him exhibited the same symptoms. He questioned Chen-o-saquani and Mea-tona at length about the boy and what he ate. Living by the confluence of the two rivers, the people of this village depended heavily on fish for their diet. Convinced that this was the problem Alvar asked that he be left alone with the child.

Alvar knew that as Wasapi-tun-Laki he had to play to the *Indio's* superstitions. Using the charms and props that he had collected, he would perform an elaborate ceremony. Most importantly, however, he would pray to God that his actions would result in a curing of the affliction that plagued the young boy.

For over two hours Alvar performed his ministrations while outside Chen-o-saquani and Mea-tona waited with a gathering of many of the villagers. Occasionally, Alvar would call in Paleowa to interpret something or just to make the child more comfortable.

The boy was conscious but much distressed with stomach pains. Alvar said "I am Wasapi-tun-Laki and I am here to treat you. What is your name?"

The boy looked up at the strange bearded white man and uttered, "Seoquana...my name is Seoquana."

Reaching into his medicine bag Alvar produced several dried roots with which he began brewing a strong tea. As the water heated he circled the bed on which Seoquana lay, repeating a *Pater Nostra* and *Ave Maria* while making the sign of the cross. All of this he did in *Spanish* or *Latin* which to the young Indian boy was quite mysterious. From the fire that burned within the hut, Alvar extracted a hot rock and lay it on the boy's stomach. This he accompanied with another prayer while circling the heated stone with an eagle feather. Finally, when all of the tea had been consumed by Seoquana he fell into a deep sleep. Alvar emerged from the hut and walked over to where Chen-o-saquani and Mea-tona waited.

"Your son Seoquana now sleeps. When he awakes, feed him with only the animals that reside on the land, for the spirits have directed him not to eat anything that lives in the water. I have talked with these spirits and if they determine that Seoquana's heart is pure they will let him survive."

Mea-tona arose and squeezed Alvar's arm in thanks and then quietly entered the hut to look after her son. Chen-o-saquani nodded and clapped Alvar on the back before, he too, entered the hut.

During the next few days, Seoquana's health improved. The rash that covered his body had all but disappeared and the stomach sickness had left him. Soon he had joined the other children of the village in play. On the night of the fourth day Chen-o-saquan, hand in hand with his wife Mea-tona, spoke to Alvar.

"Your powers are great Wasapi-tun-Laki. I give you my wife to sleep with so that your powers can enter her and pass on to our offspring." With this, he offered her hand to Alvar. Taken aback, Alvar stammered out a reply. He knew that to refuse such an offer would be a grave insult.

He took Mea-tona's hand.

It was a night like no other. From the moment she dropped her deer skin shawl and stood resplendent in front of him, Alvar was a prisoner of her grace and charms. Her lovemaking was both wild and tender without any apparent inhibitions. Finally, just before dawn, they both fell into an exhausted sleep. It was well into the morning before Alvar awoke to an empty bed. Mea-tona had rejoined her husband.

Quickly gathering his few belongings and trade items, Alvar made ready to leave the *Sana.* Summoning all his courage he made a final visit to Chen-o-saquan's hut to check on the health of Seoquana and to thank the *sachem* for his hospitality. He had trouble returning Chen-o-saquan's gaze, for Alvar's *Christian* moralities were hard to put aside and he had just slept with the man's wife.

On this, their last meeting, Chen-o-saquani slapped him on the back and immediately put Alvar at ease. "Mea-tona says you were good to her and strong in your lovemaking."

Embarrassed, Alvar looked over at Mea-tona now tending to her healthy son Seaquana. She smiled at him and then shyly looked down.

"*Sachem,* I leave you now in the hope that you and your people will prosper."

As was the custom, Chen-o-saquan began to weep and enveloped Alvar in a bear hug. As he left the village all of the inhabitants were weeping. Some ran up just to touch him.

Before crossing over the river Paleowa rejoined him. "Wasapi-tun-Laki, I will accompany you for two days and then I must return."

Alvar paused at the river's edge and looked back at the village. All of the inhabitants were crying and waving farewell to him. It was a touching scene. There in the forefront was the *sachem* Chen-o-saquan with his wife Mea-tona standing next to him. Between them was their son Seoquana, now healthy and smiling. Alvar felt sure he had impregnated her. He said a silent prayer for his future offspring and then turned to begin his long journey back.

June, 1532

South Texas

It was a decision that Alvar had wrestled with many times. With his freedom, he could continue to the south and, hopefully, reach the *Spanish* settlement at *Panuco* and safety. But, what of his compatriots back on the coast and on *Malhado Island*? The last he had heard, several of the *Spaniards* were alive and living with the *Indians* on the coast. He had no idea as to how many survived or who they were. On *Malhado* two of his compatriots, Lope de Oviedo and Jeronimo de Alaniz remained alive and lived with the *Han*. Alvar had made several visits to the island and had discussed with them leaving and traveling down the coast to unite with whoever survived. De Alaniz was in agreement, but Lope de Oviedo was hesitant. Oviedo was living with a *Han* wife and had fathered two children by her. What concerned Oviedo more, however, was the fact that he couldn't swim and that he would surely perish crossing the many bays and rivers that they would encounter along the coast. Now, on his return journey, Alvar again pondered his decision. Should he turn south and begin his journey to freedom or return and hope to lead his compatriots to *Panuco?*

He would return to the coast.

The journey back from the land of the *Sanas* had been long and arduous. Paleowa had stayed with him not two days, but four. He had chosen a different return path, they continued following the river *Sana-pana* that led east out of the *Sana* village. It was a circuitous route that required many crossings, the steep walls of the canyons forcing them to make long detours.

At the point that Paleowa left him the river emptied into a much larger waterway. He explained that this was the Pashowana, the same one they had followed north several weeks before. Paleowa assured him, however, that after aseven-day journey, the river would turn south and continue on to the "Big Waters." He further instructed Alvar to leave the river at this point and continue east until he reached the coast and the land of the *Charrucans.*

With that, the two men parted company. As was customary Paleowa sobbed and hugged Alvar repeatedly before leaving. Sitting on a large rock, Alvar watched as Paleowa picked his way back, at times disappearing from sight and then reappearing on a ridge or outcropping further on. The two men had become good friends and now Alvar knew he would never see him again. Far below Paleowa's lone figure appeared briefly and then disappeared for the last time.

After 3 days the river's course began to shift more to the east. Another 4 days journey brought him to the point where the river turned abruptly south just as Paleowa had instructed him. Once again Alvar wrestled with the decision to return to the *Charrucans.* Following the river, he could make it to the sea. A large freshwater source entering the *Golfo de Nueva Espana* would almost certainly attract an occasional ship. There, he reasoned, *Spanish* ships would eventually rescue him, but, then what? Could he organize an expedition to recover his friends and shipmates, and would they still be alive?

In the end, Alvar left the river and began his trek eastward across the hilly country. It was dry, but intersected with five rivers. The fifth river he would follow to the land of the *Charrucans.*

As Alvar approached the first river he recognized it by the multitudes of pecan trees that grew upon its banks. They seemed to stretch endlessly. Of course, with this multitude of nut trees, the squirrels were in abundance and, once across, Alvar feasted on several he had managed to bag with his bow. The *Indios* called this river *Chotilapacquen*...a river of squirrels.

From *Chotilaoacquen* Alvar continued east until he reached the next river. This arose from an impressive collection of springs that bubbled up from deep in the ground. Here the water was cold and crystal clear. Alvar rested here for a day, drinking his fill. Eight leagues further east the third river also flowed in a southeastern direction. Here he visited with a tribe of *Indios* that he was familiar with. They called themselves *Guanchas* and they called this river *Sai-la-con-tec.* Their village lay on the confluence of this *Sai-la-con-tec* and a much smaller stream. The meeting of the two waters formed a small delta.

After a day's rest, Alvar continued southeast, following the *Sai-la-con-tec* until it merged with another, larger river. He would follow this larger river until it made a decided turn to the south. At this point he would continue east He passed through country wild and hilly. From these hills and ridges, he could see great distances, a land almost devoid of any human presence. Two days out from the *Guanchas* village he paused at one of these precipices to observe a thunderstorm that was forming to the north. From where he sat the sun was shining brightly but in the distance he watched a billowing cloud jetting higher and higher into the atmosphere. Below it the horizon was dark as ink and highlighted by magnificent displays of lightning that played across the sky. The sound of the thunder was continuous. The storm seemed to be moving rapidly with diagonal bands of rain cutting across the expanse. Above, the billowing white thunderhead flattened out into what looked like a blacksmith's anvil. Below, the storm seemed to grow in intensity. Alvar watched in fascination as the sky took on a greenish hue. Amazingly, the lightning stopped and all around him, the desert became deathly quiet. The birds stopped singing, there was no wind and even the sound of the stream below him seemed subdued. Overhead, clouds moved in to filter out the sun which had been shining brightly only a few moments before. He was now on the margins of the storm.

What happened next mesmerized him.

From the angry cloud base, a white string began descending. It seemed to be a living thing as it undulated across the sky searching for the ground below. Suddenly, the white string turned black and grew in size as it made contact with the ground below. From where he sat Alvar watched as grass, trees, rocks, and dirt swirled about in the maelstrom. The string had now turned into a monster devouring everything in its path. Strangely, from where he sat the air was still and quiet. Alvar had seen tornadoes before, but never this large and certainly not this close. At its base, the churning clouds boiled about sending out tentacles of secondary whirlwinds that were quickly sucked back into the larger mass. From here heavier objects fell back to earth, crashing into the desert below. The vortex, now huge and intimidating, continued to move eastward while lightning flashed about it. Only now did Alvar become aware of the thunder again as it rumbled and crashed in a continuous cacophony of sound. The tornado slowly disappeared as diagonal sheets of rain cloud obscured its view. Overhead the clouds parted and Alvar was once again bathed in bright sunlight. The inky blackness of the storm continued to recede eastward until nothing remained but a string of white puffy god clouds.

Alvar realized he hadn't so much as moved a muscle since the spectacle had unfolded before him. He stood, collected his things, and proceeded down the hill to the valley below. Soon, his track crossed the path of the tornado. It looked to Alvar that a giant had used a garden hoe to clear a path across the countryside. Wide swatches of the ground were as bare as a plowed field. Since the direction of the tornado was the same as his own, he followed its path. He came upon many strange things. Tree trunks with stalks of grass embedded in them like so many small spears, a buzzard, very much alive, lay on the ground completely denuded of its feathers, and, most amazing of all a huge tree limb embedded into the standing trunk of another tree, forming a perfect cross. Alvar stopped and crossed himself, for certainly, this was a sign from God.

The destruction led to the fourth river and then abruptly stopped. This river was slow-moving and wide with numerous hardwood trees lining its steep banks. Large sand bars were located throughout the span and Alvar would utilize these as best he could in the crossing. Today the wind was blowing strongly from the south and the surface was undulating with waves and an occasional whitecap. Carefully he entered the water, ever mindful of the black water snakes that were common in this area. The bottom was soft and he could feel the mud squeezing up through his toes. When the depth of the water reached his chest Alvar began to swim in a sort of dog paddle, his bag of wares attached by a rawhide strip trailing behind him. At roughly the halfway point he climbed onto one of the sand bars only to find one of the black water snakes sunning itself on the surface. Seeing a threat, the snake coiled itself displaying its fangs and white skin on the inside of its mouth. Unlike other snakes these vipers were aggressive and Alvar was content to give it a wide berth...better to leave it here on the sand bar than in the water with him. After another few minutes of swimming Alvar reached the other side. The strong wind blowing from behind had actually helped him and except for the snake, the crossing was uneventful.

Three more days of travel led Alvar to the final river that marked the final leg of his journey. Luckily it was the dry season and this river was marked with several low water areas that provided easy crossing. Of all the rivers that he had crossed, this one with its collection of *El Legarto,* was the one he feared the most. These ferocious animals reached enormous sizes and to be caught in the water with one was almost certain death. He had carefully scanned the shore and the water's surface before attempting to cross. Alvar called this *Río de los legarto*. From here he turned southeast for the two-day journey to the coast and *Malhado* Island where he hoped he would find Lope de Oviedo and Jeronimo de Alaniz.

Late July, 1532

Texas Coast Near Present-Day Galveston

Arriving at the *Churrucan* camp Alvar was greeted enthusiastically and spent days displaying and trading his wares. This had been one of the longest journeys. Around the cooking fires, he talked late into the night, the *Indios* spellbound with stories of all he had seen. The euphoric mood, however, lasted only a week for the days were becoming shorter and the people needed to prepare for the winter months that were fast approaching. Alvar took this opportunity to return to *Malhado Island* to again talk with Oviedo. With only one teenage boy to assist him in the four-man canoe the crossing to the island was uneventful, the bay was calm and the weather pleasant.

He found Oviedo residing with the *Hans* as before. Squatting on the outskirts of the village Alvar was at first unnoticed. He closely watched his friend. Except for the course beard, Oviedo was almost indistinguishable from the rest of the *Indios*. Shirtless, he had tattooed his arms, legs, and body, and the skin was tanned a leather brown. The woman he had taken squatted nearby pounding some walnuts into a kind of paste. Next to her was a child that had been placed upon a deerskin. Two other children were about, one a toddler, the other about three years old. Oviedo was constructing a spear, carefully wrapping strips of deer hide around a sharpened oyster shell that had been inserted into a split pole.

When the children had moved away Alvar called in a low voice, *"Amigo!"*

Startled, Oviedo turned toward the direction of the sound. At first, he didn't see Alvar who, like himself, was deeply tanned and clad only in a piece of hide that covered his genitals. His first words of recognition were in the *Indio* language. He had to stop himself and think for a moment about the response in his native *Spanish*.

"*Senor* de Vaca...Alvar, I thought that you may have died for I had not heard of you for almost a year. Praise God you are still alive."

With this, the two men rose and embraced.

"It is good to see you Oviedo, I have traveled much since I last saw you. This land stretches far beyond the horizon and in all directions. I have seen many wonders of which I could talk hours."

"Have you heard of any others of our party? What of Fernandez, Mendez, and the others that first set out in search of *Panuco*...have you heard of them?" Oviedo seemed desperate for information.

"Friend, I have heard nothing of this party but I do hear talk of a group of our *Christians* that are further down the mainland. As to who they are I know not. I can only pray that many of our people still live and are residing with the *Indios*."

Alvar hesitated for a moment and then asked, "What of Jeronimo de Alaniz, I have not been able to locate him?"

Oviedo dropped his head and crossed himself. "Jeronimo...my friend, died last year of a lingering sickness. The *Indios* declined to help him and I alone tried to provide food and water to him as he lay and suffered."

Alvar, saddened by the news, crossed himself as well and sat cross-legged on the ground.

"His last words were of you, *Alguacil*. He asked when you were returning to lead us away from this place."

It was then that Alvar noticed that the *Indian* woman had stopped what she was doing and was staring intently at him. Like Alvar and

Oviedo she was clad only in a breechcloth Still nursing the younger of the children, her breasts hung in full sight.

"Is this the woman you have taken among the *Han* Oviedo*?*

Oviedo walked over to where she squatted and extended his hand. She rose slowly, never taking her eyes off Alvar. She was not unattractive but somewhat rawboned. Alvar saw she had a scar that extended from her right ear to her chin.

Oviedo, noticing Alvar's stare, lapsed into the language of the *Han*. "This is Wonto-lu-nika, she is the mother of my two children." Alvar nodded and extended the standard greeting of the *Han* and, it seemed of all the *Indians* of the area.

"*Ti-nok-a-la-tek-a*!" Roughly translated it meant "Greetings and good health to you."

Alvar turned to Oviedo and spoke again in *Spanish*, "Friend, we must talk once again about finding *Panuco* and returning to *Espana*."

Oviedo seemed pained and at first, avoided the subject. "Wonto-lu-nika...I call her Lu, who suffered the cut on her face when her first husband became displeased and threw her out of his lodge, but not before cutting her face with a sharpened clam shell. This was meant to discourage other men from desiring her. She was an outcast!"

"But I am an outcast as well, so I chose her for my wife." Oviedo was wringing his hands as he spoke.

Alvar thought for a moment. "Friend, you are a *Spaniard*. This is not your place, for if you remain you will die unnoticed and unconsecrated by the church. Your very being on this earth will be lost to oblivion. You need to return with me to *Panuco* to begin your life anew."

At first, Oviedo was stubbornly opposed to the idea of leaving his family and *Malhado* island. Besides, he was also unable to swim and the thought of crossing to the mainland and fording the many rivers terrified him.

They talked late into the night. Alvar, a strong swimmer, assured Oviedo that he would keep him safe in the water.

"Friend Oviedo, unless you make the decision to leave now you will never see *Spain* again."

Finally, Oviedo reluctantly agreed but only on the understanding that the true intent of their leaving was not relayed to Wonto-lu-nika and that if things didn't turn out he would return to the *Han.*

There was still a problem, however. How would Wonto-lu-nika and her three children support themselves? The *Han* were a subsistence culture and a woman alone would have to struggle for survival. Her immediate family would help her as best they could but with marriage, this responsibility had passed to Oviedo. He would not go unless Wonto-Lu-nika and his children could be cared for.

Reaching into his bag Alvar said, "I may be of some help." Pulling out a beautiful obsidian spear point he handed it to Oviedo. "Offer this to Lu's father."

CHAPTER 11

The Night Of Falling Stars

La Noche de las Estrellas Fugaces

"Shivering, we watched the sky as meteors fell in unprecedented numbers. I felt it was a sign...an omen...of good luck. We called it La Noche de las estrellas fugaces...the night of falling stars."

Mid-August, 1532

Galveston (Malhado) Island, Texas

There was much wailing in the camp of the *Hans*. Lope de Oviedo lied to his *Indio* woman that he was only leaving with Alvar for a short journey to search for the other *Spaniards*. Still, she had set into prolonged sobbing that was soon joined by other members of the group and continued throughout the day and night. Wonto-lu-nika's father had accepted the obsidian blade presented to him by Oviedo with much pride. In fact, the blade had elevated him to a higher level in the group. He strutted about carrying it at the end of a long cane pole that he had lashed it to.

Alvar watched as an anguished Oviedo hugged his three children and then turned to board the small canoe that Alvar had brought over from the mainland. Pushing off they paddled rapidly. *Malhado* Island slowly receded behind them. The sobbing and lamentations could be heard far out into the bay. Tears ran down his bearded cheeks, and Oviedo paddled like a man possessed. Soon, the lapping of the water and the sound of sea birds was the only thing that broke the silence. The journey across the bay was without incident. A pod of dolphins had joined them briefly, rolling onto their sides to observe these intruders of their marine world. As they approached the shallows, schools of frenzied mullet, besieged by predators, darted and jumped everywhere. Today the sea was alive.

It was, as Alvar could best determine, the late summer of 1533.

Amid an army of land crabs, the canoe slid onto the sand in a protected inlet that Alvar had selected. There was no one to greet them and they pulled the canoe on shore and hid it amongst some reeds. Gathering a few of the crabs the Spaniards roasted them over a small fire of dried sea grass and driftwood. With the meal, Oviedo's anguish seemed to subside. Alvar talked of *Spain* and how they would be returning to tell their story. He emphasized to Oviedo that they had to stay focused and strong for the journey ahead.

"This land is interminable and there will be many dangers, but with perseverance, we can reach the settlement at *Panuco* where we will be safe. Our immediate challenge is to cross four large rivers as we move south. There are other waterways, streams, and swamps, but these first four will be the most challenging. Hopefully, as we proceed further to the south the land becomes drier and easier to traverse."

"*Alguacil*, there is so much water to cross, I will only slow you down...surely you know that."

Alvar thought a moment, "Friend Oviedo, I could have proceeded towards *Panuco* a year ago, but my love for my *Spanish* brothers kept me here. Sadly, de Alaniz died during that time but you are still strong and we will make this journey together. I will carry you across the waterways and when it is too deep and wide we will use logs to hold onto."

The next day they came upon three *Indians* that Alvar had some association with. They were young *Deaguanes* on a hunting expedition. Alvar had spent a winter in their camp and knew each by name. After much discussion, they agreed to accompany the two *Spaniards* and guide them across the four rivers that traversed this section of the coast.

Pulling Alvar aside Oviedo questioned him, "*Alguacil*, why would these *Deaguanes* agree to help us in our quest for *Panuco*?"

Alvar laughed, "They are young and crave excitement. To them, I am Wasapi-tun-Laki, the strange bearded white trader and medicine man. They will tell stories of our journey and gain respect from others in their group."

The five travelers headed inland to avoid the broad delta basins that the rivers formed on the coast. Here the rivers narrowed and were easier to cross. The first waterway they crossed was marked by thousands of oyster shells along its bank. In places conifers and hardwood trees grew right up to the water's edge, their huge canopies overhanging and shading the area below. In other locations, broad flat stretches of grasses overpowered the trees. Both environments were marked with a variety of depressions that, filled with water, became an obstacle that the five had to navigate around. The trails were narrow and almost non-existent in places, but the *Deaguanes* seemed to know the area well. Further inland the flow of this swift river abated somewhat as it spread out over a large plain. At one of these locations and by a large oak half buried in the water the five crossed. The deepest water was only waist deep but Oviedo held to Alvar with one hand and to a large piece of driftwood with the other. The current was still strong and landfall on the opposite bank was far from where they started. Oviedo was terrified. The *Deaguanes*, all excellent swimmers, thought this extremely amusing and berated the *Spaniard*. At times they even pulled at the driftwood as if to take it from him.

After crossing this first obstacle Oviedo's demeanor seemed to change for the better. Alvar began to once again recognize the proud *Spaniard* who had been his shipmate only years before.

"We will make it home, friend Oviedo, and tell stories to our grandchildren that will amaze them."

On they marched, seeing not so much as a village or any other signs of habitation. Only the faint foot travel trails spread out before them. Occasionally one foot trail would be crossed by another and the *Deaguanes* would point out that it led to a particular village or meeting place. As they neared the next river the trail became somewhat wider and signs of recent travel by others marked the path. This river was much larger and the confidence that Oviedo had exhibited earlier began to fade.

For a time they paralleled the river inland until reaching a wide expanse marked by several sand bars. Alvar admonished the *Deaguanes* for their treatment of Oviedo and together they lashed several pieces of driftwood together for the *Spaniard* to hold onto. A visible sigh of relief came as he stepped out of the water onto each sand bar along the way. At one point, with the water lapping just above his chest, one of the *Deaguanes* jumped on Oviedo's back, forcing his head underwater. Still holding to the driftwood with a death grip, he thrashed back and forth trying to get a breath. Alvar, close by, pulled the young *Deaguane* off but not before Oviedo came up wild-eyed, sputtering and gasping for air. Luckily, they were close to the river bank and a shaken Oviedo climbed out uninjured. The three *Deaguanes* were highly amused by the dunking.

Oviedo's resolve showed signs of crumbling. "*Alguacil,* why do these people do such things?

"They are godless children with no compassion for weakness my friend. Do whatever you can to hide your fears for they will only exploit them."

"I don't know if I will be able to complete this journey, *Alguacil,* and more importantly, I feel that I will hold you back."

Alvar clapped him on the back, "Lope, you are doing fine. Look, we have already crossed two rivers and are well along to *la via de Panuco.*"

Actually, Alvar had no idea how far the *Spanish* settlement at

Panuco was, but like most of the survivors he felt it must be close in the direction they were headed...*adelante*. Even with his years of traveling across the country, he had no idea of the vastness of this continent.

Midaugust, 1532

Texas Gulf Coast

Moving southward, the two *Spaniards* and three *Deaguanes* began to pick up other travelers moving in the same direction. Two women and a male elder joined them shortly after crossing the second river. These were *Quevenes* who had been visiting relatives. Alvar immediately noted how all the *Indians* traveling with them showed deference to the elder; a tall, broad-shouldered man of about 60 years. His body was marked with numerous scars both front and back. Obviously, a warrior, Alvar learned that he was *Metova-danoca*, a name that he had heard many times before in his travels. This individual was noted for his battles with a mysterious group of *Indians* that prowled the coast in search of slaves and women. No one knew from where they came or when they would appear, but in warfare, they were ruthless and were said to eat their captives. *Metova-danoca (the man who fights like a wounded eagle)* had gotten his name from one of the first of these battles where the attackers had managed to capture his wife and son. During the melee, one of the attackers had slit his son's throat and thrown the young body on the ground before him in a taunt. Enraged, Metova killed all five in a furious battle. Covered in blood he then proceeded to dismember all the bodies and stuff the pieces into one of the canoes. To this, he set fire and pushed it into the water before collapsing. Severely wounded, it was only through the ministrations of his wife that Metova survived. Now, she was one of the women with whom he was traveling, the other being his daughter.

The land between the rivers was cut with numerous little streams and lowland swaps that had to be crossed. At each crossing, all of the travelers would procure long sticks and proceed to beat the water in front of them as they crossed the watery expanse. This was to scare off the dreaded *lagartos*...alligators who in these parts could grow to enormous size.

At a broad crossroad, more *Deaguane* women joined the group. These women, traveling together with several youngsters, were a boisterous group, laughing and calling to each other as they walked.

The third river, only about a league from the second, flowed deep and wide near the coast so the small group turned and followed a well-used trail inland. Coming to a narrow juncture in the river the *Deaguane* guides indicated this was the best crossing. Its banks were densely covered with a variety of overhanging trees that gave the narrow waterway a spectral appearance. Even the boisterous women seemed to quiet down. The river ran deep so Alvar put Oviedo between him and the makeshift raft of driftwood they had lashed together. Several of the older women held onto the raft as well, piling their belongings on top. Having the women close by seemed to calm Oviedo and he crossed with ease. Now on the opposite side, their direction turned back to the coast where the going was easier. Here they spent the night.

The following day they traveled another five leagues. The journey was marked by numerous sloughs, bogs, and small streams. Finally, The next river was upon them, its current running swift and very wide. Again, they traveled inland looking for a suitable site to cross. Here, luck was with them, and other *Indians* with canoes paddled them across. It was a good day.

On a wide sandy peninsula the group of two *Spaniards* and now, thirteen *Indians* camped for the night. A large driftwood fire was built to discourage the ever-present mosquitoes. Periodically, green leaves and other vegetation would be added to the fire, initiating billowing clouds of white smoke. Sleeping close to the fire the smoke would pass overhead, providing a relatively comfortable sleeping area. It was a calm night and the sandy peninsula was soon shrouded in a hazy cloud. The night sounds kept Alvar awake. Animals coming down to get water crashed through the undergrowth, a chorus of owls hooted late into the night, in the distance an occasional cougar would scream, and several times Alvar heard the distinct "whoof" of a black bear patrolling the river bank. The *Indians* around him fell asleep instantly, their snores and flatulations competing with the forest's sounds. At the far end of the fire, *Metova-danoca* made love to his wife, her sighs and his grunts of pleasure seemed to go unnoticed. Soon, all this faded as Alvar drifted asleep. In the morning the whole procession broke camp, and once again moved south following a now, well-defined trail.

Early September, 1532

Texas Coast Near Present-Day Matagorda Bay

The procession hadn't traveled more than half a league when, up ahead, a broad bay appeared. Upon reaching the bay they stayed on the peninsula that jutted out from the mainland. Following the shoreline was much easier walking than traversing the swamps and timber lay-downs that would have confronted them on the mainland. To the northwest, the bay was much like the area of *Malhado* that they had left, but the abundance of birds was nothing like Alvar had ever seen. They were everywhere. The cacophony of sound was deafening. Overhead Gulls, Pelicans, Frigatebirds, Spoonbills, Heron, Ibis, Egrets, Ducks, and Geese, to name a few, circled in abundance. They continued along the peninsula for two or three leagues before bedding down for the night.

In the morning they started their journey once again. Climbing a dune, Alvar looked to see the peninsula continue far into the distance, knifing between the bay on his right and the open ocean on his left. Furtively he scanned the ocean for any sign of sails. There were none.

Moving along the narrow beach they made good time. At the end of the day, Alvar estimated they had traveled 5 leagues. Still, the narrow peninsula stretched out far in front of them.

That night a storm approached from the southwest and the rain lasted until early morning. They had moved to the sand dunes which offered some protection from the wind and blowing rain, but it was a most miserable night. The next day they traveled another 6 leagues under a sullen sky before stopping just at sunset. To the west, the sky was a brilliant crimson with the promise of a clear day in the morning.

With an early start, the travelers made good time and came upon a very large inlet at mid-morning. So impressed was Alvar by the large Bay and deep inlet that connected it to the sea, he called it *la Bahia del Espiritu Santo*...The Bay of the Holy Spirit.

From the northwest side of the inlet, several canoes made their way toward them. It was the relatives and friends of the *Indians* that they had been traveling with. It was a scene of much rejoicing and, as was the custom, both parties wailed and sobbed uncontrollably for hours. During this ordeal, Alvar and Oviedo stayed apart from the rest. Up until now their relations with the *Indians* that accompanied them had been friendly, even cordial. This began to change. Several of the young boys who had arrived began to taunt them, bouncing pebbles off their heads and pulling at their beards. These *Deaguanes* were very protective of each other and to react to the provocations would surely have initiated worse treatment. Oviedo seemed to be particularly targeted by the tormentors. Alvar, seeing this, tried his best to divert attention to himself.

"*Alguacil*, why do they torment us?"

"We are different and they take pleasure in watching us suffer friend Oviedo. Try not to react to their taunts so that they will grow bored and leave us alone."

Alvar called out to one of the *Indians* who had come over in the canoes. "Have you seen other men such as ourselves from where you came?"

A particularly tall *Indio* known as Getaka stepped up to Alvar and explained that there were three men with hairy faces residing on the other side of the bay. Getaka was a *Quevene* and father to one of the young women in the group with which they were traveling. He emphasized his description of "hairy faces" by pulling on Alvar's beard which now hung down in an unruly mass to his chest.

Alvar, ignoring the slight, asked, "Do you know how these men were called?"

The *Indio* struggled with the pronunciation. Although the names were strange to Getaka he pronounced their names phonetically. "They are called *Kaas-ce-lo, Sor-ante,* and a man with skin the color of burnt wood."

Alvar suspected that the *Spaniards* ahead were Alonso del Castillo, possibly one of the Dorante cousins, Andres or Diego, and a black slave...probably Estevan. This news seemed to revive Oviedo momentarily.

Alvar pressed Getaka for more information on the other *Spaniards*. "Where you there, did you see these men?"

Getaka answered, "I have seen these men and the others."

"You have seen other "hairy faces?" Alvar was incredulous.

"The other hairy faces came over to us from our brothers the *Guaycones,* but they are all dead."

Alvar's heart sank. "Tell me of these others, for they were also our brothers?" Alvar pressed Getaka for information.

"Two of these hairy faces had marks on their arm." Getaka outlined a cross on his forearm so that Alvar would understand.

With this information, Alvar knew that two of the men were Diego Dorantes and Pedro de Valdivieso. Both of the cousins had had a cross tattooed on their forearms during a drunken spree in *Cadez* the night before the expedition sailed.

"What of the other man?"

Getaka thought a moment. "This one had a big head with much hair." Getaka held his hands up on either side of his head to demonstrate.

Alvar turned to Oviedo. "That has to be Diego de Huelva."

Alvar turned back to Getaka. "What of these three, what happened?"

Getaka seemed to smirk as he related the stories of the men. "The three hairy faces escaped from our brothers the *Guaycone*. When we learned from where they had come they were returned. I went with them!"

Getaka seemed proud of his role in returning the *Spaniards*.

"We tied them together. One with the mark on his arm kept falling down and I had to kick him to get up." Getaka pantomimed kicking something on the ground.

"The other hairy faces protested and we hit them with sticks."

Oviedo, listening to the story, shook his head and stared at the ground.

Getaka continued, "The one with the marks on his arm wouldn't get up so we tied him to a pole and carried him to the *Guaycone* camp."

Valdivieso had been the first to collapse. Now tied hand and foot to a pole he was roughly carried and dragged back to the village while Dorantes and de Huelva stumbled along.

More alive than dead Valdivieso, still suspended from the pole, was set upon a spit over a charcoal fire. Revived by the heat and pain his screams permeated the village much to the delight of the residents. They sat around the fire and threw stones at the *Spaniard* as he slowly roasted to death.

Diego Dorantes, his arms bound behind him, was tethered to a tree by a long cord. In this condition, the women of the group attacked him with sticks and sharpened clam shells. Running about trying to avoid the marauding women, he was repeatedly lacerated on his arms, legs, and torso until the ground over which he ran was saturated with blood. Finally collapsing, the women seemed to take particular delight in castrating him. Near death, he too was set upon a spit, like Valdivieso, to roast.

Diego de Huelva, forced to watch the death of his compatriots, was bound only by his hands tied behind his back. Here, the *Indian* relating the story to Alvar and Oviedo seemed to change his demeanor. No longer smirking, he nodded in approval as he related how de Huelva had sprung forward in a sudden burst of energy knocking one of his captors into the fire. The *Indio* screamed as the hot coals seared his flesh and the crowd, momentarily stunned by the action, didn't react as de Huelva attempted to escape. He didn't get far. One of the men of the village plunged a fishing spear into his chest as de Huelva ran by him. De Huelva died before he hit the ground.

"This one died honorably" was all the *Indian* said as he moved away from Alvar and Oviedo.

The story of their compatriots' deaths had shaken Alvar, and Oviedo was ashen white. They sat together not speaking for what seemed like an hour. The three that were alive and the deaths of Diego Dorantes, Valdivieso, and Huelva however, only represented part of the thirteen who had departed *Malhado Island.*

Upon asking about the fate of other *Spaniards* that may have been in the area, the *Indio* related their gruesome fates. Many had died of the cold and hunger, but others had been tortured and killed by the *Indians* ahead. This group was called the *Guaycones,* and indeed, others further ahead, Alvar had no experience with. All of his treks had been to the west where he was respected by the indigenous people, but here along the coast, he was just another "hairy face" that had come into their territory.

The *Indian* shrugged his shoulders and related he only knew of two others who had died at the hands of the *Mariames,* a neighboring tribe.

Again the *Indian* struggled to pronounce the names, but Alvar was able to identify them as Hernando Esquivel who had been on the raft with the commissary, and Mendez who had been one of the four sent from *Malhado* to seek out *Panuco.*

Both had been held as slaves by the *Mariames* and were killed because of a dream one of the tribe members had. Esquivel had died quickly with an arrow shot through his neck. Mendez had died slowly as he was dismembered with sharpened clam shells.

This was the first that Alvar had heard of anyone from another boat and he wondered what had been the fate of the others. The death of Mendez was also disheartening for he always held hope that at least one of the four "swimmers" who set out so many months ago would reach *Panuco* and bring help. He thought again of the remaining survivors, Castillo, Andres Dorantes, and Estevan.

Addressing the *Indio* one more time he asked, "What is the condition of the three men that are alive?"

Getaka had grown disinterested and wandered off without answering. The woman by his side, Alvar thought it must be his wife, answered for him.

"The hairy ones are badly treated. The young boys kick and slap them for amusement and they are forced to labor from the time the sun rises until it sets. There is talk that these people will come to this place in two days' time."

Getaka, hearing his woman speak to the *Spaniards* came back over and slapped Oviedo hard. "you want to know how they are treated, I will show you." With this, he turned and punched Alvar so hard that he fell to the ground. After this demonstration, several of the young boys in the group came over and began throwing mud balls at them. They laughed as the *Spaniards* tried to dodge them and screamed with glee when a mud ball found its mark. Eventually tiring of their game, the young men moved on but returned again and again, to cudgel the *Spaniards* with short sticks and even draw their bows only inches from the Spaniards' faces. Alvar noticed that Getaka's wife did not allow her son to participate in these activities.

By the next day, Oviedo had had enough. He would return to *Malhado* with a group of women heading in that direction. He spoke of this to Alvar.

"*Alguacil*, I can tolerate this no longer. On *Malhado* I have a wife and children, it is not much, but at least I am accepted and do not have to endure these *insultos*."

Alvar responded. "Friend Oviedo, nay Lope...we have endured much in the last few years. Indeed, it is a miracle that we still live...so many of our friends have perished."

Alvar was silent a moment as he thought of the events since the landing at *Bahia Boca Ciego* so many many months ago. It almost seemed like a dream. He continued.

"Don't you see that it is by God's will that we live? To stay with these godless savages is a life of oblivion for you will die in obscurity and no one will know of your existence."

"*Alguacil*, the world will not know of my existence anyhow if these animals kill me here and throw my body in a ditch...the chances for this happening seem very good. At least on *Malhado* I can watch my children grow and teach them the few things that I know."

"Lope, I have helped you with the four rivers, who will assist you on your return journey?

"The women and boys that followed us from *Malhado* are camped a short distance back..." Oviedo gestured with his thumb. One is my wife's sister-in-law. She has offered her help along with her young son. He is a strapping boy of about 13 and a strong swimmer. They will be returning in the morning."

Alvar felt sadness and some anger welling up inside him. All these years he had waited to help Oviedo escape his life of toil and hardship were now for naught.

"Friend Oviedo, I feel you are making a terrible mistake, and should you stay I will feel forever guilty for abandoning you."

Lope Oviedo put his hand on Alvar's shoulder. "*Alguacil*, you should feel no regrets. You have gone far and above to help me. For this, I love you as a brother, but I don't share your convictions nor do I have your strength of purpose. I choose to stay on *Malhado*, and this in no way is your fault."

The next morning Alvar traveled back to the women's camp with Lope Oviedo. It was but a short walk and neither talked much, each consumed with sadness and their own thoughts. On arrival Alvar made one last plca to Oviedo, but to no avail for he was set on returning to *Malhado*. Shaking hands, the two *Spaniards* embraced each other and Oviedo walked away. After only a few steps he turned.

"*Alguacil*, may God be with you on your return to *Panuco*. If you make it back to the world tell them of me and all of the *Christians* that have suffered in this land."

Alvar could only gulp, "I will, friend Oviedo. May God be with you as well."

Mid-September, 1532

Near the Mouth of the Texas Guadalupe River

Several days after the departure of Oviedo, Alvar had accompanied the *Quevenes* across the bay and inland to the region they called the River of Nuts. Today he was as far up a pecan tree as he could climb. Getting into position, he held on securely and started to shake the tree as violently as he could. There were two other *Indians* in the tree with him and they, likewise, were shaking as hard as they could. All around them, pecans cascaded down in what sounded like a heavy hail storm. Below, men, women, and children gathered up the nuts into woven grass baskets. The children yelped as the nuts bounced off their heads and bodies, the adults laughed and seemed to thoroughly enjoy themselves. Before coming down to join in the gathering Alvar scanned the area around him. From his perch he could see the river delta to the south, and further on the thin blue line of the ocean. In the other direction, the river snaked through the canopy of trees eventually disappearing from view. All around there were others, like himself, shaking the branches while below on the ground, it seemed like the number of *Indians* grew by the hour. Climbing down from the tree a young *Indio* of about twelve years approached Alvar and reported that the other *Christians* had arrived. The young man was the son of Getaka.

Suspicious at first, Alvar asked him, "Your father treats me badly, why do you tell me this."

The young man answered, "My mother feels sympathy for you and wants to help you find your friends. While my father is a *Quevene*, my mother is a *Yguase*, the same people that have two of your friends. The other *Christian* is with our brothers the *Mariames*"

He pointed to the edge of the forest of nut trees where the undergrowth was particularly thick. "Tonight when everyone sleeps you will flee the camp and hide yourself in that brush. Tomorrow at mid-morning my mother and her relatives will be visiting those that hold your friends. It is but a half-day walk and they will gather you up on their way."

Deciding to trust the young boy Alvar answered, "I will do as you say, but tell me the name of your mother so I can thank her."

The young boy answered, "It is Lon-on-mea."

This was no easy decision for Alvar because other *Christians* had been killed for running away. He thought of the gruesome deaths of Diego Dorantes, Pedro de Valdivieso, and Diego de Huelva. The risk was significant, but, hopefully, he could team up with the other *Christians* and begin their journey to *Panuco*.

The next morning Alvar shifted uncomfortably in his makeshift hideout. It had begun to rain and *los mosquitoes* were particularly bad. He watched through the tall grass and vines as a procession of *Indians* left the camp and moved toward the nut trees. It didn't appear that anyone was aware of his absence. He was amazed at the number of people that were in the area, they seemed to grow every hour. By mid-morning everyone was involved with gathering nuts, and the trail in front of him was deserted. It continued to rain and the mosquitoes were particularly voracious. At least now he could risk movement to swat at the dreaded pests and scratch the multitude of bites that covered his body.

There was movement on the trail and soon Alvar made out six *Indians* moving his way....four women and two young boys. He recognized Lononmea and then her young son who he had talked with the night before.

Alvar remained perfectly still.

The group stopped only a few feet from where he was hidden. The young boy moved to the edge of the clearing and softly called out. "Wan-tok-a-la." which in their language meant "bearded one."

Looking around, Alvar could see no one else on the trail. He stood up and made his presence known. Lononmea motioned for him to join them. They quickly shielded him in order to hide his presence from prying eyes. Quickly the group moved down the trail. After they had walked for half an hour the six *Indians* surrounding Alvar spread out. He was no longer in danger of being discovered by the *Quevenes.*

Alvar sought out Lononmea so that he could speak with her. "I thank you for guiding me here, I hope that someday I can repay you."

Lononmea just smiled and patted him on the shoulder.

After two hours of walking, Alvar estimated the distance at around 2 leagues, they came to a camp. These were *Mariames*, an inland group that made the journey to this spot to harvest the pecans growing by the river. The first to take notice of them was a young woman tending the fire by a crude hut. She called out a greeting. The noise caught the attention of other members of the group who came out to offer their greetings. From the far side of the camp, a bearded face appeared...it was Captain Andres Dorantes de Carranza.

Alvar rushed forward and grabbed both of Castillo's hands with his own. "Andres, it is me, Alvar, surely you recognize me!"

Dorantes sputtered and then managed to blurt out, "But I thought you were long dead."

Alvar laughed, "No friend, I am still much alive and, praise God, you are also,"

"*Alguacil*, much has happened as I'm sure it is with you. We are all lucky to be alive.

Alvar threw his arms around the captain, "This is one of the happiest days since arriving in this forsaken land."

Andres Dorantes had recovered his composure and blurted out, "Then let's make this day even better...we will travel to the camp of our neighbors...the *Mariames* and see *Capitan* Castillo and Estevanico."

Alvar answered immediately, "Is it far?"

"Only a few bends down that trail." Dorantes nodded toward the path just in front of them. "The *Yguases* camp is very close."

The *Spaniards* and Lononmea headed down the trail and, as Dorantes had noted, the camp was only a short walk distant. Alvar heard the sounds of the camp before it came into sight. It was a hub of activity as the women and children of the group were busy preparing the *Nueces Pecanas* into a variety of concoctions. Baskets of un-shelled nuts were piled in the center of the camp. A circle of children used rocks to separate the nut from the hard shell. This pounding is what Alvar had heard before entering the camp. The edible nuts were collected by the women would spread them onto hot rocks for roasting, others were ground into a meal that was used for thickening broths or adding to corn meal. Other nuts were ground with a stone mortar and pestle and added to boiling water. This produced a nourishing beverage that appeared much like milk that the *Indians* drank constantly and even fed to the infants as a supplement to mother's milk.

One of the women arose from her activity and rushed toward the visitors. It was Lononmea's sister. The two women embraced and then began wailing as was the custom. Amongst this hub of activity, Captain Castillo rose from the circle of children who were cracking the nuts. His expression was one of disbelief for, like Dorantes, he had longed believed that Alvar was dead.

"*Alguacil*, is it really you?"

"Friend Castillo, seeing you brings me unbelievable happiness."

Alvar was taken aback by his friend, for Castillo had been one of the toughest of the military captains, known for his strength and voracity. Now, like the other three, he was thin and sinewy with a full beard that covered part of his chest.

The two men embraced in the middle of the *Indio* camp. Strangely, the *Yguases* left them alone, some even wailing as was the custom for meeting friends or family long separated.

From the far side of the camp, a bearded black man appeared.

Alvar looked to Estevan, almost unrecognizable with his enormous shock of curly hair and beard. "Estevanico, you look to have fared well."

The four *Spaniards* moved to an isolated part of the camp and talked about their experiences. Castillo was the first to raise the question, "*Alguacil*, where is it that you are going?

Alvar related the story of how he had gathered up Oviedo and left *Malhado Island* and his plan to reach *Panuco*. All three were deeply saddened when they learned of Oviedo's decision to return to the island.

"He is lost forever!" lamented Andres Dorantes.

Dorantes continued, "*Alguacil*, I have long wanted to leave this place and try to reach *Panuco* but my compatriots here are reluctant to make the journey." He nodded toward Estevan and Castillo.

Castillo, somewhat upset by the insinuation, answered, "It is not of fear that I hesitate to make this journey for I fear no man."

"What is it then?" asked Alvar.

Somewhat sheepishly Castillo looked at Estevan, "We cannot swim and a journey of that distance will mean crossing countless inlets and rivers and though I fear no man, my fear of drowning is great."

Alvar smiled, "Friends, I heard the same argument from Lope Oviedo but I convinced him to put his faith in me and he crossed numerous waterways with my help."

Looking toward Dorantes he continued, "God has seen me through these years of hardship for a reason and I'm sure it is to lead us all out of this forsaken place. *Capitan* Dorantes and I will gladly carry you across these rivers and bays if you decide to flee."

Dorantes nodded in agreement. "We must at least try to return to *Espania* and the land that we love.

With no more discussion both Castillo and Estevan agreed to make the journey and put their faith in Alvar and Dorantes to help them along the way.

Although agreeing to make the journey Castillo was troubled. "*Algaucil*, I fear that telling the *Indians* of our plans will only precipitate our deaths at their hands. I would think it best not to press on immediately but to spend some time with them to earn their trust."

Both Estevan and Dorantes nodded in agreement. Alvar, not wanting to linger any longer than necessary at first argued with this reasoning but finally came to agree.

Castillo continued, "In the late summer of the year our *Indians* will make the journey to eat the fruit of the cactus. Many other groups come from far and near to join them. We could, at this time, flee from our *Indios* and go away with one of these other groups to begin our quest for *Panuco*."

All of the *Spaniards* agreed and as this time was somewhat distant Alvar agreed to give himself as a slave to the *Mariames*, with which

Dorantes was living, and wait until the cactus gathering time before making their escape. Rising, Dorantes and Alvar proceeded back down the trail but not before promising to stay in contact. They embraced and then, began their walk back to the *Mariame* camp.

October, 1532

Confluence of the Guadalupe and San Antonio Rivers

So busy were the *Mariames* in their nut harvest that they hardly took notice of the *Spaniards* during the day. Finally, in the evening hours, Dorantes was allowed to address a group of elders as they gathered around the fire. He asked if Alvar could remain with them and spoke of the virtues of the *alguacil*. One of the elders asked by which name he was called. With this Alvar rose to speak.

Over the past years, the *Indians* had assigned many names to him, but the one of which he was most proud of was "Spirit Bear Walker" assigned to him by the *Churrucans*.

"I am called Wasapi-tun-loki!"

Dorantes, who was sitting just outside the circle looked up in surprise, for this was the first time he had heard this strange name.

The *Mariames* did not speak the language of the *Churrucans* and the name mystified them as well.

One elder rose and spoke, "Tell us of this name."

Looking briefly at Dorantes, Alvar began his story of the black bear and the two cubs. In this primitive society, stories of heroic exploits were much revered and the elders sat transfixed as Alvar embellished the series of events that led to his assigned name. Even Dorantes listened with rapt attention.

At the conclusion of the story Alvar asked that he may join the *Mariames* so that he could escape the bad treatment he had had at the hands of the *Quevenes* and be closer to his friends. He went on to praise the *Mariames*, telling of all the good things he had heard about them; how they were great hunters, cared for their children, and were the "true people." With this, he regained his position by the side of the fire and awaited a decision. The elders seemed impressed and after a short amount of time, the same elder who had questioned his name rose and spoke.

"Wasapi-tun-loki we will take you in as one of our own. You will join the family of Quento-na-sah and help him in all that he commands."

Alvar was pleased because Quentonasah was also the master of Dorantes. The family group was large and his efforts would be much appreciated. Quentonasah himself was blind in one eye and it was with great effort that Alvar could look at his face without laughing for the bad eye wondered about as he was talking. So much so that both *Spaniards* referred to him as Ojo Loco in *Spanish*. When Quentonasah asked the meaning of these strange words the *Spaniards*, of course, lied and said that it meant "great man" when in fact it meant "crazy eye."

The blindness must have been a family trait because many within the family group had the same condition. Even the wife was afflicted and Alvar could only surmise that Ojo Loco had married a close relative and because of this, the condition was passed to other members of the family.

Ojo Loco treated both the Spaniards well, his position in the tribe somewhat enhanced by the addition of this white man called Wasapi-tun-loki. Estevan and Castillo lived with another group only a short distance away. The *Yguases* treated them well, but to Estevan, they paid more attention. Because of his blackness, they felt he possessed great powers. He was expected to assist with the day-to-day workload, but he was otherwise left alone. Interestingly, many of the men brought their wives to lay with him hoping that his powers would be transferred to them. Seeing this, Alvar wondered to himself why this black man would want to return to a life of slavery with the *Spaniards* when he could remain here as a relatively free man with a very active sex life.

At one of their gatherings, Alvar posed the question. "Estevanico, why is it that you would choose to journey with us to *Panuco* with all its dangers, and hardships when you can remain here as a free man?"

Estevan thought for a while before he answered. "*Alguacil*, here life is always very close to death. A storm, a snakebite, a disease, a harsh winter, or even a raid by a neighboring group can end your life. Back in *Espania,* I have an easy life and *Senor* Dorantes is a good man.

Estevan thought for a moment more, "Still, I have to admit that breeding these *Indio* women has its benefits."

He laughed and moved away, clapping Alvar on the back as he did. Even this display of familiarity would have been disapproved of in *Spanish* society but here, in this wilderness called *Amichel*, Alvar barely gave it a thought.

Late October, 1532

Mariame Camp at the River of Nuts

Alvar's life with the *Mariames* and Ojo Loco in particular was much easier than he had expected. As long as they worked hard gathering food and the other necessities the *Indians* seemed to let them be. In fact, a close relationship between Ojo Loco and the *Spaniards* began to develop. It was under his custody that their life improved. This was partially because of an incident that had occurred shortly after Alvar's arrival.

A group of unfamiliar *Indians* had occupied a section of the pecan grove adjacent to where the *Mariames* were gathering the nuts. This group did not speak their language and soon became belligerent in pushing the *Mariames* aside. This was unusual in this area because all groups usually coexisted and respected each other's gathering space. A shoving match had developed between Ojo Loco and one of the belligerents which quickly turned into a full-blown battle. Ojo Loco had grabbed a section of a stout branch and brained his aggressor who dropped to the ground unconscious. Two others immediately piled on Ojo Loco beating him with their fists. Seeing this from their perch in a pecan tree Alvar and Dorantes immediately dropped to the ground and ran to assist their patron. Alvar bowled one over while Dorantes jumped on the back of the other putting him in a headlock.

All around the other *Mariames* attacked the aggressors in a wild melee of flying fists, kicks, and gouges. The *Indian* that Alvar attacked jumped up and pinned him to the ground and was in the process of picking up a rock. Alvar tried desperately to free himself, but the *Indian* was much bigger and stronger and it was with outright terror that he watched the *Indian* raise the rock to crush his skull. At this moment the *Indian's* head exploded in a spray of tissue and blood and the rock dropped harmlessly at Alvar's side. Ojo Loco stood there with the same branch with which he had brained the first aggressor. Behind him Dorantes still held his aggressor in a headlock, both of them rolling on the ground. The *Indian*, trying to untangle himself, clawed at Dorantes eyes which were red and watering. Still, the *Spaniard* held on. Alvar watched as Ojo Loco raised his makeshift weapon and struck the *Indio* full force between the legs. Amid blood-curdling screams, Dorantes released him and rolled to the side. The *Indian*, writhing in pain, clutched his crotch and cried out in agony. Stepping to his side Ojo Loco dispatched the suffering *Indian* with another roundhouse swing to his head.

At this moment the *Yguazes* who had been camped nearby appeared on the scene and with their help the *Mariames* drove the aggressors off. Castillo and Estevan, who were with the attacking force, joined the two *Spaniards*. Both Alvar and Estevan tended to their friend whose face was marred with scratches and welts and eyes that had already begun to blacken.

Ojo Loco stepped up to both *Spaniards* and placed his hands on both their heads. He maintained this pose for several minutes while Alvar and Dorantes exchanged questioning looks. Wordlessly he removed his hands and walked off, but it was from that time forward that the *Spaniard's* treatment by the *Mariames* improved.

That night the *Mariames* and *Yguazes* celebrated deep into the night telling and retelling stories of the battle around a huge bonfire that sent sparks careening high into the air. Alvar, Dorantes, Castillo, and Estevan were left alone around a smaller fire to talk amongst themselves.

Dorantes, his eyes puffy and almost swollen shut, looked to Alvar. "*Alguacil*, we have only talked briefly of our compatriots on the other boats."

Alvar, idly drawing figures in the sand with a piece of stick, commented, "Yes, on the day of our first encounter you feared that all had died save for Natalo Figueroa who, to your best knowledge, still lives somewhere along the coast. Our conversation on the matter was cut short and we have not talked of it since."

"*Alguacil*, it pains me so...but I...I mean we..." Dorantes looked in turn at Castillo and Estevan." "We will try and relate to you everything known of our compatriots and their fates."

Dorantes started slowly. "The journey to the mainland was uneventful. We pulled our canoes onto a section of uninhabited beach and hid in the rushes until evening. After dark we began our journey to the south very much afraid and suffering from the elements. It was still early spring. The nights were cold and the winds blowing off the bay chilled us to the bone as we paddled our canoes along the shore. We dared not go inland. We ate small crabs that were more shell than meat, sea grass, roots, and an occasional fish that we were able to catch."

After pausing for a moment Dorantes continued. "On the morning of the second day, we saw ahead a structure in the sand. It was partially obscured by the blowing sand and as we hurried to it we saw immediately it was the boat of the purser Alsonso Enriquez and the friars. It had been blown far on shore as if by a storm. We looked in vain for any sign of the *Spaniards* that had been aboard but found none and, since our time was short, we proceeded to again hide in the grasses until nightfall ."

Alvar silently tried to remember each of the men who were aboard Enriquez's boat.

"That evening, as the sun was setting, we set out again and came to the first of the great rivers. The current was swift but by the grace of God, we managed to cross safely. The darkness of the night, however, caused us much grief as we had trouble finding the shore and each other on the other side. One of the canoes did capsize, thoroughly wetting the men that were in it. Since the night was cold and the wind picked up considerably they suffered much."

Castillo interjected, "It was from this experience that we decided to cross the rivers during the daylight hours."

Dorantes continued, "It was on the third day that the wind rose to such an extent that we were forced to carry our canoes along the beach. The blowing sand stung our faces and we were forced to trek further inland where the seagrasses provided some protection. We were cautiously making our way when a bearded man came running out of the rushes."

Again Castillo interjected, "We were all startled for he appeared as a madman waving his arms and screaming '*Compatriotas, Compatriotas, Cristianos*! To our surprise, it was Francisco de Leon!"

Alvar was startled. "*Senor* de Leon was on my boat. After our arrival on *Malhado,* he disappeared and no one knew what became of him."

Castillo continued, "Of his story, I know little other than he made it to the mainland and survived the winter there. Before encountering our group he had escaped from a group of *Indians* that treated him very badly. For many days he had hidden himself in the grasses and dunes not knowing what the next day would bring. You can imagine his excitement when he first spied us moving along the beach and speaking *Spanish*."

It was Estevan who spoke next. "We now numbered thirteen."

Dorantes now took up the story, "It was shortly after this that we encountered the second great river. This one was much larger than the first and the strong winds continued to blow. We were much afraid of this crossing and it wasn't until late afternoon that the conditions improved. We set out and were immediately confronted with strong currents. We paddled as best we could but were so weak from the elements and lack of food that all the canoes were dragged toward the sea. It was with much effort that we made the opposite shore, but not before two of the canoes had turned over. The first of these was swept out to sea and no sign of the three *Spaniards* aboard was found. On the other canoe, of the three men aboard, one disappeared under the waves while the others clung to the canoe. My canoe came upon these men and we pulled them to shore. We were so weak that we dared not return to the water and search for the other man or the occupants of the canoe that had been swept out to sea...may God rest their souls."

Estevan spoke again, "We now numbered nine."

Dorantes nodded. "We had become very scattered and it was on a broad delta that we regrouped. It was now evening...the winds once again picked up and the temperature dropped. We moved inland until the night became so dark that travel became impossible. We huddled under our canoes trying to find protection from the wind...and then it began to rain."

Alvar could only nod as Dorantes sat back, his eyes watering more than before. Castillo continued. "The rain, wind, and cold continued for two days. So miserable and sick were we that travel was impossible. All of us huddled together together to conserve body heat. During this time we ate nothing and only had the rainwater that ran off the canoes to drink."

Dorantes stood and walked away from the group, his shoulders shaking. He tried to hide his face but it was clear that the emotion had overcome him. Even through the thick beard, the tears cascaded from his face. Alvar, Castillo, and Estevan remained quiet but each felt the emotional stress that had overwhelmed their compatriot.

Alvar spoke, "*Amigo* Andres, come back and sit with us, for we are all distraught."

Gaining some control, Dorantes turned and walked back to the fire, but remained standing. "During the last night of our stay at this place, one more of our compatriots died. We didn't even know he had expired until that morning. I had laid next to him, Francisco de Leon, the man we encountered after crossing from *Malhado*. His face was no more than a hand width from mine and I knew not that he had died."

Emotion again overwhelmed Dorantes. He sat down in the sand and stared into the fire.

Estevan poked at the fire with a stick. Sparkles of embers cascaded into the sky. "We were too weak to bury him. We left them there in the seagrass to be eaten by the vultures and crabs. We were then down to eight men, all of us more dead than alive."

Again it was Castillo who continued. "That morning the weather improved and we trekked further down the coast, dragging our canoes as best we could, for the seas were still running high and we dared not risk them. The rain had stopped and the morning warmed so that by the noon hour the winds relented and the temperature was quite pleasant. Each of us regained some strength."

Estevan interrupted, "This was the day we came upon the injured dolphin!"

Castillio brightened, "Ah yes! An injured dolphin was thrashing in the surf, a victim of a shark attack. All of us gathered around it and dispatched the animal with rocks and driftwood. So weak were we that it took repeated blows to finally kill it."

Dorantes, back from his reverie, spoke, "We tore at its flesh there in the surf filling our stomachs with the raw meat. Many became sick, and our bodies were not able to process this amount of food. They...we...vomited there in the surf and then returned to the carcass to eat again. At long last we could eat no more and retired to the sand where we lay until early evening. Feeling much rejuvenated we continued on in the dark and came to a third river."

"The rain from the previous days had swollen this river and it was running high. We traveled inland looking for a suitable crossing point but could find none. Fearing to travel too far inland, because of the *Indios* that might be residing there, we waited at the river's edge for the current to subside. We stayed there all day. At about the hour of vespers, we made a decision to embark the next morning because our position here was exposed and we feared discovery by *Indios* that would harm or enslave us."

Castillo picked up the story. "The next morning was very cloudy and I remember a mist rising from the water. There was no wind and we embarked from the narrowest point that we could find. Pushing the three canoes into the water the current rapidly carried us downstream. I was in the canoe with two others and our combined strength carried us across the water faster than the rest. By now the two other canoes had disappeared in the mist. I remember, at midstream, seeing a very large tree float by, its branches turning like a windmill in the current. I thought then how lucky we were that this obstacle had missed us."

This obstacle had just passed into the mist when I heard the most blood curdling of screams, 'Mary Mother of God help us!' There were other screams and noises in the still air, but this is the one I remember most clearly and it lives with me every day."

Castillo stared absently into the fire before picking up the story again.

"One of the canoes with three *Christians* aboard had capsized in the strong current but all three had been able to hang onto the overturned craft. Listening to the screams we came upon them but were unable to bring any into our canoe. We paddled as best we could and finally reached the shore, dragging them behind us."

"The three had been in the cold water so long that I thought for sure all would die. There on the beach, we built a fire and tried to warm them."

Estevan continued. "The three shook so uncontrollably that we had to continually turn them so that all sides of their body would be exposed to the fire's heat. Two began to improve, but the third, *Senor* Chaves, became unconscious. He never awoke, and by evening he had breathed his last."

"We now numbered seven men and we were in the most deplorable condition. Our clothes had rotted away. I myself had only a loincloth to cover my nakedness. We were lacerated with scratches and bites from the mosquitoes and sand fleas that tore at our skin. There was no rest from these pests and so fatigued were we that even brushing them off required great effort."

Alvar could only listen and nod for he too had experienced similar hardships and understood their great suffering. He especially lamented the news of each *Christian's* death.

Castillo picked up the story again. "We walked in the surf dragging our canoes behind us for we were so weak that we couldn't carry them. That evening we came to the fourth river which was only a short distance from the last. Here we camped for the evening to gather strength. As God is most merciful we were besieged by scores of land crabs. Through all the hardships I had retained my flint and steel and after securing a fire we killed and roasted them and ate our fill."

"Feeling much refreshed we crossed over this river without incident and continued on. Quite by chance, we found ourselves on a narrow peninsula. To the west, the mainland receded into the distance but remained just visible on the horizon. Too weak to return we continued on and came to a wide *ancon*...inlet. Here the water boiled with a great current and we sat there on the beach much discouraged. To cross in such conditions would be certain death."

Estevan, having spent most of his life at sea plying the waters of the *Mediterranean* suggested that the turmoil of the inlet was a result of the tide rushing out. Perhaps if they waited for the time between tides the conditions may improve. So they waited.

As the five *Spaniards* lingered a quick-moving squall passed over, blasting their bodies with wind-blown sand before thoroughly wetting each with rain that came in torrents. Exposed on the peninsula they suffered much, huddled under the two remaining canoes.

After the storm passed the sky cleared, the winds abated and the temperature rose. Shivering there on the sand the men now tried to warm themselves.

"I had fallen asleep, there on the warm sand," recalled Estevan. "The storm had passed rapidly to the west and when I finally arose the water in the *ancon* had calmed. Seeing this we immediately entered our canoes and proceeded to the other shore which we gained with much difficulty. The waves had subsided considerably but the current was still strong enough to take us seaward. It was with the utmost effort that we finally made shore on the other side. We were exhausted and collapsed there on the sand."

For a long while no one spoke, each absorbed in his own thoughts. Alvar watched the dancing embers of the fire rise and disappear into the sky overhead. Across the clearing, the *Indians* continued their celebrations. Left to his own thoughts he again wondered what his wife Maria was doing at this very moment.

Castillo started the story once again, "Once we had rested sufficiently we continued our trek to the south. This island was long and narrow with the sea to our left side and a large bay to the west. At dark, we made our camp in the tall sea grass which provided some protection from the chilling offshore winds. I remember that night. Shivering, we watched the sky as meteors fell in unprecedented numbers. I felt it was a sign...an omen...of good luck. We called it *La Noche de las estrellas fugaces*...the night of falling stars."

CHAPTER 12

Jumping Black Frog

Frog Saltando Rana Negra

*E*stevan smiled at this and replied, *"Because of the dancing the Indios have given me a new name."*

It was Alvar who answered first. "Praise tell us what it is!"

Estevan looked sheepish when he answered. "It is Pala-see-hona."

At this, the three Spaniards convulsed in laughter.

Finally, Alvar was able to speak. "From now on, whenever I look upon you I will always see you as a 'Jumping Black Frog'!"

October, 1532

Mariame Camp by the River of Nuts (Guadalupe River)

*L*ounging by the fire, the three *Spaniards* and the black man, Estevan, continued to relate their story of survival to the new arrival, Alvar Nunez Cabeza de Vaca. It was nearly midnight and behind them, the *Indians* known as *Mariames* and *Yguases* continued their celebration of the day's battle in which they had bested an intruder tribe. Seemingly without tiring, they danced around a bonfire with strange rhythmic gyrations that somehow seemed to portray their participation in the battle. The women did not participate in the dance but remained far in the background, only approaching to bring wood to the fire. Periodically one of the dancers, excited by the activities and displaying an obvious erection, would leave the circle of dance. After satisfying his desires with one of the women he would return to the circle and continue on as before.

Ojo Loco, the *Indian* patron of Alvar and Dorantes, came over and grabbed each man in turn. He led them to the fire and motioned that they join in the dance. The *Spaniards,* having no idea of what was expected of them, tried their best to mimic the movements of the *Indians*. Their stiff *European* efforts caused howls of laughter from everyone. Even the women were laughing from the shadows as were Castillo and Estevan. Finally, Alvar and Dorantes excused themselves and hurried back to their compatriots.

Quite unexpectedly Estevan jumped up and joined the ring of dancers. His movements were like nothing the *Indians* had ever seen. He swayed with an internal rhythm and made huge jumps into the air. Alvar, Dorantes, and Castillo looked at each other in amazement. So impressed were they that they began to clap in time with *El Negro's* movements. The *Indians*, unfamiliar with this, also began clapping in time with the leaping black man. The reason for Estevan's display soon became obvious to the three *Spaniards*, for on completing the dance he retired to the shadows to mate with the *Indian* women. There was no reaction from the men, for they quickly resumed their activities, many trying to emulate his jumps.

Among the three *Spaniards,* the mood once again became somber as Castillo turned to Alvar. "After the night of falling stars, we awoke to a clear morning and freezing temperatures. We suffered grievously from the cold but continued south along this spit of land. From the high sand dunes, we could look in both directions and see water, the broad bay to the west and the ocean to the east. We knew then that we must be on an island or a very narrow peninsula."

Dorantes interrupted, "The thought of being on an island terrified us, for we questioned whether we would have to return to the inlet just crossed in order to regain the mainland. We talked about this and decided to continue and see what God's plan was for us. It took us that day and the next to reach the southern terminus of this island. Before us was another inlet, not as wide as the one previous but a vast marsh of tidal lakes and tributaries. In our weakened condition we collapsed there on the sand not knowing if we could make it to the other side."

About this time Estevan returned from his liaison with the *Indian* women. He was smiling broadly and shaking his head. He looked exhausted.

Dorantes called him out. "Estevanico, did you satisfy all of them or just a few?"

"*Senor* Dorantes, they are insatiable. Their lovemaking knows no bounds. I am a broken man...I was only able to satisfy a few."

"Ha!" Replied Dorantes, "You are a broken man only until the next opportunity presents itself."

Estevan smiled at this and replied, "Because of the dancing the *Indios* have given me a new name."

It was Alvar who answered first. "Praise tell us what it is!"

Estevan looked sheepish when he answered. "It is Pala-see-hona."

At this, the three *Spaniards* convulsed in laughter. Finally, Alvar was able to speak.

"From now on, whenever I look upon you I will always see you as a 'Jumping Black Frog'!"

The moment of levity was brief and soon Castillo continued his story once more. "As we lay there exhausted and near death, we saw the first *Indios* we had come upon in many days. They seemed to be everywhere and at closer examination, they were indulged in eating blackberries, a fruit that seemed to grow in abundance at this end of the island. They had noticed us as well and so agitated were they by our appearance that they moved further away. So hungry were we that the blackberries seemed a gift from heaven."

Estevan, sitting next to Dorantes interjected. "We gorged on them, our fingers and faces discolored by the juices." Somewhat wistfully Estevan seemed to stare into the past. " I can still taste the sweetness of those berries."

Dorantes, absentmindedly drawing designs in the sand with a stick, related what happened next. "As we gorged on the berries some of the strength seemed to return to our bodies. The *Indios* continued to stay apart from us, but then the strangest thing happened. Two *Indios* approached...or at least what we perceived to be two *Indios*. As they neared, however, we saw that one was heavily bearded. To our amazement, it was our compatriot Natalo Figueroa, one of the four who had left *Malhado* in search of *Panuco*. He, like us, was much overcome with emotion and we stood there in the sand embracing, crying, and relating stories of our exploits."

Alvar interrupted at this point. To no one in particular he addressed the question, "What of the other three *Spaniards* that accompanied Figueroa?

Castillo shook his head in exasperation, "Two of the four who had left *Malhado* died of hunger and exposure to the cold. These were Alvaro Fernandez and Marco Astudillo a native of *Zafra*. Astudillo had been a compatriot of mine for many years and I knew him well. He was very brave and the news of his death caused me much grief." Castillo hesitated, "It still does."

Dorantes laid down his stick. "The *Indio* that had accompanied them also died. Because of their weakness the two remaining *Spaniards*, Figueroa and Xavier Mendez, were forced to leave their dead compatriots there in the sand to be consumed by the animals of this place. In the end, both Figueroa and Mendez were captured by the *Quevenes* and enslaved. Their life of servitude was severe and they suffered much, but at least there was some food to eat and their health improved somewhat."

Alvar remembered his encounter only a few days before.

"An *Indio* from one of the tribes behind told me something of Mendez."

It was Estevan who answered in his blunt manner.

"*Alguicil, Senor* Mendez was killed by the *Indios*."

Dorantes looked at Estevan and shook his head before continuing. "Figuero related that Mendez was driven to continue his journey to *Panuco* and escaped the camp during the night. It was not until the middle of the next day that the *Quevenes* learned of his absence."

Alvar interjected, "Where did he go?"

Dorantes continued, "Mendez traveled south along the coast toward *Panuco*. The *Quevenes* on learning of his escape immediately set out after him, but not before beating Figueroa severely. They accused him of aiding his compatriot."

Dorantes paused briefly before continuing.

"Mendez stayed ahead of his pursuers for two days and eventually came upon a group of *Mariames* who captured him as a slave. When the *Quevenes* arrived, there was much argument and discussion but eventually, the *Mariames* killed Mendez because he tried to escape again. It was then that they cut off his head and gave it to the *Quevenes*."

Estevan again. "They brought the head back with them and Figueroa was forced to gaze upon it."

Alvar made the sign of the cross as did the other two *Spaniards*. He asked his questions slowly.

"I have so much to ask that I know not where to begin. I have learned that only Figuero of the original rescue party survived after leaving *Malhado.* I have learned that the twelve of you that left *Malhado* came upon Francisco de Leon of my boat. I have learned that by the time you met Figueroa only seven of your party remained alive."

Dorantes answered, "*Si Alguacil,* other than ourselves, there were my cousins Diego Dorantes and Pedro Valdivieso as well as Diego de Huelva and the *Asturian* cleric Pietre de Asturiano.

Alvar thought for a moment, "The *Indios* we met at the inlet told us stories of the deaths of your cousins and S*enor* De Huelva, but what of the *Asturian* cleric?"

Dorantes tried to explain, "When Figueroa first came upon us he was accompanied by the *Indio* that owned him. Together they had crossed the inlet to gather fish. We talked long with Figueroa, but as time passed the *Indio* became impatient. At that point the *Asturian,* who was in our party, said that he would go with Figueroa and, in turn, the *Indo* indicated he would provide the cleric with fish to eat. Together they went with this *Quevene* further up the island to gather fish. Before they departed Figueroa confided in me that they planned on escaping and proceeding towards *Panuco.*"

Afraid of the answer, Alvar reluctantly asked, "Were they successful in this endeavor?"

Alonso Castillo picked up the story at this point. "The *Quevenes* learned of their escape attempt and severely beat them both, even passing an arrow through the cleric's arm.

"Mother of God," was all that Alvar could mutter.

The mood brightened, however, as Castillo continued. "Natalo Figueroa is not to be trifled with, for in the end both he and the cleric were able to escape."

"Has there been any other word of these two?" Alvar was again hopeful.

Dorantes answered. "Before he was murdered, my cousin Pedro de Valdivieso had gone off with another band of the *Quevenes* to the south. On this journey, they came upon a people who talked of two hairy faces that had passed through their village. When questioned further they displayed to Valdivieso the Asturian's breviary, journal, and some clothes but had no knowledge of his death or anything else."

"Ah, so one or both the cleric and Figueroa could still be alive!"

Castillo again, "It is possible, and by the grace of God they are."

The *Mariames* and *Yguazes* continued their dancing. The night was warm and very still. Overhead the stars shone brightly in a moonless sky. Far to the west, an occasional flash highlighted some growing thunderheads.

The three *Spaniards* and the black *African* sat in silence, each with his own thoughts.

Several *Indians* came over and implored Estevan to dance for them again. This he did willingly.

Dorantes turned to Alvar. "*Alguacil*, we must talk now of the other boats."

Alvar was surprised, You know of their fates?"

"Only that of the *Adelantado* and the Friars boat."

October, 1532

Mariame Camp by the River of Nuts (Guadalupe River)

The morning was crisp and clear. A light rain in the early hours had freshened the air and now, save for the receding clouds to the east, the sky was clear. It was early and hardly a person stirred in the combined camp of the *Mariames* and *Yguzes*. The endless dancing and celebrating had taken its toll.

Alvar Nunez Cabeza de Vaca hadn't slept all night. Andres Dorantes and Alonso Castillo had told him the story of the *Adelantado's* boat and that of the Friars as had been told to them by Figueroa. Figueroa, in turn, had been told by the lone survivor of both parties, Hernando de Esquivel.

Alvar remembered his first reaction as Dorantes and Castillo relayed the story.

"You are telling me that of the 98 men aboard both the good friars and the *Adelantado's* boat only one survived...*Madre de Dios!*"

He had been dumbfounded.

Now he stared at the expanding sunrise and thought of all the men aboard the two boats...his compatriots, his friends...all dead. Even the lone survivor, the purveyor of the story, Esquivel, was gone, killed by the *Mariames* he had taken residence with; killed because one of their women had a dream that he was going to kill her son.

Only one other boat remained unaccounted for, that of Captains Tellez and Penalosa. Of this Dorantes, Estevan, and Castillo knew nothing. They had questioned Figueroa about it, but he was equally ignorant of their fate. Alvar knew, based on what he had heard last night, that their chances were not good. Still, he hoped for the best. This was a low point in Cabeza de Vacas's life. His only comfort was that God was testing him and that if he was able to bear the challenges he would be a better man.

"*Alguacil*, how are you this morning?" It was Andre Dorantes.

Alvar turned toward the cavalry officer. "Sad my friend, I can only think of the people we have lost and lament their passing. The good friar Xuarez, Campo, Bartalome Valdez, Alonso de Solis, the

Adelantado...all of the others..." Alvar trailed off, his voice quivering. "They are gone!"

Dorantes looked around him and then confronted de Vaca. "*Alguacil,* we have to talk of our plans to escape to *Panuco*. Soon the *Mariames* and *Yguazes* will go their own ways and we will, once again, be separated."

By this time both Castillo and Estevan had joined them.

Dorantes again, "*Alguacil* I have beseeched both of my friends here to join me in escaping this place and proceeding back to our *Spanish* brothers in *Panuco*..."

Anxious to get underway, Alvar exclaimed, "We should begin planning to leave as soon as possible."

Castillo was thoughtful as he addressed Alvar. "*Alguacil*, Capitan Dorantes, and I have talked of this..." As an afterthought, he turned to Estevan. "And I believe Estevanico is also in agreement."

"What is it?" Alvar asked curiously.

"*Alguacil*, you are a newcomer here, If the *Mariames* or the *Yguazes* learn of our plan to leave they will kill you for sure and, most likely, the three of us as well.

This is not what Alvar wanted to hear. Somewhat annoyed he asked, "What are we to do then?"

Dorantes spoke up. "*Alguacil*, next summer all of the Indios will venture there to eat the fruit of the cactus in that area. *Indio* groups from all over will congregate there. They stuff themselves with this fruit until their bellies swell up. When they are not eating, they are sleeping."

Alvar pondered this. "Go on."

"Our thought is to wait until this time, thereby gaining the confidence of our captors. When the time is right and the *Indios* are distracted in their gorge we can slip away."

Estevan now joined the conversation. "The tribes far to the south also congregate at the cactus fields to barter and trade. Once we have made our escape we can join one of these southern tribes in our journey to *Panuco*."

Alvar nodded his head. "As much as I would like to get underway as soon as possible, your plan makes sense. My concern is that we must endure this life with our captors for many more months."

Dorantes countered. "That is also a concern of mine *Alguacil*, but I think there is no other way."

"Are we all in agreement then?" Alvar looked around him as each of his compatriots nodded in turn.

April, 1533

Area Near Copano Bay, Texas

Alvar's lungs burned and his legs felt like lead. He had been on the move since early morning when first the *Mariame* hunters had picked up the trail of several deer. He had seen this before, but never had he been part of the hunt. Up ahead four runners followed the trail left by the animals. Behind them, Alvar and three teenage boys from the village carried water, food, and implements to dress the animals once they were dispatched. They, in turn, followed the trail of the hunters.

The hunters could run for hours with hardly any effort. Although much slower than the deer, the endurance of the *Mariame* runners would eventually exhaust the terrified animals. Occasionally the deer would jump into the water in an attempt to lose their pursuers. This was a mistake, for once in the water the hunters had the advantage. As faster swimmers, they would quickly surround the animals and drown them. More often than not, however, the animals wore out and the hunters would overtake them.

Clad in a loose loincloth they carried only a knife, bow, and two arrows. Barefoot, they talked and joked as they ran, seemingly never running out of breath. Alvar and the young *Mariames* frequently lost sight of the four but the skill of the young men he was with seemed to easily follow the trail.

It was almost noon judging from the position of the sun in the sky. It was hot and he was having trouble keeping up. The young boys running just ahead of Alvar would turn and throw mud balls at him trying to get him to run faster. Just about the time that he could bear it no longer the young boys stopped and pointed up ahead. Below them in a shallow swale, a doe and her exhausted fawn were trying to stay ahead of the hunters, jogging just behind. They were toying with the animals now.

The doe stopped and turned to face her pursuers...her tongue hung out the side of her mouth. The fawn, who had been running beside her collapsed onto the ground. The hunters spread out and approached the animal from four directions. One of the hunters waved his arms and whooped and jumped about as he approached the doe. She turned her attention to him. Directly behind her another hunter silently approached and then flung himself onto her back. With one quick motion, he severed the jugular vein with a single stroke of his knife. The other hunters approached the fawn laying motionless in the grass and dispatched it as well.

The young boys with Alvar let out a series of piercing yells and whoops and then motioned Alvar to hurry. They would field dress the animals and then cut them into sections that could be easily carried. When they arrived at the kill site the hunters were greedily eating the livers of the two animals. Nothing went to waste. The intestines were stretched and by deftly pinching them between thumb and forefinger the feces inside was forced out. The skin was flayed off the carcasses and rolled up with the viscera for processing by the women of the camp. The head was left attached to the skin. Later the brains would be scooped out as a particular delicacy. During this process, Alvar was not allowed to eat.

In a matter of only a half hour, the process was complete and Alvar shouldered his burden of the kill. With the additional weight attached to a crude frame on his back, he again struggled to keep up. The hunters started back to camp at a jog...they carried nothing.

On reaching the village the meat was quickly consumed, most of it eaten raw. Alvar and Dorantes were only given a few scraps and enlisted to scrape the skins. Because of their great hunger, they consumed any piece of fat or residue found clinging to the hide. After the hides were prepared all of the bones were pulverized into powder and mixed with water, berries, and meat scraps into a kind of thick stew. A hole was dug in the ground to contain the concoction while dirt was periodically added for flavor.

It wasn't until midnight that Alvar crawled back to his crude hut and collapsed onto the sleeping mat. Other than the few scraps given him he had not eaten for two days. By his best recollections, it was sometime in the spring of 1533.

June, 1533

South Texas

In the heat of early summer, the *Mariames* began a slow migration to the south to pick berries, dig roots, and gather bean pods. The hunger during this time was intense and that of their *Christian* slaves even worse. Along the way anything that was remotely edible was consumed. Alvar marveled at the constitutions of these people. Spiders, snakes, grubs, deer dung, ant eggs, the inner bark of trees, and even the soil was used for flavor. *Indians* caught mice and swallowed them whole, smacking their lips in the process. Grubs were especially prized and they would dig in the soft earth around rivers and marshes to uncover them. To the *Spaniards'* disgust, some even picked through their own excrement looking for undigested seeds.

A particular root, when it could be found, was consumed in large quantities. Digging these roots is difficult for they grow deep and the ground is hard. Using only stone tools Alvar's hands constantly bled from the exertion. The roots could not be eaten raw and had to be processed and roasted for two days to soften and remove the overwhelming bitter taste. Even after this process was complete, the root caused severe gas and bloating. After consumption, the *Indians* would lay about, moaning from the pain in their bellies while the whole camp resounded in voluminous flatulations. The *Indians* thought nothing of it, but even in their misery Dorantes and Alvar would laugh to themselves at the symphony of outrageous sounds.

Beginning in June the bean pods of the mesquite tree would be gathered. Sweet and nutritious, these beans could be pounded into flour and combined with berries or anything else obtained during the daily hunting and gathering routines.

The *Mariames* continued their slow journey to the south toward the prickly pear cactus fields. The *Yguases*, further to the west, were also on the move. It's not that the cactus was not available where they were, but further to the southwest it existed in great quantities. As they traveled they could see local populations of prickly pears blooming profusely with the small egg-sized fruits, called *tunas*, just starting to form.

Alvar was always impressed with the demeanor of the *Indians* he was traveling with and, most of the people that he encountered. Despite the suffering faced on a day-to-day basis, they were very happy people and sang and danced whenever possible. Sometimes they would spontaneously break out into these *areitos* for no apparent reason. Their songs were both lilting and primitive with the subject centered on great deeds performed by ancestors. Some songs were repetitive and Alvar and Dorantes would join in. They found themselves enjoying the experience and, if nothing else, it helped to diminish the drudgery and hardships that everyone experienced.

Moving ever further south and west the vegetation and animals they encountered began to change dramatically. Once again Alvar saw the large cows that he had encountered in his trading journeys. These animals, larger than European cows, were much different in appearance. They had small horns and enormous heads and front quarters. Their hair was long and shaggy. Typically they congregated in small groups of three to seven individuals. The bulls were much larger than the cows and extremely bad-tempered. The *Indians* hunted these animals but with much caution. Typically they would surround the animals forcing them to mill about in confusion. The animals' hides were thick and the archers would get as close as possible before releasing their shafts. They aimed for the area just behind the front legs hoping to puncture a lung. Arrow shots to the head were useless and many times Alvar had seen these shots bounce harmlessly off their skulls. During these encounters, the great bull was the animal that had to be watched. It was on one of these hunts that Alvar had a close encounter with.

Alvar and Dorantes had been enlisted to keep the animals distracted by waving a large blanket in the air. The infuriated bull with several non-lethal arrows lodged in him lowered his head and charged the *Spaniards*. Dorantes dived behind a thick bush leaving Alvar as the sole target. These animals, despite their size, were extremely fast and quick. Fleet of foot as Alvar was, he was no match for the angered bull. Just as he felt the hot breath of the animal closing on him, Alvar dove into a small runoff ditch. So close was the bull that he actually stepped on the *Spaniard's* shoulder as he passed over the ditch. The bull stopped a short distance away and turned to make a second charge, but it was at this moment that several of the *Mariames* rushed the stationary animal and loosened several arrows into its side. Its attention diverted, the bull tried to charge each archer only to be shot with other arrows. Now, with large bubbles of blood running from its mouth and nose, the animal sat back on its haunches with a glazed look in its eyes.

Strangely, the hunters held back and looked at Alvar. He stood, not knowing what to expect. Behind someone nudged him. Startled, Alvar turned to see his patron, Ojo Loco, handing him a spear.

"They are honoring you for the kill."

Alvar took the spear with a questioning look in his eyes.

Ojo Loco picking up on the confusion pointed to a spot just below his rib cage and instructed Alvar.

"Thrust the spear here on the bull as deeply as you can."

The dying animal watched Alvar as he approached, actually trying several times to stand. Alvar watched the animal's eyes. He feinted to his left and then rushed forward burying the spear as deeply as he could in the animal's side. A great geyser of blood rushed out with an audible "whoosh." The bull dropped to its knees and then fell forward onto the ground. Its breathing continued, but only for a moment. With a gurgle and a loud moan, the animal died. Alvar stepped back while the *Mariames* rushed forward to butcher the animal. He was handed the still-warm liver dripping with blood. He bit off a large piece and then passed it to the other hunters who greedily consumed the organ.

Coming up behind him Dorantes clapped him on the back. "I was worried about you *Alguacil!*"

"I have never been so scared." was all the Alvar could say.

August, 1533

Prickly Pear Cactus Fields Near Present-Day Alice, Texas

Each day the band would see signs of others, also moving towards the cactus fields. Occasionally they would travel together. This was both good and bad for it gave friends and relatives time to visit and compare stories, but, it also was a source of contention as jealousies and arguments arose.

It was with much relief that the band began to enter the land of the cactus. At first, only an occasional outcrop of plants would be encountered. Most of the fruit was not yet mature and those that were were quickly gobbled up, the *Indians* preferentially giving them to their children. All around other groups were steadily gathering, *Indians* from further down the coast and those who lived far inland. While much of the cactus fruits were not yet ready to eat much of the time was spent trading. The inland *Indians* brought flint and hides that were prized by the seacoast dwellers. In turn, these groups traded sea shells, reeds, and dried fish. The commodity most prized by the *Mariames* and *Yeguazes*, however, was the women of the other tribes.

Both the *Mariames* and the *Yeguazes* had no source of young women because girl babies were killed at birth.

Alvar, much to his horror, had seen newborns thrown to the dogs to be torn apart and consumed. His first encounter with this practice had left him shaken and physically ill. Since that initial encounter, he had taken great pains to avoid such events, staying as remote as possible from women who were about to give birth. It couldn't be totally avoided, however. He remembered the time he was scrapping hides and a pack of camp dogs ran past him, the lead animal with a half-eaten torso in its mouth, the other dogs trying to steal it away.

Young females were a burden to feed and because of this, they were discarded. The *Mariames* and *Yeguazes* also felt that retaining daughters would give their enemies a reason to attack them. Of all the *Indians* that Alvar had encountered only these two groups practiced this barbaric custom. The young men would barter far into the night, trading most of what they had in order to secure a wife.

September, 1533

Prickly Pear Cactus Fields Near Present-Day Alice, Texas

It was during one of these bartering sessions that a dispute arose. A *Mariame* had offered a fine bow and two arrows for a woman of another tribe, the going price for such a purchase. An older *Yeguaze* man on seeing the particularly comely women had stepped in and doubled the offer so that he could have her. Angered, the young *Mariame* had struck the *Yeguaze* with a stick causing his head to bleed profusely. Other *Yeguazes* had come to his aid, and, in turn, other *Mariames* had also entered the fray. The fight lasted for several hours and in the end, both groups gathered their stick houses and other belongings and moved apart from each other.

For Alvar and Dorantes with the *Mariames* and Castillo and Estevan with the *Yeguazes,* this was a disaster for they were now separated and their plans for escaping would have to wait until the following year.

The *Mariames* and the *Yeguazes* stayed in the cactus fields but were located far from each other. Only once did Alvar come in contact with his compatriots, and that was quite by accident. Searching for the cactus fruit, called *nochtli* by the *Indians*, Alvar wandered far from the others of his group. At midday, he entered a particularly rich area already frequented by other *Indians* that he realized were *Yeguazes*! Alvar was immediately recognized, but he was allowed to stay because he had not been part of the argument that had separated the groups. He spied Estevan sitting on the ground, legs crossed, slurping a particularly tart *nochtli* that caused the *African* to purse his lips and squinch his face.

In *Spanish* Alvar called out to him, "Estevanico it appears you have found a particularly tasty *nochtli*!"

Startled, Estevan turned quickly, cactus juice running down his chin. "Alguacil where did you come from?"

"I wandered far from my patron hoping to find you and *Senor* Castillo. In that, I have been partially successful."

"*Capitan* Castillo is far from here, maybe a league or two further to the west. I elected to stay with this group because of...well...ah..." Estevan nodded toward a group that included a particularly comely young woman.

Alvar followed his gaze and noticed the young woman looking back at Estevan. He rolled his eyes, "Estevanico these *Indio* women will be the death of you!"

Estevan only smiled and continued slurping the *nochtli*.

Sitting down next to him Alvar picked one of Estevan's *nochtli* and sampled it. "*Caramba*! I have never tasted one this tart." He pursed his lips and squinted his eyes.

Estevan laughed at him and Alvar noticed the young woman and her compatriots were also pointing and laughing.

Alvar stayed with Estevan for an hour before heading back to the *Mariames*. Together they affirmed that an escape attempt this year would be futile. They were too far apart and coordinating the escape would not be possible. Alvar asked that Estevan pass their decision on to Castillo before rising to leave.

Turning, Alvar, quite unexpectedly, extended his hand. "Until next year, take care of yourself and look after *Senor* Castillo."

Estevan was taken aback. Normally a *Spanish* slave would never be offered a handshake, especially someone as noble as the King's Treasurer. He took his hand.

"I will, and you as well *Alguacil*."

September, 1533

Prickly Pear Cactus Fields Near Present-Day Alice, Texas

It was growing late, past the hour of Vespers as Alvar struggled to return to the *Mariames* before dark. Luckily the sky was clear and the afterglow of the sunset illuminated the ground before him. The advancing darkness lent a quietness to the desert. Only an occasional hoot from an owl disturbed the stillness. It was quite unexpected then when three *Indians* bolted from their hiding place and threw him to the ground. They were *Yeguazes* and Alvar immediately recognized them. They pummeled him with kicks and slaps, accusing him of trying to escape. They had been sent by Alvar's patron, Ojo Loco, to track him down and bring him back.

Alvar tried repeatedly to explain that he had just wandered too far and become lost, all to no avail. They bound his hands behind him and led him back to the camp. It wasn't until well after dark that Alvar was placed in front of Ojo Loco. The patron slapped him heavily on the face and asked him why he had tried to escape.

"Quento-na-sah, I made no attempt to escape, I had only become lost in the desert."

Alvar could see that Ojo Loco did not believe him.

"Quento-na-sah, when your men found me I was returning to camp!"

Quento-na-sah considered this and stepped forward so that he was only inches from the *Spaniard's* face. He looked deeply into Alvar's eyes. Even with the seriousness of the situation Alvar struggled not to laugh, for though the cross-eyed *Indian* was looking directly at him, it appeared he was actually looking somewhere else.

Finally, Quento-na-sah stepped back and nodded to the three *Indians* holding him. He was cut free. Nothing else was said of the incident. Dorantes joined him then and whispered into his ear.

"That was a close one *Alguacil.*"

CHAPTER 13

Big Ears

Orejas Grandes

Ori-tan-grana, however, had a physical characteristic that gave the Spaniards much amusement...his ears were enormous! The pierced lobes were each tied with pieces of rawhide at the end of which dangled colorful stones. The added weight elongated the lobes almost to the chief's shoulders.

June, 1534

Mariame Camp Near Vales Bay, Texas

The *Mariames* and *Ygenzes* had both traveled north to their winter quarters just north of the great bay, but they had stayed far apart, the quarrel at the cactus field not easily forgotten. The *Mariames*, with whom De Vaca and Dorantes resided, located themselves at the confluence of two waterways that emptied into an estuary. The *Ygenzes*, with whom Estevan and Castillo resided, had encamped about 4 leagues to the west on the banks of a river. had They had stayed apart for the majority of the winter with only occasional visits by family groups. It had been many months since he had last talked with Castillo or Estevan. The winter months had not been easy for anyone. All suffered from great hunger. Having to do the vilest of work during these months of suffering, Alvar's relations with his *Mariame* master had deteriorated. Three times he tried to escape to other *Indians* living further inland, but all three times the *Mariame* search parties captured him. For some unknown reason, they didn't kill him, but instead, transferred him to another group of *Mariames*.

The *Mariames* and *Ygenses* had stayed apart for the majority of the winter with only occasional visits by family groups. It had come as a surprise then when Alvar was awakened by the sounds of wailing in the early morning hours. What seemed like the whole clan of the *Ygenzes* were entering camp. As they did, the *Mariame*s rushed to meet them, tears streaming down their face. The event lasted all day, the noise and discord continuing into the night. The reason for the reconciliation alluded the *Spaniards* but they were much relieved, as it gave them time together once again and an opportunity to plan their escape to *Panuco*.

Alvar and Dorantes were especially glad to be leaving, for the mosquitoes, in this area by the bay, were unrelenting. Of all the years spent in *Amichel,* they had never seen infestations such as this. Many times, when the wind was from the east, huge swarms would appear over the landscape, their mass darkening the skies. Even the thick application of greasy concoctions didn't seem to help much. Many times the whole village would pack up and move inland until the voracious pests had moved on.

It was early summer when the migration to the cactus fields began. As expected, this was the year when the nut trees would produce almost nothing so everyone anticipated gorging themselves on the swet-tasting *nochtli*, the fruit of the cactus. As before, other *Indian* groups joined them in the journey. Those traveling from the western lands brought trade items of flint and skins which the coastal dwellers traded for sea shells, roots, and dried fish.

On the way to the cactus fields the various *Indian* groups paused by a shallow bay to hunt deer. This had become an annual event. Everyone from a village would space themselves in a long line, and drive herds of deer into the bay. Here they could be swiftly dispatched. The deer hunt was enjoyed by all, with everyone engaged in driving the deer to water, butchering the meat, and tanning the hides. They remained in this area for several weeks.

In what Alvar estimated to be mid-August they arrived at the cactus fields, each group separating to find their own cache of the succulent fruit. The three *Spaniards* and the black *African* joined in the gorging, stuffing themselves until their stomachs swelled almost twice their size. Denuding entire hillsides of the fruit they would return several days later to see a new batch ready for the picking. This gourging lasted for weeks. Finally, near the end of August Alvar, Dorantes, Castillo, and Estevan decided they would make their escape. They would coordinate on the first day of the new moon thinking it to be the beginning of September.

Four days later the *Spaniards* could just see the thin curved outline of the moon as it made its accent across the desert. Alvar and Dorantes gathered their meager possessions and made ready for tomorrow. They were both excited and scared. More than that they hoped the Castillo and Estevan were also making ready.

In the morning both *Spaniards* were surprised to see that the *Ygenzes* had moved off to another location taking Castillo and Estevan with them. Conferring together, Alvar and Dorantes agreed to proceed with their plan. Hopefully, the other two *Spaniards* would do likewise.

The *Mariames* had made their encampment next to a river that flowed to the southeast called *Ocana la nochtli...r*iver of the cactus fruit. Here the cacti were particularly abundant and everyone was preoccupied with gathering the edible fruit. Alvar and Dorantes gradually drifted away from the group, stopping occasionally to feign gathering and eating. Once out of sight, they moved rapidly to the northwest, to a site that all had agreed upon to meet in case they had become separated. It was a strange zig-zag in the river that seemed to form the letter "M." This was a heavily wooded area and an ideal place to avoid the prying eyes of Indians. When Alvar and Dorantes arrived at the location they were exhausted, and quickly hid themselves in the foliage. Breathing heavily, they peeked through the grass cover to spot any sign of their two companions. They were nowhere in sight. In fact, no one was visible. This area was void of the cactus.

Concealed in their hideaway time dragged by until it was late afternoon. The sun was beating down and the mosquitoes were particularly voracious. The humidity was high and being hid away in the tall grass made it even worse. Both *Spaniards* knew that the *Ygenzes* had moved off to the north and to find Estevan and Castillo they decided to move in that direction.

Cautiously moving through the landscape they began to encounter small family groups gathering *nochtli*. These were inland *Indians* and by questioning them Alvar determined that the *Ygenzes* camp was about half a league ahead. They now moved very cautiously, stopping every few feet to scan the area. It was at one of these stops that they heard someone coming down the trail. Alvar and Dorantes hid themselves.

A figure appeared coming around the trail just under a tall oak tree. The man had black skin and Alvar knew immediately that it was Estevan. Dorantes cautiously restrained Alvar from making his position known.

"Let's see if he has been followed."

Tense moments passed as Estevan actually passed their concealed position and continued down the trail. There was no one following him.

Alvar softly called out his name. "Estevanico!"

Estevan froze in mid-stride the look of fear heavy on his face.

Alvar called out again, speaking *Spanish*. "Estevanico, it is your *Alguacil* and *Capitan* Dorantes."

Relief flooded over the black man's face as he turned to greet his two compatriots.

They briefly clapped each other on the back before hurriedly continuing down the trail talking in whispers as they walked.

Dorantes asked, "What of *Capitan* Castillo, have you seen him?"

Estevan explained that he had talked with the captain only yesterday. He was with a group of *Indians* called *Eanagodas,* searching nearby for the fruit of the *nochtli.* He had talked briefly with the captain and told him of his plans to escape the next day. Together they had agreed to use the same trail in their escape attempt.

Alvar stopped and motioned for the other two to hide themselves in some thick undergrowth.

"We will wait here until dark to see if *Capitan* Castillo comes along."

It was hot and the mosquitoes bothered them greatly but the trio remained concealed until late afternoon when they heard a twig crack. All of them froze in position and stared ahead intently. This could be an animal, an *Indian* search party, or, praise God, Captain Castillo!

It was him.

Castillo was moving quickly with frequent looks behind him. Every few feet he would dart to the side of the trail to briefly conceal himself. When satisfied he wasn't being followed he would jump up and rapidly move forward.

Alvar tapped Dorantes on the shoulder. He whispered.

"Watch this!"

Alvar called out in *Spanish*, "*Capitan* Castillo, stand at attention!"

Startled, Castillo spun about, a look of bewilderment in his eyes. On seeing Alvar, Dorantes, and Estevanico rising from their concealment, a look of relief flooded over him.

"*Alguacil,* you scared me to death, thank God it is you," was all that Castillo could say.

Dorantes, laughing, nervously called out, "We must keep moving and leave this area."

After quickly embracing and shaking hands, the four companions rapidly moved down the trail looking behind them every few feet to ensure no one was following. To be caught now would surely bring terrible consequences. They continued, *adelante*...towards *Panuco*, as fast as possible.

September, 1534

South Texas

The four men had traveled for four days, moving sporadically during the day from one concealment site to another. It was during the nighttime hours that they made their best progress, together covering as much as four or five leagues a day. In all this time they suffered from thirst, for the land was hot and dry. To remedy this they would dig a hole and fill it with the juice of the *nochtli*. Once full each *Spaniard* could drink his fill. The liquid was sweet and reminded Alvar of *arrope*, the cooked down and concentrated sweet fruit juice common to the area of *Valencia* on the east coast of *Spain*.

By Alvar's best guess, they had traveled almost 20 leagues, far from their oppressors' normal territory. In traveling south they had entered a much more desolate area. The *nochtli* were still in bloom but in much less quantity than the area from which they had fled. They began to encounter other groups of *Indians*, some traveling in the same direction.

From these people, they learned the fate of the boat captained by Enrique Penalosa and Alejandro Tellez.

A small family group of three men, father and sons, and two women spoke to the *Spaniards* of a group of coastal *Indians* who called themselves *Camones*. They related how they had killed all the bearded ones who had come ashore. This family group regularly traded with the *Camones* and had actually seen the massacre sight. They described in detail how the dead lay on the beach, hacked to pieces, their severed heads, arms, and legs spread about on the sand. They further related how the *Camone* men had strutted about, brandishing the weapons of the bearded ones and wearing their helmets and armor. Then the family group showed two of the items they had traded with the *Camones* for...rosary beads and a breviary with the name of Aljandro Tellez stenciled inside the cover.

The *Spaniards* were thunderstruck. They had long reasoned that the Penalosa-Tellez boat had encountered many of the same trials and tribulations as themselves, but to learn of its total destruction was almost more than they could bear.

This family group indicated that the land of the *Camones* was not far ahead and extended to the coast. For this reason, Alvar, Dorantes, Castillo, and Estevan immediately altered their course further inland. They would set a wide birth away from these fearsome people who had slayed their companions.

Proceeding now to the southwest they moved inland traveling as rapidly as possible. The story of the *Camones* had unnerved them and, once again, they traveled mostly at night frequently looking behind to ensure no one was following.

At about the hour of Vespers on the second day after altering course, the travelers saw some spires of smoke in the distance. Thinking the smoke was probably from an *Indian* encampment, they decided to cautiously move forward to investigate it. They were hungry, dehydrated, and tired and if there were friendly *Indians* ahead, maybe they could get some relief. Silently as possible, they moved toward the smoke which was still quite distant. Suddenly, up ahead on the trail was a lone *Indian* watching them from a distance. When he realized he had been seen, the *Indian* retreated back down the trail.

Alvar turned to the black man. "Estevanico, go after him and tell him we are peaceful and wish nothing but to find water and some food."

When the lone *Indian* saw that Estevan was alone he stopped to talk. Through hand signals and some common words, they were able to communicate. Estevan indicated that they were seeking the source of the smoke in the sky. The *Indian* explained that his village was the source of the smoke and that it was some distance ahead. He would guide them.

At about sunset, the *Indian* gave them directions and then ran ahead to prepare the village for their visit. After only a short walk the four travelers came to the village...nothing more than a collection of crude stick huts. Just outside the cooking fires were being tended for the evening meal. This was the source of the spires of smoke seen some distance back. Four of the village elders greeted the *Spaniards*.

Alvar explained, in the language of the *Mariames,* that they had been traveling long distances and would be much pleased if these people would allow them to eat and rest here.

This the elders agreed to and, in fact, suggested that the travelers were welcome to stay longer. Word of the *Spaniards* had preceded them. The elders explained that they knew of their healing powers and wished they would remain and tend to their people.

These called themselves *Avavares*.

The *Avavares* spoke a different language than any of the three *Spaniards* were familiar with, but with hand talk and their knowledge of other languages in the area, they began to communicate easily. Estevan was especially helpful. He seemed to pick up the new language with ease. These people also differed in other ways from the *Indians* of the coast. They were shorter in stature and much more impoverished. Living inland, the food sources of the seacoast were not available to them. Their diet consisted of whatever the sparse landscape could provide. Among other things, they ate the beans of a small tree with thorny branches. From this tree, they also fashioned short stout bows which they traded to the tribes of the north who prized them for hunting the large shaggy cows that frequented their grasslands.

That evening the *Spaniards* sat around the fire sharing stories with their hosts. They talked of many things and the *Avavares* seemed especially intrigued with stories of the *Spaniards'* homeland across the "big waters." During this time five *Indians* approached Castillo and complained that they suffered a sickness of the head. They suffered bouts of *maroes*...dizziness and a ringing in the ears. Castillo listened intently to their descriptions. They begged him to help.

In a dramatic show, Castillo stood, looked to the heavens, and asked for God's help. He turned to the afflicted *Indians* and made the sign of the cross over each one, commending them to God through his son Jesus Christ. For a final effect, he touched the head of each *Indian* and quickly whisked his hand away as if expelling evil spirits. With that, he rejoined the group sitting around the fire. There was a moment of silence and then, to a man, all five of the *Indians* said that the sickness had left them. They were much amazed and returned to their huts telling anyone who would listen of their encounter with the bearded spirit men.

Word spread and other people began coming forward, all with some kind of affliction begging to be cured. This lasted long into the night with the *Spaniards* asking God's help and saying *pater nostras* over the *Indians*. Each one brought an article of food, mostly pieces of dried venison, that the *Spaniards* consumed until they could eat no more. For his part Estevan also participated in the healings, concentrating on the women of the *Avaveres*. While looking to heaven he touched their most private parts and in several cases transferred his power of healing to the afflicted with intercourse.

Finally, in the early hours of morning when the last of the cures were completed, the *Indians* began to dance and sing until sunrise. The next day when the *Indians* had rested, the celebration began anew and lasted for three days.

October, 1534

South Texas

The *Avavares* had taken the *Spaniards* in, not as slaves but as healing shamans who were revered among their people. Dorantes and Estevan took up residence in the lodge of a medicine man who questioned them constantly on their methods and healing powers. Castillo was invited to join the family of one of the five he had cured on the first day. Alvar, recognized as the leader of the group, resided in the lodge of the headman whose strange name was Ori-tan-grana. In the *Avavares* language, this name translated to "Silent wind hunter" and, indeed, he was known for his abilities as a provider. Ori-tan-grana, however, had a physical characteristic that gave the *Spaniards* much amusement...his ears were enormous! The pierced lobes were each tied with pieces of rawhide at the end of which dangled colorful stones. The added weight elongated the lobes almost to the chief's shoulders. The *Christians* laughingly pronounced his name *"Orejas grandes."* Big Ears! Because the pronunciation was so similar the *Indians* never picked up on the private joke.

Big Ears had three young daughters, the oldest, Alvar estimated, in her mid--teens. The youngest, maybe fourteen. Each of these daughters was offered to Alvar as bed partners, either singularly or as a group. Big Ears expressed that he wished the power of the bearded healers be passed to his family through his daughters. It was a strange scene, especially to one with *European* standards. In the closeness of the lodge Big Ears and his wife would sleep in one corner while Alvar and the three daughters carried on their sexual escapades in the other corner. Of the three, Alvar enjoyed the youngest daughter the most whose sexual appetite seemed insatiable. At times Big Ears and his wife would watch and make comments to each other about the goings on until they too became aroused. During several of these frolics, Big Ears would offer up his wife and watch with glee as she cavorted with the bearded healer.

In each of the lodges, the scenes were similar, for sex among the *Avavares*, and indeed, any of the *Indians* so far encountered was uninhibited. Dorantes, Castillo, and Estevan reported similar occurrences and, when alone, the four *Spaniards* would laugh and joke about their encounters. It was one of the things that made life bearable so far from civilization and their countrymen.

Alvar had questioned Big Ears about the land that lay ahead, the people, and the availability of food. Big Ears responded that there was much fruit of the cactus, the *nochtli,* but that the season was all but over. Because of this all of the people had returned to their homes and the region would be uninhabited until the following summer. Without the fruit of the cactus and with winter approaching the land was desolate with few animals for meat and hides to protect them from the cold.

Hearing this and with much discussion, the *Spaniards* calculated their options. Should they venture out or stay here with the *Avavares?* Even with them, food would be scarce, but the chances of survival were far better than venturing out alone, across this wasteland in the dead of winter.

Besides, there were the women.

All agreed to stay with the *Avavares* until spring.

November, 1534

South Texas

A week after the *Spaniards'* arrival, all the people in the *Avavares* camp set out on a final hunt for the fruit of the cactus. It was late in the season and the *nochtli* were growing scarce, but further south they were known to still be blooming in abundance. The stick huts were torn down and all possessions of the meager camp were carried on the backs of the women. Food was scarce and for five days they traveled with great hunger. Game in the area was almost non-existent, the hunters only bringing back an occasional rabbit. These were preferentially distributed to the children. The *Avavares* and the *Spaniards* subsisted on anything they could find...roots, grubs, snakes, and insects. There were no *nochtli* anywhere along the route and Alvar began to have his doubts that any would be found.

On the fifth night, while the women were setting up the camp, Alvar ventured out on his own to look for two particular trees that produced edible beans that grew in pods. One was actually a small tree that grew in the driest of areas. The natives called it *mizquitl*. From it grew bean-like clusters that could be eaten. The other was a larger tree that kept its foliage year-round. It also produced edible beans. For this tree the *Avavares* did not have a word so Alvar called it simply *arbol de ebano*...the ebony tree...or more simply *ebano*, for its dark heartwood. Both trees reminded Alvar of the *algarroba* trees of southern *Spain*.

Having found a few *mizquitl,* Alvar stopped to eat the ripe beans. For five days he had hardly eaten anything and he overindulged until his stomach was much distended. Feeling tired he fell asleep, not awaking until dusk. Rising up he looked around in vain for any of the *Avavares* that he had come with. There were none. All had apparently returned to the camp-site. Now he was lost and the desert temperatures were dropping.

Choosing a direction that, he thought, led to the camp, Alvar continued on. He was naked and barefoot. In the failing light, he had to watch for thorns, scorpions, and poisonous snakes. With the approaching darkness and cold, he began to shiver uncontrollably, but still, he continued on. A dry thunderstorm passed overhead with lightning bolts that seemed to sear the very air around him, the clap of the thunder deafening. After the storm had passed a light appeared ahead and he quickened his pace across the featureless scrub. Surely this was a cooking fire from the *Avavares* camp.

As Alvar approached the source of light it was not the *Avavares* camp, but a tree aflame from one of the lightning strikes. His disappointment was great but the fire meant warmth and he knew he would survive the night.

In the morning he gathered two firebrands and as many pieces of firewood as he could carry with him. He passed through an area devoid of any wood to burn and was thankful for what he had brought. During this night he suffered greatly, only keeping warm by a very small fire from his limited supply of firewood. The next day he continued on, again with the firebrands. At the hour of vespers, he came to a river where firewood was plentiful. Here in a grove of trees, he dug a large pit with the butt end of a stout branch. Around the pit, he started four fires in the shape of a cross. The fires and the smoke that they produced kept him warm and thwarted the hordes of mosquitoes that congregated near the river. He covered himself with the grasses that grew by the river. The pit provided a wind break and he slept soundly only awakening occasionally to rekindle the fires.

Alvar stayed by the river for three more days only venturing out short distances to look for food and the *Avavares*. There was no food here and Alvar suffered greatly. His feet, already thick with callouses, were cut up and bleeding. Digging in the soft muck by the river he was able to uncover a few grubs and insects, but these only seemed to heighten his hunger. He tried eating some tender shoots of grass but this caused great stomach discomfort. By the third evening, he could feel his strength ebbing away. As darkness fell Alvar stoked the fires and once again covered himself with grass to ward off the cold.

He slept fitfully, dreaming of *Spain* and his childhood. His dream was surreal. He was helping his mother butcher chickens behind the house. They had started a fire and were singeing the feathers off the carcasses. The dream was so vivid that Alvar could even smell the burned feathers. The smell grew stronger and in his dream state, he sensed something was wrong. His eyes fluttered open to see flames licking up all around him. Somehow the grass with which he covered himself had caught fire. The dream smell of burnt feathers was his own hair. Alvar rolled to the side to escape the flames and then jumped up.

His hair was smoking.

Stumbling to the river he rolled in the water. In the cold pre-morning air the water was chilling and he quickly ran back to the warmth of the fires. By now the small grass fire had all but burnt itself out. Clearing away the singed grass, Alvar sat there in the pit and silently watched the sun as it cracked a sliver of light over the distant hills.

He must have fallen back asleep for some time because when he awoke again the sun was high in the sky. He decided then to gather his wood and firebrands, leave this place and continue down the river. Perhaps he would find food or some *Indians* that would take him in, for by now he had lost all hope of finding the *Avavares* and his compatriots.

Late in the afternoon, Alvar had stopped at a shallow pool to rest. Out of the corner of his eye, he saw something skitter across the shallows. It was a crayfish and he jumped up to capture it. He missed on his first attempt, only capturing a handful of sand. Splashing through the water he lunged at it again and was rewarded for his efforts. The crustacean's tail clicked in his hand. He ate it whole, crunching down on the hard carapace. On hands and knees there in the water, he felt the bolus move down his esophagus. It wasn't much, but it would help. Alvar rose up and proceeded to look for more of the small crustaceans.

Behind him, there was a noise. He turned quickly to discover its source.

A voice in *Spanish*. "*Alguacil* is it you?"

It was Andres Dorantes as if out of a dream. Behind him, others began to appear.

There was moisture in his eyes as he struggled to answer.

"*Si mi amigo*, it is me."

Dorantes ran across the shallow stream and embraced Alvar, now shaking with emotion.

"*Alguacil*, we thought you were dead!"

Praise God, he had been found!

CHAPTER 14
Bad Thing

Bala Cosa

The Avaveres spoke of an evil being that had come to them fifteen or sixteen years earlier. Hearing the stories the Spaniards jokingly called him Mala Cosa...bad thing, a name that the Avavares picked up!

November, 1534

South Texas

Alvar struggled to remember the year. He was almost certain it was 1534 but in the struggle to survive and the misfortunes they had experienced, the years had become muddled in his brain. Sitting on a rock, he used a stick to mark in the sand the events that he remembered and the corresponding year that they occurred. He would strive to repeat this exercise at every opportunity so that one day, hopefully, he could tell his story.

Alvar thoughtfully added his most recent encounters to the list. Being lost in the wilderness for five days, his encounter with the burning tree and his eventual discovery by the *Avaveres*. He put great significance in his coming upon the burning tree. To him, it equated to the biblical burning bush encountered by Moses at the base of *Mount Herob*. Here God instructed Moses to lead the *Israelites* out of *Egypt*. Like Moses, Alvar would lead his companions out of *Amichel*.

There were several *Avavere* children who followed him everywhere and watched with fascination as he drew the strange figures in the sand. They asked him what they meant. Alvar tried to explain but drew only blank looks from the youngsters. Other *Avaveres* had wandered over to gaze upon the strange marks in the sand and Alvar decided to give them a demonstration.

Seeing Castillo not far away he called out, "*Senor* Castillo come here, I need your help."

Alonzo took a seat next to Alvar.

"What is it that you need *Alguacil*?"

"You will see." Alvar winked at Castillo.

The crowd had grown as Alvar stood up and addressed the group.

"I need someone to whisper to me something that only they would know."

A tall lanky youth rose up and ambled over. Cupping his hand he whispered in Alvar's ear. "This morning I watched as a hawk killed a rabbit."

The youth stepped away and Alvar scratched a note in the sand and then asked Castillo to address the youth.

Castillo stood up and turned toward the youth. "You watched a hawk kill a rabbit this morning!"

The youth was so surprised that he stumbled backward and fell to the sand.

To the *Avaveres* it was astonishing. Truly the work of a shaman.

A larger crowd gathered and more people stepped up to whisper in Alvar's ear things that only they would know. In each case, Castillo repeated exactly what they had told Alvar. Soon, Dorantes and Estevan joined in on the demonstrations. Unfortunately, the demonstration turned into a fracas when one of the participants whispered in Alvar's ear that he had slept with a certain woman. Chuckling, Castillo repeated the written note.

Almost at once the woman's husband, unaware of the liaison, began pummeling his unfaithful wife. This expanded into a larger melee that included most of the family members on both sides.

The news of these spirit men spread. Reading the strange marks in the sand had elevated the *Spaniards* to a new level and they were looked on with great reverence.

As night fell the four *w*ere finally left alone and together they laughed at what had just occurred.

"We can use this to our advantage," said Alvar, "but we must be careful for, in reality, these are not miracles...only illusions."

Before he fell asleep this night Alvar was convinced it was late Fall of 1534, Maybe the middle of October or even early November. More than seven years since they had left the harbor at *San Lucar de Barrameda* and so much had happened, so many had died. If he survived this ordeal would anyone even believe his story?

November, 1534

South Texas

The *Avaveres* and their *Christian* guests continued to travel to the southwest. They traveled through a country almost devoid of anything edible. Still, there was sustenance if one looked hard enough. One plant in particular brought some relief. It was a horrid-looking vine with sharp thorns and heart-shaped leaves. With sticks and bare hands, they dug up the massive tubers. These tubers were then cut up into smaller pieces and sucked on to digest the starchy material within. The pulpy, fibrous material that remained would then be spit out. If found in abundance the tubers could be dried and pounded into flour. Big Ears explained that the vines would also produce berries during the winter months that were mostly seed but offered some nourishment.

Three days after Alvar's rescue they entered an area abundant with the cactus fruit. Some other Indians had preceded them, but there was food enough for all. Quantities of *nochtli* were consumed until everyone's stomachs were distended and they could eat no more.

Word of the arrival of the bearded white shamans had spread.

The next morning a group of *Indians* brought five sick people to Castillo to be cured. They offered their bows and arrows if he would help them. As they were lined up in front of him Castillo made the sign of the cross on each of the sufferer's forehead. He did this with great reverence, periodically looking to the sky and uttering in *Spanish,*

"Father forgive the sins of these your children and bring them to health."

Alvar, Dorantes, and Estevan stood close by and in unison repeated a *pater noster*. Of course, the spoken *Spanish* and *Latin* were not understood by the *Indians* and they looked on with great wonder.

The makeshift ceremony lasted until just before sunset after which Castillo gave them a final blessing and retired to his hut. The other three did the same. In the morning the five affected *Indians* showed up at Castillo's hut completely cured of whatever malady had possessed them. They showed great reverence and wonderment as they offered Castillo their bows and arrows as payment. He accepted and the joyous *Indians* wandered off.

The three *Spaniards* and the black man now decided to explore the area in which they were located. Not far from where they were was a wide river that ran south to southeast. Alvar thought he recognized it from his earlier wanderings. Throughout the area, others were gorging on the *nochtli*. Wherever the *Spaniards* passed the people would rise up and look upon them with great reverence. They came upon two groups who spoke entirely different languages. These were called *Cuthalchuches* and *Malicone*s. They were friendly with the *Avaveres* and often traveled with them in search of the *nochtli*. Further on were the *Coayos* and *Susolas* who spoke a language similar to the *Avaver*es but yet different in many ways. It was while sitting with the *Susolas* that the *Spaniards* were caught up in a deadly dispute. Arrows began to land around them, some embedding in the soft soil, others clattering off rocks. Everyone scattered to cover behind bushes trees and rocks. Another group who called themselves *Atayos* were at war with the *Susolas* and it was they who had launched the arrow attack.

The *Susolas* began loudly calling out, "The bearded, white holy men are with us, stop your attack or they will be harmed."

The arrows stopped.

The *Atayos* responded, "We will allow the white shamans to leave."

With that Alvar, Castillo, Dorantes, and Estevan hurried out of the area passing many of the *Atayo* bowmen as they fled.

Looking back Alvar saw that the attack had resumed, but now arrows flew in both directions as the *Susolas* defended themselves. After this both the *Susolas* and *Atayo*s, who had been at war with each other, decided on a truce.

Two days after this incident several of the *Susolas* approached Castillo. They talked of a man who seemed near death as he lapsed in and out of consciousness. They asked for his help.

Alonzo del Castillo was always a very reluctant and cautious physician. Like the rest of the *Spaniards,* he knew his abilities were limited, especially in serious conditions such as this. He turned to Alvar.

"I can not help this man who is most sick for I fear he will die no matter what I administer."

"Friend Alonzo we must do something, for these people look upon us as shamans with great power. To not treat them will bring the risk that our status as physicians will be jeopardized."

While they conferred in *Spanish*, the *Susolas* looked on expectantly.

"*Alguacil*, although I have loved God, I have sinned much in my life. I fear that I will be held accountable for these sins and fail to help this man. In so doing I will put us all in great danger." Castillo had lost his self-confidence.

Alvar considered for a moment and then turned to the *Susolas*. "Take me to this man."

Turning to Dorantes and Estevan he called out, "Walk with me."

It was an hour's journey to the camp of the *Susolas*. As they walked the three *Spaniards* were joined by some *Avavares* and a smaller group who had close ties to the *Avavares*...the *Culthalcuches*.

When they arrived at the hut of the sick man he was covered with a grass mat and perfectly still. Pulling the mat back Alvar looked down at a man who was surely dead. His skin was ashen and no pulse could be found.

Turning to the *Susolas* Alvar lamented, "We will do what we can but the life force of this man may have left him and I fear we are too late."

Several of the *Susolas* began to wail.

Alvar held up his hand.

The wailing stopped.

"I will talk with the spirits. Perhaps they will relent."

With this, Alvar began to pray over the unconscious man. He made the sign of the cross and then closed his eyes and rocked back and forth. While Alvar remained in this state, Dorantes stepped up and performed a *pater noster*. Estevan for his part touched each of the man's extremities with an eagle feather and blew upon the body. Now, Alvar, speaking in *Spanish,* beseeched God to give this man back his health. He did this while modulating his voice as if in a two-way conversation with the spirit world.

The *Susolas* were mesmerized.

At the end of an hour, Alvar asked the *Susolas* to leave the hut.

Turning to his compatriots Alvar shook his head. "This man is dead but to not have treated him would have been worse for us. We must leave this hut as if we had been in a deadly battle with the spirit world."

"I agree *Alguacil*. Let us loudly raise our voices as if we are in a great struggle."

All three began to loudly call out in *Spanish* anything that came to mind.

"*Santiago!*"

"Praise God!"

"*Espana!*"

All of this they accompanied by loud grunts and shrieks.

Finally, the three *Spaniards* left the hut of the afflicted man. For added show, Dorantes and Estevan supported Alvar between them who hobbled along on weakened knees.

The *Susolas* in their gratitude brought Alvar the afflicted man's bow and a basket of *nochtli,* the fruit of the cactus. Later in the day more sick *Susolas* were brought to the *Spaniards*. These all seemed to suffer from a strange malady that rendered its victims unconscious for short periods of time. The *Spaniards* called it a *modorra*.

In each case, the sufferers were prayed over and given the sign of the cross. Miraculously, each of the sufferers ceased to have any indication of the *modorra* when they left the hut. For these services, the *Spaniards* were brought several more baskets of *nochtli*. They distributed these baskets to the *Avavares* and *Culthalcuches* who had accompanied them.

Towards evening they were told that the man who had been near death had arisen and was walking about the camp. He had even eaten with several of his family members.

The *Spaniards* were flabbergasted that this man could have survived and immediately went to his hut to see for themselves. They found the man alert and in apparent good health. Each of them dropped to their knees and thanked God, because it could only have been through His intervention that this man survived.

Alvar was thoughtful. "God has blessed us, for this man is much like Lazarus of *Bethany* who our Lord Jesus Christ restored to life."

The *Susolas* and indeed all the *Indians* of the area were now convinced that the bearded white men and lone black man possessed great powers and they spoke of nothing else. Later, the *Culthalcuches,* who had been traveling with the *Avavares,* prepared to return to their land. Before they left they brought the *Christians* all the baskets of *nochtli* they had collected, keeping none for themselves.

"Why do you honor me this way?" Alvar asked.

A spokesman for the *Culthalcuches* stated, "We only ask that you ask the spirits to always keep us well."

"This we will gladly do."

With this, the *Culthalcuches* also presented each of the *Spaniards* with a large flint used for cutting. It was an object of great esteem highly prized by the *Culthalcuches* and indeed all the *Indians* of the area.

Again, the *Culthalcuche* spokesman stepped forward. "We have seen your many miracles and you truly are "Children of the Sun," do not forget us."

Dorantes, holding the primitive tool in his hand remarked, "I think God has smiled upon us all this day!"

March, 1535

South Texas

It was cold. Big Ears, his wife, daughters, and Alvar sat huddled around the fire inside the hut. The smoke exited through a hole in the center of the roof, but still, the atmosphere was so thick that it caused their eyes to water. Periodically each would venture outside to breathe fresh air but the fierce winds and low temperatures prompted a quick return to shelter and warmth of the hut. They had not eaten much in days, only some acorns and a few rabbits that Big Ears was able to snare. It was too cold to venture out. Two of the daughters were pregnant, presumably by Alvar. Big Ear's wife was also with child, the father being either Big Ears himself or possibly Alvar. Activities inside the hut were reduced to eating (when possible), sex, and quick trips outside the hut for water, firewood, defecating, and urinating.

As for food gathering Alvar, and indeed all the *Spaniards,* had accompanied the *Avaveres* on hunting trips, but only Castillo had mastered the bow, the other three being used primarily as "beaters" to drive the animals to an ambush site.

Today Alvar listened to the tempest outside while the little hut creaked and groaned from the force of the wind. He thought about the last few months and tried to make plans for what they would do when the weather turned. He had always watched the cycle of the moon very closely and thus had a rough estimate of the passing of months. When Alvar gazed upon the sky it fascinated the *Avavares* for they thought he was communicating with the spirit world. This fascination was not lost to the *Spaniards* who, in their healings, frequently called to the heavens for divine help. Soon, the *Avavares* began to mimic their actions, looking to the sky and talking as if someone up there was listening. It was bitterly cold today but the last week had been marked by subtle warming changes.

The full moon had passed and was now waning, only half of it exposed in the clear night sky. The sun, in its arc across the sky, was also moving noticeably to the north. Alvar estimated that the date was late March 1535. He expected that soon they would begin planning their journey to the south and, hopefully, *Panuco*.

All during this winter of 1534-35 while they remained with the *Avavares*, the four survivors had treated a myriad of *Indio* sufferers and in each case, all of those afflicted had been healed. To Alvar, Castillo, Dorantes, and Estevan it was truly a miracle from God, but a miracle that they would take advantage of. Throughout this time, however, there were some strange happenings that they could not explain. The *Avaveres* spoke of an evil being that had come to them fifteen or sixteen years earlier. Hearing the stories the *Spaniards* jokingly called him *Mala Cosa*...bad thing, a name that the *Avavares* picked up! This being appeared to be a man of very short stature with a long beard but they were never able to see his face clearly. For months they would not see him, and then, suddenly, the man appeared in the doorway of their hut holding a burning firebrand. The *Avaveres* were much afraid and retreated to the far corners of the hut, trembling. He stood there leering at each inhabitant with fiery eyes. Then, this man...this entity...this *Mala Cosa*, entered the hut and drug one of the inhabitants to the center of the hut. So afraid were the *Indians* that they did not resist.

From his belt, *Mala Cosa* pulled a large flint and made three large incisions just under the rib cage. Into these incisions, he inserted his hand and pulled out the entrails of the victim. After inspecting these entrails he cut off a piece a span in length and threw it into the fire. After this, he stuffed the coiled intestines back into the incision. Now, this demon made a cut in the arm of the victim just opposite the elbow. Reaching into the cut he dislocated the arm. This caused great pain to the victim and he was rendered unconscious. After committing these atrocities Mala Cosa placed his hands over the wounds and, amazingly, all were healed, albeit with much scarring.

Mala Cosa could also appear dressed as a woman. He would walk among them. Even when they danced he would skulk in the shadows just at the edge of the fire's glow. When angered he was capable of much destruction. Big Ears himself had seen Mala Cosa pick up one of the huts and raise it high into the air. The *Indians* were so scared that they scattered around him. With a great crash, he dropped the hut to the ground causing it to disintegrate. All that was left were the sticks and branches lying about in a great upheaval.

To appease *Mala Cosa* the *Avaveres* would give him food to eat but this he refused and never once did they see him consume anything. They asked him from where had he come, and although he never spoke, he led them to a deep cleft in the earth and indicated that his house was there below. With that *Mala Cosa* jumped into this cave and disappeared. Since that time the *Avaveres* had only seen him infrequently.

Alvar, Castillo, Dorantes, and Estevan listened to these stories with bemused interest. At one time Castillo actually snickered while the story was being told. Estevan rolled his eyes and Dorantes could not hide a half smile. Still, Alvar noticed that so afraid were these people of Mala Cosa that they shook with fear.

The *Avaveres* had closely watched the *Spaniards'* reactions and saw that they were not believed. They brought forth many of the victims and showed the scars left by the cuts that Mala Costa had made. One man had been visited numerous times and displayed terrible scars on his sides just under the rib cage. This evidence could not be dismissed and Alvar was troubled.

"What could have caused injuries such as this?" He wondered aloud.

Castillo was quick to answer. "These people live under the harshest of conditions. This man could have been gored by a bull or fallen off a cliff...who is to say?"

Alvar was still troubled. "But why would they concoct such stories? These people are many things but I have never known them to lie."

Dorantes thought a moment before entering the conversation. "We know that the devil takes many forms. Perhaps he has visited these people in the form of Mala Cosa."

Castillo shook his head in disbelief. Estevan was silent.

Alvar called for a meeting with the *Avaveres* and in the fading light of a particularly cold evening he talked of Mala Cosa.

"We do not understand this terrible demon you speak of, this Mala Cosa, for we have never seen him. Still, we have seen the terrible injuries that he has inflicted. Our advice to you is to believe in God like us and as *Christians,* you will never again be troubled by him"

The *Avaveres* all nodded in agreement and wanted to know how they could become *Christians.* For a few hours, Alvar, Dorantes, and Castillo talked of their savior Jesus Christ. They talked of His miraculous birth, His life, and, most importantly, His death and resurrection. The *Avaveres* listened with rapt attention.

In the early morning hours, Alvar collected ashes from the fire in a small bowl. To each of the *Avaveres* present, he marked the sign of the cross on their forehead and then spoke to them all.

"As *Christians,* you will no longer be afraid of Mala Cosa for he would not dare to challenge the power of our savior Jesus Christ!"

The *Avaveres* were much relieved and in the early morning hours returned to their huts. Alvar, wrapped in a thick buffalo robe walked out into the cold desert air. The moon was full and the sky was as clear as he had ever seen it. The moonlit desert stretched out before him as he stared out into its vastness.

Estevan joined him. "*Alguacil*, do you believe that this Mala Cosa actually exists?"

Alvar thought for a moment before answering.

"*Creo que si*...I think so."

Estevan stepped up beside him. "*Yo tambien*...as do I."

May, 1535

South Texas

The weather was warming. The days were longer and gone were the brutally cold nights. Everywhere the land was coming alive. Overhead enormous flocks of migratory birds filled the sky. Flowers bloomed and the sweet fragrance of spring was everywhere. Quite unexpectedly two *Avaveres* arrived in camp who had just returned from a journey to the seacoast. They talked of two bearded white men they had encountered. Alvar, Castillo, Dorantes, and Estevan listened to their story with rapt attention. From the *Avaveres'* description, the two white men were almost assuredly

Natalo Figueroa and Pietre the *Asturian* priest. For all these months nothing had been heard of any surviving *Spaniards*. Now, learning of these two there was new hope that perhaps there were other survivors as well.

Alvar questioned the two *Avaveres* at length.

"How was their health?"

"Where were they going?"

"Where had they been?"

The two answered that the two *Spaniards* appeared in reasonably good health and that they were traveling south along the coast with a small group of *Indians* called "The People of the Figs." They both appeared very nervous and apprehensive and avoided contact as much as possible. When told there were four surviving *Spaniards* inland of their location they seemed confused and bewildered. They talked among themselves about whether to continue along the coast or proceed inland to seek out the other *Spaniards*. So determined to continue south, however, they rejected turning inland and risking confrontation with other *Indians* they were not familiar with. The People of the Figs treated them well and they elected to stay with them.

The two *Avaveres* watched them continue down the coast and out of sight.

Alvar was horrified because Figueroa and the Asturian were traveling toward the area of the coast controlled by the *Camones*, the *Indians* that had massacred all of the *Spaniards* aboard the Tellez-Penalosa boat.

"We can only pray for them," was all that Alvar could say.

The next few days were a somber time for the four survivors.

Castillo was especially distraught because Natalo Figueroa had been a lifelong friend. He tried to think positively.

"Perhaps they can avoid the *Camones* and continue on to *Panuco*."

Alvar and Dorantes traded looks.

"*Si quizas...* yes perhaps."

July, 1535

South Texas

The transformation to summer had been explosive. Gone was the biting cold at night, replaced with violent storms that swept over the area with regularity. Now, the storms had abruptly stopped and the southwest was plunged into staggering heat. The *nochtili* were maturing and all around the various groups of *Indians* were beginning their annual migrations. On this day Alvar and Estevan had secretly gone on ahead to scout the land. Virtually naked and barefoot they moved easily across the dry rocky ground. The callouses on their feet had become so thick that even the cactus spines had trouble piercing the skin. It had become second nature to avoid the many dangers that walking across this barren ground presented. Most feared, of course, was the very large and dangerous snake that announced its presence with rattles on its tail...*la Yarara*. Being bit by this horrible creature could bring an agonizing death but, luckily, it most often announced its presence with the rattles on its tail. Once detected, *la Yarara* was a favorite source of food and all the *Indians* relished the taste of its flesh.

Alvar was fascinated with these "rattlesnakes," nothing like them existed in *Spain*. Besides the fearsome *la Yarara* which was easily identified by the large diamon-shaped markings on its back, Alvar had identified at least six other rattlesnakes of various sizes and markings. Some inhabited the desert, others the marshy lowlands, while still others were found in the more mountainous and rocky areas.

There were other snakes to watch out for as well. Along the rivers and waterways, *serpiente de agua de boca blanca* could be the most dangerous. This white-mouthed water snake was thick, powerful, and quick to attack a perceived threat. Alvar had watched them pursue a canoe of *Indians* until beat back by a melee of splashing paddles. During the spring these snakes congregated in large riling masses in the water and were extremely feared by the *Indians*.

In the woodlands a smaller snake the color of burnished copper existed. These Alvar called *cabeza de cobre*. Wonderfully camouflaged in the leaf and ground litter, one had to be extremely careful as to where he stepped or sat.

Another was the *serpentiene banda Amarilla*. These snakes were alternatively banded with a red-yellow configuration. Luckily, they were encountered only occasionally, but their venom was the most lethal of all, and, to his knowledge, no one had survived the bite of this small snake.

As they moved through the desert scrub-land both Alvar and Estevan were also ever mindful of the scorpions that inhabited this country. So calloused were their feet that a scorpion sting was ineffectual, but a sting to any other part of the body was extremely painful. Both had been stung by these creatures numerous times and like bees, wasps, and hornets, they were to be avoided at all costs.

Having traveled all day The *Spaniard* and the black man came to a camp of *Indians* called the *Malicones*. They were much involved with gathering and eating the beans of the *Mizquitl* tree. The fruit of the cactus, the *nochtli,* was not yet ripe and they endeavored to sustain themselves on this food source. The *Malicones* were very friendly and accepted the *Spaniards* as revered holy men.

Alvar called Estevan over to him.

"Estevanico, it is time for us to begin our journey to civilization. Return to the *Avaveres* and gather up *senors* Castillo and Dorantes. As quietly as possible return here and we will begin our journey to *Panuco*."

"*Si Alguacil*." Estevan quietly slipped out of the *Malicone* camp and disappeared into the surrounding scrub. Two days later the black man and the two *Spaniards* arrived at the *Malicone* camp.

On seeing Alvar, Dorantes hurried over to him.

"*Alguacil* we were delayed in leaving. The *Avaveres* had gathered up many sick people and asked for our assistance in curing them. We had to stay and perform the rituals."

"You are all here and that is what matters. Were you able to leave unnoticed?"

By now Castillo had joined them. "When we had completed the healing rituals the *Avaveres* celebrated long into the night, dancing around a tremendous fire until they all were exhausted. In the early hours of the morning, while they slept, we slipped away."

Dorantes chuckled. "They are probably still asleep!"

Alvar was thoughtful, "Then today we continue our journey back to civilization!"

August, 1535

South Texas

It was still about two weeks before the cactus fruit, the *nochtli*, would be ripe. During this time the *Malacomes* and the *Spaniards* suffered much. On the way another group of *Indians* that called themselves *Arbadaos* were encountered. These people were very poor and emaciated. Many were sick and all exhibited distended stomachs bloated with gas from eating the unripe *nochtli*. For two days the *Malacomes* and *Arbadaos* traveled together, but on the third day, the *Malacomes* made a decision to return by the same route. They would return back up the trail and then move toward the coast to investigate another known accumulation of the cactus fruit.

The *Spaniards* made a decision to stay with the *Arbadao*s and continue on to the south, toward *Panuco*. So, the next morning the *Malacomes* turned and trudged back up the trail. The decision of the *Spaniards* to stay with the *Arabadaos* saddened the *Malacomes* but they seemed to understand and harbored no ill will.

Alvar had approached the headman of the *Arabadaos* and asked permission to travel with them. This *Indian,* a mere youth with the strange name of Yoyo-si-waka had readily agreed, for the healing powers of the bearded white men and black *Africans* were well known.

Each of the *Spaniards* was taken in hand by a different family group and led to their houses. These houses were nothing more than an accumulation of sticks jammed into the ground, overlapped and tied together at the other end to form a loose semi-circle framework. This framework was overlaid with hides and grasses. During the summer the bottom was left open so that air could blow freely through it. Every morning the "houses" were quickly disassembled and strapped to the back of the women for the days' journey.

They traveled with the *Arabadaos* for five days eating almost nothing. Feeling their strength rapidly ebbing away, Alvar, Castillo, Dorantes, and Estevan pooled their meager resources and bought two dogs owned by Yoyo. Castillo gave up a fish net, Dorantes a flint cutter, Estevan a conch shell, and Alvar a deerskin that he used to cover himself at night.

Moving off to be by themselves, the *Spaniards* butchered the two small dogs and roasted them over a fire. Had they stayed in the village to eat, the *Arabadaos* would have stolen the meat as it was cooking. In times of starvation, the flesh of any animal was generally eaten raw by the *Indians*. Roasting meat was considered a waste of time...time that could be better utilized by finding additional food sources.

The effect of eating the roasted dog was almost instantaneous to the starving *Spaniards*. A new strength seemed to flow through their bodies. Returning to the *Arabadaos* camp they expressed their intentions to Yoyo to leave the *Arabadaos* and continue their trek to the south. Amazingly, Yoyo provided them with two guides who would take them to another group of *Indians*.

Like so many other *Indian* groups the departure of the *Spaniards* from the *Arabadaos* was met with much crying and wailing. Even the guides cried freely as they left the *Arabadao* camp.

The weather had turned and throughout the day the rain came down in torrents. At a split in the trail, the *Arabadao* guides left them. Before leaving they pointed to the south and said that a day's journey would bring them to the camp of the *Cuchendados* who were their brothers and spoke the same language. The *Spaniards* continued on alone, and in the heavy rain and mist lost their way.

At times the trail was completely covered in water, so much that it appeared as if they were walking in a shallow lake. Towards evening the rain began to abate. Finally, the ground began to rise and they came to a very great woods. It was a relief, for the wind had begun to blow and their skin was cold. It was indeed a blessing for on the fringe of the great woods was a large patch of cactus. The fruit of the cactus, *nochtli,* was not yet ripe so they gathered the pads. Carrying as much as they could hold they proceeded into the woods to build a fire and warm themselves.

Building a fire under these conditions was no easy task. Alvar and Dorantes both had fire starters; a small bow that fitted a round stick that was rotated rapidly on a wooden base. The resulting friction would produce enough heat to ignite kindling. It was tedious work, for everything was sodden from the day-long rain. Moss was gathered and Estevan busied himself with shaving off wood chips from dead branches. Once the pile of kindling began to smoke Alvar softly blew on it until a flame occurred. Slowly, they added twigs and bits of grass. The new fire struggled with the dampness but slowly, ever so slowly, the new fire took hold.

With the rocks that were in the area, they built a crude oven into which they piled the cactus pads they had gathered. All around this oven, they added more wood until a great fire roared in front of them. Exhausted, the *Spaniards* fell asleep in the warmth provided by the fire.

The next morning the fire had burned down to embers. They removed the pads from the oven and cut them into strips. These they divided equally. Gorging on the cactus pads the *Spaniards* entrusted themselves to God and continued their trek to the south.

August, 1535

South Texas

Finding the trail that they had lost the day before the four compatriots continued their march until mid-day when they came upon the houses of other *Indians*. On approaching the encampment they came upon two women and several children who, seeing them, became much afraid and hid themselves behind some large trees.

After Castillo called out the *Indians* approached the *Spaniards* with great fear. These were the *Cuchendados*.

For a moment tensions were high but when it was assured that there was no threat, the women led them back to some temporary enclosures where several *Indian* men joined them, just back from a hunting foray. After much talk, the inhabitants indicated there was a large village up ahead, about a half-days walk. Two of the men would guide the *Spaniards* while two youngsters, fleet as deer, proceeded up the trail to tell of their intended arrival.

Indeed, it was a large village, Alvar estimated 50 houses. The inhabitants had lined the trail into the camp. All wanted to view and touch the bearded white healers. As the *Spaniards* proceeded down the line of onlookers they made the sign of the cross and touched as many as they could on the forehead.

With each touch, they uttered *"Dios sea contigo...God be with you."*

This seemed to pleasure the *Cuchendados* and like the *Arabadaos*, they readily accepted the *Spaniards* into their community.

All the next day the *Cuchendaados* came to the *Spaniards* with their ailments and those without ailments came to be blessed. From the shadows, the shamans watched their every move. There were three of them. Alvar took notice of this and motioned them over. With much patience, the *Spaniards* instructed the three holy men on the ways of the cross and incorporated them into the healing process. It was a potential crisis that had been averted, for the shamans had great influence on the people and to usurp their power could have led to problems. Now they stood in line uttering the first few words of the *Pater Noster*, touching their patrons and giving the sign of the cross.

So appreciative were the people of the bearded white healers that they willingly gave the last of their food to them. After two weeks with the *Cuchendados,* another group of *Indians* appeared. These had traveled from their homeland far to the south to eat the *nochtli* that was now ripening. The language they spoke was similar to the *Cuchendados* but differed in some words. Estevan, the polyglot, was the first to master it.

Estevan relayed their intentions to his compatriots. "These people will be returning to the south as soon as they are done gathering the *nochtli.*"

Alvar gathered his compatriots and spoke of his intentions. "*Amigos*, we should ask these *Indios* if we can travel with them, for they come from the direction of *Panuco* and we must continue our journey in that direction."

All were in agreement.

On learning of their upcoming departure, the *Cuchendados* were much saddened and, as was the custom, they began to wail. They had much fear for the future, for their spiritual protectors were leaving. Alvar calmed them saying that the shamans had now been fully trained in the powers of the bearded white healers. At the end of fifteen days, the *Spaniards* left the camp of the *Cuchendados* and headed south.

August, 1535

South Texas

All of the *Indians* the *Spaniards* had encountered since leaving *Malhado* suckled their young well into their twelfth year. To the *Spaniards* with their *European* values, this was abhorrent.

"Why was this so?"

On closer examination, however, the reasoning became apparent. Because of the great hunger experienced by all of these people, it was not uncommon for them to go several days without eating. This, of course, would be devastating to a youngster. So, to preserve the next generation the children were suckled until they became of age to fend for themselves. Although this practice helped to preserve the next generation it was terribly trying on the women. Alvar noticed that the women of all the tribes he encountered died much earlier than the males, with their regime of labor and childbearing taking its toll. Although the young women in some cases were very comely, they aged quickly and by age 30 their breasts sagged to midriff and the extended nipples reminded Alvar of the milch cows on his uncle's farm in *Andalusia.*

These new southern *Indians*, however, were much different than the *Cuchendados*. They did not practice this custom and were typically weaned at the age of three or four. During periods of starvation, all available food was preferentially given to the children. Although they gathered the fruit of the *nochtli* and the *Mizquitl* tree, they were primarily hunters. In their home territory, the men traveled great distances in search of game. They hunted the shaggy "cows" that Alvar had seen throughout his travels. At times the whole community would follow the herds of these animals far to the west and north. When the animals eventually traveled into the lands of their enemies, they would break off and return to their home territory. The *Spaniards* learned of these things as they traveled with this new group. Because of their hunting prowess, Dorantes was the first to give them the *Spanish* name, *Cazadores*...hunters.

On the evening of the arrival at the *Cazadore* camp, a great *areito* was held. Amid the dancing and general rejoicing, a pit was dug in the ground to which large quantities of beans from the *Mizquitl* tree were added. The men of the village took turns pounding the bean pods with wooden poles until only a fine powder remained. The finely ground beans were then removed and put into two-handled baskets. Water and earth were added by the shamans in precise quantities until a thick gruel was produced. Of this, all the members of the *Cazadore* and the *Spaniards* ate.

Alvar liked the sweet taste of the strange concoction but disliked the gritty residue and, like many foods relished by the *Indians,* it produced large quantities of gas. Not used to its effects, the *Spaniards* rolled on the ground in agony, their stomachs greatly distended. Much to the *Cazadore's* amusement, their only relief came from the colossal flatulations that resounded throughout the night.

The *Cazadore* were so protective of the bearded white healers that they posted a six-man guard outside their dwelling every night and no one was allowed to enter until daybreak. They explained to the *Spaniards* that a constant war existed with two other groups that lived to the west. It was not unusual for a raiding party to enter the camp after nightfall in an attempt to steal their women and food.

After a week with the *Cazadore,* five *Indian* women from the south entered the camp. They were visiting relatives and had brought trade goods. All in the camp were happy to see them. They provided information on food sources and told stories of their encounters. They also came to observe the bearded healers whose presence was becoming known across the area. They also talked of their village on the other side of a great river with many houses. The *Spaniards* listened to their stories with rapt attention.

Pulling his comrades aside Dorantes spoke to them, "We should continue our journey, for to stay in one place too long puts us in jeopardy. Surely these women would help guide us to their brethren up ahead."

All agreed, and they delegated Estevan to ask for help. Ever since their arrival, the women had shown great interest in the black *African,* to the point where one had grabbed his crotch and then communicated with the others as to the size of his member. After that the five would not leave him alone and it became a joke among the *Spaniards* and the *Cazadore* as each of the women pestered him unmercifully. They would follow him around the camp pulling him into the bushes when an opportunity arose, either singly, two, or even all five.

As expected, the women agreed, but wanted to stay in the *Cazadore* camp for one more day with their relatives. The *Spaniards,* anxious to move on, decided to leave on their own, gradually moving to the south until the women caught up.

Estevan relayed their intentions to the women and they gave him rough directions as to which way to proceed. The *Cazadore* lamented their departure and begged them to stay...all to no avail. That night the four wanderers blessed each and every inhabitant of the village.

In the morning the *Spaniards* collected their belongings and proceeded south down the path from which the five women had come. In the background, the wailing and cries of the *Cazadore* subsided until there were only the sounds of the wind and the crunching of their feet on the path. By Alvar's best estimate, it was late summer, maybe early September, 1535.

CHAPTER 15
The River Of Gourds

El río de calabazas

It was then that Alvar learned the Indians' name for the river that was just ahead...Cheloawanna. He struggled with the translation, but after much discussion determined it meant "Rio de Cealabazas"... river of gourds.

Early September, 1535

Five Leagues North of the Rio Grande

Andres Dorantes sat, *Indian* style, on a patch of grass and looked at the vastness and desolation that spread out before him. To the west, the horizon disappeared into a flat, almost featureless, expanse. Cactus, rocks, scrub trees, and grass as far as he could see. High in the north sky three buzzards circled in an almost cloudless sky. Certainly, below them, somewhere, was a carcass of some unfortunate animal that had met its end. He watched with rapt attention as the three tightened their circle and descended earthward. He was much too far away to see what it was that had attracted their attention. In the harshness of this place, it could be a rabbit, or maybe the remains of a cougar kill. There was always the possibility that the rotting cadaver could be human.

Andres shook his head.

Here, life was cheap and death was looked at almost nonchalantly. Rival groups of *Indians* killed each other regularly. Even among the inhabitants of a single group, arguments, and life taking was not that uncommon. If a child was born sickly or with deformations it was discarded ...left in this wilderness to die of hunger and exposure, its body consumed by the wild animals and insects.

How he yearned for the civility of his native *Spain*.

The foot-path they were on meandered through this infernal wilderness, sometimes leading them south, sometimes bending east or west. Now they were at an intersection with two other foot-paths and they argued amongst themselves as to which route to take. The directions given by the women at the village were vague at best and now the travelers were hopelessly lost.

An exasperated Alonzo Castillo threw up his hands. "All we can do is continue to the south and hope that the women of the village find us."

Alvar and Estevan nodded their heads in agreement and each looked to Andres for his answer.

Rising from his sitting position Andres chose the most southerly of the faint footpaths and silently started down it. Wordlessly, the others followed behind him.

The heat and humidity were oppressive. The years of exposure to sun and wind had seared their skin to a leather-like appearance. Like snakes the dead dermal layer would shed periodically, falling off in flakes or patches. Except for facial hair, they were almost indistinguishable from the *Indians* around them. That is, all but Estevan who, being a black *African*, was obviously different than the other three. His skin, with its higher pigment content, suffered far less than his *European* counterparts in the blazing sun.

Today all four trudged down the southerly trail that Andres Dorantes had chosen. They had come to other intersections but by their unanimous agreement always picked the most southerly.

It was Estevan who noticed it first.

"*Huelo agua*...I smell water."

The procession stopped and each of the men sniffed the air. It was unmistakable, the smell of water was close.

Alvar, "We must be close to the river of which the women spoke."

Each of the four scanned the area ahead of them. The land was flat and featureless, but far ahead was a line of trees that extended in both directions.

Castillo, "Let us continue on in this direction for I am sure that tree line marks a river channel."

It was at this moment that the four travelers heard a commotion behind them. They froze in their tracks and listened intently. Drifting to them with the wind was the unmistakable sound of women talking and laughing.

Alvar, "I think the women of the village have finally found us!"

Next to the trail was a small seeping spring, no more than a trickle that quickly disappeared in the dry rocky ground. Here the four *Spaniards* sat down by the side of the trail to await the arrival of the women.

Estevan watched as the procession moved along the trail in their direction.

"They have arrived!"

It was the four women plus three other inhabitants of the village they had just left. Each went to the small spring to lap up the life-giving water after which they descended on Alvar, who they considered the leader of the *Christians*, and chided him for getting lost and taking the wrong trails. It was good-natured criticism, however, and soon everyone was laughing and telling stories. It was then that Alvar learned the *Indian's* name for the river that was just ahead...*Cheloawanna*. He struggled with the translation, but after much discussion determined it meant "Rio *de calabazas*"... river of gourds.

It was getting late in the afternoon and still, the women and their fellow travelers sat by the spring apparently not anxious to move ahead. It was Dorantes who finally stood up and made it known that they would be continuing along the trail. Almost reluctantly, the *Indians* followed suit and soon the whole procession was moving toward the tree line that loomed in the distance.

September, 1535

Crossing the Rio Grande

It was early evening when they came to the banks of a large river. It was The River of Gourds. The current at the point of crossing was brisk but, at its deepest, the water only came to their chests, much to the relief of Estevan and Castillo who were non-swimmers. Still, each carried a large piece of driftwood with them in case they stepped into a hole or were swept downriver into deeper water. The river had been swift and in crossing they were pushed downstream. On the far side of the river, they clambered up a muddy bank and then, finally onto dry ground. Alvar stopped briefly and looked back at the river they had just crossed. It reminded him of the *Guadalquivir River* in *Spain*. A strange feeling passed over him. For some reason it seemed to be more than a river, but a boundary, a point where the hardships of the last few years were left behind them. Ahead was a new beginning and, hopefully, they would find their way back to people of their own kind.

The four *Christains* and their entourage of *Indians* milled around the far side of the river for several minutes before, finally heading down a well-worn trail. The women were excited, because their village was close at hand.

September, 1535

Across the Rio Grande Near Present-Day Reynosa, Mexico

A league beyond the River of Gourds the long shadows began to spread across the ground. Evening was coming fast. On a small hill spread out before them were a hundred or more houses of a large village, its inhabitants already lined up to see the strange bearded healers and the black man they had heard so much about. As the procession neared, the people began to shout and slap their thighs in anticipation. So ruckus was the display that the *Christians* hesitated. Seeing this the four women took each by the arm and led them forward.

Once in the village the *Christians* were swept up by the crowd and carried along, their feet not touching the ground. Many of the people carried gourds filled with small rocks. These they shook constantly. It seemed that all the inhabitants wanted to touch the *Spaniards* and receive their blessings but with the noise and confusion communication was almost impossible. Finally, the procession stopped in front of two huts that had been specifically prepared for the travelers. Alvar and Castillo would share a hut while Dorantes and Estevan the other. Outside, the revelers begged them to join in a celebration, an *areitos*, in their honor, but Alvar and the others refused. Undeterred, the *Indianas* sang and danced throughout the night in a wild melee of celebration. At some point during the night, Estevan left his hut and joined in the festivities. Once again the *Indians* were fascinated by his jumping ability and wild undulating dancing. The women of the village were also attracted to him and he had sex with as many as he could. Finally, just before dawn he came back into the hut and collapsed, exhausted onto the bed of animal skins that had been prepared for him.

Dorantes, still awake, looked over at him and asked, "How many tonight?"

Before falling into a deep sleep Estevan mumbled, "*Trecee*...thirteen, I think!"

On the morning of the next day, a large crowd gathered outside the huts of the *Spaniards* all wanting to be touched and blessed by the bearded shamans. Until mid-morning Alvar, Castillo, and Dorantes shared in performing this ritual until Estevan, finally awake, joined them. When they had completed the task the *Indians* presented them with dried fish, venison, and *nochtli,* the fruit of the cactus. To the women who had brought them, they showed their appreciation by presenting each with many arrows. This was to be a day of rest and for the remainder of the daylight hours, the *Spaniards* walked amongst the villagers talking with them and gathering information on the way ahead.

Alvar questioned the *Indians* about the gourds he had seen on entering the village. To this question, the *Indian* replied that the gourds were sacred and served to protect these people.Alvar asked from whence the gourds came, for this was the first time he had seen any since leaving *The Isle of Horses*.

The *Indians* replied that they came from the sky...*vienen del cielo*, from the spirit world, and that they occasionally find them along the banks of the river, after floods, deposited there by ancestors long dead.

Fascinated by the story of the gourds Alvar conferred with his three compatriots.

"I am convinced that these *calabazas*...gourds...are swept down the river from other *Indios* far up river, for none appear to be grown in this area. The *Indios* in their ignorance think they are gifts from the sky."

Alvar nonchalantly waved his hand toward the heavens.

It was Castillo who answered, "It shows that there are inhabitants all across this land...in all directions."

Dorantes agreed and then continued, "We need to go on as soon as possible."

"But, in what direction?" Castillo spread his hands in question.

After some thought Alvar answered, "There is still talk of the fierceness of the *Indios* along the coast."

Dorantes, Estevan, and Castillo all nodded in agreement.

Alvar continued, "To avoid the fate of our compatriots in the boat led by *Capitans* Tellez and Penalosa I suggest we do not go east to the coast but rather continue to the south."

All agreed.

"It is settled then, let us tell our guests that we will be leaving in the morning."

September, 1535

Across the Rio Grande in the Mexican State of Tamaulipas

First light had not permeated the moonless darkness of morning as the three *Europeans* and one *African* left the village of 100 houses. Even at this early hour, it seemed as if every inhabitant would be accompanying them. As they moved down the trail that led to the south, the people pressed upon them. It was a caravan. Children ran alongside the trail playing tag, throwing sticks, and causing mischief. The *Indians* belabored the travelers, asking for a healing touch or a blessing. Estevan was surrounded by the young women of the village who, much to his enjoyment, flirted with him continuously.

After a journey of less than two hours, the bearded healers and their caravan arrived at another village. Here they were again well received. As they entered the village a deer that had been killed that day was presented to them by a group of elders and a younger man that appeared to be the hunter. Dorantes stepped forward, thanked the hunter and shook hands with all the elders. This action mystified them, for shaking hands was something they were unfamiliar with. Dorantes followed this up by blessing the deer and directing the elders to have it cooked so that all may eat. This act was well received.

On entering the enclosure of huts and fire pits a strange thing happened. The people traveling with the *Christians* took whatever they pleased from the people of this new village. They confiscated arrows, beads, shoes, food from the cooking fires...whatever they desired. Strangely, there was no animosity. After pilfering what they could, these *Indians* returned back up the trail to the village of a hundred huts.

Bewildered by this action, Castillo, spoke to Alvar. "*Alguicil*, the customs of these people are very strange!"

"I agree friend Alonzo...strange indeed!"

Castillo rushed to question some of the people of this village as to why this was happening for he feared that there would be reprisals against the *Christians*.

He explained that they were much dismayed by this escalating ritual. He feared that if it continued one of the groups would rise up against the other in all-out war. Seeing his anguish the *Indians* approached all of the *Christians* and said not to worry. The people of this village were so contented by being cured and blessed by the bearded shamans that it was well worth it. Besides, as the new group, they would be compensated by those up ahead who would suffer the same fate. It was a concept that the *Europeans* could not understand but were forced to accept.

This pattern of ritual pillage and exchange continued the next day and, in fact, to every village that they encountered. The people from the preceding village would accompany the *Christians* to the next, taking anything that they desired. Once satisfied, this group would return to their village. Those of the new village would then accompany the *Christians* to the next, and so on. The practice became more pronounced as they continued inland. Not only were things of value taken but, in many cases, the entire village would be destroyed...huts torn down, fire pits scattered.

September, 1535

In the Mexican State of Tamaulipas

Less than two leagues further on The convoy of *Spaniards*, one *African,* and throngs of *Indians* followers came to another village where the people came to them in droves to be touched and blessed by the bearded shamans. The crowds pressed upon them all day and by nightfall, the exhausted *Christians* were finally shown to their sleeping quarters, but the revelry and merriment that continued through the night did not let them sleep. They departed this village drawn and haggard the next morning and anxious to leave.

On the trail Castillo addressed Alvar. "*Alguacil* we have seen many celebrations and *areitos*, but nothing like last night.

Alvar shook his head. "Of all the places we have been that was truly the *pueblo de mucha alegria*...the village of much merriment!"

Their journey for the next two days was hectic. Moving southwestward they passed many villages each of which begged the travelers to stop and administer their healing powers. The crowds continually pressed upon them in greater numbers, impeding their progress.

Alvar was frustrated. He estimated that at this rate they would travel less than 2 leagues a day with all the confusion and delays. He stopped the procession and ordered the people to stay behind them.

Feigning great anger he spread his arms to the sky and lamented in *Spanish,* "Father forgive me for what I am about to do!"

Turning to the throng of people he spoke to them in their language. "Let us continue unimpeded or a curse will fall upon you and your villages."

The effect was electrifying. The people seemed shocked and terrified. They withdrew several hundred yards behind the *Christians.* Even the women that had surrounded Estevan backed off. From here on the four travelers continued along the trail entirely unhampered moving at a fast walk. Still, the throng of villagers followed, at a distance, their mass extending far down the trail.

September, 1535

Village of the Blind

Finally, after several more days of travel, they stopped at yet another village whose people swarmed over them. In their appearance, these *Indians* were well-proportioned with very good features. Intriguing was the lightness of their skin. Could it be that other Europeans had visited these people long ago? The four travelers could only speculate about this.

The *Christians* worked far into the night evaluating and blessing as many people as possible. When they had become much fatigued each was shown to their own separate hut where they could spend the night. Women were brought to them, but all declined, even Estevan, for the day had been long and grueling.

In the morning more people were brought from another part of the village. These people were affected by a strange eye affliction. Some were blind or partially blind in one eye, others were completely blind in both eyes. On closer examination, the eye was covered with a *nube*...a white film that obscured their sight.

Castello turned to Alvar while evaluating one of the non-seers. "What are we to do with these people from this Village of the Blind?"

"Tell them that if they accept and love our God they will find peace" was Alvar's only answer.

"But *Alguacil* this will not cure them and they will leave here as they arrived...still blind!"

"This is true friend Alonzo, but all we can give any of these people is hope. Hopefully, God will hear their suffering."

The *Christians* blessed and touched their sightless eyes, asking God to watch over and protect them. Strange as it seems, this seemed to satisfy the afflicted and they left with spirits uplifted. All of the *Indians* responded with gifts of food and arrows. Again, Alvar directed that the gifts be distributed among the *Indians* that had brought them to this place.

From this village, the travelers could make out the outline of mountains. Still low on the horizon they seemed to run in a line roughly northwest to southeast. The *Indians* accompanying them begged that the *Christians* continue across these mountains to the coast. Here they said many people would welcome them and give them many things, but the *Christian's* declined, taking a course over a flat plain instead.

September, 1535

Little Bags of Silver

The day was warm and dry. The caravan made good time on the well-worn path. At mid-morning Alvar estimated they had traveled some three leagues. About this time the Indian guides that were with them started to become very excited for, just ahead, was the village of their relatives. The trail led up a small rise, and at the top, the *Spaniards* looked down on a small village next to a pretty stream. The inhabitants, perhaps sixty in all, were standing outside their huts anticipating the arrival of the bearded shamans.

The Indian guides and indeed all of the people of the caravan rushed by the *Christians* and began sacking the village of their relatives. They took weapons, food, clothing, and anything that was seen of value. Still on the hill Alvar, Costello, Dorantes, and Estevan looked on and felt sadness for the people of the village. When things had calmed down the foursome walked down the hill and entered the village. Amazingly, as they entered, the people were in a festive mood. Dancing and singing many rushed forward to greet and touch the strangers.

The celebration continued. Soon several of the elders approached the *Christian* shamans. Knowing the custom of their relatives they had managed to hide some things before the sacking of their village began. They brought the *Christians* beads, red ocher, and little bags of silver. The silver was looked upon by Alvar, Dorantes, Castillo, and Estevan with much interest but here in the wilderness, it was worthless. Still, Alvar made mental notes of its existence.

When questioned as to where the silver was obtained, the *Indians* nonchalantly pointed to the mountainous west saying, "In some places it lies scattered all about."

From this encounter, the travelers began to formulate an alternate plan. Perhaps they should further investigate this land of *Amichel* before trying to reach *Panuco*. The three *Spaniards* talked much of this, for as much as they wanted to return to civilization it was believed that there was a vast fortune somewhere in *Amichel*. This collection of silver brought to them by the *Indians* proved that. Returning to *Spain* with a working knowledge of the rich hinterland of *Amichel* would be invaluable.

As was the custom of the Spaniards gave all the gifts, including the silver, to the *Indians* that had accompanied them. Late in the afternoon other people from a nearby village arrived and brought with them additional gifts of bows beads and other things. These were distributed as well. Now the dancing and celebrating began in earnest and by nightfall three huge bonfires lit up the camp.

The next morning as the *Christians* were making preparations to leave, the distraught *Indians* begged them to spend one more day. Finally, Alvar relented. They would stay with these people and leave at first light the next morning. During the day they blessed and made the sign of the cross over most of the inhabitants to which these people seemed immensely satisfied.

That evening Alvar called a conference with his cohorts.

"If these primitive people can obtain silver so easily then surely it must be very plentiful."

All nodded in agreement.

Dorantes answered first, "Surely if it is so plentiful just lying about there must be untold veins just below the surface that can be mined."

Castillo articulated what everyone else was thinking. "Perhaps we should proceed further inland to investigate this source of riches." With that, he pulled out a small piece of the silver given to them earlier.

Alvar laughed, "Friend Alonzo, your sleight of hand amazes me. I had thought we returned everything to the *Indios* that brought us."

"Not everything *Alguacil*, this piece I hid in my waistband."

Alvar thought a moment and then put it to a vote. "Who here thinks we should proceed further inland to investigate the source of this silver?"

All raised their hand except Estevan.

Alvar turned toward the black *African*. "Estevanico, why did you not raise your hand?"

"*Algaucil*, I belong to *Senor* Dorantes. If he wishes to go, then I will follow him."

Still much afraid of the coastal inhabitants, therefore, the *Christians* found it preferable to maintain their move inland where the *Indians* appeared more peaceful. Additionally, Alvar, Castello, and Dorantes agreed that traveling through this unknown region would result in beneficial knowledge that, once rescued, would enhance their worth to *Spain*. This became a predominant goal and it was even discussed that maybe they should continue overland to the *Mar del Sur*...the South Sea, the location of which was general knowledge, although obscure in its exact boundaries. The early voyages of Dom Henrique of *Portugal*, Bartolomeu Dias, Vasco de Gama, and the more recent adventures of Vasco Nunez de Balboa and certainly the world circumnavigation by *Portugal's* Ferdinand Magellan had proved that this "South Sea" was there. In fact, it was Magellan who had given it a name...*Pacifico*.

In the morning the *Christians* set out once again accompanied by many of the *Indians* who served as guides and porters. The decision being made, the *Christians* altered their course and turned to follow the river to the northwest. Seeing the determination to continue in this direction the *Indians* showed great sadness as they bid the bearded shamans farewell and returned to their homes. For the first time in many days Alvar, Dorantes, Castillo, and Estevan were alone.

At mid-day, two women approached the trail ahead. When they came to the travelers they laid down their load to rest for awhile. Alvar, with surprise, saw that they were carrying maize flour. The *Spaniards* had not seen any maize since leaving the Bay of Horses, now several years ago. When questioned, the women said that there was a village a few leagues ahead with much to eat, including the fruit of the cactus and maize flour. These women indicated that further up the river they would find many houses with much to eat. After resting for awhile the women took up their loads and moved down the trail while the *Spaniards* continued upstream.

October, 1535

Village of Twenty Houses

Along the river path, the shadows were growing long, and evening was approaching. Overhead scores of bats fluttered and darted through the air, gorging on the multitude of insects that were now rising into the cool evening air. Here next to the water the mosquitoes were unbearable even with the thick layers of mud the travelers had spread on themselves. They moved higher up the riverbank and just past the thick stands of trees that followed the river's path. Here the wind was not blocked and its effect drove some of the insects away.

Just as the sinking sun's orb began to touch the horizon a small village appeared up ahead. As they approached Alvar counted the dwellings.

"*Amigos*, I count twenty houses and already the inhabitants are coming to greet us."

Unlike the other villages that they had visited these people seemed much bothered by the approach of the shamans. They were weeping and apprehensive. Puzzled by this Dorantes asked one of the village elders why they were so full of sorrow.

One elder stepped forward and related that wherever the shamans went the villages were sacked and robbed of everything.

Dorantes turned and pointed down the trail from which they had just come.

"Have no fear because we are alone."

With this, the *Indians* seemed to lose their fear and offered the bearded shamans the fruit of the cactus. This was well received for the walk along the river had been tiring. The people of this village all appeared healthy so after a brief ceremony of touching each inhabitant on the head and giving the sign of the cross the *Spaniards* asked if they could spend the night in the village. This was agreed to.

The next morning Alvar, Dorantes, Castillo, and Estevan had just gathered their things in anticipation of continuing their travels when there was a commotion in the village. Further downstream from where they had just come the same *Indians* that had supposedly returned home the day before descended on the village. They took everything. All manner of food, weapons, and animal skins were carted away. The people of the village wept uncontrollably for they were left with virtually nothing.

As the looters left the village with their spoils they turned to the inhabitants and told them how the bearded shamans were children of the sun and to guide them and do anything that they asked. When the next village was reached they, in turn, could take whatever they wanted. The people of this village now treated the *Spaniards* with new reverence and offered to accompany them on their journey up the river.

October, 1535

Mountain of Bright Birds

On the first day after leaving the village, the *Christians* continued on the trail to the northwest. Traveling with the *Indian* guides from the Village of Twenty Houses they passed through a country that became increasingly hilly and more beautiful. Gradually they began to outdistance the throng of followers that strung out behind them, for they walked quickly and with a purpose. The *Indians,* however, seemed in a party spirit as they stopped frequently to socialize and compare booty from other villages they plundered along the way. They were learning fast.

At the hour of vespers, Alvar called a halt after making a decision to stop here for the night. He estimated that they had traveled 8 leagues. The entourage of *Indians* had swelled to more than fifty people. Alvar noted that even after they stopped scores of *Indians* continued to swarm into the campsite, Impromptu shelters were built, fires started and hunters brought in freshly killed game. They would eat well tonight.

The next morning the travelers, much refreshed, headed out, leaving before daybreak in the hopes of outdistancing their following. They forded the river with some difficulty because it was running high and swift. Once underway there was a heavy ground fog that obscured everything but, looking up, the travelers could see blue sky.

"This will burn away by mid-morning and then we will have a clear day." It was Dorantes.

This would be welcome news because they had been traveling under an overcast and rain-laden sky for the last few days. As predicted, the fog began to dissipate. Moving along the trail, Estevan, who had the best eyesight of the *Spaniards*, was first to bring to Alvar's attention that, up ahead, a mountain ridge line was emerging through the fog.

"I think *Alguacil*, that there is a *Sierra* ahead."

Several of the *Indians* accompanying them were brought up and questioned.

Yes, it was true, they were approaching what the *Indians* called, the *Mountain of Bright Birds.*

Alvar asked why they used this name.

The *Indians* spoke in hushed tones. The "bright birds" existed here in great quantity and represented their dead ancestors. It was a place of much reverence.

The name "bright birds" puzzled Alvar.

By noon the sky had completely cleared. All around them, the vastness of the land was astounding. Up ahead the little mountain grew in size with each hour of walking. It towered above the landscape. What's more, other mountains appeared. Further to the north another, and much larger Sierra, loomed in the distance. The *Indians* that accompanied them seemed to grow more excited with each step.

As evening approached *The Mountain of Bright Birds* towered above them and one could pick out the ridges and valleys on its surface. Soon, flocks of birds seemed to fill the sky above. Their presence seemed to mesmerize the *Indians* who continued on, not speaking. The *Spaniards* immediately identified them as parrots, but in such quantities, as they had never seen.

There appeared to be two types of parrots; one was a brilliant iridescent green, the other a darker green. As they flew, the undersides of their wings appeared blackish. The darker green parrot was by far the most abundant. On closer study each sported a deep maroon coloring on the forehead and their eyes were ringed in yellow.

The mountain seemed to be out of place in the flat landscape like it had dropped from the sky. The *Christians* could see thick stands of pine and oak extending up the steep slopes. Higher up, mountain ridges of bare rock and steep cliffs punctuated the higher elevations. All about, the parrots circled in never-ending profusion, their combined calls deafening at times.

They would camp here tonight at the base of this "Mountain of Bright Birds"

October, 1535

Entering the Foothills of the Sierra Madre De Oriental

This day also dawned bright and clear and the procession was underway at first light. The trail the *Indians* had been traveling turned north-northwest and followed the base of *The Mountain of Bright Birds* for 5 leagues. There the mountain abruptly ended, disappearing into a broad valley that bordered the other larger Sierra they had seen. This was much larger and was marked by continuous, towering, rocky peaks that appeared like the spine of a long-dead dragon laid out on the desert floor. Further on more mountain peaks appeared, seemingly running in a continuous chain. During discussions with the *Indians,* the *Spaniards* determined that this range sliced across the land from northwest to southeast.

The trail continued on through land rich in wildlife. Deer grazed openly in this valley between the sierras; most abundant were those with a whitetail that was prominently displayed when frightened. Other, much larger deer, had enormous ears that seemed out of proportion to their bodies. These reminded Alvar of mule ears and he called them *ciervo mulo.* Of course, the small swift *antilope* was present as well. They traveled in small herds of ten or less and astounded the *Spaniards* with their speed and agility. Now and then black bears were seen at a distance. Occasionally small groups, of what Alvar called, "shaggy cows" moved through the valley.

That evening they camped between the two sierras. As darkness enveloped them animal sounds of all types drifted through the air. It was a symphony. First came the owls, each species with its own characteristic sound. One in particular had an unnerving and shrill call. The *Indians* called this one *tah-huna asio* or cries like a baby.

Next were the collective howls of a small dog-like animal the *Indians* called *"coyotl."* Like the wolf, the *coyotl* hunted in packs and was admired by the *Indians* as a trickster with the ability to assume the form of a man.

The much deeper and resonant howl of the wolf was also recognizable. Strangely, when a wolf call was heard the *coyotls* fell silent.

Later in the evening, everyone heard the distinctive "whoof" of a bear patrolling just outside the firelight. This was a concern because bears were known to invade a camp. The men grabbed their bows and spears and began to advance into the darkness yelling and beating sticks together to scare off the animal. This was successful and everyone heard the animal crashing through the underbrush to escape its tormentors.

Early in the morning hours, prior to sunrise, Alvar was awakened by the scream of a cougar. He heard it twice, but it was far off and of no concern. With this animal, he was well acquainted. The *Christians* learned that this was also the habitat of another much larger cat, one much revered and feared by the *Indians*. Alvar and his three compatriots had heard of this animal many times from stories brought back to *Spain* from Cortes and his conquistadors who called it *"El Tigre."* Alvar had seen its brilliant spotted coat on display in *Seville* but none had seen the animal in the wild. The *Indians* called it *"yaguara"* and spoke of it as a supernatural being. A night hunter, it roamed the land like a ghost, unseen until it pounced on its unsuspecting victim. Indeed, the *Aztecs*, whom Cortes had so recently conquered, revered the animal. Their ruling class dedicated statues and even wore the animal's skins as a sign of power.

With bears, cougars, wolves, snakes, and poisonous insects; in this land of *Amichel, El Tigre* represented just one more way to die. Alone, naked, and barefoot, they were no match for these fearsome beasts. Safety for the four *Christians* and the *Indians* accompanying them resided in staying together.

October, 1535

Two Gourds

The *Christians* continued their journey to the northwest, skirting several hills...*Colinas*...and staying in the valleys between them. Estevan called them *"Colinas Grande"* because they were not really hills and not really mountains. The Indians still followed behind but it was obvious that the caravan of people was shrinking in number. Dorantes fell back to ask them why this was so. He returned to say that the next village ahead was the last to which these people had a connection. Beyond that another group of *Indians* known as *Guachichile* were not necessarily friendly to them. These people spoke a different language and were very warlike. Although the *Guachichile* occasionally came to trade in the town ahead, they just as frequently would send raiding parties to gather food and women.

Dorantes continued, *"Aguacil,* they say that these *Guachichile* paint their heads red and are experts with the bow and arrow."

Alvar looked worried. "We should try to make contact with these "redheads"...*cabeza roja,* before venturing into their land."

All were in agreement.

Before noon, they came upon a village situated close to a river. It was a picturesque setting and the largest village they had yet seen in their journeys. People surged out of their houses and across the shallow stream to meet these strange newcomers with healing powers. Each of the *Christians was* taken by the hand and led down the hill.

It was a very large encampment, the number of thatched huts of all different sizes continued up and down both tributaries. It looked to be a major trade center for the Indians of the area. Two holy men greeted the *Christians* and gave them two gourds, each of which was elaborately painted with a red ocher.

Not knowing how to react to the receiving of the gourds Castillo asked one of the holy men to explain.

Taken somewhat aback, the holy men hesitated and then, seeing that Castillo was sincere in his question, answered that the gourds were sacred symbols of authority and power. From this moment on the four white shamans always carried the sacred gourds with them.

The few Indians that had accompanied the travelers now began to sack the village, but they were few and the village large. They could not carry everything they took and soon returned down the trail taking only what they could hold.

All through the evening and into the night the *Spaniards* performed their rituals, blessing the inhabitants and making the sign of the cross. For the more serious cases, Dorantes began to mark the foreheads of the afflicted with ashes from a "holy fire." This, of course, was reminiscent of the *Spanish Cuaresma*...Lent...where the sign of the cross is marked on Catholics' foreheads by priests symbolizing repentance and mourning for one's sins. The ashes are to remind each that they come from dust and to dust they will return.

That night Alvar prayed long and hard that these actions by the four travelers would not be misinterpreted by the creator. They were not ordained men of God, only desperate castaways traveling in a strange and fearsome land, struggling to survive.

The next day they departed, this time moving inland through the rugged foothills of the Sierra. Only a few *Indian* guides stayed with them. The remainder stayed behind knowing that the route ahead was long and there were few, if any, villages to plunder. Only occasionally would they run across isolated hunters or family groups. On many evenings the skies were like being at sea, the stars so numerous and bright that one felt like reaching up and touching them. At night the *Spaniards* would lay on their insulating cover of pine branches and watch as the *Meteoritos* punctured the starry spectacle. Most were brief stabs of light that disappeared in a moment. Others flared up briefly. Occasionally, one shown so bright that it bathed the ground around them in an eerie glow. These the *Indians* called *Kawatch do lopuna*...tears of their ancestors.

After days of trudging through this rugged and desolate country, they entered a lush land bordered by the confluence of two streams. Alvar estimated that in this journey they traveled 50 leagues. Here on the higher ground, they came upon a large village.

From his vantage point, Castillo looked down at the village and counted. "*Alguacil*, I count 39 dwellings and one long house."

Even this far inland the inhabitants had heard of the bearded shamans. They rushed out onto the footpath to greet them. These people were well proportioned and both women and men wore their hair long. The men wore a breech-cloth and leggings made of deer hide. The women were, for the most part, bare-breasted with a loose garment attached at the waist and extending down to their ankles. It was winter, however, and the people further wrapped themselves in deer skins, and the furs of many mammals. One cloak was very distinctive, for it was entirely skunk fur. Estevan even made a comment as to how anyone could stand the god-awful smell long enough to prepare the skin.

Andres Dorantes was the first to enter the village. A group of three village elders presented him with a large copper bell onto which was engraved the outlines of a face. They indicated that this was their prized possession and that they believed so strongly in the bearded shaman's powers that they were giving it to them. Additionally, they passed out cotton mantles to the *Spaniards*.

When asked from where these articles came, they spoke of people far to the north. This astounded the *Spaniards* for the bell was obviously cast by people that had some understanding of metallurgy, something they had not seen since entering this land of *Amichel*.

Studying the bell, Dorantes related to Alvar. "*Alguacil* if this technology exists further to the north then there must be mines to extract the copper. If there are mines then they must have knowledge of other metals as well."

"I agree Andre, it might be best if we investigate this further."

Castillo and Estevan nodded their heads in approval.

The next morning while still in their hut the travelers heard a commotion outside. Peeking through the covered doorway Estevan gasped.

Castillo noticed. "Estevanico, what is it pray tell?"

"The ridge above the river has many strange *Indios* and..."

The other *Spaniards* rushed to the door. "And...what Estevanico?"

Estevan gulped, "They are all painted red!"

CHAPTER 16
Dead Crow

Cuervo Muerto

The Indian was named Soonaloka-Dia and he was the leader of the Guachichiles. In their language, Soonaloka-Dia meant "Dead Crow," a name that was feared by all their enemies.

October, 1535

At the Villages of 40 Houses

At the Village of Forty Houses, the travelers had encountered the *Guachichile* or *cabeza roja,* as the *Spanish* called them. They had surrounded the village and for a time things looked quite dire. But then, an opening appeared in the line of fearsome warriors and a procession of elders and a lone individual made its way down the riverbank toward the village below.

By now all the inhabitants and the leading men were lined up watching the approaching *Guachichiles.* As soon as the column had crossed a shallow ford there was a brief discussion as the leaders of the village walked down to greet them. Suddenly all heads turned toward the *Spaniards* and fingers pointed to where they were standing. The procession began moving toward them.

Estevan was the first to speak. "*Alguacil* what do you think is happening?"

"I would think that the answer to that question lies with the man who walks alone, he looks to be a chief of some type."

The procession stopped directly in front of Alvar and then spread out, surrounding the *Spaniards.* The man who walked alone came to stand directly in front of Alvar. He was tall and very fearsome.

Like the others, his head was painted with red ocher, indeed, most of his upper torso was colored as well. His chest, arms, and face bore the tell-tale scars of battle and tattoos adorned his arms and legs. From his pierced ear lobes deerskin thongs hung to the shoulder, each with a crow's foot tied at the end. Pierced through the septum of his nose was the baculum of a raccoon. He wore no head covering and his black, unbraided hair hung below his shoulders. He wore only a thong and carried a lethal-looking club.

Alvar took great care to stare directly into the Indian's eyes and not to show any signs of weakness in his presence.

The Indian spoke a strange lilting language that was interspersed with some words that Alvar understood. An interpreter from the village stepped up and Alvar called for Estevan, the polyglot, to assist him.

The Indian was named Soonaloka-Dia and he was the leader of the *Guachichiles*. In their language Soonaloka-Dia meant "Dead Crow," a name that was feared by all their enemies.

Looking directly at Alvar, Dead Crow began to speak, his words translated by the village interpreter and listened to intently by Estevan.

"I have heard that Wasapi-tun-loki, his people and the black man have great spirit powers."

Alvar thought a moment before answering. "Our God and Savior is all-powerful."

Alvar stopped and briefly looked up to the sky, then continued. "We are here only to help and to pass on His words so that all may believe in His powers."

Dead Crow thought about these words for a moment before continuing. "At our village, my son lies in much pain. The spirit of death is very close and I cannot bear to lose him. I would ask that you come with us so that your powers and the one you call God, can save him."

Alvar looked back at his compatriots and then at the multitude of warriors that surrounded them. He chose his words carefully.

"It grieves me that any man must lose his son. Our business is done here so we will gladly see to your son."

Dead Crow's countenance visibly softened but he went on to explain. "While battling one of our enemies my son was struck by an arrow and it now remains in him."

Dead Crow went on to explain that his village was only one day's walk from here and if they left now they could be there by evening.

After conferring with the other three, Alvar accepted, for Dead Crow's village was further to the northwest and in the direction that they desired to go.

The *Guachichiles* and the four *Spaniards* set out immediately for Dead Crow's village.

October, 1535

Dead Crow's Villages

The trail to the village was rugged and steep. It crossed a Sierra at least seven leagues in length. The footing was treacherous with stones that resembled iron slag under their feet. Castillo identified the rocks as volcanic in origin and was sure that the peaks they were crossing were ancient volcanoes. Even for hardened travelers, this journey was a real challenge. Dead Crow set the pace and walked with a purpose. Alvar understood his haste and struggled with the rest of the *Spaniards* to keep up.

As evening approached, the caravan of *Guachichiles* and four *Spaniards* dropped into a beautiful river valley. Dead Crow halted his relentless pace to stand on a precipice overlooking the valley. He pointed to the many houses set along-side the river and turned to Alvar, Dorantes, Castillo, and Estevan standing behind him.

He said simply, "This is our village, I hope life has not yet left my son's body."

Entering the village, the inhabitants lined the path to stare at the strange bearded shamans. The mood was somber for all knew the reason these strangers had arrived. Dead Crow's son still survived but his condition was grave. He hurried the *Spaniards* along to a large hut. This was his home and within it, a boy lay on a litter while his mother and several women attended him.

With that, Alvar, Dorantes, Castillo, Estevanico, and Dead Crow walked to the litter.

Dead Crow, his eyes glistening, spoke softly. "My sons name is Hewaha Kona."

Before them was a young man, Alvar estimated his age at 15 or 16. The boy was very confused and drifted in and out of consciousness. His face had an ashen pale to it. He was in bad shape.

Alvar peeled back the blanket that covered the boy and saw the reason for his condition. The broken shaft of an arrow projected just above the boy's left nipple and a trickle of blood emanated from the open wound. Alvar pulled the skin apart on either side of the shaft to better see the flint arrowhead. It extended deep into the chest cavity and as Alvar gently pulled, the shaft would not budge.

After that, the other three looked at the wound in turn and made comments.

Dorantes noted that the point appeared to be very close to the heart and any movement would surely puncture it. Castillo and Estevan agreed. While they talked Dead Crow looked on expectantly.

Castillo looked worried. "We will have to do something. I feel that our lives are in jeopardy if we don't save this young man."

"But what are we to do, "asked Dorantes. "The arrowhead is deeply embedded in cartilage only a very short distance from the heart."

"The boy is in bad shape now," countered Estevan, "Cutting it out will be extremely risky."

Alvar listened to his compatriots and then turned to Dead Crow.

"How did this happen?"

Dead Crow related that a raiding party had attacked their village while most of the men were out on a hunt. The residents of the village, the young the old as well as the women, had bravely fought back. One of the enemies had attempted to take the boy's mother, Dead Crow's wife. As she was being dragged by her hair, Hewaha Kona grabbed a flint scrapper and deeply slashed the attacker's leg. His mother escaped but the boy was shot with an arrow while he resisted.

Dead Crow stiffened with pride as he related the story. "My son is already a brave warrior."

Alvar looked at Dead Crow and his wife. "We will do what we can."

Castillo spoke, "*Alguacil*, this boy may be beyond our ability to help him. What will happen to us if he dies?"

Alvar looked about at the fierce *Guachichile* warriors. "Friend Castillo, we have no choice. It is in God's hands now." He immediately ordered a sharp implement. Dead Crow pulled a flint dagger from his waistband and handed it to Alvar. Alvar tested it with his thumb...it was indeed, very sharp!

Making a show for the Indians surrounding him, Alvar blessed the flint blade and held it toward the sky before handing it off to Castillo to do the same. It was passed to the other two and then returned to Alvar.

The fearsome countenance of Dead Crow seemed to wilt as he sank to one knee and reached for his son's hand.

Alvar responded immediately. He took hold of the chief's shoulder and said, "We will fight these demons with all our power to save your son."

The translators along with Estevan passed these words onto Dead Crow. Through tear-stained eyes, he looked up at the *Spaniard* and only nodded.

With four men holding the boy immobile, Alvar began his cut. A yellowish fluid oozed from the wound and then mixed with blood as Alvar cut deeper. The boy lurched and screamed and then passed into unconsciousness. Estevan cleaned the wound as Alvar cut. With his hand on the boy's head, Dorantes repeated the *pater noster* while Castillo stood behind Alvar ready to assist.

Careful not to cut any obvious veins or arteries, Alvar extended his incision until most of the flint arrowhead point was visible. Blood oozed from the wound as Estevan struggled to keep it clean and visible. Gently Alvar rocked the arrowhead back and forth while carefully chipping out the cartilage material it was embedded in.

It loosened but still couldn't be extracted.

Alvar dug out more cartilage, carefully collecting it so it wouldn't remain in the wound. Pulling ever so gently on the shaft he pried with the flint blade and suddenly, unexpectedly...the point came free.

Alvar asked for a gourd of water and then proceeded to irrigate the area until he was satisfied that no foreign material or pus remained.

Now, using a small bone awl Alvar made a series of holes in the skin on both sides of the wound. Through these, he passed thin pieces of deer sinew and drew the skin tightly together. The heavy bleeding slowly abated and then stopped altogether. A new poultice was applied and Alvar stepped back.

"We have done all we can do."

He instructed the *Guachichiles* to make the boy as comfortable as possible and to report any change in his condition. With that Alvar picked up two short sticks and laid them on the boy's chest in the shape of a cross. Dead Crow asked for the flint arrowhead that had been removed from his son's body. He showed it to all and then passed it around. All the people of the village touched the projectile with great reverence.

October, 1535

Dead Crow's Villages

Dead Crow's son did not regain consciousness the rest of the day. At nightfall, Alvar checked on the boy. Peeling back the poultice he was encouraged to see that the wound still looked clean with no apparent infection. While Dead Crow and the other Red Heads looked on, Alvar made a show of praying over the prostrate body and then looking up to the sky.

The next morning there was a commotion in the village. The *Spaniards* rushed out of their hut to see what was the matter. Almost as soon as they stepped into the sunlight Dead Crow was before them and next to him stood his son, now awake. To be sure, the boy was leaning on his father for support, but he appeared clear-eyed and was without fever. The *Spaniards*, always in awe of the healing powers of these Indians were flabbergasted, they stood there just staring at the young boy.

Alvar was the first to break the repose. He chastised Dead Crow for getting the boy up and ordered several red-heads to carry the boy back to his bed. He explained that his concern was that the wound would break open. Dead Crow helped carry his son back.

Alone now, Dorantes spoke for the other three. "We have been blessed this day by the saving of this young man's life. God does work in mysterious ways."

A unison of "Amens" was repeated by Alvar, Castillo, and Estevan as they all knelt to pray.

Later, as the morning brightened, gifts began to arrive at the *Spaniard's* hut. Meat, nuts, ocher, dressed hides, beads, and all manner of flints. Most notable was a deerskin bag of silver presented to each Spaniard. At noon Dead Crow himself walked to the hut with a procession of his followers and presented Alvar with a fine bow and quiver of arrows. To the other three, he presented shoes made of soft deerskin.

"Wasapi-tun-loki, you and your spirit healers have saved my son. You are now one of us.

Several *Guachichiles* now appeared and began to apply the red ocher to the faces and bodies of the *Spaniards*. With his contrast of black skin, Estevan's coating was the most ridiculous looking of the four, to the amusement of the other three.

After the application of the ocher, Alvar approached Dead Crow.

"We are honored to be accepted as one of your people, but I would ask only one thing of you."

Dead Crow listened to the translation and then answered. "What is it that the great shaman, Wasapi-tun-loki, requests of me?"

"Our journey will follow the setting of the sun." Alvar pointed to the west. "We will need someone to guide us, for this island that we have never traveled."

Dead Crow brightened. "Wasapi-tun-loki, I will lead you myself!"

The village now erupted in singing and dancing. A giant bonfire was constructed and all through the day and night, the celebration continued. Just before sunrise of the next morning the village finally fell silent as the exhausted revelers fell asleep.

In his hut, Estevan looked at the three naked women lying beside and across him. It had been a wild night, one that he would surely remember.

October, 1535

Dead Crows villages

The travelers had remained in Dead Crow's village for another day and then continued northwest with Dead Crow and a small group of *Red Heads* leading the way. Before leaving Alvar had removed the stitches from the arrowhead wound. This time Dead Crow left a strong contingent of warriors in the village to protect his people from attack while he was gone.

They traveled up the same river that the village had been on. The country they passed through was both rugged and beautiful. Sierras, valleys, steep-sided arroyos, cliffs, peaks, and lush mountain forests. Everywhere traveled they met a diverse group of people who spoke a multitude of languages. At times only hand talk could be used for communication. It was mid-winter and the travelers avoided the higher elevations. Even so, many days were spent trudging through snow-covered trails. In the lower elevations, the snow disappeared but the biting wind and cold persisted.

The processions that followed the *Spaniards* were becomming extensive. Each of the children of the sun had their own following, their favorites, and their woman. Estevan, with his insatiable sexual appetite, had the largest following, but there were many others of both sexes as well. Some carried gifts and burdens that had been given to them. Among the throng were hunters who, in this part of the country, carried enormous clubs. In the open country, they would form lines with fifty or more, and walk forward through the brush flushing out the huge hares that frequented this area.

The *Spaniards* would watch in awe as the long lines of club-wielding hunters flushed out one of the fleet animals. They would immediately fall upon it with their clubs in a flurry of motion. Then, all would stop and a hunter would hold up the dead and battered animal. The lines would again reform until another hare was located.

Usually, five dead hares would be tied together with strings of deer hide fastened around their hind legs. These were called "loads," and at the end of a hunt, the *Children of the Sun* would be presented with eight or ten "loads" each.

Other hunters, carrying their bows, spread out into the hills and mountains to hunt deer. In the evening they would return bringing as many as six animals to each of the *Spaniards*. Along with the deer, all manner of birds including quail and parrots were brought as well. Even the women participated, bringing cactus pads, spiders, worms, and whatever else they could find that was edible.

All of the game would not be eaten or even prepared by the *Indians* until the bearded shamans made the sign of the cross over it. Then, the women of the camp would gut, skin, and clean the carcasses. At the direction of the *Spaniards* and the native leaders, the game would be roasted and distributed to all the people who went with them. On receiving his or her proportion, each of the Indians would ask the *Spaniards* to blow on the food before it was consumed. It was a time-consuming process and one that typically kept them busy until well into the night.

Upon arriving at a camp site the women would construct huts for each. The shaman leader, Wasapi-tun-loki, was slightly larger, but it was Estevan's hut that was the most populated. Before retiring, each of the white shamans would be surrounded by the women so that he could choose which they would sleep with. It was important for these women to become impregnated by one of the *Children of the Sun*. This selection process could last for some time, with each viewing for attention and demonstrating their sexual prowess as best they could.

Once in the hut, the unchosen women would position themselves around the outside perimeter of the hut, listening to the goings on and hoping they would be called to participate. Others would even assist in the lovemaking, providing support or stimulation. In the morning all the participants would gather up and get ready for the day's journey as if nothing had happened. The *Spaniards*, with their fading *European* moralities, could only shake their heads in disbelief.

November, 1535

Traveling North in the Present-Day State of

Coahuila, Mexico

The travelers continued north into brutal wilderness. The caravan followed rivers whenever possible. These rivers passed through lofty canyons that had been cut deep by the eternal flow of water. When the waterways eventually played out there was only a barren, dry landscape of sand, stone, and towering precipices of tortured rock. It was terrifying and at the same time awesome to behold. Striations on cliff faces were laced with colored strata that changed hues with the position of the sun.

Continuing north and west with Dead Crow and the throng of people, they came to a river valley and a river flowing from the north. They rested for a day before proceeding 30 more leagues across a high plateau. At the end of this seven-day trek, they came to a great crossing of the trails. Here, many people awaited them while still others were constantly arriving. As the newcomers arrived they quickly constructed huts until the area around the roads was crowded with people and shelters.

Ahead lay a deserted land with rugged sierras. Beyond that, a great river. The *Spaniards* elected to remain at the crossing for two days before continuing on. The newcomers, always eager to please the bearded shamans, offered to accompany them through the rugged country ahead.

On the day of departure the caravan left early. Many stayed at the crossing of trails or began their journey homeward. Those remaining to follow Alvar, Dorantes, Castillo, Dorantes, and Estevan only numbered about one hundred people. It was a grueling journey across uninhabited desert mountains that most were not willing to undertake. Every morning more and more of the followers would wish the shamans well and then return back from where they had come. The trail itself was barely legible, sometimes not at all. Often they followed the crude drawings on rock faces or intermittent piles of stones that marked the way. Several times the trail was lost altogether and the travelers would come to a stop while scouts were sent out to reestablish the route. The food that had been so plentiful just days before was now unavailable. Water was even more scarce. If not for a rare rainstorm the travelers may all have perished from thirst.

As hardened as the *Christians* were this land presented an extreme challenge. It was brutally rugged. The footpaths they followed traversed rivers, streams, steep inclines, dangerous cliffs, ridges, and wild animals that could kill. Poisonous snakes, scorpions, spiders, cougars, jaguars, wolves and bears. Most fearsome were the bears. For the first time, they began to encounter a new, larger, and more ferocious bear. The black bear that they were familiar with was somewhat predictable but this new brown bear was to be avoided at all costs. Much larger, it was totally fearless and could rip a man in half with its huge claws. The *Indian* name for this bear was *chaka toni.* The *Spaniard's* called him Oso *Diablo*...devil bear!

One evening, the *Christians* and their host of followers camped at an enclave overlooking an expansive valley below. Dorantes and Estevan stepped up to a steep precipice to survey the scene below them. As they looked and chatted a lone animal emerged from the shadows. Unaware of the human observers far above the animal was obviously stalking something. At first, Dorantes thought that it was a large puma but when it emerged into the light the coat was spotted and of a yellowish hue. It was also much larger than any puma Dorantes had ever seen. Several *Indians* joined the two *Christians* and began whispering "*Yaguar.*" Now in deep grass, the animal periodically advanced forward and then crouched down motionless in the grass. Estevan was the first to notice several antelope warily grazing in an open area. They were vigilant but the wind carried the scent of the big cat away from them. Again the animal advanced and stopped. Its coloring blended with the grass so well that at times all that was visible was the slight twitching of its tail.

Ever closer *Yaguar* crept. Above, on the precipice, Alvar and Costello had now joined the onlookers. Everyone seemed to hold their breath. A lone male antelope wandered closer, unaware of the danger. The predator tensed...even its tail stopped twitching. Then, in a moment, it sprang! The antelope, with amazing reflexes, spun around to escape but before it had made two strides the *Yaguar* was on it. The sheer weight of the large cat knocked the much smaller animal to the ground. As it struggled the *Yaguar* sank its fangs into the antelope's neck. It was over...after only two or three kicks the doomed animal ceased to move. In the distance, the antelope herd raised a dust cloud as they fled across the valley.

The *Christians* and the *Indians* drew a deep breath, for all had momentarily stopped breathing as they watched the drama below. After warily looking around, *Yaguar* began to feed, first opening the abdominal cavity and then tearing at the flanks.

Again, it was Estevan who first noticed another animal approaching the kill. It was a large brown bear, a *chaka toni.* Among the *Indians* watching from above, there was a low murmur.

"Now there will be trouble!"

Both animals were revered by the *Indians*. The *Yaguar* for its cunning and the *Chaka toni* for its strength.

Yaguar sensed the bears approach and raised up to survey the scene. The bear, totally fearless and testing the wind with its nostrils, moved steadily closer to the kill.

Chaka toni was the larger and more powerful animal but the *Yaguar* was more agile. Normally in a confrontation such as this, the cat would back off, but today, *Yaguar* stood its ground.

The bear warily approached the kill area expecting *Yaguar* to retreat. Instead, the big cat attacked, catching the c*haka toni* off guard. The bear retreated a short distance and then began circling the kill site.

Again *Yaguar* attacked, raking the bear with its sharp claws. *Chaka toni* turned to attack, but the cat moved out of range. Again he circled but now, much more warily.

Chaka toni charged as *Yaguar* moved nimbly aside, landing a stinging swat to the bear's muzzle. The bear grabbed the carcass and began dragging it backwards but now *Yaguar's* attack was fast and decisive. It sunk its sharp canines into the bear's exposed flank.

From the valley below the sounds of the battle pulsed through the evening air. The muffled "whoofs" of the great bear mingled with the growls and screams of *Yaguar*.

Chaka toni dropped the carcass to protect his flank and seemed confused as the agile cat now circled him alternately making brief charges to swat or nip at him. This went on for several minutes with *Yaguar* apparently getting the best of the battle. But then the big cat made a mistake and got too close. A swipe from the fore paw of *Chaka toni* sent the jaguar sprawling. The bear followed up with a vicious attack but *Yaguar,* ever agile, leaped high into the air and retreated from the kill site. It had enough. *Yaguar* moved away, only looking over its shoulder once before disappearing into the scrub.

Chaka toni watched *Yaguar* for a moment and then moved to the slain antelope and began feeding.

Now the *Indians* and the *Christians* began talking about what they had just witnessed.

Whispering, one of the *Indians* relayed to Alvar. "This is the first time I have seen this. Many times I have witnessed animals stealing each other's food, but never between *Chaka toni* and the great *Yaguar*."

The *Indians* were pointing at the kill site. Unsure of what the commotion was about, Alvar watched as *Chaka toni* briefly stopped feeding to defecate. At that moment *Yaguar* emerged from the tall grass, rushed forward, picked up the carcass, and in the blink of an eye disappeared into the bush. The big cat had been hiding downwind waiting for just the right opportunity. *Chaka toni* forlornly watched *Yaguar* disappear, sniffed the kill site one last time, and then ambled off.

There was much excitement among the *Indians.* In a way, both of the revered animals had won this contest. The brute strength of *Chaka Toni* had defeated *Yaguar* in an all-out fight, but the cunning of the big cat had triumphed in the end.

Alvar addressed his compatriots. "This story will be retold many times over the fires of their children and grandchildren."

Dorantes replied. "Not just theirs *Alguacil*, but mine as well!"

CHAPTER 17

Leaving The People Of The Cows

Gente de las Vacas

*F*inally, on the third day, the women returned. They related that the land ahead was populated by the "The People of the Cows" and since this was the season, hunting parties were in the north in search of the great beasts. Only a few people remained in the villages that they encountered.

Convinced that an advanced culture existed in Amichel further to the west and maybe further north, the four survivors had abandoned their quest for the Spanish settlement at Panuco. At first, they bypassed the coastline of the North Sea and trekked further inland to avoid the terrible Indians that had massacred all of the Christians aboard the Tellez boat. In each of the villages they encountered, however, little hints pointed to riches that might exist further to the north. Gourds, cultivated maize, pieces of silver.

In the village of 40 houses, they had been presented with a copper bell. This was significant, for it indicated that somewhere in Amichel the technology existed to mine metal, cast, work it, and engrave a design. In the minds of the survivors, this warranted further investigation and they completely abandoned all ideas of reaching Panuco. If they could find this civilization they could return to Spain as heroes, and like Cortes, wealth beyond comprehension.

After years of captivity and hardship, their position now was relatively good. By the grace of God, they were revered shamans able to safely travel anywhere. Mostly they had plenty to eat and scores of women to share their bed at night. Now, after traveling north to the Great River they would continue west, then north, and then finally west until they reached the South Sea. They would continue to search for this great empire.

November, 1535

Traveling Through the Mexican State of Coahuila

After 13 days the group, now numbering many people, came to a large river that flowed from the north. There were people here. Many people. Upon the *Christians*, and those that had traveled with them, these people gave many gifts. Red ocher, beads, skins, deer fat, flints, and most of all, pine nuts, which were in abundance. Here they passed through high plateaus and immense grasslands. They followed the river for 30 leagues. At times, the river's path was marked by lush grasses, and huge cottonwood, pecan, and oak trees. The towering summits and sheer cliffs closed upon them such that there would be only a small trail paralleling the river. Other times, the footing was so steep that the procession was forced to leave the river and follow the trail into the high plateau country. Here, it was very dry and the game was scarce.

Finally, the travelers crossed a broad river flowing to the east. The *Spaniards* had reason to believe this was the same River of Gourds they had crossed several months before. Other *Indians*, traveling from very far away, came to greet the newcomers. They had heard of the *Children of the Sun* and their great healing powers and all wanted to touch or be blessed. With them they brought food and gifts and, of course, pine nuts. So plentiful were these pine nuts that the *Christians* jokingly identified all the individuals here as *People of the Pine Nuts*.

After crossing the barren plains and sierras during the previous days the *Indians* accompanying the *Christians* had suffered much. Food and water had been scarce and the great suffering had taken its physical toll. As was the custom they would claim the gifts and return to their homes. There were so many gifts that the *Indians* that accompanied the white shamans could not carry them all. They left the unused offerings abandoned at the river before returning by way of the tortuous route just completed.

It was here that Dead Crow notified the *Spaniards* that this was as far as he would go.

He talked to Alvar. "Wasapi-tun-loki, this is as far as I have ever traveled. I know nothing of the land beyond. I have heard that there is a great village with many people further to the west. Further north still they say it is so cold that a man will freeze while he is walking."

The *Guachichiles* gathered up their booty, but, like the others, they could not carry it all and left much on the banks of the great river.

The four *Spaniards* gathered around Dead Crow, each shaking his hand and thanking him for his guidance. Shortly after this the *Guachichiles...* redheads...turned and began the long trek back to their village.

Estevan questioned the *People of the Pine Nuts* why they didn't reclaim the gifts. To this they said it was not their custom, after having offered it, to take it back again.

The *People of the Pine Nuts* were a loose confederation of several villages, each led by a head man or *cacique*. There was no overall leader. The other groups who had traveled from afar were also represented by a loose contingent of *caciques*.

Alvar gathered up all the leaders and spoke to them with the assistance of hand talk and Estevan, the polyglot.

"We desire to go in the direction of where the sun sets." Alvar pointed to the west. "We would ask that you send people in that direction to inform those ahead that we are coming."

The various *caciques* considered this but after some discussion, at first refused, saying that those to the west were their enemies. Because they feared the power of the shamans, however, they finally agreed to send two women ahead. Alvar agreed and understood; that women could safely travel between warring groups and serve as intermediaries.

The next day the two women headed out. One was from the *People of the Pine Nuts*, the other was a captive who had lived with them for several years. Her name was Tanikia. It would be her people that would be encountered in the West. They would talk with the people ahead and then return to tell of what they learned. The *Christians* accompanied these women one league up the river where they agreed to wait for their return.

Each of the *Christians* had their own retinue and in a large clearing by the river, they set up camp to await the return of the women. Days passed while they became increasingly frustrated. Finally, on the fifth day, the two women ambled into camp at about the noon hour. Strangely, they conferred with the *caciques* before talking to the *Christians*.

Alvar confronted the *Indians*. Again, through interpreters and hand talk the *caciques* replied sheepishly that there were no people in that direction and that there was nothing to eat or water to be found. They said the women had found nothing. They again declined to lead the *Christians*. Alvar knew this to be a lie, for Estevan had become involved with the one called Tanikia, the captive, and she had related that her people were ahead and anxiously awaiting the shamans.

As *alguacil* and leader of the *Christians,* Alvar feigned anger as did the other three. They all stormed out of the camp and went out into the countryside to be away from the *Indians*. No sooner had they made a fire and bedded down than the *Indians* appeared. They were terrified, begging them not to be angry anymore and that they would lead them wherever they wanted to go even at great risk.

The *Christians* persisted in their ruse and by the next morning, a strange thing happened. So terrified were the *Indians* that many became ill. Those affected would lie on their mats as if in a stupor. Life seemed to drain out of them. By the next day, eight people had died from this strange malady and many more were becoming sick.

Gathered together, Dorantes spoke to the other three. "These people are terrified of us. If we persist in our anger, I fear they all might die."

Castillo added, "This fear of us could spread and scare off any who might want to help us."

Alvar and Estevan agreed.

Dorantes continued, "Let us make a show of beseeching God for their forgiveness."

And so the *Christian* shamans reentered the camp. All who were sick were prayed over in an elaborate ceremony of the sign of the cross, repeating the *Trinitarian invocation* and laying on hands. Finally, after repeating the *pater noster* they moved from one victim to another.

Within hours the afflicted began to show improvement. By the next day, most who had suffered appeared healthy once again. There was now great rejoicing that extended far into the early morning hours.

Although the *Indians* had shown great concern over those afflicted with the illness, there was no sentiment for those who had died. Even mothers did not lament the loss of a child. One woman who did show emotion over the loss of her small baby was taken away and severely lacerated from her shoulders to the bottom of her legs. The instrument used for this punishment was the sharp teeth of a rat's mandible.

Seeing the bloody woman's injuries, Alvar asked why this was done. The *cacique* of her group responded.

"This is her punishment for weeping in front of you and displeasing the *Children of the Sun.*"

November, 1535

Following the Rio Grande Through South Texas

Again the *Christians* sent out the two women to scout the land ahead and tell the people of their coming. For three days they remained in the camp by the great river awaiting their return. During this time most of the Indians who had been ill, recovered. Other *Indians*, continued arriving, to see, touch and receive a blessing from the four holy men, the *Children of the Sun*. Some had traveled many leagues and were in poor shape. The *Christians* did what they could to help feed and comfort everyone, all the time collecting information about the land and what it had to offer.

Finally, on the third day, the women returned. They related that the land ahead was populated by the *"The People of the Cows"* and since this was the season, hunting parties were in the north in search of the great beasts. Only a few people remained in the villages that they encountered.

De Vaca, Dorantes, Castillo, and Estevan huddled together to talk about what to do next. Together they decided to leave the next morning and continue their journey in the direction that the women had just come from.

"Alguacil, the people here will try and follow us. Many are still recovering from the sickness and others are too old or too young to make this journey. They will surely slow us down."

"I agree, friend Castillo," was Alvar's reply. "We will instruct that only the most hardy will accompany us."

Estevan had an idea of his own. *"Alguacil*, before we arrive at these villages it would be better if only a few proceed ahead so that they can receive us without fear."

"Ahh Estevanico, a good thought!" Dorantes and Castillo nodded in agreement.

"Once we are a days walk from the village we will instruct the women guides to lead two of us to these People of the Cows. They can then make known our upcoming arrival and good intentions to these people."

The following morning, just after sunrise, the *Christians* and their troop of followers began their journey to the northwest. In the lead were the two women. The one who was a captive, Tanikia, was accompanied by Estevan with whom she had formed a strong relationship. Walking side by side they frequently touched and at rest stops, disappeared into the bush.

The three white *Spaniards* typically walked together and at times took the lead to pick up the pace. Behind them the *Indian* followers trailed in clusters of friends, family groups, and women burdened with the camp paraphernalia. Each day, a little after noon, hunters would forge ahead in an attempt to procure food for the evening meal. The hunters, returning a little before sunset, waited by the trail at a campsite they had chosen. On arrival, the women would construct the crude shelters, start fires, and prepare the evening meals before darkness was well upon them.

On the evening of the third day, the women guides announced they would go on alone, with two of the shamans accompanying them. At sunrise, Castillo and Estevan shook hands with Alvar and Dorantes and then proceeded up the trail.

In the camp, Dorantes and Alvar settled in with their individual followers and awaited the return of Estevan and Castillo.

November, 1535

Confluence of the Rio Conchos and the Rio Grande

For a day and a half Castillo and Estevan with the two women guides traveled up the river. Three other *Indian* men accompanied them, but the rest of the following had stayed back with Alvar and Dorantes. *The People of the Pine Nuts* were enemies of *The People of the Cows* and as such, were not willing to go ahead.

At noon on the second day, the small troop came to another river that flowed from the south. It intersected the great river they were traveling on at a location between several mountains. Here just north of the confluence was situated a village. The woman that accompanied Estevan became very excited, for this was the village of her father who served as the *casique*.

Castillo remarked, "Estevanico, do you see that the houses here are much different than others we have seen in our travels?"

"*Si Senor* Castillo they appear to be permanent structures. Houses that you would live in year-a-round."

Tanikia ran on ahead to greet her father and the people of the village. When Castillo and Estevan arrived the whole population had turned out. As they walked along the people would touch them and then run back to their lodges only to return and touch them again. At the center of the village, waiting to receive them, was Tanikia and her father. He was called Quitilla. She ran to Estevan and embraced him. Estevan, startled, looked toward her father. The only reaction was a slight nod of the *cacique's* head.

Now, what erupted was quite strange. The people all began to celebrate. A circle of *Indians* surrounded Estevan and Tanikia, all dancing and singing. Food was brought out and the celebration extended well into the night. Throughout it all Estevan and Tanikia seemed to be the center of attention. Oblivious, Estevan enjoyed himself, joining in the dancing to the obvious delight of the *Indians*. Castillo, however, was mystified by the goings on and questioned the *casique* as to the reason for the celebration. Somewhat limited by language and hand talk Castillo finally was able to discern that this was a wedding celebration.

A wedding between Estevan and Tanikia!

Castillo was thunderstruck, for nothing had happened like this before. He walked over to where Estevan was dancing.

"Estevanico, stand still for a moment!"

"Estevan, with a questioning look in his eye, responded, *"Capitan* Castillo, you look troubled."

Castillo had to yell because of the noise. "Did you know this is a wedding ceremony?"

Estevan still smiling and looking around said, "No *Capitan*, who is getting married?"

"You are!"

The smile disappeared from Estevan's face. He suddenly understood.

Castillo had to stifle a laugh. He put a hand on Estevan's shoulder.

"Congratulations, you will make a fine couple."

Unable to hold back Castillo laughed aloud and then turned away, still laughing.

For a while Estevan looked sad and forlorn, but as the night wore on he accepted his fate and, once again, joined in the rivalry. Around midnight Tanikia's father had the two join hands while he grasped both on the shoulder. After only a few words he announced they were married. Again, there was great celebration. The women of the village gathered up Tanikia and took her away. Quitilla draped a beautiful fox pelt over Estevan's shoulders and inserted two eagle feathers into his hair. They stood there watching the festivities until Tanikia returned adorned in a beautiful soft deer skin skirt with braided roping and fringes that hung to her ankles. She wore a necklace of small colorful pebbles that had been pierced to accept the rawhide cord that held them. Her long black hair, festooned with many colored feathers, hung to the small of her back. Even Castillo was taken aback by her beauty.

With this, the women of the village led the couple to a hut at the far end of the village.

Estevan and his bride were not seen all of the next day. That evening, after dark, Estevan sauntered up to where Castillo was sitting by the fire.

"Well, *Senor* Estevanico have you had enough of love-making for a while?"

Estevan could only smile.

Castillo continued, "I have been thinking. It is probably a good thing that you are now married to the daughter of these "*People of the Cows*" for they will now be our allies and assist us in whatever we do.

Estevan answered, "What of the *Alguacil* and *Senor* Dorantes?"

"I will leave in the morning and return to them. The other woman guide, the three *Pine Nut* men, and five of the *Cow People* will accompany me. You will stay here with your...ah...bride until we return."

"There is one more thing *capitan*." Estevan looked away from the fire.

"What is it?"

"Tanikia thinks that she is with child!"

Castillo sighed, looked up, and then stared into the fire. Finally, he spoke.

"This may be a blessing!"

Estevan looked at him with a questioning stare.

Castillo continued. "We will be leaving here and continuing our journey. Better you convince her to stay here and raise the child.

Estevan nodded and then walked away.

Early December, 1535

Journey to the West:

The weather had turned and a chilling wind was blowing from the north. Tired and cold, the small group including Castillo, the woman guide, three *Pine Nut* men, and five *Cow People* arrived at the site where Alvar and Dorantes waited for them. Both *Spaniards* warmly greeted Castillo.

Dorantes looked around questionably. "Where is Estevanico?"

Castillo could only stifle a smirk. "Ha, he is fine but it is a long story. Let us sit and talk about it over the fire for I am chilled to the bone."

The story of Estevan's marriage caused much laughter among the three *Spaniards*. They talked late into the night discussing the implications of the marriage and the other things that Castillo had seen.

"*Alguacil*, The permanent structures indicate that they have resided in their valley a long time. They also grow squash and beans in their fields of maize. I ate *frijoles* until I thought I would burst." Castillo rubbed his stomach in mock pain.

Castillo further related that the black man, Estevan, had said he would accompany many of the *Cow People*, and meet them on the road.

"We had better leave early then. Tomorrow will be an interesting day." Alvar rubbed his eyes and retired to his temporary shelter.

By the time the sun rays began to fall on the river valley, the troupe of *Spaniards* and *Indians* were well on their way. It was still early morning and they had traveled no more than a league and a half when up ahead a large throng of *Indians* appeared with Estevan at their head with Tanikia and Quitilla by his side. The *Spaniards* rushed ahead to greet the black man.

Castillo clapped him on the back. "Estevanico, how did you get here so fast?"

"*Capitan*, I could not hold them back. So badly did the *Cow People* want to greet you that we left that very afternoon after you had departed."

The *Cow People* lavished many gifts on the *Christians,* all of which were turned over to the *Pine Nut People* who were accompanying them. Shortly thereafter all these people took their leave and returned down the trail.

As soon as the *Pine Nut People* had gone, the *Christians* and their following continued back up the trail. Arriving long after night had fallen, the village once again erupted in celebration that lasted well intothe morning of the next day.

In the afternoon Alvar called the other three over to him.

"We will leave in the morning and continue our journey to the west. The *cacique* has offered to guide us on this journey."

The next morning none of the *Christians* were prepared for what they saw. Virtually the whole village had turned out to accompany the four shamans. All that would remain were the very old, the injured, and women with children too young to make the journey. At the recommendation of Estevan, however, Quitilla had ten men remain in the village to provide security.

They traveled along the river for six or seven leagues until coming to another village similar to the one they had just left. The inhabitants turned out to meet the shamans, but also their relatives from Quitilla's village. Here the shamans blessed a group of hunters scheduled to leave the next morning to hunt *ayani* or what the *Spaniards* called shaggy cows.

It was Dorantes idea to collect all the hunting weapons in a pile such that they could all be blessed in one elaborate ceremony. So, there in the village center, next to a roaring fire the various tools of the hunter's trade were neatly arranged. Bows, arrows, spears, flint blades, and clubs. The group of hunters, ten in all, plus four women stood in a line. The shamans had roughly rehearsed how this would proceed.

First, Estevan with his fox pelt and eagle feathers appeared. He silently walked around the fire chanting some unintelligible lyrics in *Spanish*. Then the three *Spaniards* appeared, looking very somber and lordly. The four came together next to the weapons. The *pater nostre* was given and then, looking up, all three appealed to God to watch after these men and women. The four then walked over to the assembled hunters and touching each on the head, gave the sign of the cross. With this, the ceremony was concluded.

The effect was immediate. The hunters strutted around the fire after collecting their weapons. The people of the village surged forward to touch each one of them. After that, the usual singing and dancing commenced late into the night. They ate *frijoles*, pumpkins, and stewed meat. The *Cow People* had no pots, but instead filled dried gourds with water. To these they placed hot rocks into the water, constantly replacing them until the water boiled. Once hot enough they would add cut-up strips of meat and other things.

Scenes like this occurred for the next two days in every village that the shamans came to. Finally, at the end of the second day, they sat down with Quitilla to determine what to do next.

Alvar questioned Quitilla why there was so little maize among the *People of the Cows*. The *casique* responded that the seasons had been unusually dry and for this reason, they dared not plant their crop for fear of it drying up.

Alvar thought for a moment and then asked, "When the seasons become wet again, where will you get seed for planting?"

Quitilla pointed to the west. "It comes from where the sun sets. There the rain falls and the people have maize.

Alvar told the *casique*, "It is our desire to go to this land of maize. What is the fastest route we can take without difficulty?"

Quitilla answered, "It is a journey of seventeen days if you follow the great river, but the people along the river are our enemies. The path is bad and you will find nothing to eat but a fruit that is so bitter that most men and animals will not consume it."

Alvar *questioned,* "Is there a better way to travel to the land of the maize?"

Quitilla seemed to brighten. "You must leave the great river and go north. Four days journey from here there are great numbers of *ayani;* as far as the eye can see. The land is very populous and there is much to eat. From here you can then travel to the sunset and in seventeen days turn again toward the river and the *People of the Maize*."

Alvar spoke in *Spanish* to his three companions.

"It is my opinion that more advanced cultures of these people will be associated with the growing of maize, much like the *Aztecs*. This northern road to the cows seems a very great detour. I suggest we continue up the river even though it will be more challenging."

There were nods all around.

Turning to Quitilla Alvar asked, "Will you guide us, for we have determined to follow the great river?"

The *casique* looked disappointed. After some thought, he answered. "We do not wish to go this way but I will send five of my people to guide and watch over you."

The *Christians* left the *People of the Cows* the next morning and continued up the great river. With them went three men and two women from the *People of the Cows*. Tanikia had stayed behind at the bequest of Estevan.

Castillo had questioned him on this. "What did you tell Tanikia to convince her to stay back?"

Estevan struggled with his reply. " I told her, *capitan*, that I would return to see my child.

"Estevanico, you cannot believe this will happen! We will never return to this place."

Both men had stopped walking and stared at each other.

Estevan finally spoke. "Again, *Capitan*, I will try and find a way to return and see her...and my child."

With that, Estevan turned and continued up the trail leaving Castillo to ponder what had just been said.

CHAPTER 18

The Corn Road

El Camino de Maiz

*T*his part of the journey the Spaniards began to call the El Camino de Maiz or The Corn Road because of the abundance of food and, more specifically, corn as the major staple.

January 1536

Following the Rio Grande to Present--Day El Paso,

Texas

Just as Quitilla had said, the *"Children of the Sun"* and the people with them had difficulty traversing the 17-day journey up the great river. Food was scarce. Before they set out, however, Tanikia had prepared balls of deer suet for each of the travelers. Deer fat mixed with various grass seeds made up this concoction. Because they were well into the winter months and the weather was cool, this suet would last almost indefinitely on the trail. In the end, the suet and an occasional fish would sustain them.

Estevan had become quite proficient at spearing fish. At the evening campsites, he would stand motionless in the quiet eddies and cane breaks of the great river. He would strike suddenly with a spear when a fish of decent size ventured into his view. More often than not he missed, but occasionally his actions would be rewarded. On the third day, he was able to provide three large catfish to the cooking fire. Other days only a small brim or bass or nothing at all would be offered up, but everything helped.

The people along the river were very poor. They also hunted the great shaggy cows, but the season for this was over and the remaining winter months would be spent close to the river where they could gather the berries of the *chaca,* and fish. They lived from day to day, for this was the season of starving. What was in abundance, however, was buffalo robes and they offered many of these to the *Christians* who, in turn, gave them to the *Indians who* traveled with them and others along the river trail. At each small village, a few more *Indians* would join the procession.

Finally, at the end of seventeen days of travel, they came to an area where there seemed to be a break in the mountains. The river at this point had turned sharply northward, a direction that the *Spaniards* did not want to go. Alvar called the other three to a meeting.

"*Amigos,* I think we must leave this river and continue our venture towards the setting sun. Only in this direction will we come to the South Sea and the people that grow maize."

They carefully questioned the other *Indians* traveling with them. By all accounts, the way in which they wanted to travel was across a dry desert and tall sierras. There were few inhabitants in that direction but after many days of travel, they would come to people who grew maize in abundance, and further on, the waters of the South Sea.

The next morning the four shamans crossed the great river and began their journey towards the setting sun.

Late January, 1536

Crossing the Desert Highlands of Northern

Chihuahua

The *Christians* struggled to cross the dry highlands and rugged mountain ridges. Fierce winds from the north blew across this bleak terrain. The thick buffalo robes kept them warm, but finding a protected campsite at night was a challenge. The women that accompanied them carried the necessary sticks, rawhide, and hides with which to erect temporary shelters. Once the campsite had been chosen the sticks would be lashed together to form a crude framework. Brush and skins would then be thrown over this framework and secured to the sticks with rawhide ties. Around the base, rocks and soil were piled up to keep the air from blowing under the structure. Although not completely rainproof they would protect the inhabitants from the fierce night winds. All of the brush structures were erected in a semi-circle around the upwind side of a central fire, that is, if there was fuel enough to gather for a fire. These crude dwellings were never more than a few feet high and only large enough to hold two or three people at most. Surprisingly, the combined body heat of the inhabitants kept the structures quite comfortable inside. Each of the *Spaniards* slept with two women. These same two women might be repeated on the next night but generally, one or even both would be replaced by others.

The people that lived along this route were very poor. They hunted bison in the autumn but were generally ostracized by the larger and better-equipped people to the north. During the difficult winter months, they subsisted almost entirely on powdered herbs and thelong-legged *conejas*...hares. The hares were constantly hunted as the caravan moved across the landscape. Some days two or three would be brought in and presented directly to the shamans, who, after keeping only a small portion, would present the remainder to the people who followed them. Since it was now winter the *Spaniards* also tried the powdered herbs that the *Indians* seemed to relish. They were ground and mixed with water to form a sticky and tasteless paste that the *Spaniards* found quite inedible. Still, the horrible concoction helped sustain them when food was scarce.Finally, after the grueling days of travel, the *Christians* and their entourage came to a river valley and many permanent houses. Surprisingly, the *Indians* here knew of their upcoming arrival and greeted the newcomers with great quantities of maize, cotton mantles, squash, and frijoles. These gifts were given to the people who had accompanied the shamans. Their numbers had swelled to about fifty individuals and after receiving the gifts many began the journey back, to the way they had come. As they proceeded back up the trail there was much singing and rejoicing which continued until they were out of sight.

This was a permanent settlement and to the Spaniards, it looked as if the *Indians* had resided here for many years. Many of the houses were made of earth that had been packed tightly to form low walls. Across these walls, beams were laid to support a slanted roof of woven grasses. The flooring was usually grass mats that were laid along the interior of the structure. The *Indians* called these structures *buhios*.

The *Christians* remained in this village for three days, feasting on the abundance of food. The inhabitants flocked around them wanting only to be touched by these strange medicine men. Of Estevan they were especially curious, rubbing his black skin and then looking at their hands to see if any of the black came off. In the evening husbands brought their wives and fathers brought their daughters to be impregnated by the *Christians*. The feeling was that the offspring would inherit the powers of the shamans and bring honor to the families. The women patiently waited outside their huts to be called next.

The *Christians* tried hard to please, for to turn down any of the women presented to them would be would bring disgrace to the woman and her family. Young and old, fair and ugly, all were given equal opportunity. Each of the shamans, however, could only perform for so long, and at the end of two days, they were exhausted. On the morning of the third day, they announced they would be leaving the next morning. Still, the women lined up outside their huts.

Alvar was exasperated as he talked to the other three over the morning meal.

"*Amigos*, I cannot continue this. I will tell their *cacique* that we will need time alone for prayer and meditation before we leave."

"Good idea," was Castillo's reply, while the other two nodded their heads in the affirmative.

The next morning the men arose early and began their journey before the sun rose. They started out alone, but as the morning progressed, *Indians,* running to catch up, would join them. By mid-morning their numbers had swelled to thirty or more individuals.

As a new group jogged up the trail behind them Dorantes turned to ask,

"Why do you follow us?"

"Because you are *The Children of the Sun.* You will protect us from all things evil and cure us when we are sick," was the reply.

Now turning south they encountered many permanent settlements. The land was rich and food was abundant. Each village had fields of maize, beans, and squash. Cotton grew abundantly and the *Indians* presented the *Spaniards* with blankets woven with such dexterity that they exceeded anything found in *New Spain.* This part of the journey the *Spaniards* began to call the *El Camino de Maiz* or The Corn Road because of the abundance of food and, more specifically, corn as the major staple. The *Indians* in this area called themselves *Eudeve* which, in their language again meant "The People."

The villages began to display more and more artifacts brought from the South Sea. Shells, decorative corals, and even shark's-teeth that the men wore as pendants. The larger shark's teeth were quite impressive, some as large as a man's hand. The *Spaniards* could only imagine the size of the creature from which they had come.

Overall the people encountered along the corn road appeared more advanced than any previously encountered. The women wore ankle-length deerskin skirts over which they donned dyed short-sleeved cotton shirts that extended down to their knees. The men usually dressed more scantly than the women with breech clothes and short hide skirts. Over this, the men would occasionally drape themselves with a cotton shawl. Both sexes wore footwear.

There was a plant the *Indians* called *iczotl* and the *Spaniards* had seen it many times in their travels. These *Eudeve* people, however, utilized this plant in ways not seen before. They ate the fruit, stems, roots, leaf bases, and flowers, weaved sandals, rope, and baskets from the fibrous leaves, and used the root pulp for a kind of soap. Alvar and the other three watched in amazement as one *Eudeve* woman made each of the *Spaniards* a set of sandals. They laughed when the women struggled to find leaves long enough to fashion Estevan's footwear...he had the biggest feet of any of the *Spaniards*.

The language of the *Eudeve* differed from any encountered so far. Unlike other languages, the tone of the speaker was used for major emphasis. These tone and volume changes produced an effect that was quite alien to the *Spaniards* and although some words and phrases were universal, most of the communication was by hand talk. The *Spaniards* were now fluent in at least six languages besides *Spanish* and semi-fluent in numerous languages they had picked up along the many miles of their travel. Estevan was the exception. Wherever they went, the *African* seemed to become conversant after only two or three days ofcontact with the new cultures.

February, 1536

The Village of Hearts

They arrived at a large river. Dorantes stepped up next to Alvar with a question.

"*Alguacil*, I have a good feeling about this part of our journey. This is indeed a beautiful waterway...we should name it."

Alvar thought a moment and then pulled a folded piece of deerskin from the light pack he was carrying. On this deerskin was a likeness of the Virgin Mary that he had drawn only the day before. The drawing was crude but he had used it to demonstrate the Savior's virgin mother to the *Indians* that had surrounded him.

"Friend Dorantes, I also feel good about our journey today. I look here at my modest attempt to capture the likeness of the Holy Mother and think that it would be fitting to call this river *Nuestra Señora de las Angustias*...Our Lady of Anguish."

Dorantes thought a moment and then said, "Then that's what it will be."

However, when this name was presented to the *Indians*, they could not pronounce it, for in their language, there was no hard "n" sound. They quickly dropped most of the nomenclature and referred to it as only "*Sonora.*" The *Spaniards* simply shrugged their shoulders and from then on it was called the *Rio Sonora*.

Alvar was presented with beautiful turquoise and emeralds that the *Indians* had fashioned into large arrowheads or spear points. These were quite beautiful and as the *Spaniards* marveled at them they asked the *Indians* from where they had come. They answered that they had come from high mountains far to the north in trade for plumes and parrot feathers.

Here again, the *Spaniards* were tempted to reverse their direction in search of this northern land of riches. They talked late into the night, but all eventually agreed that they should concentrate on returning to civilization. There they could relate their findings and organize another expedition into *Amichel*.

To Alonzo Castillo, the Indians presented one of their prize possessions....brightly colored shells from the South Sea. Estevan was given a finely crafted bow.

In addition to the gifts made to the other three, an offering of 600 deer hearts was presented to Andres Dorantes. These deer hearts and other dried meats were stored in earthen huts and hung from poles. For this reason, the *Spaniards* called this place, *Pueblo de los Corazones...Village of the Hearts.* Through the hand talk and translations the *Spaniards* learned that they also called themselves *"The People."* It was an oddity that so many *Indian* groups called themselves "The People. A subject that Alvar and Dorantes discussed by the evening campfires.

As always, the *Spaniards* distributed most of the gifts between the people who had come with them, but not before they had feasted on some of the deer hearts. Alvar kept one of the emeralds and Estevan kept the bow.

The *Village of Hearts* seemed to be a central trade hub for items coming from the *South Sea* and the mountains to the east. Resting there for three days the travelers noted groups of burdened merchants entering the village at all times of the day and night with items to barter and trade. From them, they learned that the land to the west was heavily populated but along the coast, there was no maize and the sea people lived a much different life of fishing and collecting sea-weed that they eat. These people have no canoes and venture out into the water with crudely made rafts.

At the *Village of Hearts* the four *Spaniards* discussed which way they should turn once they reached the south sea.

Castillo spoke first. "*Alguacil*, we have encountered hundreds of cultures in our journey and seen things beyond description. In all our travels, however, the people have been hunters, gathers, or farmers. Some villages are better off than others but I see no proof that there is another civilization such as the great Cortes encountered."

Dorantes agreed. "God has walked with us on this journey and protected us from much harm. Now I dream of returning to the civilized world. I suggest that we turn south with the hope that we may find a *Spanish* settlement."

As usual, Estevan had little to say except, " I have enjoyed the freedom of this land but will follow whichever direction you decide."

Alvar thought for a long moment. He looked down at his heavily calloused feet, so tough that he could run down a rocky path with no discomfort. He looked at his arms, legs, and torso, burnt almost the same color as the Indians and covered with scars, scratches, and insect bites. His hair, beginning to show gray, was long and his beard unkempt.

With a sigh, he nodded, "I agree. If we turn north we will eventually die in this land of *Amichel*. When we reach the south sea let us follow the shoreline and, hopefully, we will once again find our own kind."

From the *Indians* in this area, the *Spaniards* learned that instead of continuing west toward the *South Sea* a better trail existed that ran almost due south from The *Village of Hearts*. Its terminus was another large river that emptied into the sea. The river was a two-day journey. Along this river were many villages that grew maize, beans, and squash.

And so, after three days at the *Village of Hearts,* the *Spaniards* set out once again, having made the decision to take the well-worn trading path to the south and then follow the next river to the *South Sea.*

This trail was very circuitous and mostly unpopulated over some very rough terrain. On the second day of travel, the four stood on a precipice and gazed out across the endless expanse. The foot trail meandered below them, finally disappearing in the distance behind another large hill. As barren and lonely as the land appeared, this trail was well-worn. They periodically met travelers coming from the south bearing trade goods who assured them that a major river was only a few days distant.

They pushed on, traveling about five leagues a day. Along the trail, the *Spaniards* ate very little, only consuming a few morsels in the evening. The *Indians* were amazed at how little they ate and how they never seemed to tire. They were convinced that these bearded shamans had truly come from heaven. When entering new areas even those *Indians* at war would make peace with each other.

At the end of two days of travel, the trail ended abruptly in a lush river valley inhabited by many people. The river at this juncture was nothing more than a stream, but the guides claimed that it grew rapidly in size further down the mountains. Their name for it was quite unpronounceable at first but roughly translated to *"Little River that flows to the Big Waters."* The *Indians* swarmed around the bearded shamans, for news of their arrival had preceded them. Many had traveled some distance to see *The Children of the Sun,* explaining that many of their villages were two days further east, near another river called, by some, *"Large River that flows to the Big Waters"* and by the people who lived there, *"River of the Yaquis."* They called themselves *Hiake* or *Yaqui,* the *Spaniards* were never quite sure how to pronounce it.

Once again, their presence was highlighted by singing and dancing that lasted late into the night. They stayed here for three days, resting from the arduous journey they had just completed.

On the evening of the third day, Alvar stood at the bank of the river skipping flat rocks across its placid surface. He turned as Captain Castillo approached.

"Capitan Castillo, what are your thoughts this fine evening?"

"*Alguacil*, we are now well-rested in a land that seems very plentiful and the natives are more than friendly. I think tomorrow we should begin our journey down this river."

"I agree. Seek out Capitan Dorantes and tell him of our intentions and I will strive to find Estevanico so that he can make ready."

Castillo smiled and looked around. "Good luck, there are probably forty or fifty huts in this village and my guess is that our amorous black friend is in one of them bedded down with one or more *chicas*!

Alvar just shook his head and turned toward the village. "I will find him."

February, 1536

Indian Village by the Present-Day Rio Matape

On the first day, the journey down the river was a pleasant walk. From village to village the people prevailed on the *Children of the Sun* to touch and bless them. Newborns and children of all ages were brought to be blessed and women begged to sleep with them.

On the second day, the sky became darkened with storm clouds and by afternoon a light mist had begun to fall. In the distance, thunder rolled across the river valley. The mist turned to a light drizzle and the wind began to bend the top of the trees. By mid-afternoon, the rain was falling heavily and staccato blasts of wind blew so strongly that the surface of the *Little River* was replete with whitecaps. The wind blew across the trail causing the men to stumble as they walked.

Finally, on reaching another village Alvar called out to the other three. "*Amigos*, this is crazy, I am cold, wet, and miserable. Let us stay in this village until this tempest subsides." He had to yell to be heard over the sound of the wind, the rain, and the thunder.

As always they were welcomed warmly by the people. Each of the *Spaniards* was taken to separate huts that were inhabited by family units. Castillo's hut was larger than most, but it had to be, for inside was a family of 7. This was the hut of the village *cacique* who shared it with his wife, three daughters, and two sons. It was crowded inside but the warmth of the shaggy cow robes felt good. Outside, the rain increased in intensity.

Castillo was sitting idly at one end of the hut while the family silently stared at him from the other side. At long last the buxom wife asked Castillo, almost apologetically, if he would touch and bless each of her children.

He stumbled through the difficult language, pantomiming with hand talk as he spoke. "Yes, *Senora* I would be most happy to do that."

He called each child over individually and made the sign of the cross for each while repeating, "Father in heaven, watch over this child." He looked up toward heaven with each sacrament.

After the last child had been blessed Castillo asked the parents if they would also like to receive a sacrament. The woman seemed overjoyed. Quite unexpectedly she threw off her cotton shawl and knelt before him. Her enormous breasts were now exposed and it was with difficulty that Castillo finished the sacrament.

He thought to himself. "What a hypocrite am I. Here I am blessing these people in God's holy name while lusting after this woman's breasts. There must be a special place in hell for sinners like me."

As the woman returned to her end of the hut the husband threw off his cotton garment and also knelt before the bearded shaman. It was then that Castillo took note of the necklace he wore...it looked strangely familiar. Tied to a leather thong that hung around the husband's neck was a buckle from a sword belt, the kind used by many a *Spanish* soldier. Also tied to the buckle was a horseshoe nail. Castillo asked for the necklace with the promise that it would be given back. The husband readily turned it over.

"From where did you get these items?" Castillo asked.

"From the sky," was the man's response.

As the rain lessened somewhat, Castillo told the husband that these items were very important and that he would like to show them to his compatriots. The husband nodded enthusiastically and rushed out of the hut to gather the other three.

Soon, all four of the *Spaniards* were huddled together in the hut passing the necklace back and forth between them.

Dorantes studied the belt buckle and horseshoe nail. Then, turning toward the husband asked, "Who brought these things from heaven?"

"They were bearded men like you. They rode atop a large deer that was very fast. They had swords and long lances with which they speared two of our people over by the river." The husband pointed in the direction.

Alvar spoke in *Spanish*. "We must not act too interested in this story for they may associate us with these *Spaniards* that brought them harm."

Dorantes arose and handed the necklace back to the husband. Acting as if ready to leave he looked over his shoulder and asked very unassumingly.

 "What happened to these men?"

"They returned to the water from where they had come. As the sun was setting we saw them moving across the water toward a white cloud just above the surface and after that, they disappeared back into the sky."

The rain had almost stopped. Outside the hut, the four survivors pondered on what they had just seen.

Alvar spoke, "We should all give thanks to God for I have begun to doubt we would see signs of other *Christians* ever again."

Castillo answered, "But, who were they and what were they doing here?"

Estevan had a thought. "Perhaps they were *Spanish* slavers."

Dorantes just shook his head. "We have no answers to these questions but I think we should go faster on our way to the south and by the grace of God we may find other *Christians*."

Alvar returning to the hut said over his shoulder. "Let us ask our hosts if there is a faster way to the sea."

Inside, the *cacique* related that the river to the east, the one they called the *Large River that flows to the Big Waters* was a faster route to the sea.

In the west there was much lightning and, for sure, another storm was about to come upon them. The meeting of the four broke up and each returned to their respective hut as darkness and more rain fell upon the village, which the *Spaniards* now called *Pueblo hebilla...Buckle Village.*

For two days more it rained incessantly. The common area around the village was a sea of mud and almost no one ventured outside. The *Yaquis* did not seem to mind the weather, for it was the work of *Yuku,* their god who controlled all things. The moisture would make the maize grow and for this they were pleased. The *Spaniards*, however, were anxious and wanted to be on their way.

Finally, on the morning of the fourth day, the clouds passed to the west and the sun shone brightly. Now, well out of its banks, the river was a swirling mass carrying huge trees and other detritus down its channel. They would have to wait. And, wait they did. For two weeks the river remained impassable.

Early March, 1536

Crossing the Rio Matape En Route to the Rio Yaqui

It was very early spring. The weather was warming and each morning Dorantes and Estevan would venture out to check the condition of the swirling mass of water that coursed by *Buckle Village*. Even now as they looked for a shallow area the banks were piled with uprooted trees, branches, and knee-deep in mud.

This day the two walked a league or more downstream, investigating any possible site for a crossing. At a sharp turn, the river bifurcated into two channels, each separated by a large sand bar. It was a sprawling flat area and the water flowing in each channel was relatively shallow. Dorantes, who could swim, even waded out about halfway to the sand bar. The current made him unsteady, but the water never rose above his waist.

"Estevanico, If we are careful, I think we can cross here. It looks shallow all the way to the sand bar and I think the other side is the same."

Estevan, who didn't like the water, merely nodded. "*Capitan*, I hope you are right. The faster I can cross this river the better!"

Coming back up the bank Dorantes laughed. "How is it that you were a fisherman and sailed all over the *Mediterranean Sea* and never learned to swim?"

Estevan sat down on a log. "*Capitan*, when I was a boy working on an *Arab* dhow the captain learned that I could not swim. In a drunken stupor, he threw me off the boat saying this was how he learned."

Dorantes. "What Happened?"

Estevan gulped. "I was terrified...I moved my arms and legs but still sank like a rock. The last thing I remember was the burning of the saltwater in my nose as I breathed it in. Next, I was laying on the deck coughing up water and vomiting."

Dorantes sat down next to him. "So, who saved you?"

Estevan laughed. "It wasn't the *capitan*! He passed out right there on the deck. One of the other fishermen, a black man like myself, dove in the water and pulled me out."

"I see now why you hate the water so. I wonder if *Capitan* Castillo has a similar story?"

Both men looked at each other and laughed.

Estevan. "We should ask him when we get back."

Dorantes rose. "Let us hurry back and tell the *Alguacil* of our finding. I feel we will be continuing our journey in the morning."

The crossing at the river bend had been without incident. Only once did Castillo stumble on a hidden rock beneath the water's surface and fall face-first into the river. But, the water was only thigh deep and the commotion regaining his footing caused much laughter from all that were around him.

Upon reaching the other side of the river, Alvar explained to those who accompanied them that they would find the other *Christians* and tell them not to kill or take slaves of any more *Indians*. The *Indians* wept at this news. The *Children of the Sun* and their guides now headed up into the hills and sierras that separated the two rivers.

At the end of three days, the travelers and their guides began their descent into a narrow river valley and a much larger river than the one they had left a few days before. The guides that accompanied them proudly explained that this was their river, the river of the *Yaquis*!

Now the travelers turned south and followed the river valley, sometimes next to the water, other times skirting the twists and bends by walking overland, This was rugged and yet beautiful country highlighted by deep canyon arroyos, cliffs, fast-moving white water, and placid pools. All along the *River of the Yaquis* other, smaller streams emptied into it, some forming broad deltas, others a hardly noticeable trickle. For nine days they followed the river. They were rapidly losing altitude. On the tenth day the river abruptly turned to the west and before them was a flat alluvial plain that extended to the horizon. It was a beautiful and fertile land filled with lakes and rivers. Beyond this, twelve leagues distant was the South Sea.

What they now saw was disturbing. Villages were burned and abandoned, and the signs of *Christian* slavers were all around them. Horseshoe tracks in the ground, an occasionally thrown shoe, a discarded broken lance, and crossbow bolts.

The people that were encountered were haggard, thin, and sickly. No longer did the shamans have a trail of admirers with them but now the people abandoned their fields and hid. There was no food to be had. The four travelers now, once again, had to endure hunger as they proceeded south.

Slowly a few *Indians* came to them, hopeful that these *Children of the Sun* could stop the terrible bearded men who burned their villages, killed, raped, and took away their people.

Although no food was available, the *Indians* brought them blankets and other things that they had managed to hide from the marauding *Christians*. Many had to survive by eating the bark of trees and roots that they pulled from the ground. It was truly a heartbreaking scene.

After two days of travel and seeing all of this Alvar addressed the other three. "What I am seeing here gives me great grief. These people, if treated correctly, could easily be converted to *Christianity* and would make for fine subjects of our Imperial Majesty. We must find these misguided *Spaniards* and tell them to cease their bad treatment of the *Indians*."

All through this area small groups of *Indians* skulked along always staying close to cover. So terrorized were these people that they dared not stop in any place for long. They now were determined to die rather than be captured. The fields that had once been lush with corn, beans, and squash were now left unattended. Everywhere the villages were deserted.

As the four survivors continued toward the coast the number of people that accompanied them began to increase in size. Strangely, the *Indians* didn't associate them with the *Spanish* who were terrorizing the country. Rather, the *Indian*s began to have hope that these *Children of the Sun* would protect them.

Finally, after a week of travel, the smell of the sea permeated the morning air. It was invigorating and the thought of seeing the ocean once again quickened their step. On gaining the top of a high hill the majesty of the *South Sea* was suddenly spread out before them. It was a clear day with a deep blue sky and as far as they could see in either direction the shoreline continued uninterrupted. They looked longingly toward the horizon wishing to see a sail, a *Spanish* sail, but done was there.

Taking in this view, the memory came to them of all they had been through and the people that had been lost. They wondered what had been the ultimate fate of companions like Lope de Oviedo, Natalo Figueroa, Pietre the *Asturian* cleric, and indeed, the last moments of their leader *Adelantado* Panfilo Narvaez as he was swept out to sea with Campo and Anton Perez. So many terrible times, and yet, so many amazing experiences. Now, here they were, still alive at the *South Sea* after traveling by foot across *Amichel* and all its dangers. The enormity of the moment overcame all four survivors of the Narvaez expedition. For a long while they stared at the panorama before them, each in his own thoughts.

They traveled down to the sea by themselves. So terrified were the *Indians* to be caught in the open by the terrible men that came from the sea that they stayed on the hill, hiding in the grass and bushes. It took longer than expected and it wasn't until noon that the four men finally walked out into the surf. Alvar sat in the sand letting the waves break around him, the cuts and bruises on his legs stinging slightly in the swirling salt water. Dorantes and Estevan waded out waist-deep and started splashing each other. Castillo just stood by the water's edge and stared.

CHAPTER 19

Hideaway

Escondite

They continued along a ridge and then up and over a steep crest that was difficult to climb. From here the trail dropped into a deep and spacious cleft. Spread out below them was the village. Huts of all sizes and shapes extended on both sides of a main thoroughfare and even up the mountainsides. It was the perfect hideaway. Not visible from the valley below and is easily defensible from the steep approaches.

March, 1536

Returning to the Sierras From the South Sea Beach

It had been a long day. They had tarried while at the beach and during the hike back had stopped frequently to scan the horizon. When they arrived it was late afternoon and all of the people that had waited for them were terrified that exposed on the beach, such as they were, the *Indians* were sure that the bearded men from the sea had captured them. It was almost dark before Alvar and his companions were able to assure the *Indians* that there were none of those terrible men around...at least not here. Everyone was anxious to move inland again where the hills and valleys provided cover for the people to hide.

It was late in the evening when exhausted, the caravan of Navarez survivors and their followers finally bedded down in a grove of trees by a sheltered valley. No fire was started and everyone spoke in a whisper, so afraid were the *Indians* of being detected.

The next morning Several of the *Indians* approached Alvar and Castillo who were gathering their things in preparation for the day's walk. They communicated that there was a village fortress high in the mountains that the terrible men from the sea knew nothing about. It was a long journey. Many of the people had fled there and now, they as well, would like to go.

This was the first that the *Christians* had heard of this village fortress. They were told that many people were now there and that there was food enough for everyone.

To the *Spaniards,* this new revelation was very interesting. It immediately conjured up thoughts of the *Aztec* capital of *Tenochtitlan,* itself an isolated fortress concealed in a mountain valley until discovered and conquered by the great Cortes. Could it be that another site existed with wealth beyond belief and that the four survivors of the Narvaez expedition would be the first *Europeans* to see it?

Alvar looked out at the crowd of followers, most were emaciated and some were sick...all were hungry. Children no longer played and frolicked around the campsite but sat listless just staring ahead.

Further conversations with the *Indians* indicated that this fortress was twelve days' walk from where they now were. Alvar estimated that the distance was 40 leagues or more.

"I think, *Capitan* Castillo, that we should visit this protected hideaway so that we can bring relief to these poor people and see for ourselves what this fortress in the mountains truly is."

Castillo nodded, "I agree *Alguacil* and I am sure that *Capitan* Dorantes and the *Negro* will also agree. Once there we can refresh ourselves and then carry on in the search to find our countrymen."

The decision was made. At mid-morning the four survivors and the *Indians* that followed them would set out inland across the coastal ranges heading directly toward the towering *Sierras* that loomed to the east. Once near the mountains, they would continue south while skirting the foothills. Near the fortress, they would proceed further into the *Sierras* until they reached their destination.

March, 1536

Campsite After Leaving the Beach at the South Sea

Dorantes watched the *Indians* as they passed and tried to make a mental count.

When they had passed, Estevan stepped to his side.

"What is the count, *mi capitan*?"

"I think about a hundred and ten. Some were bunched together and I may have missed a few, but it is close."

The land they traveled over was very fertile with many waterways and rivers making their way to the ocean. Alvar concluded that it was a fine area for raising crops and cattle, an area that the *Spanish* should investigate in the future. Now, however, the land went untended and, for the most part, the villages were deserted. As they made their way toward the *Sierras* other small wandering groups began to join them. All had heard of the *Children of the Sun* and their promise to protect the people from the bearded men from the sea who rode on huge beasts and wielded terrible weapons of destruction.

On the second day after leaving the *South Sea* the caravan of people now numbered around 250; it had more than doubled in size. The line of individuals following these *Children of the Sun* now extended down the trail such that more frequent stops were required so that all could catch up.

Turning southeast the long line of travelers kept the looming *Sierras* on their left. Castillo and Dorantes organized the *Indians* to send scouting parties up ahead to determine the best route and keep on the lookout for any *Christians* that might be in the area. Periodically these scouting parties would send a runner back to guide the procession and to tell of any discoveries on the trail ahead.

On the sixth day, the party entered a valley between two *Sierras*. Here they set up camp for the evening. At the hour of Vespers a runner entered the camp area and, addressing Estevan, told of a river two days ahead. The scout had found a good crossing by a deserted village, but most discouraging were the signs that the terrible *Christian* slavers had been there. The village had been burnt with much destruction.

Although the scout reported that these *Christians* were no longer in the area the *Indians* became terrified. Some left the camp and disappeared into the *Sierra*. Alvar tried to convince the people that their best chance was to stay together. If the slavers were encountered the *Children of the Sun* would protect them. With this reassurance, many returned and the panic subsided. The number of *Indians* in the camp now numbered around 400 and was increasing every day.

In two days, at the noon hour, the procession came to the river. There it was! From a distance, the river treeline stretched across the hilly expanse almost from horizon to horizon, and they could see the water twinkling in the afternoon sun. A short walk later the castaways were standing on the grassy bank looking across to the other side. Higher up, on a raised section, were the remains of an abandoned village. Scattered about were the burnt-out remains of huts and other personal belongings. It was a sad sight. A small group of *Indians* came to them and related what had happened there. It was their village.

Three days before, the *Christian* slavers had entered the village on their terrible beasts. The *Indians* held up ten fingers to indicate how many of them there were. With their long lances, they herded the young men, women, and children into a circle. Some ran away but many were overtaken by the riders on their swift animals and brought back. Several *Christians* dismounted and began tying the captives' hands behind their back. One of the *Spaniards*, they thought the leader, dismounted and took one of the comely young girls into a hut and had sex with her. Inside the hut, the girl was softly crying as the *Christian* came out and remounted his animal. Amazingly, another dismounted and entered the hut and had his way with the girl and then another...and another.

Once the captives' hands were tied they were all joined together with a long rope. During the process, the women were freely groped and abused. One *Christian* even had sex with one of the women as she lay bound on the ground. Any resistance by the men was dealt with severely. Heads were bashed and ribs were broken with savage kicks. One young *Indian* boy managed to escape and ran towards a group of trees. Before reaching this cover, however, one of the *Christians* fired his crossbow and its shaft passed through the boy's right thigh. He cried out in pain but continued to crawl towards the trees. The *Christians* didn't pursue him...they were too busy subduing the others. The boy escaped.

When the *Christians* were finished they took a torch to the village and then, crossing the river, led the band of captives away to the south.

The four survivors listened intently to the story. All seemed deeply distraught. From the group of *Indians* telling the story limped a boy of about twelve. On his right thigh was a deep wound. It was the boy in the story. Luckily, the bolt had passed completely through his leg without hitting bone or major blood vessels. Alvar touched the wound and prayed aloud, his voice cracking with emotion.

What happened next was even more disturbing. Another *Indian* carried a young girl of about fourteen and set her in front of the Spaniards. Except for a blanket around her, she was quite naked and obviously in some pain. When the Indians lifted the blanket covering her private parts the *Spaniards* gasped. Her pubic area was severely bruised and blood still seeped from her vagina. In addition, her right arm and leg had suffered burns. After recovering from his shock at seeing such a sight Alvar held her hand and repeated a

Pater Noster. This was the girl that had been repeatably raped by the slavers...only there was more to the story.

So weak was the girl after the repeated attacks that she remained in the hut unable to move. Upon their leaving, the slavers torched the hut knowing full well that someone was within. As the hut ignited she screamed and begged for help. The slavers just laughed and rode away. Somehow, someway, the young girl found the strength to crawl across the dirt floor to the back of the hut. There was only one entrance and it was blocked by the fire, so she tore at the interlaced branches at the rear of the hut until she made a hole just large enough to wiggle through. Laying just outside the burning mass her energy ran out. The heat was becoming intense and she lost consciousness. Luckily, at that moment the *Indian* girl was dragged to safety by her brother...the one who had been shot by the crossbow.

March, 1536

Camp by the Fuerte River

At the river's edge, the *Spaniards* made a decision. Dorantes spoke up.

"Let us find a crossing and then we will camp on the other side. In the morning we can continue our journey to this fortress."

Once again, Alvar questioned the guides

"Wasapi-tun-Loki, we will follow this river to the south for one day before again returning to the *Sierras*. From there it is a day's travel to another stream. Once we come to the stream it is but a short journey to the *Sierra* fortress.

As an afterthought, Alvar instructed Estevan to ask what was the word for this river.

The Indian guide, a boy of about seventeen, gave a description to Estevan that lasted longer than expected.

Finally, Alvar asked, "What did he say?"

Estevan repeated what he had been told. "Tell Wasapi-tun-Loki that the spirits of our ancestors live on this river. The river always flows clear and provides us with water to drink and fish to eat. Because of this, we call it the strong river."

Alvar nodded. "Then that's what we will call it, the strong river...*El Rio Fuerte*."

They had found a crossing not far downstream from where they first encountered the river. Upon arriving it was evident from tracks in the mud that steel-shod horses had crossed at this same location. This immediately caused fear and consternation among the *Indians* but closer examination indicated the tracks were not recent.

Castillo conferred with the scouts. Although there were other signs around, they had not seen any *Christian* slavers. With that the *Indians* seemed to relax...a bit. The crossing was without incident except for Estevan stepping into a deep hole as he was halfway across the river. For a moment his head disappeared under the water only to explode to the surface moments later with much thrashing and cursing. The cursing was unique, for Estevan had command of at least six languages and Alvar claimed that he hadn't neglected any of them in his vocal tirade. Three women immediately came to his rescue and led him to the other side.

Castillo, also a non-swimmer, floated on a large piece of driftwood and paddled his way across as best he could.

"Where are the *Indio* women when I need assistance?"

The camp was made, cooking fires were lit and the women began assembling their crude structures. There was little to eat. Until well after dark the *Indians* walked the river looking for anything edible.

Shortly after sunrise the procession headed out...or tried to. As they started moving the *Indians* clustered around the *Spanish* shamans in such a mass that it was impossible to make any headway.

Alvar called for quiet and stood on a stone so all could see him. "My children, come with us and we will find these terrible people who have done this and put an end to this madness.

De Vaca, Castillo, Dorantes, and Estevan had to push their way to the front and even then they were beseeched by the *Indians,* wanting to touch them or have a blessing made upon them. Once free of the crowd, Alvar strode out at his fastest pace while the others followed suit. These years of walking across *Amichel* had given them all one advantage; they could walk for hours and walk fast!

Soon, the crowd of people at the front began to thin out so that only the fittest stayed with the *Spaniards*. Now the crowd of people extended even further down the trail, the numbers totaling in excess of 500. The *Spaniards* maintained their pace during this day, only stopping briefly while the guides reconnoitered the ground and the scout runners arrived to tell of the conditions ahead. They traveled almost due south as they paralleled the river they had just crossed. To their left were the foothills and high peaks of the *Sierra Madre Occidental*. On this day Alvar estimated that they had traveled six leagues.

Finally, toward evening the four relaxed their pace and located a campsite close to the river. It was a narrow valley shielded by low hills to the north and south. It wasn't until late in the evening that the last of the line of followers made their way into camp. Many were exhausted and all were hungry. Children cried and people wandered about while many tried to find an isolated spot where they could rest or build a haphazard shelter. Some ventured back to the river in the hope of finding food. Fish, snakes, insects, mice, birds, roots...anything that was edible was consumed.

Alvar called for the *Indian* guides. He questioned them about tomorrow's journey. In the morning they would be leaving the river and following the edge of the *Sierras* as they proceeded to the east.

Alvar turned to Estevan. "Ask them how many days travel until we reach the mountain fortress."

The guides talked amongst themselves for a moment and then answered by holding up three fingers.

Today they had traveled about six leagues, but this was unusual. The *Spaniards* had surged ahead to free themselves from the crowds of people and the ground over which they traveled was relatively flat. Tomorrow they would have to slow their pace. In the *Sierras'* the steep grades and torturous paths would slow them down even more.

Anxious to move on, Alvar merely said, "We will leave before dawn."

March 1536

Camp by the Fuerte River Near Present-Day San Blas, Mexico

This morning the *Spaniards* were on the trail well before sunrise. The path became increasingly more difficult with steep climbs, numerous switchbacks, and loose shale. Each step had to be taken with care. At noon they rested while the scores of people following them caught up. After resting they followed a valley which extended northward for about a league. At that point the guides once again turned east into a mountainous area where the trail was but a narrow foot-path, at times not even a path at all. Steep climbs and slippery downhills greeted them until turning south on a dry stream bed and its narrow gorge. Here the travelers had easier going, but not for long. The guides once again turned eastward up a mountainous path. The guides explained to the *Spaniards* that this would temporarily lead them out of the mountains. In the late afternoon, the footpath abruptly descended and they entered a beautiful valley. Here the travel was easy, but it wasn't to last. A league further and they climbed once more into the rugged foothills. It wasn't until the end of the day that the procession, once again, dropped into a wide flat plain. They would make camp here.

Now a decision had to be made. The fastest route to the fortress was across this plain to a small *arroyo*...stream. They would then follow this stream to the north. This direction, however, would leave them exposed should any slavers be in the area. The other alternative was to turn further northward and follow the base of the *Sierras*. This, of course, would provide cover but add a day to their journey.

Dorantes approached Alvar. "*Alguacil*, these people are terrified of venturing out into this open country, but to follow the mountains would put undo hardship on us all."

"I agree Andres. I talked of this earlier with *capitan* Castillo and, like you, he feels we should take the shorter more direct route."

"And you *Alguacil*, which route do you prefer?"

"I agree with you and *Capitan* Castillo of course, but we have to convince these people that we will protect them from any harm should any of these *Spanish* slavers find us."

Andres Dorantes thought on this for a moment. "*Alguacil*, this is a strange paradox that we are put in. After so many years I long to return to our *Spanish* brethren and our way of life, and yet, I feel a responsibility for these people."

"As do I *capitan* Dorantes, as do I."

Both stared out across the rolling plain that lay before them.

Alvar broke the reverie. "We will take the shorter route. At some point in time, we will have to face these slavers and try to convince them of their wrongdoings. The sooner we can begin this process the better."

"*Alguacil*, do you think they will listen?"

"I can only hope, but a truthful answer is that this slave trade will most likely go on and these people will pay the price. They will be used as laborers in the fields and mines throughout *New Spain*. Perhaps our story will make a difference. If they can be converted to *Christianity* and give up their heathen ways our Majesty will have compassion and make them full citizens of *Spain*."

"*Alguacil*, it has been many years since we were stranded...I think seven or eight. We are not even sure who is King of *Spain*!"

Alvar grimaced. "This is true. So much has happened. This will be one of the first questions I ask when we find other *Christians*."

As the evening progressed the four talked at length with the people that followed them. Headmen, Families, and individuals clustered around the *Children of the Sun* as they tried to convince their followers that they would protect them. To be safe they would assign additional scouts to precede the caravan who would report back if there was trouble ahead. At last, just after midnight, everyone settled down. Some left the camp, afraid to proceed any further, They would take an alternate, and longer, route to the fortress. Alvar retired to a hastily built structure put together by an Indian woman who had shared his bed since leaving the village by the river. She was thin and well-proportioned with long black hair that hung to her waist. Her legs and stomach were adorned with tattoos which wasn't to Alvar's liking but she was otherwise attractive, attentive to him, hard-working, and had an insatiable appetite for sex.

Looking down at her lying naked on a hide blanket Alvar thought to himself. "Like *Capitan* Dorantes, I dream of returning to my people but there are times when this is not all bad...God forgive me!"

April, 1536

Leaving the Camp by the Plain

It was raining when Alvar awoke early the next morning. The *Indian* woman was tightly clinging to him as she snored blissfully. He had trouble extricating himself from her grasp and in the process, she woke with a start.

She referred to him by his *Indian* sobriquet. "Wasapi-tun Loki, are we leaving so early? Come back and lay with me."

Looking at the weather, the offer was tempting, but they had a long way to go. The desire to reunite with civilization and other *Christians* was growing stronger day by day.

 "Make ready to leave woman. I will go awaken my friends so that we can get an early start."

Alvar strode across the campsite. Castillo was already up, sitting on a rock and rubbing his eyes.

"The Lord be with you on this fine morning *Capitan* Castillo!"

"And to you *Alguacil*, but I'm not so sure how fine the morning is."

Alvar laughed as he made his way to the *Negro's* lean-to. He stopped just outside and stared in disbelief. Three naked *Indian* women lay on top of the black *African*. Arms, legs, buttocks, and bare breasts were intertwined in one mass. Estevan's foot extended out onto the dirt. Alvar reached down and pulled on it.

"What...who...Oh, *Alguacil* it's you!"

The women were waking up around him.

"Estevanico, we will be leaving here shortly. Find *Senor* Dorantes and join us as soon as you can."

"Yes *Alguacil*, I am getting up now." The women seemed to fall off him like water off a duck's back. Alvar just shook his head and walked away.

Sunrise was subdued as heavy clouds scudded across the sky. The soft rain had been replaced by a light mist and gusty winds blew across the hilly plain in front of them. It was cold and each of the men wrapped themselves in a buffalo robe as they walked. Their legs and feet were bare and the wind blowing up from underneath chilled them.

The four were preceded by four *Indians* who jogged on ahead to scout the trail. They would leave markers indicating the correct path to take. It could be a pile of rocks, a broken twig, or even a scuffing in the dirt. Behind the shamans, others were following and the line of travelers soon spread out across the countryside. Only a short way into the journey they crossed a narrow stream. The path that they were following led to the water's edge and a relatively shallow area with a rocky bottom. The rain that was falling had not yet affected the stream's depth and the *Spaniards* hurried across with the deepest water only to their knees. Here they turned north and followed the stream into the mountains.

From here the guides indicated that the Hideaway was only three or four leagues distant.

Alvar, Dorantes, Castillo, and Estevan now set a fast pace for they had learned long ago this was the best way to stay warm. So fast did they move that the scouts were frequently overtaken. When this happened the four would slow their pace while the *Indians* jogged up ahead.

As noon approached the skies began to clear but the wind remained strong. Luckily it was blowing from the northwest and actually pushed them along. To the east the *Sierra Occidental* loomed ever present, its blue outline contrasting with the hilly plain they were now crossing.

The plain behind them, they were once again headed up into the foothills of the *Sierra*. By mid afternoon the skies had cleared to a bright iridescent blue. Even over the *Sierras* to the east the clouds had all but disappeared. It was now a gloriously clear day.

As evening approached the *Indian* scouts indicated that camp should be made. In the morning all the people would begin their climb to the *Indian* fortress. It would be treacherous and steep and a whole day would be needed to get all the people moved.

April, 1536

Leaving the Camp on the Ocoroni and the Climb to the Hideaway

Morning broke clear. Unbelievably, *Indians* were still crossing the river into the camp. Wet, tired, and haggard, men women, and children staggered up to the fire to rest and dry off. These were the people who had taken the long way around the valley. Alvar watched these people and felt tremendous compassion. He wondered how he would feel if he had not experienced the years of existence with these people. A disturbing thought, for he still remembered the disdain he had felt for these people when first encountered them in *La Florida*.

Alvar muttered to himself. "That was a different time."

He shouldered the few burdens he was carrying and strode out. Castillo, Dorantes, and Estevan were close behind him.

Looking up, Estevan watched a wake of buzzards circling en masse over the *Sierras* just to the west. These were large birds with white wingtips, white trailing edges, and reddish heads; all clearly visible in the clear mountain air. They seemed to be circling something near the mountain peak. Estevan had seen buzzards before but today a larger more ominous bird was circling just above them. It was not a buzzard, but appeared to be a very large eagle.

Stopping, Estevan plopped down on a rock to observe the aerial spectacle above.

"What do you see Estevanico?" It was Dorantes who had just come up the trail behind him.

"Ah *capitan*, it is sometimes beautiful just to watch the buzzards as they circle high in the air."

Dorantes noted the eagle. "What do you think that eagle is doing?"

"Ah *capitan*, he is waiting for the buzzards to locate a kill so that he can steal it!"

"Ha, Ha, of that I am sure! We had best hurry along for it looks like the *Alguacil* is far ahead of us."

Indeed he was. The gorge seemed to close in while the trail became narrower and steeper. Up ahead the advance scouts were returning with two individuals that Alvar didn't recognize.

The scouts saw Alvar approaching and pointed, the strangers headed directly to him. Both were men of middle age, obviously of some importance. The first to reach Alvar grasped his hand and held it to his chest. He addressed Alvar by his *Indian* name.

"Wasapi-tun-Loki, welcome, we have been waiting for the arrival of the children of the sun."

One of the scouts approached and explained that these were emissaries from the hideaway. They had come to intercept the caravan before it arrived. They looked nervous.

The elder of the two emissaries asked Alvar to sit with him. Castillo now joined the group and they all sat cross-legged in the grass.

"Wasapi-tun-loki we grieve for all these people and want to help them." He gestured toward the mountain cleft that Alvar had just passed through. Even now the line of stragglers was beginning to emerge into the valley.

"There are so many people and their numbers extend far into the distance. It would be an easy thing for these cruel men that kill and enslave us to follow this line of people to our encampment." He turned and pointed vaguely toward the *Sierras*.

"He is right *Alguacil*." It was Castillo. "The *Christian* slavers would welcome such an opportunity."

Alvar turned to the emissary. "What do you suggest we do?"

The elder stood. "We would ask that you remain in this valley until all have cleared the trails behind you and we have hidden all signs that people have passed this way. Once we are sure these cruel men are not following we will lead you to our hideaway in small groups."

"This is a good plan, *Alguacil*."

"I agree *capita*n." Alvar nodded to Castillo.

Castillo addressed the elder. "How far is the hideaway from here?"

The elder was deliberately vague. "We will take you along a very difficult route, one that will not be able to be tracked. High into the *Sierras*." Again he pointed towards the mountains.

April, 1536

In the Valley Below the Hideaway

The camp in the valley continued to grow until the line of stragglers coming through the mountain cleft dwindled and finally stopped. It had been two days since they had entered the valley.

Dorantes looked at the spectacle before him. Small lean-to structures and huts were spread out before him on the valley floor. The evening was clear and the smoke from the cooking fires traced vertical white lines into the sky. Behind this, the sharp contours of the *Sierras* looked dark and ominous in the fading light.

He had tried to count the number of people but finally gave up. There were hundreds and hundreds. They represented people from all over the country. Some had resided by the South Sea, others from the grassy plains, and many were mountain dwellers. Farmers, hunters, fishermen, old, young, women, children...they were all represented here. All were hungry and destitute.

In the morning the people of the hideaway would begin leading small groups up into the *Sierras* to the *Indian* fortress they had heard so much about. Dorantes was anxious to get moving.

That night the four castaways made ready for the final trek to the *Indian* hideaway. They didn't know what to expect. Almost certainly it would be nothing like *Tenochtitlan*. There were no indicators of a great civilization anywhere near here...No roads, no bridges. And yet, who knows what resided in those mountains?

At first light, a group of 100 people began their journey across the valley and into the rugged mountains. At the front of the column were De Vaca, Dorantes, Castillo, and Estevan. The guides lead them along steep rocky trails and very rugged terrain. The *Spaniards*, conditioned as they were, felt the pull of the steep uphills. Even more so, the people behind them struggled mightily. Soon, the fittest were helping the less able along the pathway. Estevan carried two small children while Castillo steadied a pregnant woman up a particularly treacherous climb. Dorantes had moved to the back of the procession, giving encouragement and helping people along as they needed it. Alvar, still at the front, walked hand in hand with two elders, at times pulling them along behind him.

After a league and a half the procession stopped to rest at a panoramic overlook, a bald spot on the mountain with a rock outcropping. Below stretched a beautiful valley.

One of the guides approached Alvar. He pointed to the valley below.

"Wasapi-tun-loki. These are our fields by which we feed the many people that have come here."

Indeed, far below the patchwork of cultivated land was clearly visible.

The guide continued. "From here the village is not far. We shall be there when the sun is still high in the sky."

They continued along a ridge and then up and over a steep crest that was difficult to climb. From here the trail dropped into a deep and spacious cleft. Spread out below them was the village. Huts of all sizes and shapes extended on both sides of a main thoroughfare and even up the mountainsides. It was the perfect hideaway. Not visible from the valley below and is easily defensible from the steep approaches.

It was immediately evident that there was no advanced civilization center here. Alvar's thoughts of another *Tenochitlan* or even something close were not to be.

They descended into the village, careful not to slip on the loose rocks that seemed to cover the trail. Everywhere there were huts and lean-tos. Children were playing along the side of the road. The people began to accumulate so as to watch these newcomers as they approached. Word of Wasapi-tun-loki and his three shamans had spread rapidly.

The crowds grew as they neared the village center until finally, the procession stopped at a location where several longhouses had been constructed. The chief elder approached the *Spaniards* and welcomed them. Loads of maize were given to the shamans who in turn gave it to the people who had followed them. Each load consisted of a woven basket full of un-shucked ears.

For the rest of the day and into the night, the scouts returned from the camp in the valley with more and more refugees. On each arrival the newcomers were given maize...so much maize that by the next morning Dorantes estimated there were over a thousand loads distributed among the people following them.

As they walked through the village that evening, it gave the four castaways great satisfaction to see the miserable, starving people they had brought with them finally get enough to eat.

April, 1536

In Camp at the Indian Hideaway

Alvar rubbed his eyes in the early morning light. The air was brisk as he pulled the buffalo robe tightly against himself. Walking to a tree in a secluded part of camp he relieved himself. Others were there. The cool air smelled strongly like urine.

Back in the camp Dorantes, Estevan, and Castillo were talking with four *Indian* boys.

Alvar joined them.

"Ah *Alguacil*, We have instructed these four to go out and gather as many people as they can and meet us three days from here. Each one of these messengers represents one of us. Your messenger is this fine young lad." Castillo signaled one of the boys to step forward.

Standing before De Vaca was a boy of about fifteen years old. He was tall and rangy with thick black hair that hung to his shoulders. He carried a bow and three arrows. He proudly met Alvar's gaze without blinking.

"What is your name boy?"

"Wahton," was the reply.

Alvar thought about the name and then turned to Estevan for clarification.

Estevan spoke in *Spanish*, "The name means 'fast rabbit' *Alguacil*."

Alvar turned back to the boy, "They say you are a fast runner."

"I have never been beaten, Wasapi tun Luki!"

Alvar put a hand on the boy's shoulder and laughed aloud. "Then, Wahton you are the right messenger for me."

Wahton puffed up and looked around proudly.

Alvar then gave instructions to all the messengers. "Tomorrow we will begin our journey to find the men that are tormenting you. Today, the four of you will proceed ahead of us. Always be on the lookout for the bad *Christians* and report to us as soon as you see them."

With that Alvar made the sign of the cross and blessed each one. "God be with you!"

The boys trotted out of camp, heading south.

The next day the castaways began their journey down from the mountain hideaway. Behind them swelled an army of refugees. Some followers were from the *Village of Hearts*, now far behind them. Others had continually joined them along the route. Now, many of the people from the hideaway joined them as well. To these people, the bearded holy men meant redemption from the horrible depredations of the *Christians* who raped, killed, and enslaved their people. It was felt that only they could put a stop to this madness.

At midday, the four messengers returned, quite to the surprise of the castaways.

Wahton stepped up to Alvar. "Wasapi-tun-loki there are no people anywhere!" The young *Indian* gestured with his hand in a sweeping motion. "They have all run away and hidden in the mountains. They are fleeing from the terrible men and the beasts that they ride on."

Castillo, Dorantes, and Esevan had joined De Vaca. Castillo asked. "Did you see any sign of these men?"

"Yes!" Last night after we left we moved quickly down the trail. Early the next morning, before the sun was up, we came to their camp. We watched from behind trees as they gathered up the many people who were in chains. At first light, they mounted their beasts and moved off to the south leading the bound people behind them."

Other people had begun to gather around the guides as they told their stories. Many became sorely afraid and began drifting away. Word of mouth spread quickly and soon an exodus of people jammed the road returning to the hideaway.

It was only midday but the castaways decided to camp for the night here on the road, out in the open, to show the people that they were not afraid. This seemed to placate some, but many others fled to the mountains.

Again the messengers were sent on ahead.

The next morning before leaving, Dorantes stood staring at a sandy patch of trail. Castillo came upon him. "What is it in the trail that is so interesting *amigo*?"

"Ah Alonzo, I did not hear you come up. Look at this patch of ground and tell me what you see."

Castillo studied the tracks. "It is covered with many footprints and hoof marks from shod horses...*Spanish* horses! But, Andres, these signs are everywhere...why is this patch of ground so interesting?"

"The hoof marks are almost obliterated by the footprints."

Castillo looked at Dorantes questionably.

"It means, friend Alonzo, that the people were behind the horses probably being led in chains. I can only imagine the suffering."

Castillo looked again at the prints with a new understanding. "Years ago we would have thought nothing of this."

"Yes, many things to think about." Dorantes looked up at the throng of *Indians* that were preparing for the day's travel. Men, women, and small children were all terrified of what lay ahead. "It is like a dream, Alonzo. After all these years we may be rescued from our plight. We will return to civilization but these people will continue to be tormented."

Both were now staring at the ground in deep thought when De Vaca called to them.

"*Capitans* let us be underway, for we have a long journey ahead."

April, 1536

Searching for the Christian Slavers

It had been a long day of walking. Apparently, the slavers had come this way as well, for signs of their passage were everywhere. Many *Indians* still followed the castaways but with every sign of the slavers' presence more would leave the caravan.

That evening the messengers returned to report on the conditions ahead. Again, Wahton served as their spokesman.

"Wasapi-tun-loki, tomorrow we will come to the place from which we watched the slavers."

"What else did you see?"

Wahton talked briefly with the other three messengers before he answered.

"Wasapi-tun-loki, we met several *Indians* well armed with lance and bow. They also were looking for the slavers, but to kill them. They said there were many more in the mountains who would now fight for their homes and families."

Alvar chose his words carefully. "Wahon, did these armed *Indians* speak of us and are we in danger?"

"No Wasapi, these *Indians* only hunt the slavers that are killing and taking their people.

Again Alvar paused before continuing. "Yes, Wahton but these slavers are like us...we are the same."

Wahton looked confused. "Wasapi you heal and help our people. You are not the same as these other men."

Not wanting to draw more attention to the issue Alvar dismissed the messengers.

The next morning dawned hot and clear and as they moved along a dust cloud hung over the column, a sure signal to anyone of their whereabouts. For a while, the four castaways were together at the front of the procession.

"*Alguacil*, with this dust cloud and clear sky anyone will know we are here." It was Dorantes.

Alvar answered. "I don't know if I'm more apprehensive of the *Christian* slavers or these *Indios* that have now taken up arms."

"I agree *Alguacil*. We are very close to being rescued from our plight but still, there is the possibility of a quick death."

"Let us pray for that not to happen friend Dorantes."

Just before the hour of vespers, the four messengers appeared on the trail ahead. They explained that the campsite used by the slavers two nights ago was very close. It was located somewhat off the trail, so Wahton gestured for them to follow.

Only a short walk later they crossed a very shallow brook and came to a secluded glen. There were horseshoe tracks everywhere and Castillo was the first to spot tether stakes for the horses. There were other signs as well. By the fire pit, Dorantes found wood chips next to one of the sitting logs. One of the slavers had sat here and idly whittled a stick to pass away the time. Isolated from the main camp was another area where many people had congregated. Here there was human feces and still the smell of urine.

"This is where they kept their captives!" Estevan spoke with a strange look on his face.

"We will make our camp here tonight." Alvar directed the messengers to move the people coming up the trail to this location.

That evening Alvar called a conference with the other three.

"Compatriots, I believe we are very near the *Christian* slavers. This is very good news, for after all these years of our wretched captivity our rescue may be close at hand. We can only give thanks to God our Lord."

"It is hard to believe *Alguacil*. So much has happened." Dorantes was doodling with a stick, drawing circles in the sand.

"It hasn't happened yet, there is still much danger out there." Castillo was pessimistic and of foul temper. All day he had struggled with a disease of the bowls. He was dehydrated and fatigued.

Estevan remained quiet.

Alvar cleared his throat. "We are moving too slow as a group to catch the *Christian* slavers. I would suggest that one of you and the *Negro* go on alone in search of these men. Either of you is younger and hardier than I and chances of finding them would be much better."

Dorantes looked uncomfortable with this request. He didn't say anything.

Castillo stood and slowly paced back and forth. "I would like to excuse myself from this endeavor. Although I feel somewhat better tonight I am much fatigued and don't think I would be up to the hardship."

"Nor I *Alguacil*," was all that Dorantes said.

Alvar looked askance at both of them. He couldn't believe his ears. These were men who had been with him all these years, sharing in the hardships and deprivations. Never once before did they seem intimidated by a hard task. But, their minds seemed made up.

A long silence fell over the meeting. Finally, stifling his anger, Alvar announced, "I will take the *Negro* and set out in the morning to find these *Christian* slavers. If we are successful I will send word back for you to join us."

With that De Vaca abruptly got up and left the meeting.

April, 1536

In Search of the Christian Slavers

Andres Dorantes felt like a coward as he watched De Vaca, Estevan, and eleven *Indians* move down the trail and disappear from sight. Normally he would have had no problem going on ahead in search of the slavers but now something in his head told him to hang back. He felt awful. He confided in Castillo.

Alonzo Castillo was thoughtful as he listened to Dorantes. "*Amigo*, there have been a few times in my life where I have turned away from a challenge. For some reason, I felt that something wasn't right. Maybe it was God's way of warning me and maybe this is God's way of warning you!"

"But Alonzo, I feel like such a coward. We are so close to rescue. The thought of leaving this infernal place made me lose my nerve."

Castillo was quick to reply. "Ha! I have been with you for many years now and at no time did I ever consider you a coward. We have suffered much together. I would suggest you confess your feelings to the *Alguacil* when we see him again and I'm sure he will understand."

"I hope we see him again!" Dorantes felt no better.

Alvar had set a blistering pace following the trail of the slavers. He passed three sites where these men and their burden of captured *Indians* had stopped to rest. With each step, the trail seemed to become fresher. He knew that he was not far behind. By evening he estimated they had walked ten leagues. As darkness closed in around them the exhausted thirteen travelers stopped for the night. The eleven Indians, Wahon among them, had managed to start a small fire. So fatigued was De Vaca that he only took a small bite of the dried deer meat that he carried in his waistband before falling asleep. Estevan was already snoring under a small tree next to the trail.

In the very early morning, Alvar awoke. He felt refreshed but somehow different. It was still very dark and the stars of *The Road to Santiago* shone brightly above him, so bight that he could faintly see his shadow.

Everyone else was sleeping.

Alvar knelt and crossed himself. He felt so insignificant under this mantle of stars and the vastness of the land. He prayed that this would be the day of his delivery back to the civilized world. And, he prayed for the multitude of *Indians* that he had encountered and who now were suffering grievously at the hands of his own countrymen. He ended his prayer by giving thanks for sparring his life when so many others had died.

Alvar Nunez Cabeza de Vaca sat there then just staring out across the vastness until a faint pink glow appeared over the *Sierras*.

Wahon touched him lightly on the back. "Wasapi, are you ready?"

Quite surprised, Alvar turned around to see all eleven *Indians* and Estevan standing behind him.

They moved quickly down the trail.

April, 1536

First Contact with the Spanish Slavers

Corporal Juan Lopez shifted in the saddle and scratched the back of his neck. There were three others with him, but he spoke to no one in particular. "*Hijo de puta!* These damn mosquitoes are bad this morning."

The other three indiscriminately swatted at the clouds of insects that seemed to be rising out of the grass. Even the horses were jittery as they tossed their heads and stomped their feet.

"Don't worry corporal, as soon as the morning sun burns off this dew it will get better." It was Martino Rodriquez, one of his riding companions.

Lopez continued, "The *capitan* sent us out here to find the trail to *Culiacan*. Surely it must be close by.

The four horsemen were now configured in a loose semi-circle as they discussed their plight. Lopez was facing north the others were facing him. All were armed with swords and lances.

"How I long to return to *Mexico City*! I have a *chica* there with *tetas* like this..."

Lopez shifted his lance so it was supported in the crook of his arm. He held out both of his open hands.

There was laughter all around.

He continued. "And this *chica*, she can..."

Lopez stopped in mid-sentence, his eyes wide and staring.

The other three riders looked at him questionably. Still staring, Lopez pointed. No words were spoken.

The riders turned in their saddles to look behind them. They quickly swung their horses around.

On the trail, Wahon, the *Indian* guide, was the first to see the riders. All he said was "Wasapi!"

Alvar saw them then. Four armed *Spaniards* on horseback.

For a moment everyone just stopped and stared. A strange quietness descended on the area.

Alvar was the first to gather his wits. "Estevanico, come with me."

De Vaca and the *Negro* moved toward the riders.

Martino Rodriquez finally found his voice. "Juan, I thought I heard that *Indio* in front speak our language...and there is a *Negro* with him!"

One of the other riders blurted out, "That's no *Indio*, he has a beard, a blond beard!"

All four riders grasped their lances tightly, not knowing what to expect."

De Vaca and Estevan advanced toward the riders and then stopped. Summing up his most commanding voice Alvar called out.

"I am Alvar Nunez Cabeza de Vaca from the Narvaez expedition. Can I speak with your leader?"

Lopez was dumbfounded. This strange-looking man on the trail in front of him with a *Negro* at his side was claiming to be from the lost Narvaez expedition. Everyone knew of the Narvaez expedition. He was only fifteen when he first heard of it. It was the talk of all *Spain* at the time. All were presumed lost...yet...here in front of him were two survivors.

Lopez spurred his horse forward. Before him was a man deeply tanned and lean with a scraggly, unkempt beard that hung down mid-chest. His blond hair was bleached almost white. For clothing, he wore only a loincloth and no shoes. His feet, thick with callouses, were cracked and scared. Around his waist hung a flint knife and on his shoulders a crude backpack. Two eagle feathers festooned his headband. Like the *Negro* he carried two gourds symbolizing that they were *Indian* holy men.

Lopez shifted his attention to the *Negro*. He was younger than the white man but equally lean and ill-clothed. His curly black hair had been tied back and, like the white man, two eagle feathers fluttered in the wind.

Dismounting, Lopez now stood directly in front of them. He looked beyond at the eleven *Indians* on the trail. They stood immobile.

"I am corporal Juan Lopez."

CHAPTER 20

The Village At Culiacan

El pueblo de Culiacán

The village was large and sprawling and only less than a league from the Spanish settlement of San Miguel. It was a place where many Indians had gathered to escape the atrocities of the slavers.

April, 1536

First Contact with the Spanish Slavers

The awkwardness of the encounter soon wore off as Cabeza De Vaca and Jose Perez began to talk. It was obvious to Corporal Perez that this half-naked man, with leathery skin, burnt dark by the sun and smelling of animal grease was a nobleman. He spoke *Spanish* like an *Andalusian* aristocrat and had a commanding presence about him.

Alvar's first question to the amazed slaver confirmed that they had been away for a very long time.

"Corporal Perez, can you tell me what the date is?"

Perez had to think a moment.

"*Senor* De Vaca it is April, 1536, but my apologies, for I have lost track of the exact day."

"And Corporal Perez can you tell me who rules Spain?"

"Charles the Fifth is our king."

"Praise God!"

Perez motioned for the other three riders to join them. They tentatively came up and two dismounted. The other, Jose Hernandez remained on his horse eyeing the eleven *Indians* who stood with Estevan a short distance away.

"Corporal, I have so many questions but I have to ask, where is your *capitan* and where is your base of operations?"

"We left the river where we are camped this morning on the orders of our *capitan*, Diego de Alcaraz, to search the area for *Indios*. We were returning when we saw you."

"How far is your campsite by the river?" Alvar asked.

Perez turned to his comrades and thought out loud. "Maybe a half league or so."

The other three all nodded in agreement.

"Corporal, would you do me the honor of taking us there so I can talk with your *capitan*?"

Perez hesitated and then looked up the road to where Estevan and the eleven *Indians* were standing.

"What of the black and the *Indians* that are with you?"

Alvar turned and motioned to Estevan to approach. "They will accompany us."

"No disrespect *Senor* De Vaca, but the *Indians* are armed with *Turkish* bows and arrows. Will they be a threat to us?"

Alvar could see the concern in the eyes of all the *Christians*. "Not at all, Corporal Perez. They are our guides and protectors."

"Then most assuredly *Senor* De Vaca, I will be happy to take you to our camp."

April, 1536

Slaver Camp on the Sinola River

They had moved quickly down the trail. Corporal Jose Perez was amazed at how fast the barefoot men could walk and how they didn't seem to tire. At times he actually had to goad his horse into a jog to stay ahead of them. For protection Perez had Jose Hernandez and the other horseman stay at the rear of the procession. De Vaca had assured him that the *Indians* where no threat but here in *Indian* country, one could not be too careful.

As they entered the camp by the river the inhabitants looked up with startled looks on their faces. Because the *Indians* had all fled this part of the country it had been fifteen days since they had even seen an *Indian*. And now, they watched Corporal Perez leading a band of thirteen into camp.

As the procession got closer some were startled to see a black man among the thirteen. And then, someone yelled, "The one in front has a beard!"

A few grabbed their lances when they saw that the Indians were armed.

Perez called out, "*Camaradas*, put down your weapons, they are friendly."

Stirring himself from his hastily built lean-to, Captain Diego de Alcaraz rubbed his eyes and watched as the procession approached him.

Wasting no time Corporal Perez separated himself from the column with one of the captives. It was then that Alcaraz noticed with a start that the "captive" had a long white beard and his facial features were definitely not *Indian*.

"*Capitan* Diego de Alcaraz, allow me to introduce Alvar Nunez Cabeza de Vaca of the lost Narvaez expedition." Perez seemed to puff up with the announcement.

Alcaraz was speechless. Had he heard Perez correctly?

Alvar walked up and extended his hand. "*Capitan* I have waited for this moment for so many years."

Like in a dream Alcaraz looked at the hand and then back at De Vaca. He automatically reached out and shook it.

"How...who...where did you come from?" Was all he could say.

Alvar seemed amused as he shook the captain's hand. "It has been a long and frightening journey *capitan* but right now I need to bring up the other survivors."

"There are other survivors?"

Yes, besides me and the black man walking behind me, there are two others, several-days journey from here.

It was then that Alcaraz noticed the black man for the first time.

As Estevan approached Alvar explained, "Estevan is the property of *Capitan* Andres Dorantes de Carranza and along with *Capitan* Alonzo del Castillo Maldonado we are all that remain of the Narvaez expedition."

Recovering somewhat from his initial shock Alcaraz asked, *"Senor* De Vaca that expedition was lost nine years ago and one of the great mysteries of our time. How did you get here?

Alvar shrugged. "*Capitan,* we have much to talk about but right now I would like to get word back to my compatriots so that they may join us."

"Of course *Senor* De Vaca, how far from here are they?"

"I would guess ten leagues or so *capitan*. Not only are my two *capitans* there, but the many *Indios* that have brought us here. I would like to send the *Negro* and the eleven *Indians* back to retrieve them."

"Then let them get started as soon as possible. I will send three of my horsemen and our *Indian* guides to accompany them." Alcaraz quickly gave orders to Corporal Perez who lost no time in rounding up two other riders and fifty of the *Indian* guides.

Within the hour the rescue column, with Estevan walking in the lead, was heading back up the trail.

Alvar watched them disappear from sight and then turned to Captain Alcaraz. "Thank you for this *capitan*. Both of my *capitans* are so looking forward to being rescued from this life of toil and hardship."

"I can only imagine *Senor* De Vaca! Come, let us sit and talk of the things you have seen and experienced."

Five days passed and in that time Alcaraz and the men with him never seemed to tire of the stories that De Vaca told of his journeys through *Amichel*. More importantly, however, Alvar began to have reservations about the disposition of the many *Indians* that would be joining them. Alcaraz, and indeed, his men, could secure much profit from their sale. The *Spaniards'* quest for gold and silver was insatiable and mining operations were springing up all over *Mexico*. The *Indian* men and boys were needed to work these mines, working until they literally dropped, then to be discarded and replaced with new workers. The women and young girls would be sought out for their beauty, sent back to *Mexico City*, and sold as mistresses, whores, and personal servants. The undesirable women and children would be used as farm workers. All over *Mexico,* these slave operations were decimating the populations.

De Vaca's argument was that the *Indians* should be *Christianized* and brought into the *Spanish* culture. It was a losing argument, however, because the slave trade profits were enormous.

In the middle of one of these heated arguments between Alcaraz and de Vaca Corporal Jose Perez came galloping into camp and slid his horse to a stop just in front of where the two men were seated.

"*Capitan*, we have returned with the two *Spaniards* and...and..."

"What is it corporal?" Alcaraz demanded.

"Sir, there are hundreds of *Indios* with us. They stretch for a league or more up the trail."

Alcaraz jumped up and ordered his men to arm themselves and make ready.

"*Capitan, capitan!*" It was de Vaca. "These people come in peace, put away your weapons."

"How can you know that *Senor* de Vaca!"

"Because *Capitan*, these people follow us, they do what we tell them and we have promised them safety."

Alcaraz thought a moment and then ordered his men to stand down but to be ready in case there was trouble.

Soon Estevan, Dorantes, and Castillo were seen advancing toward them. Behind them, a sea of bobbing heads and a dust cloud that indicated many more to come.

April, 1536

Slaver Camp on the Sinola River

Senor de Vaca, how are all these people to be fed?" Alcaraz paced back and forth. "My men and I are starving and now we have untold numbers of *Indios* to worry about. I beseech you to call out to the people who have hidden from us and ask for food to feed us and these multitudes."

Alvar did as he was asked, but was told by the head men that people were already on their way with food and would be arriving the next day.

True enough, word came to the camp the next morning of another mass of *Indians* moving down the trail. At noon they arrived...six hundred of them...most carrying clay pots filled with shelled maize. By now, the *Christian* slavers camp by the river had swelled to over one thousand individuals.

Now the discussion came up again between Alcaraz and the survivors about the fate of the Indians. Although he obviously couldn't take all of the *Indians*, he planned on enslaving a select few. In this discussion, Dorantes and Castillo now took an active part.

Dorantes argued. "*Capitan* Alcaraz these are peaceful people, they are farmers who mean you no harm. Let them return to their farms and villages to grow maize, beans, and squash so they can feed themselves."

"*Capitan* Dorantes, we have been given orders and this is how we are compensated. I care nothing for these heathens."

Castillo, always the one with a short fuse, now spoke up. "What is wrong with your thinking, Alcaraz? These people have fed you when you were starving and now you will turn on them? You are without honor!"

Alcaraz turned scarlet and advanced toward Castillo, his hand on the hilt of his sword.

"You dare be impertinent with me!"

Castillo did not back down, but instead looked to one of the other cavalrymen.

"Give me your sword and I will show this fool how to fight."

At this moment Alvar stepped in. "*Capitans*, we are all gentlemen here, let us resolve this peacefully!"

Alcaraz continued. "I see no gentleman there." Nodding toward Castillo. Only a half-naked, barefoot, half-*Indio* who has forgotten he is a *Spaniard*.

"*Bastardo*!" Yelled Castillo as he advanced toward Alcaraz. Dorantes stepped in his way as several of the cavalrymen began to move closer.

Alvar was a little more forceful. "*Capitan* walk away from this. It does us no good to fight among ourselves."

Alcaraz glared at Castillo for a moment then turned on his heel and walked away.

Over his shoulder, he told de Vaca. "I want you out of this place!"

What happened next was an effort by Alcaraz to discredit the survivors. Through his interpreters, he told the *Indian* leaders that de Vaca, Castillo, Dorantes, and Estevan were all *Spaniards* just like themselves and that they had no god-like healing powers. Furthermore, Alcaraz told the *Indians* that he and the soldiers with him were the real Lords of the land and the *Indians* should obey them.

To all of these charges, the Indians replied to the interpreters that they did not believe these things for they had seen the bearded shamans comfort and heal the sick while the slavers killed and enslaved their people. They had seen the shamans walking naked and barefoot while the slavers were well-dressed and on horseback.

The shamans shared their hardships and gave everything they had to the less fortunate. The shamans came from where the sun rose and they, the slavers, came from where the sunset. No, the lies of the *Spanish* slavers could not be believed.

This conclusion spread throughout the *Indian* community which had now become considerable. Although there were many different languages spoken, all understood the trade language of the area, *primahaitu*, and word spread quickly.

Early the next morning, Alcaraz, frustrated by his efforts to discredit the survivors, sent one of his men to request a meeting with Alvar.

Corporal Perez came upon Alvar offering assistance to a young *Indian* girl who had fallen and badly cut her leg.

"*Senor* de Vaca, a good morning to you."

"And to you Corporal. To what do I owe this honor?" Alvar liked the corporal, since their first meeting the young soldier had always treated him with respect.

"I have been asked by my *capitan*, to ask if you would meet with him. I will take you to him."

Alvar considered this a moment. "Certainly Corporal, let me finish up here and we shall walk together."

It was hot and Captain Alcaraz was sitting under an oak tree trying to avoid the heat. "Ah de Vaca, you are here."

Corporal Perez turned to excuse himself.

"You can remain here corporal, for this concerns you as well."

"What is it that you wish to speak with me...us about *capitan*?" Both Alvar and the corporal stepped into the shade of the tree.

"*Senor* De Vaca, your presence here along with *capitans* Costello, Dorantes, and the slave Estevan has become a problem." Alcaraz paused.

Alvar said nothing.

Alcaraz continued. "I am assigning Corporal Perez and three of my men to accompany you away from this place. But first, I would ask that you use your influence to disperse the many *Indians* that follow you and have them return to their homes and farms."

Alvar countered. "And *Capitan* Alcaraz, how many of these *Indios* will you take away as slaves to be sold in the markets of *Mexico City*?"

Alcaraz bristled, but avoided the question. "*Senor* De Vaca I only wish to make this land peaceful and productive again so that we can bring the inhabitants...these *Indios*...to *Christianity*.

Alvar didn't believe the captain, but what choice did he have? It was obvious that Alcaraz wanted him out of here and it was beyond his capabilities to do anything about it. His only hope would be to influence the higher authorities when he got back to civilization.

"*Capitan* Alcaraz, if we do this where shall you send us?"

"*Alguacil* De Vaca." It was the first time Alcaraz had addressed him by his official title in the expedition. "When we left the settlement of *San Miguel* several weeks ago we rode with an *alcade* named Lazaro de Cebreros."

Alvar didn't recognize the name.

Alcaraz continued. "About ten leagues from this place we decided to split our forces. I would continue on to the *Sierras* and he would turn to the west. After three weeks we agreed to meet up again and return to the settlement at *San Miguel*."

Alcaraz paused and then continued. "I will have Corporal Perez and two men escort you back to our rendezvous place and from there, *Alcade* Cebreros will take you to *San Miguel*."

Alvar nodded. "How far is this settlement at *San Miguel*?"

"From our position here I would think it to be 25 leagues, more or less."

Alvar thought for a moment...finally, he said, "*Capitan*, I will need two or three days to convince the *Indios* to return to their homes."

"Unfortunately I can only give you the rest of this day, for it is critical that you leave early tomorrow morning if you are to meet up with *Alcade* Cebreros."

"I see," replied Alvar. It was obvious that the slaver captain wanted them gone as soon as possible. "We will talk with the *casiques* this morning and try and convince them."

"Excellent, I will allow two *Indians* to care for your needs and to be your servants.

The older of the two was Quetux, the other was Sestroni-ki. Their names roughly translated to Raven and White Bear. Their village in the *Sierras* had been raided by Alcaraz's men early one morning. A few of the men of the village had resisted and at least one of the slavers had been injured by an arrow. So enraged were the *Spaniards* by this that they burned the village and killed anyone who challenged them. The women suffered immeasurably, each *Spaniard* taking his liberties before chaining all the captives. Quetex and Sestroni-ki had tried to escape but were ridden down by one of the slavers and severely beaten. Their scars were still very visible. Not knowing quite what to expect next, their assignment to care for the survivors was an unbelievable reprieve from the death sentence of working in the mines in the *Spanish* empire of *New Spain*.

After the meeting with Alcaraz, Alvar hurried to the other three survivors. Together they talked to the many *caciques*, headmen, and shamans that accompanied the *Indians*. They told them that all the people needed to return to their villages and work the land as before and, if they did this, the *Christian* slavers would leave them alone.

At first, the *Indians* refused, saying that they must accompany the Children of the Sun wherever they went and it was their responsibility to ensure they were passed on to other *Indians* who would also protect them. The negotiations took time and it was not until the hour of Vespers that the *Indians* were convinced to return to their farms and villages. It was with great regret that they would let the Children of the Sun continue on alone. There was much weeping at the conclusion of the talks.

Alvar, Dorantes, and Castillo confronted Alcaraz as night was falling andtold him of their meeting, and emphasized that the Indians must be treated fairly. If not they would surely return to the hills or take up arms against the *Christian* slavers.

Alcaraz readily agreed but Alvar read his face and felt the captain was telling them what they wanted to hear. In the end, Alvar felt, he would gather slaves and do whatever it took to enrich his own coffers. Dorantes and Castillo were in agreement.

As the three excused themselves Alvar turned to Alcaraz.

"*Capitan*, on our return to *Mexico City* we will be writing a full report as to the series of events that has befallen us. In addition, I will include a summary of our agreement here."

Alcaraz only nodded and said. "I look forward to reading that report *Senor* De Vaca, it will be most interesting."

Inside Alcaraz was seething. He called for Corporal Perez.

When Corporal Perez showed up a few minutes later, Alcaraz was to the point.

"Corporal, I want them out of this camp before the sun is up."

"Yes, *capitan!*"

"Move as rapidly as possible and take them on a path that will ensure that none of their *Indio* patrons will follow them. Do you understand?"

"Yes, *capitan!*"

"After you have delivered them to *Alcade* Cebreros, return here as quickly as possible, for there is much work to do.

"Yes, *capitan!*"

May, 1536

Rendezvous With Alcade Cebreros

They had been traveling for two days through a country so dense and rugged that everyone suffered grievously. There was no water. Besides the four survivors, Corporal Perez was accompanied by three other cavalrymen and twelve *Indians* who served as guides and porters. Only Perez and the three cavalrymen were mounted.

It was mid-afternoon when the troupe stopped to rest. Alvar approached Corporal Perez, sure that he was being devious in his movements through this country.

"Corporal, why do you lead us through this terrible dry land of scrub and tangles? We have had no water for two days and already seven Indians have laid down unable to continue on. I fear that they will perish."

Perez hung his head before answering.

"*Alguicil*, I must apologize. I was ordered by my *capitan* to take you in this direction to discourage any *Indio* patrons from following you. In doing this, however, we became lost."

De Vaca noted that Perez had addressed him as *alguicil*, an indication of his respect.

"Corporal, it saddens me that *capitan* Alcaraz means to deceive us. I cannot assign any blame, however, for you are under orders. Of more concern is our lack of water." Alvar hesitated. "Are we still lost?"

"*Alguicil*, just an hour ago the scouts identified our location. We are very close to the rendezvous location with *Alcade* De Cebreros. There is a small spring there which will give us much relief."

Another half an hour passed as they trudged along the dusty trail. The horses were the first to indicate there was water close by. They became noticeably excited and it was with difficulty that the riders held them back.

Up ahead a thicket of trees and grass stood out from the dry and brittle scrub that they had been traveling through. It was green! As they came closer it was apparent that there were already *Christians* there. Horses were staked out in the lush grass surrounding a small spring that bubbled up from the rocks. The water collected in a small pool that drained out in a small rivulet that disappeared into the dry ground only a few *yara* from its source. Around the pool were clustered a group of men, some *Spaniards,* and a few *Indians.* Further from the spring were ten or fifteen wretched Indians chained together and guarded by two more *Spaniards.*

Corporal Perez spurred ahead and as he approached the pool the *Spaniards* turned to greet him. An impromptu discussion ensued and all eyes turned toward the approaching column.

The *Indians* accompanying the column broke first and rushed to the pool to slake their thirst. When the four survivors reached the water's edge it was a melee of *Indians*, horses, and *Spaniards* gorging themselves.

As Alvar and Dorantes were returning from the pool for the second time Corporal Perez and another *Christian* approached them.

"*Alguacil* and *capitan* Dorates I would like to present *Alcade* Lazaro de Cebreros."

The man standing before Alvar was short, stocky, and middle-aged. His hair and beard were disheveled and his eye darted about as if looking for something that wasn't there. His face was deeply tanned and pockmarked. He was clad in a loose cotton tunic that showed several scars on his arms. It was obvious that this man had been a warrior.

"Ah, the Narvaez survivors! All these years and now you return from the dead. Most amazing." Cebreros extended his hand in a greeting.

Alvar took his hand while deciding almost immediately he didn't like this man. There was a cruelness in his eyes that was hard to ignore.

Dorantes shook his hand as well but eyed him suspiciously.

Castillo and Estevan approached. Alvar introduced the two.

"*Capitan*, so good to make your acquaintance!" He pumped Castillo's hand but made no effort to acknowledge Estevan.

"We must talk of your journey. Tonight we will rest, but tomorrow morning we will begin our journey to the *Villa de San Miguel*. A place that we now call *Culiacan*."

That evening the survivors talked at length with Cebreros and the men with him about their adventures in *New Spain*. Cebreros listened intently, interrupting frequently as to the numbers of *Indians* that the survivors encountered. And, Cebreros talked of his own achievements. How he had joined the governor of *Panuco*,

Nuno Beltran de Guzman, in exploring and conquering the areas to the west. By 1531 they subdued this land and called it *"la Conquista del Espíritu Santo de la Mayor España"* (the Conquest of the Holy Spirit of Greater Spain). However, when the name was submitted to the acting regent in *Spain*, Mad Queen Joanna, it was disapproved. She instead bestowed the name *"Reino de Nueva Galicia"* (Kingdom of New Galicia). Cebreros said he and Guzman had laughed heartily at that.

The survivors were familiar with the name Guzman. Panfillo Narvaez on many occasions had expressed a deep hatred for the man and let it be known to whoever would listen. Guzman was granted the governorship of *Panuco* in 1525 to counterbalance the influence of Hernan Cortes who the crown believed was becoming too powerful. Guzman arrived in *Mexico* just a month before the Narvaez expedition left the port of *San Lucar de Barrameda*. He wasted no time in solidifying his position and infringing on the lands granted to Narvaez by Charles V. Knowing full well what Guzman was up to Narvaez itched to confront him when the expedition landed in *Panuco* as planned. But, of course, the expedition never made it to *Panuco*

By the end of the night, the conversation had turned away from the experiences of the four survivors and centered on the achievements of Lazaro de Cebreros and his patron Nuno Guzman. They learned that both men had founded the city of *Culiacan* and how in appreciation Guzman had made him the first *alcade* mayor, a title that Cebreros never relinquished. Having heard enough, Castillo was the first to excuse himself from the discussion. Alvar and Dorantes followed shortly thereafter.

Leaving the fire Dorantes only said two words. *"Bastarda arrogante*...arrogant bastard!"

Alvar's response was equally short. *"Si!"*

The next morning the procession of Narvaez survivors, slavers, and chained *Indians* moved down the trail toward *San Miguel* and *Culiacan.*

May, 1536

Meeting Melchior Diaz the Alcade Mayor of San Miguel

It was a long slog towards the settlement at *San Miguel.* For six days they journeyed on primitive footpaths and animal trails over terrain that was both rugged and beautiful. Behind them was the *Sierra Madre Occidental* with its dense evergreen forests of pine and fur trees. In front, the mountains gradually descended toward the coastal plain. Now tall oak trees became the dominant species of this ever-changing ecotone. On the sixth day, the caravan came to a village of peaceful Indians by a large river. Here, Cebreros dropped the survivors off before proceeding down the river.

Before leaving, however, Cebreros had a conversation with Alvar, Dorantes, and Castillo.

"I will leave you here in this village and proceed with our captives to *San Miguel,* which is only a half-day ride from here. I will personally inform the *alcade* of *San Miguel* of your coming. He is a good man named Melchior Diaz and I am sure he will send horses for you to ride. From *San Miguel,* I will continue on to *Mexico City.*"

Not waiting for an answer, Cebreros spurred his horse and was gone.

The two *Indians* that had remained with the survivors doted upon them, looking after their every need. They quickly constructed crude shelters. Estevan spent time with them both, learning much. In the slave markets of *Mexico City, Indians* of this age were worth the least, a fact which Alcaraz undoubtedly considered before assigning them to stay with the survivors.

519

The next morning there was a commotion in the village just after daybreak as a group of riders entered the camp. The *Indians* of the little village were terrified, but it soon became very apparent that these *Spaniards* meant no harm. It was the *alcade* mayor of the settlement of *San Miguel* who came to see the survivors of the Narvaez expedition. The mayor and his entourage stopped only briefly to ask the whereabouts of the survivors. The *Indians* pointed to the quickly constructed shelters toward the back of the village.

The *Spaniards* reigned up outside the shelters. Castillo was just returning from the woods after emptying his bowels beneath a giant oak tree. Still clad only in a loincloth the guests didn't immediately recognize him. It was only after he called out to them, "*Saludos amigos!*" that they took a second look and saw a half-naked, bearded *Spaniard* walking toward them.

A man of obvious importance dismounted and approached Castillo, hand extended. "I am Melchior Diaz the *alcade* mayor of *San Miguel.* I have just learned of your amazing journey and have ridden all night to properly greet you and your comrades."

Castillo grasped his hand, he could tell he liked this man immediately. "I am Alonzo del Castillo Maldonado, *capitan* of Infantry for the Narvaez expedition."

By this time the other three survivors had come up. Dorantes shook his hand and introduced Estevan as his friend and servant. Amazingly, Diaz reached out and shook Estevan's hand. Next, Alvar shook the mayor's hand and introduced himself.

"*Alcade* Diaz, it is an honor that you have taken the time to greet us in such a manner. We have dreamed of this moment for many years."

Diaz responded, "Praise God, the honor is all mine *Alguacil* De Vaca. I have brought four horses for your return to *San Miguel* where you will be my honored guests. On behalf of the governor of our province, Nuno de Guzman, I bid you welcome."

Alvar hesitated and looked at his companions. "*Alcade* mayor, I hope we remember how to ride!"

There was laughter all around.

May, 1536

Ride to the Indian Village of Culiacan

The *alcade* mayor Diaz stayed at the *Indian* village that day listening to the stories of the Narvaez survivors. Together they laughed and wept at the adventures, torment, and suffering they had experienced. Indeed, Diaz had acquaintances that had been lost on the expedition. That night Diaz also expressed deep remorse for the way the survivors and the *Indians* had been treated by the likes of Diego de Alcaraz and Lazaro de Ceberos.

"They are a breed of men without a soul. Unfortunately, in the beginning, we needed men like that to tame this land. Now, with their cruelty and greed, they stand in the way of progress."

Diaz was so sincere in his feelings that Alvar was prompted to say, "*Alcade* Mayor, I feel certain if you had been there in their stead none of the things done to us would have happened."

The next morning de Vaca, Dorantes, Castillo, and Estevan mounted horses for the first time in almost 9 years. After having traveled everywhere by foot the experience was exhilarating and the day's ride very pleasant.

As they rode Alcade Mayor Diaz talked at length with the survivors. He told of how this land, *Nueva Galicia*, under Guzman's control suffered. In this immediate area, most of the *Indians* had fled to the *Sierras* terrified by the slavers such as Alcaraz and Cebreros. Their villages and farms lay abandoned. Further south many of the *Indian* tribes were at war with the *Spaniards* and it was very unsafe to travel.

Diaz reigned in his horse and turned towards them, "Of you brave survivors I would ask a favor."

Alvar answered for the others, "Whatever is the favor *alcade* mayor we will try to grant your request."

"I would ask, *Senor* de Vaca, that all of you use your influence with the *Indios* to ease their fears and bring them out of hiding so that once again they can settle themselves as *Christians* and farm the land in the name of God and Your Majesty."

Dorantes answered, "*Alcade*, we have lost our following. We have been separated from those *Indios* who believed in us and who were skilled in these matters. It will be very difficult now to convince other *Indios* of our wishes."

Castillo added, "But, of course, we will try."

Alvar interjected, "*Alcade* there is still the issue of men like Alcaraz and Cebreros whose brutality scares the *Indios* into hiding."

Diaz continued, "I would be in your debt if this could come about so this land could at last be profitable and many lives would be saved...both *Spanish* and *Indio*! Let me worry about the likes of Alcaraz and Cabrero."

Alvar offered a suggestion. "We do have two *Indios* that have been with us since we came upon *capitan* Alcaraz's men. They have knowledge of the *Indios* that accompanied us and held us in high regard. Perhaps we could call on them to assist us."

Unexpectedly, Estevan entered the conversation, though only briefly. "I will talk with these two about what you have discussed."

There was a moment of silence before Dorantes continued. "*Senor* Estevanico has established a friendship with these two and will be the best qualified to ask for their help."

Turning to Estevan he continued, "Go to them now and let us know what they say."

With that Diaz looked at all four survivors. "*Gracias*, I know you will do your best." He turned his horse and spurred it forward.

Later that day the entourage of Melchior Diaz and the four survivors entered the *Indian* village of *Culiacan*. Here the survivors would instruct their two *Indian* captives. The village was large and sprawling and only less than a league from the *Spanish* settlement of *San Miguel*. It was a place where many *Indians* had gathered to escape the atrocities of the slavers. They readily accepted *Christianity* as their new religious observance. This, of course, was out of necessity more than anything else. Everywhere crosses could be seen adorning individual living quarters and, indeed, a church was under construction in the middle of the village. Alcade Mayor Diaz was a fair man, and as long as the *Indians* were industrious and accepted *Christianity* he would protect them.

The survivors spent a lot of time with Quetux and Sestroni-ki after reaching the village of *Culiacan*. They talked much of the *Christian* God, his son Jesus Christ, and the holy virgin, Mary mother of God. It would be their job to go out and convince the *Indians,* hiding in the hills, to embrace *Christianity* so that they could be free of the slavers and return to their farms and villages. Both men were receptive and very eager to learn all they could. Other *Indians,* hearing of their mission, joined them, eager to help. Soon, an assortment of people from all over the area gathered around the survivors as they exhorted everyone to spread the word. Alvar, Dorantes, and Castillo instructed the people for two days while Estevan acted as interpreter for those people whose language they had not yet mastered. Frequently the *Spaniards* would have to pause in their instructions to let Estevan catch up with the hand talk.

The concept of an all-powerful God was surprisingly easy for the survivors to relate to. Most, if not all, of the indigenous people, already believed in a powerful deity that watched over and controlled everything. He was known by many names, depending on the culture, but His predominant title was Aguar. It was an easy exercise to convince the Indians that Aguar and the *Christian* God were one and the same.

More of a challenge was convincing the people that God's son Jesus Christ had been sent to earth to save men's souls from sin. The virgin birth and the subsequent life and death of the Savior was such a persuading story, however, that soon everyone was won over.

After five days of instruction Quetux and Sestroni-ki, and the now large contingent of followers, were sent out into the *Sierras* to talk with the people and convince them to embrace *Christianity* and once again populate the area now known as *Nueva Galicia*. Quetux and Sestroni-ki were presented with one of the holy gourds that Alvar, Dorantes, Castillo, and Estevan had carried with them. This was the insignia of the survivors' holy status and would be well received by all who saw it.

The Alcade mayor Diaz also provided Quetux and Sestromi-ki with an official document that would protect them should slavers try to interrupt their mission. As well prepared as they could be, the two Indians set out for the *Sierras* to talk to their people. During the time they were gone, the survivors had numerous sessions with the *Indians* all around *Culiacan*.

After one meeting Dorantes spoke with Alvar, "*Alguac*il, I think we are making some progress. There is much talk and many *Indios* have left the village to bring their friends and families out of the *Sierras*."

"Ah, friend Dorantes, that is indeed good news but I have concern of our messengers. Tomorrow will be the seventh day since they departed for the *Sierras* and we have received no word."

De Vaca's fears were put to rest the very next day. It was a beautiful morning with a luminescent clear sky. In the distance, the line of the *Sierras* rose majestically into the sky.

About mid-morning a runner breathlessly entered the village. "They have returned, and with them are three lords and fifteen others!"

The four survivors hurried to the trailhead at the entrance to the village. In the valley below were the two messengers, Quetux and Sesroni-ki, followed by three elegantly adorned *Indian* leaders and their retinue of followers.

"I'll be damned," Castillo was the first to speak.

Dorantes answered, "Looks like our messengers have made contact. Let us hurry out there to welcome them."

Each of the *Indians* that had come down from the *Sierras* carried a crude wooden cross, many constructed from just two sticks lashed together. The three *Indian* lords brought gifts of beads, turquoise stones, and plumes. The rest of the day was filled with joyous celebrations. The survivors sat with the three *Indian* lords and gave assurance to them that as long as they accepted *Christianity* no harm would come to them.

At the end of the day, as the survivors were returning to their quarters, Estevan turned to Alvar, "*Alguacil,* will these *Spaniards* really honor this agreement with the *Indios?*"

Alvar turned to Dorantes and Castillo but both hung their head and looked away.

Finally, after some thought, he indirectly answered Estevan. "There are some good *Christians* who, I am sure, will watch out for the best interests of the *Indios*. I think *Alcade Diaz* will do his best to fulfill his promises."

Estevan was not dumb. He knew that however good were *Alcade* Diaz's intentions, his power was limited in this sprawling land and the greed of the *Spanish* slavers would probably prevail.

Alvar continued "We have done all we can do to bring peace to this country. We must now concentrate on returning to civilization and telling our story. *Alcade* Diaz will be here tomorrow to accompany us to the *Christian* community at *San Miguel.*

CHAPTER 21
Assimilation

Asimilación

After so many years, civilization's pull was unmistakable on the survivors. They embraced it, their spirits lifted and they began the process of assimilation with thoughts of the future.

May, 1536

The Indian Village at Culiacan

When notified of the positive happenings in the village of *Culiacan*, Alcade Melchoir Diaz immediately set upon gathering gifts for the returning *Indians*. He put together large quantities of blankets, robes, and agricultural tools. This, of course, took time and it wasn't for two weeks before he returned to *Culiacan* with several wagons piled high with supplies.

While they waited, the survivors had been busy convincing the *Indians* of the good intentions of the *Christians*. People continued to stream into the village, many bringing gifts of beads and plumes. During this time all four survivors assisted in baptizing the many *Indians* who now were eager to embrace their new religion. Others were taught the rudiments of constructing churches so they could return to their villages and start the process.

When *Alcade* Diaz arrived at the village of *Culiacan* with his entourage and wagons he was amazed by the number of people and the activity.

"*Senor* de Vaca, what you and your men have done here is amazing. There are rumors that all over *Nueva Galicia* the *Indios* are laying down their arms and returning to their villages and farms."

Alvar answered, "*Alcade*, we have tried to do our best, but our great fear is men like *Capitan* Alcaraz will continue to terrorize these people, taking them as slaves against their will.

Diaz thought a moment before replying. "*Senor* de Vaca I will make a solemn oath to you, the other three survivors of the Narvaez expedition, and to the *Indios* gathered before us. My oath is this. I will not make or consent to any action to take slaves in this land among the people who have accepted our *Christian* doctrine. I will forward my feelings on this to the viceroy, Antonio de Mendoza, and to the governor Nuno de Guzman."

"That Sir is all we can ask." Was Alvar's reply. All three of the other survivors nodded in agreement.

"Now *Senor* de Vaca, you and your compatriots gather your things. I have brought four horses and we will leave for *San Miguel* as soon as possible."

Such as they were, there were few things to gather for the survivors. They were still clad in the scant garments that they had worn for the last eight years. Each had a few trinkets and the sacred gourds that they carried everywhere.

The villa at *San Miguel* was only five leagues distant and only sparsely populated by *Spaniards*. There was the inevitable church, parts which were still under construction. It rose almost majestically in the center of the ramshackle town, its adobe walls brightly whitewashed. On a wagon just outside the church *Indians* wrestled with block and tackle to raise a bronze bell into the church belfry high above. Everywhere there was activity. The *Alcade* mayor's residence was a line of adobe buildings hastily constructed side by side. Behind these was a much grander residence only partially completed.

Diaz took the survivors on a brief tour. They saw the blacksmith shop busily repairing everything from tools, bridles, and wheelbarrows to making nails. Next to the blacksmith shop was a line of stables and barns for storing hay and fodder. Close to the stables was another line of crude barracks that billeted the contingent of soldiers assigned to the town. On the outskirts was the foundry, with several *Indians* busy preparing hides. Next to them, leathersmiths were preparing a multitude of products; belts, reins, saddles, and straps. Several corrals housed cattle, hogs, sheep, and goats, each watched over by *Indian* herdsmen.

Cooking fires sent their curling spires of smoke into the air accompanied by the tantalizing smell of baking bread, fajitas, and tortillas. Chickens were everywhere, scurrying and squawking while avoiding being trampled by the horses.

After so many years, civilization's pull was unmistakable on the survivors. They embraced it, their spirits lifted and they began the process of assimilation with thoughts of the future.

After the tour, Diaz billeted the three *Spaniards* in his own personal residence. He apologized for the crudeness of their accommodations.

"*Amigos*, soon I will have a much grander residence." He gestured to the building under construction. "But, for now, this is as best that I can do."

All the survivors laughed aloud. Castillo answered, "*Alcade* mayor, in the many years we have been gone we have bedded in places you would not have consigned your horse."

Diaz joined in the laughter. "This will only be temporary, soon we will continue our journey to *Compostela* where you will meet with Governor Guzman, and then on from there to *Tenochtitlan* and the great Cortés."

Diaz thought a moment and corrected himself. "*Tenochtitlan* is no longer the accepted name. We now call it *Mexico City*!"

Alvar spoke up. "*Alcade*, when will we leave for *Compostela*?"

"That could be a problem *Alguicil* for we will be traveling the coastal road. This area is occupied by warlike *Indians* who have deserted their farms and are at war with us. No one is safe on this road unless accompanied by armed horsemen. Our soldiers are currently occupied in areas south of here and it may be some until they return. We will definitely need an escort."

The survivors all nodded in understanding.

"In the meantime, you are invited to share in the pleasures of our humble village. Tonight we will have a fiesta in honor of your arrival."

Each of the *Spaniards* proceeded to their quarters, Estevan would stay in the cook shack adjacent to the residence.

May 13, 1536

Village of San Miguel

Early on Friday Morning, the slaver Diego de Alcaraz rode into *San Miguel* with fourteen men. They had only three *Indians* under chain. When *Alcade* Diaz questioned him about the captives Alcaraz replied.

"*Alcade,* these three were taken after they harmed several of my men. The other *Indios* that we had captured were released by my command. What we have seen is most amazing. Everywhere we went, the *Indios* were coming down from the *Sierras* holding crosses and professing their desire to become *Christians*. It is like nothing I have ever seen."

The survivors listened to the words of Alcaraz, but this man was untrustworthy and Alvar was sure there was something he was hiding. Indeed, when Estevan secretly questioned the three captives they told how the captain had sent many slaves, under separate guard, directly to *Mexico City*.

Together the four survivors talked. Castillo and Estevan wanted to bring the transgressions of Alvaraz to the attention of *Alcade* Melchoir Diaz.

Alvar intervened, "*Amigos*, what Alcaraz is doing is indeed wrong but it is apparent that his unlawful practices are widespread throughout *New Spain*.

Castillo objected, "Should we do nothing?"

Alvar thought a moment. "I feel our voices will be lost in the avalanche of violence and greed so prevalent in this place. We have done all we could, but now we are close to returning to the life we once knew. It is my opinion that we should continue in that direction as quickly as possible. To further involve ourselves in the politics of *New Spain* may not be in our best interest."

Castillo could not argue with the logic but Estevan merely shrugged and looked away.

Later that day Alvar did mention his distrust of Alvaraz to *Alcade* Diaz. Diaz listened but lamented that Alvaraz had a powerful friend in Lazaro de Cebreros who, in turn, was close to Governor Guzman.

"I do what I can *Alguacil*, but many times I have to look the other way and this is one of those times."

Alvar thanked Diaz for his sincerity and was now sure, more than ever, that returning to *Spain* should be his, and the other survivors, primary objective.

The next day a contingent of *Spanish* cavalry rode into *San Miguel* to report to *Alcade* Diaz. Accompanying them were six *Christians*, rough-looking men, leading hundreds of *Indians*, all in chains. The survivors could only watch as the pathetic procession shuffled along in despair.

The war to the south was going badly. The *Indians* were attacking *Christian* settlements and travelers wherever they could. In the pursuit of a rebellious band one of the cavalrymen had been killed and three injured. Diaz saw the wounded men and then walked among the soldiers thanking them. He talked with their captain.

"*Capitan*, rest your men today. Tomorrow you will accompany our guests and five of my personal bodyguards to *Compostela* to meet with Governor Guzman. Once your mission is complete you and your men can continue on to Mexico City for rest and refit. He handed the captain the appropriate paperwork.

"Many thanks, *Alcade*, my men deserve it for they have fought hard."

Diaz shook the captain's hand. "Good luck *capitan*!"

The next day, May 15, 1536, the four survivors, Diaz's bodyguards, and 20 cavalrymen left *San Miguel* and proceeded south toward the village of Compostela. The distance was 100 leagues. The procession was hindered by the 500 pathetic Indian slaves that accompanied them. The horsemen and the six slavers tried their best to keep the procession together but, at best, they could only manage four or five leagues a day. The land they traveled through was deserted, danger lurked at every turn. The *Indians* of this area were in revolt and they took every opportunity to attack the unwary procession. Indeed, the evening campsites were the most vulnerable. Sites were chosen that were open and unimpeded by trees, brush, hills, or valleys. Still, several attacks did occur and several of the slaves were carried off. The *Spanish* horsemen spent most of the nights riding perimeter guard. Luckily, during this journey, there was only one slight injury...a mare was struck in the flank by an arrow that was easily removed. As they traveled along, the South Sea loomed to their left. From high vantage points, Alvar would rest his mount and gaze out at the beauty before him. Further out, the ocean stretched endlessly to a hazy blue horizon.

On this day Castillo joined him. "*Alguacil*, what is it you see out there?"

Startled at the question Alvar thought a moment. "Friend Castillo, it is not what I see but the memories that flood through my head.

Castillo nodded. "*Si*, I have the same thoughts. So much has happened. We have seen so much, cheated death, and lost so many friends."

Alvar turned towards him then. He addressed Castillo formally. "*Capitan*, why have I...we...survived while the others lost their lives? This one thought continues in my head...round and round." Alvar made a spinning motion with his finger.

Castillo shook his head. "For that, I have no answer, only that God makes the final decision about who lives and who dies."

After this exchange, the two survivors sat atop their mounts not speaking, taking in the grandeur that lay before them.

Finally, after twelve days of travel, the procession entered an area that was secure from any attacks. Here, the *Spanish* under governor Nuno Guzman had cleared all of the insurgents and reestablished the farms and villages of the area. The 20 horsemen, anxious to be relieved, left the procession and took a different route to *Mexico City*. With forty leagues yet to go, it took another week for the survivors and the Diaz bodyguards to enter the village of *Compostela*.

Compostela was the regional capital of this new part of *Mexico* called *Nueva Galacia*. Everywhere there were signs of progress. It seemed that every day more people flooded into town. Their arrival caused a considerable stir, for the survivors were still only clad in their Indian breech clothes and skins. Nuno Guzman himself greeted the four, shaking hands and welcoming each to *Compostela*...even Estevan.

Guzman addressed them and the crowd around him. "Survivors of the Narvaez expedition, through God's mercy you have been returned to us after these many years of wandering in the wilderness. We all grieve for those that were lost but revel in the fact that you have finally come back to us."

The governor then led the survivors into his official state house where he offered them proper clothing and food.

"*Senors*, it is only fitting that with your return you dress again as proper *Spanish* gentlemen."

Each accepted the clothing but it was very apparent that none of the four was comfortable in wearing it.

To Guzman's questions about the clothes Dorantes answered. "*Adelantado,* we have gone naked for almost nine years. Our skin is tough and scaly and accustomed to the extremes of weather. It will take time before these garments will feel good upon our bodies."

And so it was with their bedding as well. Each was given a room with a fine bed and straw mattress. To a man, however, each chose to sleep on the floor. The softness of the mattress was something they could not get accustomed to.

After ten days the survivors made ready to continue on to *Mexico-Tenochtitlan.* While in *Compostela,* however, the governor and many others had questioned them about their journey, with particular interest in any valuables that they encountered. They relayed as best they could the vastness of the land. It was all of their beliefs that, of the many civilizations in Amichel, there was much more to be seen and possibly, further north, a civilization rivaling the great *Aztec* empire.

23 July 1536

Entering Mexico City

The journey to *Mexico-Tenochtitlan* was a surreal experience for the survivors. Since the 1521 defeat of the *Aztecs,* tremendous changes had occurred in *New Spain*. There was now a regular trade route between Compostela and, indeed, all of the large villages in the area. The roadway was cluttered with people on the move. Farm wagons carried produce, chickens, turkeys, timber, and all sorts of trade goods while herds of cattle, swine, and sheep were being driven along by their handlers. The survivors studied the mass of humanity, still a little awed by their new life and the quantum changes that had occurred to them.

Castillo rode easy in the saddle as the procession moved along. Since mounting a horse for the first time in eight years, his leg muscles had finally become used to the saddle. He reflected on how nice it was to sit in relative comfort as the road passed beneath him. They traveled with a full contingent of 25 armed horsemen and a line of wagons piled high with trade goods.

As they entered the city it was a sight to behold. An island metropolis situated in the middle of *Lake Texcoco*, its shimmering waters glistened in the high mountain air. Off to the southeast were the twin volcanoes *Popocatepetl* and *Iztaccihuatl,* their white icecaps vivid against the deep blue sky. *Iztaccihuatl,* now long extinct, was in contrast with the higher *Popocatepetl* which, even now, emitted a trailer of white smoke. Between the two peaks lay the *Paso de Cortes* from where Hernan Cortes and his soldiers had first entered the *Valley of the Mexica* in 1519.

There was construction and destruction everywhere. Many of the majestic structures-temples, towers, shrines, and sculptures, had been torn down, the material used for fill and new buildings. More importantly, the dams and drainage areas for the lake surrounding the city had been destroyed. As a result, flooding was becoming an increasing problem. The general layout of the city had been preserved. The *Zocalo* was the central plaza where the three main roads converged. Here the *Aztec Templo Mayor* had existed. This great temple had been devoted to the *Aztec* gods *Huitzilopochtli, Tlaloc,* and *Quetzalcoatl.* Now, the temple was being obliterated, the huge stone blocks stacked in neat rows for future use. It was said that these stones would be used to build a cathedral. Along the edges of the *Zocalo* were the *Spanish* administrative offices and other buildings that, even now, were being expanded.

Arriving at the *Zocalo* the survivors were met by Viceroy Antonio de Mendoza. Alvar, Castillo, Dorantes, and Estevan sat astride their horses as the viceroy approached. He was surrounded by officials and guards, for although the *Aztecs* had been defeated, there were still insurrectionists around and it was not unusual for *Spaniards* to lose their lives.

The viceroy rode up to each of the survivors, shook their hands, and said a few words. Even Estevan was warmly greeted. "Ah, *Senor* Estevanico, I have heard that you are the one that speaks a hundred languages...very amazing...welcome back!"

Then, still astride his horse Mendoza gave a short speech of welcome.

"Men of the Narvaez expedition, for so long we had thought you all were lost but now a great providence has determined to bring you back. Although we are saddened by the fate of so many of your comrades we revel in the fact that you and your many stories have been returned to us...welcome! Now, if you will follow me I will show you to your quarters ."

The survivors went with Mendoza while the rest of the caravan continued on to their respective destinations.

They were escorted to the governor's house where a line of adobe guesthouses had been built. Each survivor would have his own room. Again the viceroy shook each of their hands and then announced that they would be the honored guests that evening in a gala ball.

"Rest yourselves, gentlemen, for there will be many people wanting you to tell, and retell, your story. The *Marques del Valle* will also be there to honor your arrival."

The survivors were confused by this title and looked at each other questionably. Seeing this Mendoza explained that this was an honorary title granted to Hernan Cortez by His Excellency Charles V.

Mendoza continued, "Cortes has taken a sharp interest in your return. I'm sure he will have many questions."

Dismounting, Alvar stepped inside the room assigned to him. Two *Aztec* women were in attendance to see to his every need. Both middle-aged, they stood at the doorway with a pitcher of water. They offered him a drink which he accepted.

"Gracious senora!"

After drinking he thanked both women and sent them away, saying he wanted to be alone.

Inside the single room was a four-posted bed with a soft mattress...*el jergon*...filled with sweet-smelling straw, the pillows were goose down. Alvar sat on the bed and immediately lost his balance as he sank down. He lay there a moment staring at the ceiling. The events of the last few weeks swirled through his head. For eight long years, he and his compatriots had existed in a primitive society with starvation, violence, and death as their constant companions. Now, in only a few weeks he lay here in these opulent surroundings, secure and safe once again.

He was uncomfortable. The softness of the mattress hurt his back and the body heat generated from the down pillows made him sweat. He got up from the bed and sat in a chair across the room. Next, he removed the riding boots given to him before leaving *Compostella*...they were confining and uncomfortable. He would have removed the pantaloons but decided against it as he walked outside. Across the *Zocallo* were the remains of the *Aztec Templo Mayor,* all but gone now except for a section of the stairway leading nowhere.

Barefoot, Alvar walked across the courtyard and up the stairs of the once-great temple. At the top he looked down at the rubble, even now being hauled away. He scanned the city around him and was overwhelmed by its size and complexity.

A noise from behind startled Alvar from his reflections. He turned to see Castillo coming up the stairs, and behind him, Dorantes and Estevan. They were also barefoot.

"*Alguacil*, may we join you?"

For a moment they joked about the softness of the bed and how the boots and other clothing seemed to restrict them, then they became quiet.

Dorantes spoke, "We have seen and experienced so much...where do we go from here?"

Alvar looked at his friends. Like himself they were hard, gaunt men who had suffered much. He shook his head. "I'm sure God has a plan for us."

In the distance, the volcanic peaks stood as sentinels in the sky. Like the smoke cloud emanating from *Popocatepetl,* the future of the survivors would be subject to the fickle winds of life.

It was Sunday, one day before the eve of St James, 1536.

www.ingramcontent.com/pod-product-compliance
Lightning Source LLC
Chambersburg PA
CBHW051129300726
48978CB00011B/206